CHASING THE SUN

JUDY LEIGH

Boldwood

First published in Great Britain in 2021 by Boldwood Books Ltd.

Copyright © Judy Leigh, 2021

Cover Design by Debbie Clement Design

Cover Photography: Shutterstock

A CIP catalogue record for this book is available from the British Library.

Paperback ISBN 978-1-83889-581-5

Large Print ISBN 978-1-83889-580-8

Harback ISBN 978-1-80162-695-8

Ebook ISBN 978-1-83889-582-2

Kindle ISBN 978-1-83889-583-9

Audio CD ISBN 978-1-83889-575-4

MP3 CD ISBN 978-1-83889-576-1

Digital audio download ISBN 978-1-83889-579-2

Boldwood Books Ltd

23 Bowerdean Street
London SW6 3TN
www.boldwoodbooks.com

For Liam and Maddie

1

Friday 13th August

Whoop whoop! Today, it's my 70th birthday and I'm going to have fun. A Leo, that's me – I just looked up my characteristics: 'confident, drama-adoring, loyal, fiercely protective of their nearest and dearest, generous, sunny, and big-hearted, with a tendency to be reckless and rootless'. That's definitely me to a tee. So, three birthday cards just arrived in the post – one from my lovely Samantha in Cumbria, one from dear Nell. The other one's from R's sister in Scotland, who must be eighty now, bless her. A new decade starts today – it's going to be brilliant, I just know it. Carpe diem – seize the day. I can't wait to get started...

Molly stopped writing, turning the turquoise diary over in her hands thoughtfully. 'Seventy...' She stretched her arms above her head. 'A whole new decade. I wonder what I'll do.'

She gazed around the living room, looking at the paintings on the wall, the untidy sofa covered in cat hairs and squashed cushions, the mantelpiece crammed with knick-knacks brought back from her many travels: miniature clogs, an oversize mug sporting the word 'Croatia', a kora-playing Gambian Jali carved from wood, a tiny metal Eiffel Tower.

'Seventy,' she murmured again and wandered upstairs to her bedroom where she'd left the vacuum cleaner. She could vacuum up quickly before breakfast. A big birthday was a new start, as good a reason as any to clean the house. Molly scratched her head. 'What I really need to do is to get the chores out of the way, then it's time for some fun.'

She picked up the vacuum cleaner, listening to the deafening whirr of the motor, and began to shove it across a rug, singing at the top of her voice to block out the noise. Fluff had collected in straggling shreds in the corner of the room. She watched it slide into the nozzle, twizzle and disappear. Then she paused, turning off the motor, and shook her head in disbelief.

'Home is where the heart is,' Molly observed, matter-of-factly. 'But my home is full of cobwebs and dust. Maybe I need a new one. Perhaps I'll move somewhere exciting... Now that would be a thing. Florida might be nice...?' She let the nozzle of the vacuum cleaner fall from her hand, suddenly changing her mind. 'August's too late for spring cleaning. I'll just change the bedding.'

Molly bounded towards the bed but as soon as she glimpsed her reflection she stopped, staring into the wardrobe mirror. A woman with a cheerful face, a mane of slate-grey hair, wearing a baggy T-shirt and loose jeans paused for a moment too and stared back. Molly turned sideways and gazed over her shoulder. A smiling woman gazed boldly into her eyes. Molly laughed.

'So, this is as good as it gets at seventy, is it? I see...'

She raised her arms above her head and howled in protest, a wild throaty yell, shaking her hair over her face. She was a strong cave woman, primitive and self-sufficient. She was fierce Boudicca. She was valiant Joan of Arc. But she was still seventy.

She told herself she didn't care how she looked. It was too late to worry now; anyway, it didn't matter. Then a new thought came to her, a brilliant idea.

'I don't have to be reminded every day that I'm seventy.'

Molly rushed into the third bedroom, the one she used as an office, which was piled high with artist's materials and all sorts of once-useful junk. She saw an old cricket bat standing upright in the corner, heaved it over her shoulder like a professional batsman, muttered, 'Howzat!' and marched back into her bedroom. There was nothing to be gained from looking at herself. She spoke directly to her reflection in the mirror.

'Right,' she grinned. 'That mirror has got to go. I'll smash it out and leave a hole, maybe put a colourful painting in there. Then I won't keep noticing that I'm no longer twenty-five. That's how to start a new decade – I'll love the person I am – and I won't focus on small imperfections.'

She lifted the cricket bat high: a woman with a primitive weapon raised over her head stared back at her, dressed in a voluminous T-shirt and jeans that were two sizes too big, rolled up at the bottom, bare feet splaying out below. Molly smiled at the ludicrous image of herself, poised, ready to attack. Of course, it would be dangerous to chop out a mirror. There would be fragments, shards, flying slivers of glass. And smashing the mirror to smithereens would not change the stark reality: she was a single, solitary, seventy-year-old woman who always claimed to be sixty-five when people asked because age didn't matter. She never considered that pretending to be sixty-five would make her two years younger than her half-sister Ellen Spencer – always called Nell since childhood – who was pretty, happily married and perfect in every way.

Molly knew she shouldn't care. Nobody noticed how she looked anyway. She had arrived at this point in life and her face and body had arrived with her. It had been an interesting journey. It was a shame to destroy the mirror, Molly conceded, just because she wasn't young any more. She would still look the same, and there would be a lot of clearing up to be done afterwards.

Molly took one last look: she hardly believed how much seventy years had changed her. She still felt the same person as she had been at thirty, at forty, but the years suddenly seemed to have accelerated away. Molly stood sideways and pulled in her stomach, thrusting out her chest. She turned away from the mirror and smiled over her shoulder, wiggled her bottom, posed, waved an arm in the air to acknowledge her fans, like a pop star. Her body wasn't as bad as she'd first thought, it was strong and solid. She posed again. She looked all right really, she thought, if you didn't look too hard at the chin. And the wrinkles.

Molly shrugged, the bat dangling in her hand. Her former prettier younger self may have gone forever, but it had been replaced by a wiser, stronger older woman. She had her health and her humour: she was fine as she was. Who cared? Not Molly, not really, not any more.

Molly decided she'd put the cricket bat back in the small bedroom, then she'd make a cup of coffee and a slice of toast with peanut butter and concentrate on enjoying her birthday. The weather outside was perfect: it was a hot summer's day. She would welcome her new decade by sharing breakfast in the garden with her cat who definitely believed she was still young and beautiful, especially at mealtimes.

Fifteen minutes later, sitting on a bench in the garden with a tray on her lap, Molly hummed a little birthday tune. She sipped strong coffee, the delicious aroma in her nostrils, and nibbled at peanut butter on wholemeal toast. Birthdays were good: she intended to have many more. She gazed over the lawn and into the neighbour's garden, where the sound of clipping suggested that Vanessa was attending to the hedge. Molly noticed her side was unkempt and overgrown, and resolved to trim it later for the sake of her pleasant, cheerful neighbour who, despite being single now too, managed to hold down a busy job and keep her house immaculately tidy and the garden ship-shape.

Molly surveyed the lawn, covered in thistles and in need of a good mowing; the bird bath was broken; the shrubs were straggly and untidy and the small cluster of fruit trees resembled a meadow: weeds, dandelions and daisies sprouted everywhere. She didn't mind; she had to admit that chaos suited her, and she'd rather be chomping through a second slice of toast than attending to a rambling disorderly garden. The thought that she and the garden were two of a kind made her smile. Vanessa popped her head over the newly clipped hedge and smiled, waving a slim bare arm.

'Hi, Molly. I thought I heard you moving around. Are you enjoying the sunshine? It's beautiful out here today.'

Molly stretched her legs in the baggy jeans and looked down at her tanned feet, wriggling long toes. She had forgotten that it was her birthday. 'I should be cutting the hedge, I suppose, but it's too nice out here to do any work.' She sighed. 'Besides, it's August – I can cut the hedge back in the autumn, can't I?' She offered her neighbour a hopeful look.

Vanessa smiled cheerfully. She was an apple-faced, rosy-cheeked woman in her forties, always positive despite being ditched by her serial-cheat of a husband several years ago.

'The hot sun doesn't bother you. You have the right skin type.' She shrugged. 'I just go lobster-red and burn.' She laughed, as if having sunburn was an asset. 'If you need your hedge sorting out, I'm sure I could get Jack round to do it. He's home now.'

'I thought your son was living in Bristol? Wasn't he at uni

there?' Molly munched the last of the toast and brought the coffee mug to her lips.

'He's finished, back home now. He's found a job in Yeovil. His girlfriend is coming to live with him. She'll be looking for work too.'

'You'll have a houseful then?' Molly gazed up at the sky. The deep blue brightness made her close her eyes for a moment.

'They are looking for their own place together: they don't want to stay here with me, although I've offered. It would be nice to have the company...' Vanessa waved the shears in her hand. 'Kids today – it's really hard for them to start out. Especially in their twenties. Renting can be expensive.'

'I'm sure.' Molly met Vanessa's eyes and smiled encouragingly. She had no idea what life was like for youngsters. Molly's daughter Samantha was in her early fifties, married to a sheep farmer in Cumbria. She rang once a week just to keep in touch, but they rarely had much to say to each other. Samantha was nothing like Molly; she was practical and sensible like her father, Trevor. Molly pursed her lips: she hadn't thought about Trev in years. She shook her head, dispelling a misty memory of a hapless young man with huge brown eyes and a personality that was yet to be formed. They had both been too young, too eager. Then an idea occurred to her, the thought that she could help Vanessa's son and herself in one move.

'Vanessa, my garden is in need of a bit more work than just the hedge – why don't you ask Jack to pop round, if he's up for a bit of gardening at the weekend? I'm sure we can sort out something to suit us both.'

Vanessa's pretty face broke into a delighted smile. 'Oh, that would be lovely. He could use the extra cash – thanks, Molly.' She disappeared behind the hedge and, seconds later, the clipping began again. Molly swallowed the last of the coffee and sighed. Life wasn't too bad.

The sun warmed her skin. Molly felt happy: it was her birthday. She stretched her arms luxuriously. No, life wasn't all that bad on a warm August day, sitting in the garden with nothing much to do but bask in the strong sunlight.

Molly thought fleetingly about her half-sister in Yeovil, ten miles away, in her tidy semi-detached house on a smart estate, with its neat lawn, the car parked outside, a well-vacuumed, orderly and clean-smelling interior. They were meeting up tomorrow for dinner at Nell's place to celebrate her birthday. She adored Nell, who was a much better home-maker: her house was always fragrant with candles or room fresheners or both; everything was up to date and top of the range, including the huge television on the wall so that Phil could watch rugby from the huge squashy sofa, a whisky in his hand.

She compared Nell's place to her own ramshackle cottage a few miles from town, with only two neighbours for company; the dusty interior was cluttered with stuff she'd had for years and couldn't bear to throw away. She thought about the tattered sofa and armchair covered with multi-coloured throws, the sooty woodburning stove, the cobwebs in the corners, the array of knick-knacks from her travels and the small television. Home was warm, comfortable, unashamedly disorganised, but then so was Molly.

The Berlingo, abandoned at an angle on the gravel outside the cottage, was full of debris: recyclable shopping bags, garden implements, empty boxes of cat food. It occurred to her that, as Nell had often suggested, she ought to move somewhere modern and easy to clean, but she couldn't imagine herself in a neat house. She liked chaos.

There was a scrabbling of claws on the bench next to her: a

shabby ginger cat clambered onto her knee. Molly rubbed the tousled fur, scratched the crumpled ears that had been tattered in a fight with a squirrel years ago. The cat rolled on her lap, purring, and Molly flattened the top of his head affectionately with her hand.

'Is it food time, Crumper?'

Her voice was soothing, and the ginger cat closed his eyes and the end of his tail twitched with excitement. Molly picked up the ragged cat and cuddled him.

'All right, let's take you inside and give you some biscuits, then I'll pop over to the colonel and make him a sandwich.' She clamped her lips together, a gesture of determination. 'Afterwards I'll have a spot of birthday lunch and maybe we can put the hammock up for the afternoon? I can finish my book and you can laze in the sun with me.'

Ten minutes later, Molly was puffing hard as she rushed up the hill towards Colonel Brimble-Dicks' house, several minutes away. She opened the little wooden gate, secured with a length of twine, and strode down the path that dissected the lawn to the heavy wooden door. Molly bashed the knocker, waited a few minutes and knocked again. She listened hard for any sound of the colonel shambling through the hallway, but she heard nothing.

She rapped again, thinking that if there was no response from him, she'd call the police or break down the door. She imagined peering through the living room window, noticing the old man slumped in a chair, smashing down the door, rushing in to help, giving him the kiss of life: he'd probably wake up, open his eyes in shock and yell at her to fetch him a stiff drink. He was ninety-six years old now: it was inevitable that he'd become ill one day. But four days ago, when she'd visited to check on him and fix his lunch, he'd been as cantankerous as ever. Other than the cataracts that he said plagued him due to the hot sunlight in the Far East where he'd served in the 1960s, and being a bit slow on his legs, he was impressively fit. Colonel Brimble-Dicks said his good health was down to the whisky he drank daily with each meal. Molly knocked again.

Finally, the door opened and a thin man with sparse white hair and red-rimmed eyes glared at her. His voice, although a little throaty, was barking and loud.

'For God's sake, woman, can't a man have fifteen minutes with the *Daily Mail* on the khazi without somebody disturbing him?' He looked up and down and shook his head. 'Come in then, Polly.'

'Molly,' Molly grinned, her face glowing with positivity but, as ever, Colonel Brimble-Dicks paid no attention.

The house smelled stale, of over-dried washing and over-fried onions. The hall was draughty, as was the living room, where the colonel kept his vast collection of ancient books on rickety shelves, and heavily framed family portraits hung on the walls proclaiming his military ancestry. The kitchen was warmer, a little wood-fired stove in the hearth pushing out dry heat. Pegged socks and yellowing underpants hung overhead from a little string line. There was a pile of unwashed dishes in the sink.

The colonel sat down in the bucket chair at the table and picked up a half-full glass of something golden yellow that Molly fervently hoped was whisky. He turned sharply. 'I thought the other woman was coming round today, the young one, Vanessa.'

'No, Colonel, she'll probably pop in tomorrow. I'll give you a hand today. Has the nurse been?'

'She's no nurse. She's just the woman I pay to come in and do things. I get her in just so that she can complain about how much I drink.' He made an indignant sound in his throat, his veined cheeks wobbling with irritation and he stared at her through milky eyes. 'Anyway, what sort of name is Amber? She's named after a traffic light setting.'

'She's very nice, Colonel. It's good to have someone to check how you're doing. She keeps you on your toes.'

He coughed, irritated. 'She's in the family way. She's leaving. I'm getting another one. Jo. Probably just as bad, or worse.' He tilted his head and looked at Molly. 'Since you're here, I could do with a sandwich. And clean socks. And the floor needs sweeping. There are cobwebs everywhere.'

Molly reached for the dustpan. 'If you had a vacuum cleaner, Colonel, it would make the job much easier.' She began to sweep up dust mixed with errant peas. 'I might get you one – for your birthday.'

He leaned forward, watching her. 'I thought I'd see the other one today – your neighbour...'

'Vanessa,' Molly repeated as she brushed dust and debris. She was aware of the colonel's eyes on her as she bent over with the hand brush.

'Pretty girl, Vanessa. Don't know why her husband left her. She does a proper thick sandwich, not those thin flapping things the wind would blow away that you make.'

'I always get you a healthy lunch when I pop round.' She watched him bring the whisky to his lips, his hand trembling a little. 'What do you want on your sandwich today? How about a nice egg mayo?'

'Egg what? I can't be dealing with these modern faddy foods.' He spat out the words as if they tasted horrible. 'Mayonnaise and eggs? What kind of mixture is that with whisky? I'd be violently sick.' He cleared his throat. 'Beef and mustard. Beef, or ham, and English mustard.'

'I'll see what's in the fridge, shall I?' Molly replied good-naturedly, but he didn't hear her. The whisky glass was a quarter full. She lifted a dustpan and dropped the rubbish into a flip-top bin, then washed her hands under the tap.

'Molly's special tasty lunch coming up, Colonel.'

'Not milk and a cheese sandwich, Polly. All that stuff makes me bunged up and then I can't go.'

Molly opened the fridge door. 'You're a bit low on food, Colonel – you need someone to get you a bit of shopping.' She found two slices of ham wrapped in plastic and half a tomato. 'Shall I pick a few things up for you?'

'Vanessa orders it for me online now.'

'Oh, yes, I remember.'

He sniffed. 'You're getting senile, Polly, forgetting what I've told you.' He held out the glass. 'Fill this up again, will you?'

Molly took the glass. 'How many have you had this morning, Colonel?'

'Never you bloody well mind. You're worse than a nagging wife.'

Molly chatted as she buttered bread. 'Did you never want to marry, Colonel? Didn't you meet anyone special? Someone who'd be a nice wife?'

'No such thing as a nice wife. Harridans, all of them, women. No time for any of you.' He grumbled, his face taking on an expression of someone who'd just tasted something unpleasant. 'I've always managed to look after myself. The army taught me discipline and cleanliness. I don't see any point in keeping a dog and barking myself.'

Molly smiled hopefully. 'Really, Colonel, what about companionship and love?'

'Rubbish.' He took the sandwich she placed in front of him. 'I don't know what you're wittering about. The days of any man wanting you for much are gone. Vanessa's a pretty woman though.' He nodded towards the glass. 'Fill it up, Polly, right to the top.'

Molly opened the woodworm-riddled cupboard, finding a bottle of whisky that was almost empty. She poured the remains into a fresh glass and handed it to the colonel. 'Don't you ever feel like a change, going on a journey? I do. All the time. I'd love a break somewhere nice... I get bored, stuck in one place for too long.'

'If you say so.' The colonel took a bite of his sandwich and chewed for a moment. 'The butter's rancid and the ham's stringy but I suppose you did your best. I'll get it down me.'

Molly sat down at the table and gazed at the old man.

'Bon appétit, Colonel. I know it's only a sandwich but you should enjoy every mouthful. That's my philosophy of life – relish each moment. It's best to stay positive.'

He picked up the sandwich again and turned his rheumy eyes on her. 'Do you believe in God, Polly?'

She shrugged. 'I suppose so – I don't think about it much, to be honest.'

'I always wonder about it: the vicars say that God is love but I think He has a warped sense of humour.' His face was sad. 'Think about it. We're born full of innocence and we grow up strong and we have so much hope for the future. But it doesn't last. I remember wondering about that when I was in the war. Many of my men died young in battle in Borneo, good young men, fit, brave men too.'

He reached for his glass. 'Women were left without husbands, children without a father. And I thought I was one of the lucky ones, because I came home. But – and here's why I think God's sense of humour is twisted – now I'm not that soldier any more, I'm nothing, just old and alone and forgotten. My legs are weak and every day I wonder if I'll see tomorrow. Perhaps I'd have been better off dying out in Sarawak with all those good young fellows.'

Molly patted his hand, full of sympathy. 'There's always hope, Colonel.'

'Hope? You must be bloody mad, woman.' His expression was haggard. 'I remember your husband, Richard – such a pleasant, cultured man. He was lucky – he was taken in his sleep. He never knew the aches and pains of being old and alone.'

'Oh, I didn't mean to upset you.' Molly shook her head and turned away. It was definitely time to go. 'Well, I'll get off now, Colonel Brimble-Dicks. I'll pop in on Monday and get you some lunch.'

'Hope. You must be mad.'

'No, I'm just being positive. It's my birthday – and I'm going to make the most of it.' Molly beamed. 'I'm seventy years old today.'

He chortled for a moment and then barked one loud shout. 'Anus.'

Molly jerked back to face him. 'Pardon?'

'I just remembered it... from my schooldays.' His eyes were filling with water as he laughed at his own joke. 'That's the Latin word they used for an old woman, a crone.' He lifted his glass, waving it in Molly's direction. 'I thought you'd like that one.'

She shrugged. 'Well, it's my birthday all day today and I'm celebrating. I'm going to treat myself to something special.' Molly noticed he was staring into the distance, not interested. She took a breath. 'Right. I'll see you on Monday. Take care of yourself, Colonel.' As she walked into the hallway, she heard him bellow after her.

'And it's neuter, anus. No use to man or beast, old women.' She heard him pause, a fit of coughing, and then he raised his voice. 'You can bring another bottle of whisky next time you call in, Polly.'

Molly closed the door behind her, rushed down the path and through the gate, replacing the twine to secure it. 'Bless him, he's a sad, lonely old man,' she muttered to herself as she hurried down the hill towards her cottage. Colonel Brimble-Dicks' last words were echoing in her ears. Molly stopped for a moment, thinking, full of sympathy for him. He had a point: life was for living, for seizing each day, and Molly had been feeling restless. It was time for change to happen. She started to walk, accelerating into a trot, then cannoned down the hill towards her cottage, smiling and humming a little birthday tune. It was her birthday. She was going to do something new.

2

Friday 13th August – still

It's my birthday. Seventy is no different to being sixty-nine except that it sounds so much older. So far, the day has been all right – but I need to celebrate properly – I feel the urge to be outdoors, take a long walk, do something wildly creative. The house feels too small – I need adventure.

That evening, Molly sat in the armchair with Crumper on her knee, the diary in her hand and a cup of tea next to her on the table. She hadn't eaten anything since breakfast – she'd forgotten she'd promised herself a birthday lunch. She wondered about watching television. There might be a nice travel programme on, animals in far-off countries, or something about nature.

In her youth she had travelled to several countries; at first, it had been holidays to France with little Samantha; she'd been to the Gambia with David and later, when she met Richie, she'd travelled through Europe and beyond, both of them relishing the experience of discovering new places. She knew the reason for her innate wanderlust was because of her mother, who had moved on soon after Molly's birth. Her parents hadn't married. In fact, Molly's mother hadn't even stayed with her and her father until Molly's first birthday, so she had no recollection of what she was like and only knew that her name was Kezia Lovell, and that Molly had inherited her dark hair and her erratic ways.

Her father had just once shown her a faded photograph of herself, a baby in a shawl, in the arms of a woman with black hair and a direct, intense gaze: he'd mumbled that he'd loved Molly's mother but she had left him. He rarely spoke of her again and she'd never seen the photograph since. Molly guessed that Kezia Lovell hadn't lasted long as a mother because she was unpredictable and she assumed that she'd inherited her traits: impetuosity, wilfulness, recklessness. Her father never said as much, but she knew what her failings were and who she took after. Molly had not been the perfect child like her half-sister Nell, who was adorable and faultless, exactly like her step-mum, Jean, who had always been wonderful. She recalled Jean with a fond smile.

Molly suddenly decided it would be a good idea to open some wine to celebrate her birthday. There was a bottle of Côtes du Rhône in the kitchen. But Crumper was purring contentedly and it seemed a shame to disturb him as he rolled over on his back with his legs in the air. His eyes were closed, and his back leg was twitching intermittently; he was probably dreaming about the starlings splashing in the broken bird bath. Molly reached for a book on the table next to her teacup. It was beautifully bound in turquoise silk, with a line drawing of a woman's profile in emerald stitches on the cover. She picked up her pen, chewed the end thoughtfully, and read her last entry.

Wednesday 11th August
  Rainy today. Crumper caught a shrew and I rescued it. Watched too much TV and felt frustrated, stuck indoors. I think

I'll take up jogging. I'll get up early tomorrow and run to the signpost for Yeovil and back. That's probably almost a mile. I'll be fit as a butcher's dog, whatever that is, by the end of the summer.

Molly smiled. She'd forgotten she intended to try to run a mile every day. She'd stayed in bed yesterday until after nine listening to the radio. She lifted the pen and began to write.

Friday 13th August, continued

She contemplated the diary entry so far, her scrawl proclaiming an uneventful day, and wrote again.

Today has been a strange landmark birthday.
   I don't mind that I've become older – it's better than the alternative – but that doesn't mean I have to be stuck in a routine. I need to up my game and not end up like the poor colonel, alone and bitter. I need more fun in my life.
   Now I've entered a new decade, I need a hobby...

Molly sighed, closing the book with a clunk, and thought for a moment.

'I do need a project.'

She inhaled strongly, deliberately, and put the diary down. She had been keeping a diary for the last five years, since Richie died. It had been consolation at first, then company, a friend, someone to listen. She rubbed the ginger cat's chin.

'Right, Crumper. I'm going to have a glass of wine and eat something substantial to keep body and soul together then you and I can curl up together and watch a bit of David Attenborough. How would that be?'

She kissed the cat's tattered, flat forehead before pushing him from her knee and smoothing down the baggy T-shirt, then she stood up, focused and ready for action.

Twenty minutes later, the kitchen was filled with the warm aroma of sizzling onions, garlic and mushrooms. Molly splashed red wine into the frying pan and added basil from a pot growing on the window ledge. Boiling water made the little tubes of penne rise in the saucepan. She slurped a mouthful of wine from a very full glass and began to sing a little song: U2's 'I Still Haven't Found What I'm Looking For'.

Molly had a strong voice and she sang it loudly, with abandon. She and Richie had loved U2. They'd seen them in Paris in 2007, holding hands, not able to take the smile from their faces throughout the entire concert. Richie had loved the Edge's strong guitar sound and Molly had adored Bono's voice. But not as much as she'd adored Richie McCracken. He'd been the love of her life and losing him had changed everything.

She was still bawling out the song as she slopped pasta onto a plate and poured more wine into the glass. She sat at the scrubbed table in the kitchen and started to eat. Crumper arrived, leaping up on the table, and he stretched out a skinny paw to steal a piece of hot pasta. Molly reached for her wine and smiled at his efforts to pilfer food, holding out a piece of pasta, blowing on it to cool it.

'Oh, Crumper – we were going to eat supper in front of the television.' She patted the flat furry head. 'I know – after this we'll take some birthday ice cream into the living room and see if we can find a nature programme, shall we?'

An hour later, Molly was sitting in the armchair with her feet up in worn furry slippers, finishing the last of the wine. Crumper was sprawled on the arm of the chair, his nose snuffling in the empty bowl of pecan caramel ice cream. Molly rubbed her stomach.

'I'm full.'

She pressed the remote to find something to watch on TV and roamed the channels disinterestedly. There was a programme about people painting portraits. She watched it for a few minutes. Someone had finished a picture of a Scottish actor and got him just right: the twist of his mouth, the contemplative gaze of his eyes. Molly exhaled and stared at the wall above the desk.

She was gazing at a painting of a naked woman standing, her arms raised in the air, dark hair over her shoulders, her expression impetuous and joyful, the light in her eyes a luminous gaze into the distance. At the lower right-hand corner, where the woman's thigh ended was a signature, 'RMcC'.

Richie had painted her in 1991, two years after they'd met. He had been the only one who'd ever truly understood her, and he had captured her mood perfectly in that painting.

Molly stared at the picture, her hand over her face to suppress a smile. She'd been self-assured, unabashed, carefree in those days. She hadn't minded him painting her naked. He'd seen her strutting around the house with hardly a stitch on one Sunday morning and abandoned his usual practice of painting landscapes in order to paint her. He had rendered her in an abstract way, her skin ochre, her hair so dark it was almost blue, making the whites of her eyes gleam and the irises soft.

The painting did not focus solely on her capriciousness or her mischief; it was a study of her in a moment of complete trust and love, her eyes uplifted all the time. Richie had been so proud of it. Molly had laughed and said it made her look brazen and fat.

She thought, with a shrug, that she'd be glad to be as slim as she had been. But it wasn't Richie who had inspired her confidence: she'd been buoyant, light-hearted and independent by nature then. He had just brought out the best in her and she had encouraged the best in him. She had never worried about anything in those days; she had lived for the moment, happy.

There was a space on the wall next to the painting. Molly glued her eyes to the blank pale wall with a crack in the plaster as an idea came to her. She could fit in a second painting; one she would create of herself now. In all her glory, naked. It would complement Richie's painting perfectly and it would be, Molly thought, her mind fuzzed by alcohol, a perfect way to celebrate her seventieth. Painting herself could be her new project: an up-to-date portrait of Molly on the wall next to the old one would bring her into the present day.

She rushed upstairs into the third bedroom, the office where Richie's easel and acrylic paints and canvasses were still kept. There was a painting of a deer, antlers high, one eye proud and alert, the other simply sketched in pencil, the body and background still a few random lines. Richie had left it unfinished.

Molly dragged out a large canvas and some paint, a tube of deep emerald and another, lurid blue. There were no brushes to be found. Molly waved a hand, unfazed. 'Who needs brushes?' She tugged off her clothes, flinging them out through the door onto the landing until she stood naked, cold and laughing. 'I can paint myself. Oh – I know...'

She hurried downstairs and padded into the kitchen. In a drawer, she found some cling film and began to wrap it around her body like a huge adhesive bandage.

Back upstairs, she squeezed the emerald paint from the tube and smeared it over the cling film, covering her torso and shoulders, as far as her belly button. She slopped extra paint to the front of her body so that the protective wrap was thickly coated, then she lay down on the canvas as heavily as possible, wriggling, making a human print. She stayed this way for almost a minute, rolling against the canvas, then she stood up carefully and surveyed her handiwork.

'This body needs some work.' Molly smiled as she stared at the rough impression of round flattened breasts, a curve for the stomach and small flimsy arms and shoulders. She placed the picture upright, turned her head to one side and scrutinised her work. It was clearly a woman's body, an impression of crushed voluptuousness.

Molly dipped a finger in the lurid green paint and added a few random swishes for shoulder blades, the hint of a neck, a thumb print for a belly button, then she signed MM at the bottom, for Molly Mitchell. She grinned: it wasn't bad. Richie would have loved it, the freedom of expression, the immediacy of it. She'd let it dry and then tomorrow she'd hang it next to the painting Richie had done all those years ago. Two companion paintings: a diptych. Molly then and Molly now.

For a moment she was lost in thought: all those years ago Richie had laboured over the first painting for weeks. Now she had created the companion one in under two minutes. Her skin was becoming cold and sticky beneath the cling film. She rushed into the bathroom and turned the shower on full, waiting for the water to steam before she leaped in. She had smudges of acrylic paint on her arms and thighs.

She was about to plunge into the stream of water, cling film and all, when she heard the sound, a persistent ringing downstairs. Someone was at the front door and, by the elongated hum of the bell, they were keen to be heard. Molly gasped. She hadn't time for a shower. She rushed into her bedroom, seeing the image of herself fly past the wardrobe mirror, an oven-ready chicken wrapped in shiny green cling film. She pulled her hair from the knot as if the slate-grey mane that tumbled beyond her shoulders would somehow make her wrapped nakedness more acceptable.

She tugged the dressing gown around her body and rushed downstairs.

The doorbell was still ringing. When she dragged the door open, a small woman, her hair cut in a neat blonde bob, wearing a pretty blouse and smart blue jeans was facing her. She was carrying a handbag and a suitcase. Her eyes were puffy and red. She simply said, 'Happy birthday, Molly,' and burst into tears.

Molly extended two green hands and gasped. 'Nell? I wasn't expecting you today. I thought we were meeting up tomorrow. Are you all right?'

She glanced over her sister's shoulder to see the silver Ford Fiesta parked outside her gate, in the lane. Then she became aware of her sister's slumped body, the bulging suitcase, the tear-filled eyes, the wobbling chin and she threw her arms around the smaller woman, oblivious to the shower running in the bathroom, the sticky paint squelching on her skin and the desperate need to remove it straight away with soap and water. She hugged her visitor, breathing hurriedly, anxiety in her voice.

'Nell, what on earth's happened? Come in at once. Let me put the kettle on.'

3

Friday 13th August

I made a painting to celebrate the arrival of a new decade. Then Nell turned up out of the blue – I'm there for her a hundred per cent, poor love. Don't worry, Nell – your big sister will try her best to sort everything out.

Molly ripped off the plastic wrapping, showered quickly, scrubbed off most of the slimy green paint spattered on the sides of the cubicle and rushed downstairs in clean pyjamas to the kitchen table where Nell was huddled over a steaming cup of chamomile tea, dabbing her eyes, the tissue squeezed in her fist. She stared at Molly. 'You have a splodge of something green on your chin...'

'Oh.' Molly lifted a hand without thinking and rubbed hard at the skin below her mouth. 'How's the tea?'

Nell shrugged. 'It tastes like cat's pee but it's doing the trick and calming me down. I'm sorry, Moll...' She sniffed. 'I haven't brought you anything for your birthday – everything has gone wrong.'

'I got your card... and it doesn't matter.' Molly pushed damp hair from her face. 'So, what's happened? Is everything all right? Is Phil okay?'

'Phil.' Nell forced a laugh that wasn't a laugh at all; her eyes filled with huge tears immediately. She tucked the sweeping fringe behind her ear and took a deep breath. 'I've left him.'

'Oh, that's awful, Nell.' Molly's eyes were wide. 'Well, you're welcome to stay here as long as you like.'

'It might be forever.' Nell clamped her lips tightly together.

'That's not a problem. Can I get you food? A sandwich? Then you can tell me all about it.'

'I'd be sick, Molly. I'm so...' Fresh tears welled up. 'It's really over.'

'Are you sure?' Molly reached out and squeezed Nell's small hand affectionately. 'You've been together for forty years... How on earth has that happened?'

'Over, in a split second.' Nell dabbed at her eyes with the tissues. 'I can't go back now. Anyway, it's too late for that.'

'For what?'

'He's found someone else.'

'No,' Molly gasped. 'Phil's not the type.'

'He wasn't.' Nell met Molly's gaze grimly, her eyes red. 'He is now.'

'I don't understand.'

Nell took a deep breath. 'He told me this evening. He met her in the coffee shop in town. She works there – a barista or a waitress, I'm not sure. She's called Nikki. It's the real thing, apparently.'

Molly leaned forward, her fingers rubbing her temples. 'But you two have always been so comfortable together...'

'Comfortable.' Nell's face contorted, a mixture of anger and resignation with a dash of gallows humour. 'That was the problem. Now he's met her, he knows what real love is, believe it or not.'

'Phil said that to you?' Molly's eyes were wide with amazement. 'Phil? Steady, sensible, stick-in-the-mud Phil?' She flattened a hand over her mouth. 'Oh, sorry, Nell.'

'He came home tonight and told me all about it. He said he'd leave and I could stay but I just packed a case and walked out.' Nell reached for the tea and breathed in steam. 'I couldn't believe it at first. It's just not like Phil. But...' She sipped the tea gratefully. 'It just shows how wrong you can be about someone.'

'Perhaps it's a mistake.'

'My mistake. For trusting him, for believing we had a good marriage. He was really sorry, he said, but he loves her. He told me all about it tonight. We sat at the table and he explained it to me like I was a child. He loves her. She's the one. And the worst thing...' Nell clutched the teacup. 'She's thirty years younger than him. She's thirty-seven.'

'No – she can't be.' Molly shook her head again, disbelieving.

Nell blew her nose with the tissue; when her hand came away, the tip was pink. 'So, it's over. I've been married to Phil for longer than his... his mistress has been alive.' She gave a little snort. 'He's moving her into our house. I won't go back, not ever. I don't want to see him; I don't want to have to talk to him. I'll never put my foot inside that house again.'

'She's moving in?'

'Yup. Into our home, our bed...' Nell swallowed the rest of the tea, pulling an unhappy face. 'He said at first that I should have the house and he'd move in with her, but I don't want to go in there ever again. So, he said he'll buy me out after the divorce. I can find somewhere else to live.'

'Divorce?'

'Oh, yes, we talked about that too, Molly. That's how "over"

Phil and I are.' She ran a hand over her face and her neck, the skin starting to mottle. 'I don't suppose I could have a medicinal drink?'

Molly's heart was swollen with sadness for Nell: she slid her chair back and moved to a cupboard, taking out a bottle of brandy and two glasses. 'Medicinal? Just a small one then.'

'Large, please. In fact, just give me the whole bottle.'

Molly poured a small drink for herself and passed Nell a glass and the bottle, ruffling her sister's silky hair affectionately. Nell filled her glass with brandy, a little spilling onto the wooden table, and lifted it to her lips with shaky fingers. 'So, why were you covered with green paint?'

Molly shrugged. 'I've been painting myself.' She grinned at her joke. 'New project. I'm trying to branch out.'

'I need a new project. In fact, I need a whole new life.' Nell swallowed the drink and pulled a face. 'So, can I stay here with you?'

'Of course – you don't need to ask.' Molly reached out and grabbed her sister's hand. 'The spare bedroom's all made up.'

'The spare room...?' Nell's chin quivered. 'That's about right. I'm spare now.'

'Not at all. This is your home. *Mi casa, tu casa.*'

Nell had finished her brandy and began to pour herself another. 'I'm glad to see you're still keeping up the Spanish classes...'

'No, I've forgotten most of it. It must be well over fifteen years ago when Richie and I learned it together...' Molly sat still for a moment, remembering them both repeating phrases, copying a nasal voice on a CD and laughing. Richie had been a natural linguist. She reached for the brandy bottle and topped up her glass. 'Oh dear, Nell. I suppose it's you and me by ourselves now – but I promise you'll be all right.'

Nell's eyes were glazed. 'Sisters, alone, unwanted, miserable for the rest of our days...'

Molly shook her head, sliding the bottle just out of Nell's easy reach. 'No, we won't let that happen. It's Phil's loss.' She took a breath. 'We can turn this around, make it work for you. You'll see – it's an opportunity, not a disaster...'

'My husband dumping me for a younger woman is an opportunity? Really, Molly...'

Molly was aghast – she'd said the wrong thing. 'No, I don't mean that, just... you'll be fine, Nell, really you will. You just need time.' She looked at her sister's face, tears streaming down her blotchy cheeks, and exhaled slowly. 'Time and a good night's sleep and...' She pushed the bottle back to Nell. 'And maybe just a teeny bit more brandy...'

An hour later, the bottle half-empty, Molly helped Nell struggle upstairs, tugging her suitcase in the other hand, and deposited them both in the guest room. Then she washed her face and brushed her teeth before ambling into her own room and snuggling under the duvet. Her mind was crammed with thoughts leaping up and down, first an overwhelming anxiety about her sister and then her busy day, the new painting of her at seventy, the reflection of herself in the mirror and the colonel's mocking words. The red light on the alarm clock informed her that it was approaching midnight, but Molly still could not sleep.

It would be lovely to have her sister to stay, and Molly was desperate to help. Nell was distraught, and Molly wondered momentarily about Phil's side of the story. An affable Yorkshireman, Phil had always been mild-mannered, honest, cheerful. Molly would never have considered him to be the roving type and she certainly couldn't imagine him falling in love with a younger woman: he was far too pragmatic. Molly wondered if her sister had somehow got it wrong. But it wasn't the sort of thing one made a mistake about, adultery. Molly liked Phil and it occurred to her that she should go and talk to him. It might even save her sister's marriage.

Molly imagined that Nell must be feeling awful right now, alone in the guest room, with her thoughts. Molly always felt loneliest at night-time. She thought of Richie again. She'd hung onto the bed they had shared: she couldn't bear to part with it, the idea that somehow his DNA lurked in a fold or a seam of the mattress, that he was somehow not far away. But, of course, he was very far away. He was gone and that was the stark reality. Molly was alone and, no matter how nice it might be to enjoy her sister's company for a while, she didn't want Nell to suffer the loneliness that was stitched permanently into the fabric of her own life. She'd become used to being by herself; she was tough, resilient. But poor Nell was made of more fragile stuff.

Molly rubbed her eyes and she was suddenly resolute. She'd get up early tomorrow and drive to Nell's house; she'd speak to Phil and he'd see the error of his ways. Perhaps, miraculously, he might forget about Nikki from the coffee shop and beg Nell to come back to him. Then everything would be all right again – Nell would be happy. Molly sighed and closed her eyes.

4

Saturday 14th August

My mouth feels like the inside of a log. I drank too much brandy with Nell last night – sadly, we weren't celebrating my birthday. Poor Nell. I think I know how to solve all her problems, though. I just want Phil to see sense...

Molly checked on Nell at nine o'clock. As she peered round the door of the spare bedroom, Nell was fast asleep, her body twisted beneath a dishevelled duvet. Downstairs, Crumper had occupied his usual place first thing in the morning, next to his dish, and was yowling for food. Molly fed him, rubbing the flattened fur, then she grabbed a banana from the fruit bowl. She'd be back home by half past eleven, wake Nell and make them both coffee and lunch. Molly smiled sadly: Nell mightn't be feeling her best. She had polished off a lot of brandy.

Molly glanced at her silk notebook on the small table and resolved to update it later. There were more things she needed to write down after last night. She would order her thoughts by setting them down clearly and, hopefully, she'd have good news. She'd put up her painting, too, next to Richie's painting of her younger self, the celebration of her at seventy in all her mature emerald glory.

Molly glanced out of the window: the sky was leaden and overcast, so she reached for a light coat and stepped outside. As she pushed her car keys into her pocket, she heard a friendly voice calling from over the fence. She turned and was met by Vanessa's smiling face.

'You're up early, Molly.'

'Just running a few errands.'

Vanessa smiled. 'There's a silver car parked on the side of the road by your fence – is that yours?'

'It's my sister's. She's staying with me for a few days.' Molly pressed her lips together. It was best not to tell Vanessa the whole story, not yet.

'By the way, Molly, did you visit the colonel yesterday?'

'I popped in and made him a sandwich...'

'I think he's getting grumpier.' Vanessa shrugged. 'He told me I was getting thin the last time I called in. He said if I stood sideways, he wouldn't be able to see me.' She shook her head sadly. 'He went on and on about how women should have proper flesh on them, like cattle.'

'He tells me how lovely you are. He's just lonely,' Molly replied. 'I think I'll have a word with him. I'll take him a bottle of whisky round and have a quiet chat. I might suggest he holds back with the misogyny.' She grinned. 'Being nearly a hundred years old and a war hero is no excuse for rudeness.'

'I think he's unwell,' Vanessa said. 'He's in a lot of pain all the time – you know how his arthritis flares up. Perhaps the anger keeps him alive.'

'That and the whisky, poor man.' Molly made a mental note to pick up a bottle for him later. 'I think that's all he has now. It's a shame. Still, I'll point out a few ground rules. The days when women were objects for men to judge are gone. He has a new carer coming, apparently. Maybe she'll keep him in line.'

Vanessa gazed up at the sky. 'I'm hoping the weather will lift. Jack said he'd pop round to see you later and chat about doing the garden.' She beamed. 'It was so kind of you to offer to let him do a few odd jobs.'

'It's not as if I'm going to keep the garden looking tidy by myself, is it?' Molly grinned, rattling her car keys. 'Right. Good luck with Colonel Brimble-Dicks, Vanessa. Don't take any of his cheek.'

Vanessa gave a little laugh. 'I suppose it's the nearest I get to being paid any attention nowadays.' She raised her voice as Molly opened the Berlingo. 'What I'd give for a good-looking man to take me out on the town.'

'You and me both,' Molly called through the open window as she started the engine. She drove away steadily, taking the turn for Yeovil.

The radio was blaring out a tinny pop song from the 1980s but she wasn't listening. Her words were still rattling in her head. *You and me both*, she had said without thinking. It was a throw-away comment, but Molly wondered if it was true, whether she would really like some male attention, whether a date would do her good. It would be nice to be flattered, to have some kindness, affection even. The thought puzzled her: she'd believed she was fine alone but, for the first time in years, since Richie had died in his sleep, she wondered if she needed someone new to spend time with.

She thought briefly that she could suggest to Nell that they signed up for internet dating or speed dating. It would certainly be a project for them both. They could support each other to meet intriguing strangers. Molly grinned, thinking it might be sisterly fun to dress up, to go out on dates, to compare different men, to laugh like teenagers as they gazed at potential men friends' photographs on their phone screens and made decisions about whether to swipe left or right.

She turned the car onto the busy main road; as she accelerated, she realised that dating would be a terrible idea. Nell didn't need a new man. She still wanted the one she was married to. And Molly didn't need a man either. She'd had one she'd loved beyond words and that was that: she wouldn't bother with another. As she often said, who would want flat lemonade after sampling champagne?

So instead, Molly contemplated what to say to Phil when she arrived. She was determined to be calm, she would be sympathetic, non-judgemental, but above all, she would be loyal. Poor Nell. Then, when she'd spoken to Phil, she'd have a clear idea about the next move, and she'd go home and discuss the plan of action with her sister.

Molly admitted to herself, as she pulled on the handbrake outside Nell's house – Phil's house now – that she truly believed Phil was making a mistake and probably needed to have it pointed out to him. He was temporarily blinded by bubbly barista Nikki from the coffee shop and, after a few wise words from his sensible sister-in-law, he'd realise the error of his ways and beg his wife to come home. Realistically, Molly thought, it had to be the case. Phil and Nell had been married for years. They'd had their ups and downs; in the early days they had struggled on Phil's low income as an apprentice until he became manager on the shop floor at Westlands; Nell had devoted herself to being a classroom assistant in a primary school, immersing herself in others' children in order to deal with the sadness of not being able to have one of their own.

But they'd enjoyed a kind of symbiosis. Phil would always help Nell on and off with her coat; he'd always ask her if she was warm enough, drape an arm across her shoulder as they left a restaurant. They had shared the household chores, the weekly shop; they'd been on annual holidays, mostly to the Greek islands. They appeared devoted to each other. Molly sighed. None of those things meant that he loved her, of course. He was a caring partner and they shared responsibilities. That was consideration; it wasn't love. Molly wondered now what love was, and how you recognised it amongst all the other things that filled a long-term relationship: duty, habit, tolerance.

But Molly had loved Richie and he'd adored her. It had always been there in the fun, the laughter, the shared words, the joy of being together: even in the bickering quarrels and the hugs and kisses they'd shared afterwards. It had broken her heart when he died, when his huge generous heart gave way.

She hadn't loved Trev, Samantha's father, but in the inexperienced rush of youth she had thought she loved him enough to find herself pregnant at seventeen. She and Trev hadn't lasted long after that. He'd been too young and wasn't ready to be a father at eighteen: he and Molly had little in common. He'd kept in touch with Samantha even when he had a new family and, as far as Molly knew, they still got on well. He hadn't been her type, though, Trev. She had liked David more. They had met when Samantha was ten years old. He had helped her move house from the flat in Yeovil; it had been his removal firm and, a year later, she had moved herself and Samantha into his house.

But, on reflection, that wasn't love either. She had simply been a woman lurching towards hope again, clutching at straws, changing her mind, striving for happiness in the arms of a nice-enough man; hoping for someone to share time with, to fill the hours when she wasn't furiously rushing around trying to be a competent mother. But it hadn't worked: they'd drifted apart; the conversation ran out. She had left him six years later and that had allowed her to be independent for a while, to stutter impetuously through a few rash relationships until Richie had met her at a Christmas party, where she'd been dancing wildly on the tables before she'd thrown herself into his arms and later into his bed. As usual, she had rushed into a situation without thinking first but Richie had been the right one by accident and this time she'd known it immediately.

Molly slammed the car door behind her and set off down the little path, reaching number three, and ringing the bell. In her mind, she had prepared her first sentence, practising it with a smile and a calm, reassuring tone: 'Hello, Phil, how are you? We need to talk about you and Nell.' It sounded dramatic but it was reasonable enough. She waited a moment, then the door creaked open and Phil filled the frame. She took a breath and the words spluttered from her lips.

'Well, if it isn't Phil the philanderer.'

Molly had intended to be calm and persuasive but suddenly she couldn't stop herself. 'Have you any idea what you've done to my poor sister? And goodness knows what you were thinking of, having a relationship with that coffee shop woman...'

She stopped. She had expected Phil to look pleased with himself, smug, his face flushed with the success of his young conquest. She'd expected to see him wearing youthful, trendier clothes, to have grown his short grey-brown hair over his collar or even to be sporting an inappropriately jaunty moustache. But Phil was wearing an old T-shirt and baggy jeans. He had lost weight; he looked haggard and miserable; his eyes were red-rimmed. He slumped against the door frame.

'Molly.' His voice was heavy with sadness and regret. 'You'd better come in...'

She followed him into the house without another word. She hadn't planned to start an argument. They went into the lounge and sat down in the armchairs. Molly gazed around. The house had always been impeccably tidy: Nell was a very particular home-maker. But Phil's breakfast of congealed eggs and toast was abandoned, half-eaten, on the coffee table next to a cup of coffee. Two crumpled socks lay on the carpet. The curtains were still closed and the television was blaring out the daily news. Phil reached for the remote and switched it off, then he turned sad eyes to Molly.

'I'm not surprised you're angry. I don't blame you. Nell's staying with you, then? I thought that's where she'd go.'

Molly met his gaze. 'You've hurt her, Phil.'

He nodded. 'I know. I'm not proud of what I've done...'

Molly huffed. 'Going off with a woman from the coffee shop? I never thought you were the cheating kind. Whatever were you thinking?' Her eyes flashed. 'And what are you going to do to put it right?'

Phil wiped a hand over his forehead. 'There's nothing to be done, Molly.'

Molly was about to launch into a tirade, pointing out that Phil had caused the mess and could darn well sort it out, but something about his slumped shoulders stopped her. Then she noticed his face was streaked with tears. 'I can't abandon Nikki.'

Molly folded her arms. 'So, you're going to abandon Nell instead?'

'I didn't intend for this to happen, but it did.' He sighed and pushed a hand through his hair. It needed washing. 'From the moment I met her, something changed. I can't turn back.'

'So, how long has this been going on?'

'About eight months.'

'Eight months?' Molly was horrified.

He looked away. 'I go to the bowling club with the lads on a Thursday afternoon and afterwards we all go for coffee in the trendy new café, Le Loup.'

'The French place? I've never been there...'

'That's where I met Nikki. I mean, we struck up a conversation. There was a spark... more than a spark. I looked at her and I felt like I wanted to take care of her. She was vulnerable, sweet. I'd never felt that way before.'

'You should have ignored it, Phil. You could have walked away. You have a wife. She's vulnerable now.'

'I should have. But I couldn't stop myself. It was like Nikki was a magnet and I couldn't hold back. I tried at first; I wanted to think of Nell but I couldn't help what I felt. I went back to the café on my own a few times, and there was Nikki in her uniform looking at me. I couldn't take my eyes off her. We'd always talk and laugh together, and one day I asked her to meet me, just the once. Then it escalated – she knew I was married but – I'd wait in the street for her after she finished work and then we met up on her days off. We tried to stay apart. We both knew it was wrong, but one thing led to another...'

'What about Nell? What about her feelings?'

'I know... I didn't want to hurt her. If there was any way I could have stopped it, I would but Nikki and I are right for each other. Then it was too late. And I lied to Nell, which is terrible. I shouldn't have, but she thought I was out with the bowling boys.' He shook his head. 'Nikki is... special.'

'So that's it, you've made your decision, Phil?'

'I'm afraid so. It's a mess. I'm sorry.'

'And she's in her thirties?'

'Thirty-seven...'

'So – you're having a fling with a woman thirty years younger than you and you think it's the real thing? Phil, seriously...' Molly grabbed his arm, her eyes wide. 'Isn't it just a moment of madness or something? Infatuation? A passing fancy?' She leaned forward. 'Think about it. Think about Nell. You had years together...'

'But for many of those years we were just co-existing, Molly. Nikki makes me feel alive...'

'It's just temporary passion, Phil: just lust. Nell and you are real – a marriage, a home, a life together, sharing...'

'You're wrong.' Phil sighed. 'It's not just about sex. I mean Nell and I don't... we haven't... for years. We have separate beds. There's nothing between us, no affection, we don't share anything, we don't hug; we just bumble round the house and hardly say a word to each other. It's been that way for twenty years and I've given up trying to do anything to bring us together. I thought we'd be all right, that we rubbed along together, me and Nell, but then Nikki came along and...'

'And you betrayed Nell? You just went off and found a young replacement and fell into her bed because things were a bit boring with your wife.'

'It's not like that; it's not sordid. We love each other, Nikki and me.'

Molly shook her head. 'Go to counselling, Phil, marriage guidance: go with Nell and ask for help – it's not too late to sort something out between you both.'

'It is too late.' Phil's voice was a murmur, a sadness caught in his throat. 'Nikki's pregnant.'

'No.' Molly suddenly felt a layer of ice spreading across her skin. She chewed her lip, her face troubled. 'But Nell had two miscarriages...'

'Five,' Phil whispered. 'We didn't tell people about all of them...'

'She told me she couldn't have children...' Molly's eyes blazed. 'Now your fancy woman is expecting a baby? Phil, this will crush Nell.'

He sighed. 'Nell doesn't know.'

Molly puffed air out of her cheeks, suddenly feeling sorry for everyone. 'This changes everything.' She thought for a moment. 'I can't say congratulations, Phil...'

'I've always wanted a child. Nikki has a son, who is sixteen – but a baby of our own. Oh, Molly...'

'I don't know what to say.' Molly examined her fingers, thinking. 'I came here hoping you'd see sense, that you and Nell could patch things up and you'd dump Nikki but now...'

'I've promised her we'll get married... when the divorce comes through.'

Molly exhaled. 'Poor Nell.'

Phil agreed. 'I feel so awful.' He rubbed his hands through the grey-brown hair. 'I've known Nell for forty years; we've been through a lot. I'm fond of her but... Molly, this is such a mess.'

Molly grabbed his arm and blurted. 'Nell mustn't know about the baby.'

'Yeovil isn't such a big town – and people talk.' Phil sighed. 'We can't keep it a secret for very long – Nikki's started to show already...'

'Right. We need a plan. This is what's happening, Phil. I'll look after Nell.' Molly was resolute. 'Go and pack her stuff into cases and put them in my car. Everything you can, so she doesn't need to come back here. And you can communicate with her and me through text and email. She can't find out about the baby, not yet.'

'All right.' He rose obediently, his face tired. 'What are you going to do, Molly?'

'I'm going to take care of my sister,' she retorted, although in fact she had no idea at all what she would do next except to make sure Nell didn't know that her husband's girlfriend was pregnant. Molly sighed as she watched Phil stumble towards the hallway and up the stairs. She'd need to play for time. She needed a plan.

5

Saturday 14th August

I'm not sure what to do for the best. Nell's life has changed forever in twenty-four hours. And she has no idea yet about Phil's baby. Poor love. I'll make sure she's fine. I'll think of a way to cheer her up.

Molly had deposited her sister's three bulging cases in the hallway and was currently trying to balance her new painting on a nail she'd hammered into the wall. It hung precariously at an angle. She stood back and admired her artwork. It was a rough representation of a woman's body in a vivid green, although, on second thoughts, it could have been mistaken for a lurid smiling face. Or a rickety tree. It would have made Richie smile.

She remembered the luggage blocking the stairs and scratched her head thoughtfully. She'd take the cases upstairs in a moment, make Nell some lunch – it was that time already – and hope that a plan would just pop into her head about how to stop her finding out about Phil, Nikki and the baby. Perhaps it might be better just to tell her the truth. Molly wasn't sure. Her thoughts were interrupted by a knock at the front door. She'd left it open as she'd hauled Nell's luggage into the house.

'Hello. Molly?' A young man with a cheerful face and a thatch of blond hair was standing in the doorway, stretching out his hand enthusiastically. 'It is Molly, isn't it? You're expecting me.'

Molly showed him a confused face. 'Am I?'

'I'm Jack, Vanessa's son, from next door? She said you'd like me to do a bit of gardening?'

'Oh, yes.' Molly took his hand. 'Yes, that would be a good idea. I'm afraid I have let it go to waste a bit… I didn't recognise you. You've cut your hair. Come in, Jack.'

He followed her into the living room, his eyes taking in the furniture: the small television, the bookcases bulging with too many books, the ornaments, the paintings on the wall, Crumper sprawled on the sofa surrounded by colourful cushions.

'I could start on clearing the garden now.' Jack looked eager. 'In a couple of hours, I could sort out the lawn and pull up some weeds.'

'Perfect. Would twenty-five pounds do?'

Jack's face flushed with delight. 'Oh, that would be great. I'm saving up – we're saving up. My girlfriend is coming down in a few days and we're going to look for our own place.'

'Vanessa told me you'd found a job?'

'In Yeovil. Mel is going to look for work here too. We'll need a car and once we get our own place there will be bills…' His smile broadened. 'We can't stay with Mum too long. I mean…' He pulled a face to indicate that the idea was ludicrous. 'So I'm happy to work in your garden as often as you like.'

'It's a deal, then.'

'I'll make a start now.' Jack's gaze fell on the paintings again. 'I like your paintings. Especially the one of the green fruits.'

'Fruit?'

'The apples and the bendy green bananas...'

Molly was about to explain to him that it was her body wrapped in cling film but she thought better of it. 'Yes, that one.' She spoke without thinking. 'It's a copy... of a Jackson Pollock... abstract... expressionist. It's called *Vision in Emerald – number seventy.*'

Jack was impressed. 'Right. Nice. I'll start today, shall I?'

'Start? Oh, the garden. Yes, okay – tell me when you're done and I'll pay you – in cash.'

'Thanks, Molly. Will do.'

She watched him wander into the garden, momentarily wondering how such a slender young man was going to wrestle with all the weeds and overgrown bushes. Then her mind flitted back to Nell. She would delay telling her about Phil as long as possible and instead concentrate on keeping her sister occupied: eating, talking, maybe shopping, although Molly reminded herself to stay away from Yeovil and especially from the French-style coffee shop. She bustled into the kitchen with the intention of making an omelette for Nell. As she burst through the door, she saw her sister seated at the table drinking coffee.

'Oh, you're up? I was going to make you some lunch.'

Nell shook her head. 'You were busy chatting at the door when I came down.' She sighed. 'I nearly fell over all the luggage. So, you saw Phil?'

Molly nodded.

'And I take it his answer is out there, with all my things stuffed in three cases. That's it, then. It's over?'

Molly nodded again.

Nell rested her head on her arms. Molly stood, mouth open, wondering what to say, then she blurted, 'He's very upset, Nell.'

Nell looked up, her face flushed with sudden anger. '*He's*

upset? *I'm* upset. How dare he whine at you about his feelings when he's the one who dumped me?'

Molly sat down at the table and took her sister's hand in hers. Her face was sad. 'Oh, Nell. It's such a mess.'

Nell met her eyes. 'So, we're definitely done, me and Phil, after all this time? It's over?'

Molly paused, then her voice was quiet. 'I think so, yes.'

'I don't know whether to be angry, whether to go round and scream at him, whether to put my nose in the air and pretend I don't care or just to get blind drunk.' Nell closed her eyes.

Molly patted her hand. 'Don't do anything. Give yourself space. We'll work something out. Think of it as—' She was about to say 'a fresh start' but she stopped herself. She took a breath. 'We'll play for time, watch this space. Think of it as a holiday.'

'A holiday?' Nell was distraught. 'He's cheated on me, Molly.'

'Yes – sorry, Nell – I meant – time for change...' She had said the wrong thing again. Molly sighed: whatever she said wasn't going to help, so she muttered, 'Shall I make lunch?'

'No thanks – I couldn't.' Nell sipped her coffee. Molly noticed her eyes were ringed with a tinge of blue. Silence hung on the air then Nell suddenly jerked her head. 'My necklace. Did he put it in the case?'

'Necklace?'

Nell scraped back her chair and rushed into the hall, moving at speed. She wrenched open the first suitcase, throwing clothes and underwear out, a frantic whirling of her arms. Then she repeated the exercise with the second case and then the third while Molly watched, her hands on her face.

'It's not here.' Nell turned wild eyes on Molly. 'She's not having my necklace.'

Molly raised her brows quizzically. 'What necklace?'

'The one Mum gave me. It's gold, a little heart and a letter N on a chain.' Nell leaped up and grabbed Molly's hands. 'He's not giving it to Nikki. You'll have to go back and get it, Moll.'

'All right. I'll make us some lunch first and...'

'Go now, please?' Nell's eyes were huge, begging. 'I want to make sure he doesn't give it away.'

Molly sighed. 'Phil's not likely to do that...'

'He's given her everything else,' Nell said grimly.

'I'll go now, then.' Molly sighed, reaching for her keys. A sudden thought had popped into her head. Perhaps there was one last way she could save Nell's marriage with a little honest persuasion. And she was ready for a cup of coffee – she could try one in the new French café in town before she visited Phil.

* * *

It was midday. Nell watched Molly's Berlingo careering down the road. A smile fluttered on her lips temporarily, fondness for her crazy half-sister who could always remain positive in the face of adversity. And poor Molly hadn't had it easy, losing Richie like she did, having to make her own way by herself. Richie had left her fairly well provided for, but that wasn't the point. Her sister lived alone but Molly seldom seemed lonely or sorry for herself. Nell, on the other hand, was feeling extremely sorry for herself right now. Her eyes filled with tears again and her eyelids felt heavy and raw. She had barely slept.

She stuffed most of the clothes back in the cases and lugged the largest one up to her room. *Her* room. It wasn't her room; it was Molly's spare bedroom. Strange curtains, a duvet cover that wasn't hers, unfamiliar knick-knacks. She could fill the wardrobe with her clothes, put her own things in the room but it would still be Molly's house. Nell thought again: just like the room, she was spare now, empty, a second choice. She thought of all the framed photographs she and Phil shared, from their wedding photographs to all the pictures of their holidays in Corfu and Crete. She knew each snap, each pose, Phil with an arm round her, both smiling into the lens. But it was all a sham now, their marriage, their happiness, their past together. It was just a lie. He had found someone else and that had changed everything, cancelled it all out.

Nell trundled downstairs and picked up the other two suit-cases, dragging them against each step as she stumbled back upstairs. She began to unpack methodically but her mind wasn't on the mechanical task of putting clothes on hangers and arranging them in the wardrobe. She was wondering what her life would be like now. Her heart was breaking; she missed Phil, the familiarity of him, the sharp scent of his aftershave, the sense of another person in the house, the company, the routine. Her old life was all gone in an instant.

Immediate images, like a film running in her head, showed Phil, the new Phil, with Nikki in an embrace. Nell had never seen Nikki, but she imagined her tall and slender, elegant, a smile like Julia Roberts's, bubbly and blonde like Cameron Diaz, affection-ate, playful, sexy: everything she probably wasn't any more. Nell was just one thing now: alone. She'd be that way for ever.

Of course, she was lucky to have Molly. They'd always been close as sisters. Nell's mum had treated both girls the same, even though Molly wasn't her own child, and Molly had seldom spoken about her real mother, the one who had left her. Nell breathed in deeply. She wished she could be more like Molly, tough, able to cope with whatever life threw at her; Molly would always be all right. Nell didn't feel she was carved from the same tough stuff as her sister at all.

Then the film in her head changed: Nikki was a seductress,

laughing at Nell as she led a grinning Phil by his necktie into the bedroom. Nell imagined the red lips and the black lacy under-wear – and she felt angry. Nikki was a tart who'd spotted Phil, an older man with a comfortable house and a comfortable car, and she had made her move. She was a gold-digger and she'd won. Phil was weak and susceptible: he was a fool.

Nell sighed deeply. She knew really that none of that was true. They were all just victims of life's twists and turns. She took a dress from her case and held it up in front of her. It was an old favourite, at least six years old, one she'd often chosen when she and Phil were going out together. It was a pretty dress, fitted, black and grey; she'd thought it elegant and she remembered she'd worn it a month ago, on their wedding anniversary, their thirty-ninth.

Nell wondered if Phil would be back in a few weeks, begging her to come home so that they could carry on with their simple, comfortable life. Maybe he would become bored with his new mistress; maybe he'd even miss her, his loyal wife.

Another thought popped into Nell's mind. She wasn't sure she could ever trust Phil now. What if she changed, grew, became stronger, independent? What if she even liked her new life? What if she found someone else?

Nell gave a scornful laugh. She was in her late sixties. Who would want her, an abandoned woman, soon to be a divorcee, someone else's unwanted wife? The thought made her shiver. She had no idea what life held for her now; all she knew was that she felt miserable and that she'd have to take each day at a time. She was like the black and grey dress she had just shaken from her suitcase and placed in the wardrobe, an old favourite that might never be worn again

She'd wait and see: she had no other choice. She was grateful to Molly for being there for her. Perhaps this was an opportunity to connect, to laugh, to drink wine and share memories. But that wasn't what Nell wanted at all. She just wanted her old life back. She wanted Phil.

6

Saturday 14th August

Maybe if I have a chat with Phil's new woman, she'll see sense and back off, even with the baby on the way. I feel sorry for her and I feel sorry for Phil. But my priority is my sister. Nell comes first every time...

Molly gazed around the café from her seat, at the gold décor and the long bar where two women in black and white uniforms were preparing drinks. One was a middle-aged woman, the other was a small dark-haired teenager, neither of whom could be Nikki. Molly drummed her fingers on the table, a polished pine surface holding a menu that offered croissants and various beverages beneath a smart black logo of a wolf and the words Café Loup.

'Your latte?'

Molly stared into the face of a young man with brown hair in a ponytail. His name badge said he was called Tobey. Molly noticed the 'e' and thought she'd never seen it spelled that way before. She watched as he carefully placed the cup in front of her and she reached for the steaming liquid, taking a sip. Then she waved a hand at the young man.

'Can you tell me, does Nikki work here?'

'Nikki Grindley? Yes.'

'So – which one is she?'

'Oh, she's not in until later.' The young waiter beamed. 'She starts at two. Enjoy your latte.'

'Thanks.' Molly brought the drink to her lips again. It burned her tongue as she took a gulp. Perhaps it was for the best that she hadn't found Nikki, she thought, as she imagined accosting the adulterous waitress by the throat, arguing and making a scene in the café with Nikki shrieking back at her, yelling that she and Phil loved each other and they were going to have a baby, and what did she know about love anyway, she was just an older woman in tattered jeans and grey hair that sprayed around her shoulders like a long, wild Brillo pad.

Molly smiled as she imagined the other people in the café turning to stare in horror as Nikki, whom she imagined to be thin with a hugely pregnant belly, threw her tray laden with full cups of cappuccino into the air and burst into tears, proclaiming that Phil was a love god and the man of her dreams. Yes, perhaps it was a good thing that Nikki wasn't at work yet. Molly finished her drink and reached for her handbag.

It was past one. She drove through the familiar roads of the estate and parked the Berlingo outside Phil's house, acutely aware that she had started to think of the tidy semi-detached with its ordered lawn out the front as belonging to Phil now. Poor Nell was homeless. Molly determined she'd find ways to look after her as she pressed the bell. Phil came to the door, his face still wan, smelling of aftershave that was reminiscent of detergent mixed with pine. His expression was surprised.

'Molly...'

'I've come for Nell's necklace – the one Mum gave her, with the heart and the letter N.'

'It's in her bedside drawer, I think – wait a minute, Molly, and I'll nip up and get it.'

Molly heard him rush up the stairs. She stepped into the hall, treading softly on plush carpet, and called up, 'I'll be in the lounge, Phil.'

As she walked into the too-warm room with the huge television and the squashy sofa, a woman looked up at her, huge round brown eyes anxious, her brow furrowed. Molly took in the untidy blonde hair that came to her shoulders, the shapeless blouse and light jeans, the strappy sandals and red toenails, and said, 'Nikki.'

Nikki was nervous. Her hands gripped a mug of steaming herbal tea that smelled of fruit. Molly recognised the design, one of Nell's set of six blue ones with the motto 'Keep Calm and Drink Coffee'. Nikki didn't look very calm.

'I'm Molly.' Molly glared at Nikki. 'Nell's sister. I've come for some of her things.' She took a deep breath and was about to launch in with the words 'I hope you're pleased with yourself after breaking up a marriage of nearly forty years...' but she pressed her lips together. Nikki's mouth was trembling, and her eyes had filled with tears. One of them rolled down her face, then another.

'We're really sorry, Molly. Really sorry how it's all happened. It's such a mess.'

Nikki's voice was soft, with a gentle Midlands lilt, kind and full of remorse. She let her head droop forward and her shoulders began to shake. Molly flopped down next to her and placed a warm hand on her shoulder.

'You're right, it is a mess, but these things happen and now there's a baby on the way, there's nothing you can do...' She stopped, feeling a sudden pang of guilt. She should be defending her sister. She took a breath. 'Nikki, look at me. You and Phil—'

Nikki glanced up and wiped mascara across her cheek. 'We love each other.' She seemed fragile, nervous, and Molly felt sorry for her.

'It shouldn't have happened like this...'

'I know.' Nikki's eyes were wide, a trapped animal's. 'Phil said you'd be angry, that you'd stick up for Nell. But really, we never intended to...'

Molly sighed. 'The baby is the important one now, I suppose...' She sighed. 'How pregnant are you?'

'She's due in December. The week before Christmas.'

Molly's brain started to count. It was August. That made Nikki about five months pregnant.

Phil had entered the room and he was staring at them both, holding out a hand containing a delicate necklace with two pendants.

'I've found it, Molly. This is the one.'

Molly leaped up and took it from his palm, staring from Nikki to Phil and back again: one was sitting forlorn, round-shouldered, wiping her face and the other stood awkwardly, his body tense and his eyes full of sadness. She slipped the necklace into her jacket pocket and sighed.

'Thanks, Phil. Well, I'll be going.' She glanced at the huddled woman on the sofa. 'I can't say it was nice to meet you, Nikki, but I wish you all the best with the baby and stuff.'

She whirled round to Phil and was conscious her heart was thumping. 'And as for you...' She shot him a frown. 'You make sure you give my sister everything she's owed. She'll need it. And, well, take care of this baby and Nikki.' She folded her arms. 'Try to do a better job this time around, Phil.'

Phil nodded, his face miserable. Nikki had started to cry

again, a soft snuffle. Molly had no idea what to say to help either of them. Besides, she was Nell's sister and her loyalty lay with her, although she felt strangely sorry for the fragile pregnant woman and the floundering father-to-be who were staring helplessly at each other.

Phil murmured, 'You've got a shift this afternoon. I'll run you in, love.'

'Right – thanks.' Nikki nodded and wiped her eyes, then struggled up from the sofa.

Molly decided it was best to leave; she turned on her heel and fled to the door, running down the path to the car. She had no idea what else to do. She leaped in, slammed the driver's door and started the engine. The car jolted forward and sped to the end of the road.

She called in at the supermarket for a few groceries and a bottle of whisky and headed towards home, the necklace in her jacket pocket. She stopped outside Colonel Brimble-Dicks' drive and reached over to the passenger seat for the bottle. He'd be pleased with the tipple, poor man, but Molly resolved to have a gentle word with him about his flagrant misogyny and, in particular, she'd ask him not to upset Vanessa, who called in voluntarily out of the goodness of her heart and might stop doing so if he continued to be so grumpy. Molly doubted that her reminder would do any good.

She knocked hard and was surprised when the door sprang open seconds later. Colonel Brimble-Dicks was still in his pyjamas and dressing gown, gaping at her.

'What are you doing here, Polly? I wasn't expecting you today …'

She charged past into the kitchen. He followed her at a steady pace. She noticed an empty plate on the table, a few breadcrumbs sprinkled across the surface, and a cup of half-drunk tea. She plonked herself down on a wooden chair, brandishing the bottle of whisky.

'Well, Colonel, I'm here and I've brought you some more of this.' She noticed him staring at her. 'It's clear you've run out of whisky completely if you've had to resort to tea.'

He rubbed his red-rimmed eyes. 'Ah, Polly...'

'Molly,' she reminded him. 'And another thing, Colonel, please can you be nicer to Vanessa. The poor woman comes here out of the kindness of her heart to help you. So please stop all this business of talking about women being too thin or too old or saying that anus means a crone in Latin...'

The colonel looked uncomfortable, shrunken inside his dressing gown. Then suddenly a scraping sound came from upstairs as if someone was moving furniture. Molly was alarmed, thinking of bats – or burglars. 'What was that noise, Colonel?'

'Ah, that's my new helper.' Colonel Brimble-Dicks gazed up at the ceiling. 'Started today.'

A cheery male voice came from upstairs. 'I'm all done up here, Lionel. There will be no lumps in the bed now.'

Molly stared at him amazed, and mouthed, 'Lionel?'

'He's very good,' the colonel explained with a little smile.

There was a flurry of footfalls from the stairs, then a fresh-faced man in his twenties, his brown hair styled in a high immovable quiff, rushed in. 'We're all done and dusted, Lionel.' He grinned. 'Your bed will be so much better now. I've turned the mattress and... Oh, hello. You must be Polly. Lionel's told me all about you.'

Molly raised her eyebrows and was about to tell the young man in no uncertain terms that her name was Molly Mitchell and she didn't want to be called Polly ever again, but the young man thrust out a hand. 'Joe Kemp. Lionel's new personal carer. We're making some changes around here, aren't we, Lionel? We're going to make you much more comfortable.'

The colonel smiled beatifically. 'Joe has brought me some audio books and I'm getting a smart speaker thing. He's showing me how I can play my favourite music and he's going to help me get news updates and Radio Four.'

Joe noticed the bottle of whisky on the table and frowned. 'Ah, I'll put this in the cupboard, shall I? Remember what we agreed about a little tot a day, just one and no more?'

Molly glanced at the colonel, expecting his face to cloud over and for him to bark about being able to drink what he bloody well liked when and where he liked, but she was surprised to see him smile in an acquiescent way, gratitude on his face. 'Joe's making me dinner for tonight. I'm having steak and kidney pie.'

Joe gestured towards the colonel. 'We've got everything organised, Lionel and me. He'll have his favourite foods, regular baths, some treats and a proper night's rest. He's asked me to pop in every day and I'm quite local so I can come over at any point and check he's comfortable.' Joe pushed a hand across the back of his neck where the hair tapered to bristles. 'I think we'll have a really good routine now.'

The colonel nodded. 'Much better. Joe knows what's what. The previous woman, Amber, she didn't sort things out like Joe has. He understands discipline, routine, cleanliness – and he's a man.'

'Well, that's ideal.' Molly took a step back and breathed out. 'I'll let Vanessa know she doesn't need to pop round quite so often.'

'Lionel's very grateful to have visitors.' Joe glanced at the colonel, putting a gentle hand on his shoulder. 'Aren't you, Lionel?'

The colonel coughed. 'My neighbours are fine women, both

of them – damned fine. I'm very grateful – I don't know how I'd have managed without them before you came, Joe.'

'And I'll chat to Vanessa about the shopping she orders online for Lionel,' Joe added. 'There's some collaboration to be done about his diet. I've told him he needs to make a few small changes. In fact, I might as well do the ordering for him now I'm here.'

Molly was bewildered. She caught Joe's eye and hoped her expression showed how impressed she was that he had made such an immediate impact.

Colonel Brimble-Dicks piped up. 'Joe is going to lend me some films to watch. There's one about a soldier called Private Ryan and another about some German chap who had a list.'

'My favourite is *Top Gun* with Tom Cruise.' Joe patted his arm. 'I'll bring that one round and we can watch it together. There's nothing like the old classics.'

Molly pressed her lips together; she hadn't thought of mid-1980s films as being classics; in her view, classics were the films made before Technicolor, with actors like Humphrey Bogart. She grinned. 'Nice to see you've managed to tame – I mean – to make the colonel comfortable.'

'Oh, I'm much happier now Joe is here.' The colonel actually smiled. 'So you and Vanessa can have a bit of extra time to yourselves. You should enjoy life more, Polly. Get out, meet people. You're stuck in your ways living here. You younger ones should have fun while you can. Because, before you know it, old age has crept into your house and then into your bones and you can't get it out again.' He paused for a moment, his face serious, then he waved a finger at the young man. 'But I've got Joe to help me now and that's made all the difference. He's going to make a treat for this afternoon; he says I'll like it. What is it, Joe?'

'Just a scone and jam and cream for tea; that's for later,

Lionel.' Joe turned to Molly and put a warm hand on her shoulder. 'I think we've straightened things out a little for him here.' He walked with her towards the door and lowered his voice. 'I'm trying to establish some sort of routine. If you and your neighbour would like to come round to make him a cuppa some mornings, that would be great. I'm insisting he naps more in the afternoon from now on.'

'It all sounds very good,' Molly agreed. 'What about the whisky? He's always loved it.'

'Oh, a little of what you fancy does you good, I always say.' Joe grinned enthusiastically. 'But not too much, too often. He was beginning to use it as a prop and that's not helpful. Thanks for popping in, Polly. Lovely to meet you.'

'Molly,' Molly corrected, but Joe had closed the door. She shook her head, not yet able to process what had happened. As she wandered towards her car, she smiled: one thing was for sure – now there was a new carer who would spend more time at Colonel Brimble-Dicks' house, she and Vanessa were definitely off the hook, which meant she could dedicate more time to her sister.

* * *

Nell opened the door of her Fiesta and slid in, gazing around furtively, like a spy. She placed her handbag determinedly on the passenger seat and started the engine. Molly might arrive back at any moment and she didn't want her sister asking her where she was going or trying to change her mind about what she intended to do. It had to be done.

Nell accelerated away, telling herself she was a strong woman: she had to say her piece and no one was going to stop her. She noticed a Berlingo approaching. As Molly's car sailed by, Nell noted that her sister was singing; she probably had the radio on and hadn't the first clue that Nell had driven past her.

That was for the best, Nell decided grimly, as she turned the corner: she didn't want Molly to know where she was going. She was on a mission. Now she would think about what she was going to say, and work out the best place in Yeovil to park in order to visit the trendy new coffee shop.

7

Saturday 14th August

Today was busy. Things are changing fast. Nell's old life is unrecognisable. Phil's life will never be the same again now his new lady friend Nikki has a baby on the way. The colonel is a reformed character with his helper and new best friend, Joe, who calls him Lionel like they have known each other for years. Maybe the universe is telling me it's time for me to move forward too. I still can't believe I'm seventy. It's time for something new – I can feel it in the air.

Nell ordered a chai latte and a young girl in a black and white dress and apron, probably not yet twenty, brought it over to her, but she wasn't interested in the frothy drink. Her eyes were on a blonde woman who was clearing tables, and whose name badge Nell was sure read 'Nikki'. Nell observed her like she was studying for an exam. The woman was taller than she was; she had shapely legs and messy blonde hair tied back with a rubber band, and she moved hurriedly. Her waistline wasn't slim beneath her apron; she was pleasant-faced and pretty but she was hardly the sex kitten Nell had feared.

Nell frowned. She was in her late sixties, but she was small, neat, well groomed; she took care of herself. This Nikki looked so flustered and busy, as if she didn't have time to bother with her appearance. Nell wondered how to speak to her, how to frame what she was determined to say. Then Nikki moved to the table next to her to pick up three empty cups, and Nell caught her eye.

'Excuse me,' Nell boomed in her best irritated-customer voice.

Nikki scuttled over and Nell noticed the hurriedly applied mascara, the troubled eyes, the pale skin. She offered Nell a smile. 'How can I help?'

'This latte isn't hot enough.'

Nikki bent forward and seized the cup. 'Oh, I'm so sorry about that. I'll just get it warmed up for you.'

Nell watched as she rushed towards the counter and wondered whether to call after her, 'Like you warmed up my husband behind my back?' But no words came.

She watched Nikki bustling about and thought about the soft Midlands lilt of her voice, the compliant smile, the trusting eyes. Nell wasn't sure what to say to her when she returned with the drink so she decided she'd settle for something indignant like, 'Do you know who I am? No? But you know my husband, don't you? You know him very well, from what I've heard.'

Nell wondered if Nikki had ever seen a photograph of her; she might have recognised her from one of the holiday snaps in Greece with Phil, but her attitude had been simply professional. No, Nikki had no idea at all who she had just spoken to. Nell pressed her lips together: her husband's mistress was about to find out.

Nikki hurried back with a steaming cup and put it down gently on the table. She smiled. 'Here you are, madam, I popped an extra biscuit on your saucer for you.' Nell glared at the wrapped cinnamon biscuit and back at Nikki, who smiled, her eyes sad. 'We all need a bit of something sweet to cheer us up sometimes. I know I do. You have a lovely day, now.' She whirled away to the next table, clearing up debris left by coffee and a flaky croissant.

Nell picked up the biscuit and watched Nikki again. She was simply a sweet-natured, ordinary girl and Phil had chosen her over his old, stale wife. Nell thought about Nikki's words, about needing something sweet to cheer her up. She imagined Phil was sweet to her; she was sure he cheered her up. She wasn't sure whether she was angry with Nikki, whether she felt sorry for her or whether, in fact, she felt anything at all. If she was honest, she was furious with herself for wasting forty years.

Nell crushed the biscuit in her fingers, still in its cellophane wrapper, watching the crumbs move around inside like trapped grains of sand. She threw it on the table and picked up her handbag. She'd leave the hot chai latte, the sweet-natured Nikki wishing her a lovely day and her old life behind her and she'd go back to the Fiesta and cry her eyes out.

* * *

Molly rushed into the house, her hair and handbag flying behind her and threw her bag of groceries on the floor. She grabbed the notebook, beautifully bound in turquoise silk, with a line drawing of a woman's profile in emerald on the cover. 'Right. Let's get my thoughts straight,' she muttered.

She glanced back at yesterday's entry, reading the last lines twice.

Friday 13th August
I need to do something exciting – a holiday, a long walk,
something creative perhaps. The house feels too small – I need
adventure.

Molly picked up a pen and nibbled at the end. She paused
and then wrote a few words.

Saturday 14th August, continued
Exhausted! I've been rushing about all day and everything
is such a mess. I met Phil's new partner Nikki, and I actually felt
sorry for her. I'm so proud of Nell, though – she's being so
strong—

Molly stopped mid-sentence and frowned. 'Where's Nell?'
She rushed over to the window, not able to remember if the
Fiesta had been parked outside. It wasn't there. 'Oh no!' she
gasped, guessing that Nell had gone to speak to Phil, to give him a
piece of her mind. She wouldn't put that past her sister: she was
not one to hold back on matters she felt strongly about, although,
Molly thought with a smile, Nell was a lot more sensible and
considered about her opinions than Molly, who was inclined to
blurt out the first thing that came into her head and regret it later.

Molly decided she should ring Nell and check she was okay.
She rummaged in her bag as the front doorbell rang.

Molly darted towards the front door, which was still wide
open. Vanessa was smiling and holding out a jam jar full of a
golden liquid. 'Molly, I brought you some apple jelly. The first
batch of the summer. It's still warm.'

Molly took the jar. 'Lovely. Thanks, Vanessa.'

'Well, I thought you and your sister might enjoy a jar. And I wanted to say thanks for being so nice to Jack and letting him do your garden.'

'He's a lovely young man, and he's doing me a favour.' Molly folded her arms, the jam tucked under her armpit.

'We're picking up Melissa, his girlfriend, this evening from the station. It's lovely to have Jack home again. He starts work in Yeovil next week...' Vanessa looked sad for a minute. 'It's natural for young people to want to be independent.'

'Have they found anywhere to live yet?'

Vanessa shook her head. 'Most places are quite expensive. Maybe when Melissa finds work...' She stopped suddenly, a thought in her head. 'Oh, Molly, have you been to see the colonel?'

'I have. What a changed man he is.'

Vanessa leaned forward. 'Did you give him a good talking to?'

'I didn't need to.' Molly raised an eyebrow, her face mischievous. 'He has a new carer who's got him trained already. Joe, he's called, a lovely lad. Incredible quiff and very personable. Anyway, Joe says to pop in for coffee and a chat one morning and he'll take over the shopping. The colonel's cutting down on the whisky and Joe says he's doing extra hours... oh, and the colonel's first name's Lionel.'

'Oh, dear.' Vanessa sighed. 'So, I'll have even more free time to fill...'

'Well, then, we both need a new hobby,' Molly joked. Then suddenly she noticed a car approaching. 'That's Nell – she's back.'

'Is your sister staying for long?'

'Who knows?' Molly rolled her eyes. 'Come in and have a cuppa, then you can meet her properly.'

Vanessa's face flushed with delight. 'I don't mind if I do. I haven't had a good chinwag with the girls for a long time.'

* * *

The kitchen clock showed the time was after five. There were three coffee cups and an empty biscuit packet on the scrubbed table; Vanessa and Nell were getting on famously. The conversation was mostly about the problems with men, how they were all nothing more than liars or cheats and how, when they'd dumped you for another younger model, it was somehow your fault for not pandering to them more. Nell thought all men were feckless and weak; Vanessa said that, in her experience, too many men were predators, always looking for fresh game, expecting the little woman to stay at home and clean the house, cook the dinner and mind the children while they ran their own lives from bars and gambling houses and behaved like single men. Molly shook her head.

'I don't agree. I think men are nice.'

'Then you've been lucky,' Vanessa suggested. 'Do you think there are any nice ones out there? I live in hope.'

Nell drained the last of her coffee. 'I liked Richie. He was eccentric but he was a lovely man. He had a great sense of humour and he was very generous. Mind you, I liked Phil once. I thought he was funny and affectionate. I didn't see this coming, not at all.' Nell thought for a moment and forced a grin. 'So, Molly, I wonder – have you met any nice men recently? I mean, are there any around at all? I'm asking for a friend.'

Nell and Vanessa collapsed into peals of laughter, then Molly sighed, her head filled with memories. The room became still, all three women thinking their own different thoughts. Molly stretched out her legs. Nell reached across the table for the crumbs of a biscuit and crushed them with her fingernail. Vanessa glanced up at the clock.

'Goodness, it's late. Jack and I have to go and fetch Melissa.'

She wriggled from her chair. 'Well, thanks for the coffee, Molly. Lovely to meet you, Nell.'

'Thanks for the apple jelly, it'll be great on toast at breakfast time,' Molly called after Vanessa, who was already making for the front door. She met her sister's gaze as she leaned across the table, picking up the empty cups. 'So, where did you disappear to this afternoon, Nell?'

Nell tapped her nose. 'That's for me to know...'

Molly's eyes widened. 'Did you go and see Phil?'

'No.' Nell glared at her. 'I went to see his fancy piece in Café Loup.'

Molly caught her breath. Her first thought was whether Nell knew about the baby. She examined her sister's face: she was clearly pale and not beaming with happiness, but she didn't look like a woman whose world had been crushed to pulp this afternoon.

'And?'

Nell leaned her chin in her cupped hands. 'She was working in the coffee shop. She didn't know who I was. I felt sorry for her and then I left.'

Molly breathed a slow sigh of relief. 'Oh.'

Nell steeled herself, taking a deep breath, narrowing her eyes in a show of being tough. 'It's over between me and Phil, Molly. Well and truly over.'

Molly glanced at the windowpane. Huge droplets of rain had started to spatter against the glass. She felt something damp rub against her ankles. It was Crumper, who'd just slithered in through the open door. He leaped on the table and she stroked him, flattening his damp ginger fur. She put the cups in the sink, her back to Nell, and shook her head.

'Look at this weather. And it's August. I was thinking of barbecuing outside and now we can't. What shall we do this evening?'

'TV? Pizza? Bottle of wine?' Nell raised an eyebrow.

Molly stared out of the window at the tin-grey skies. 'You and I, we need something new in our lives.'

* * *

Hours later, the bedroom was in darkness, heavy rain still thudding against the window. Crumper was purring next to Molly's feet as she slumbered. Then suddenly, she sat completely upright.

'Of course. I've got it. I know what we'll do.' She recalled the right word to use at exactly this moment. 'Eureka!'

Molly slithered out of bed and wriggled into her dressing gown, tying the belt tightly, pushing her feet into slippers. She'd get a cup of water; she was still full after the take-away pizza and her mouth was dry after she and Nell had shared a bottle of Shiraz, but that wasn't her primary mission. She padded downstairs and into the kitchen, filling a tumbler from the tap; then she silently took it into the darkened lounge where the laptop sat on a small desk in the corner. Molly flicked on the light switch and settled herself at the desk. She pressed a button on the laptop, wriggled the mouse and the screen brightened.

'So far so good.'

She typed the word 'apartments' and considered the options.

'Hmm,' she frowned, thinking. 'Where is always warm this time of year?'

8

Sunday 15th August

Got it! The perfect plan for us both in one smart move! I need to travel, to explore new places – and it's just what Nell needs too. I'm so excited!

Nell and Molly sat comfortably at the scrubbed wooden breakfast table in their dressing gowns, pyjamas and bare feet. Molly had insisted that it was the most civilised way to start a Sunday, with coffee, breakfast and newspapers. She and Richie had done the same every week, spending a leisurely two or three hours at the table nibbling pastries and bagels, filling up coffee mugs and discussing articles in the *Observer*. Molly had retained the ritual for the last five years, even though she'd had breakfast alone other than Crumper, who usually sprawled himself across the newspaper, but who was currently mauling the curved end of a croissant beneath the kitchen table.

'So, Nell,' Molly smirked, her face shining with mischief, 'I might have a really nice surprise for you.'

'Goodness, Molly – I think I've had enough surprises for one week,' Nell exhaled, fingering the delicate necklace around her neck, playing with the little gold heart.

Molly closed her eyes and took a breath. She was sure that her idea would work; there was one surprise she certainly didn't want her sister to have, the new and sudden knowledge that after she had had five miscarriages, her husband was about to become a father. Before long, she'd find out: someone would let it drop into a conversation or, worse, she'd be in a supermarket and see Phil and a huge-bellied Nikki tottering around the corner with a trolley full of disposable nappies. But her plan would certainly go some way to preventing Nell from finding out until she was better prepared. Molly poured hot coffee from a metal jug. 'This surprise is a nice surprise.'

Nell rolled her eyes playfully, pretending to be showing extreme patience with her crazy sister, and sipped coffee, enjoying the rich flavour of Brazilian beans. She felt in a better mood than last night, when she'd ended the evening sobbing into her Shiraz and claiming she'd never love a man again as they all had treachery in their DNA. She sighed. 'Ah, this is lovely, Moll. I needed coffee after the wine we drank.' She wriggled up straight in her chair. 'Mind you, I'm going to have to cut back on the carbs after that enormous pizza last night.'

Molly shook her head. She wasn't sure that it mattered very much – she just ate what she liked. She held out the plate to Nell. 'Bagels or croissants?'

'Just coffee,' Nell smiled. She put a hand on Molly's arm. 'Well, what is it, this great surprise?'

'Surprise?' Molly had momentarily forgotten. Then a grin spread across her face. 'Oh, yes – come on. We need to talk to Vanessa right now – she doesn't know yet, but she's the missing part of the jigsaw.' Molly lurched out of her seat, taking a quick gulp of coffee from her mug.

'Shouldn't you get dressed first?'

Molly glanced down at the dressing gown, the pink pyjamas with an elephant print and her bare toes, and laughed. 'Oh, good point. I'll only be a few seconds.'

Ten minutes later, Molly and Nell were standing at the garden fence talking to their neighbours. Vanessa had been picking tomatoes from the greenhouse and Molly had called her over, then insisted she ask Jack and Melissa to join them. A few moments later, all three of them – Melissa, a tall girl with a freckled face and her light hair tied in a ponytail, Jack, in shorts, and Vanessa, wearing a mystified expression – were all looking expectantly at Molly. Nell decided she'd hurry things along. 'Molly has something she'd like to talk to us all about.'

Molly lifted Crumper, hugging him in her arms and fondling the folded ears. 'It's about Crumper, too. I mean, it concerns us all.'

Jack raised his eyebrows hopefully. 'If it's extra work, I'd be glad to give it a go, Molly. I mean, the Yeovil job starts on Monday and Mel has seen online that there might be some work in a pub down the road, but we could share extra gardening.'

'The Globe,' Mel added, her voice enthusiastic.

Molly nodded. 'Well, the thing is – I've booked a little holiday for me and Nell in Spain.'

'Really?' Nell was astonished.

'That's nice,' Vanessa added, confused.

'I've booked an apartment.'

'An apartment?' Nell repeated.

Molly was pleased with herself. 'We need to get away for a break, Nell.'

'So – what can we do to help?' Jack asked, hopefully.

'Well, the owner is away until Christmas – she's from Cheshire. Her mother isn't well and she's coming back to the UK to nurse her. So, I said, if we like it, we'd stay on until the end of December.' Molly met each surprised gaze, her own eyes sparkling: by the end of December, Phil and Nikki's baby would be born and, perhaps, Nell would be having such a great time in the sun that she wouldn't care.

Nell found her voice. 'Until Christmas?'

'In Spain. It'll be glorious. We'll have plenty of time to do whatever we like,' Molly reassured her. 'And the break in the sunshine will do us good. So I've told Lisa, the woman who owns the apartment that if we like it, we'll stay on.' She gave a little jump. 'It's a two-bedroomed luxury apartment with a sea view and a roof terrace and a hot tub.'

'I wish I was coming,' Vanessa enthused.

'When did you dream all this up?' Nell asked, still astonished.

'Last night. Midnight. I contacted Lisa, who replied first thing, then I booked flights, one way of course, to Murcia airport. It's all paid for from my savings.' Molly folded her arms, pleased, with herself. 'We've a week to pack and get organised. We're off next Saturday.'

'So, do you need a taxi to the airport?' Jack asked. 'I could borrow Mum's car. I'd be glad to help.'

'I want you to stay in my house, Jack,' Molly smiled. 'Free of charge, of course – just do the garden and feed Crumper until we get back.' She breathed out, satisfied at the delighted expression on Jack's face. 'If you stay on here until the end of the year, it will give you time to settle at work and save up towards your own place.'

'Wow.' Jack was almost speechless. 'Thanks...'

Vanessa was gaping, tears in her eyes. 'So, Jack and Mel can live next door to me? For four months?'

'That's the idea,' Molly grinned.

'Well, you might have spoken to me before you organised it...'
Nell was still shaking her head.

'It's a surprise,' Molly claimed, triumphantly. 'And it works
perfectly.'

'That's such an incredible thing to do,' Mel gasped.

'We're so grateful.' Jack took his girlfriend's hand, his eyes
wide.

'I could even sort out the insurance on the Berlingo so you
could drive it.' Molly was on a roll, her generosity boundless. She
hugged the ginger cat, who had seen a starling and was
attempting to wriggle free. 'It will be lovely for us all.'

'Well, that certainly was a surprise.' Nell draped an arm
around her sister's shoulder. 'But I have to say, a holiday in Spain
might be great. But four months, Molly?'

'Why not?' Molly's expression was gleeful. 'We can have
adventures; we can do as we please, we can take up jogging...'

'If I wasn't going to be living next door to my lovely son and
his girlfriend,' Vanessa gushed, 'I'd come with you instead – you
wouldn't have to ask me twice.'

Nell smiled. 'You're right. It's a great idea. We need to have
some fun; I know I certainly do. Yes, thanks Moll – I'm looking
forward to it already. Sun, sea, sand...'

'Sangria...' added Mel.

'Stunning scenery,' Jack suggested.

'Siesta? Salsa? Singing?' Molly added.

'Seduction? Sex?' Vanessa burst out laughing. She put both
hands to her cheeks as everyone stared at her and she flushed
with embarrassment. 'Who knows what fun you'll both have
there? Oh, you'll have such a wonderful time, I just know it.'

* * *

It was early in the morning but Molly was wide awake and full of energy. She had thrown most of the things she thought she'd need in one suitcase: shorts, T-shirts, a swimsuit, two pairs of jeans, some undies and a few scarves she could wear as sarongs. Nell was still upstairs packing, deciding on evening wear and whether she should wear a one-piece or a tankini on the beach. Molly was poised over the turquoise notebook, pen in hand. She thought she'd write her last entry and pop the diary in her handbag.

Saturday 21st August

I'm packed and ready to go today. Can't wait. Murcia sounds lovely. It's somewhere in the south-east of Spain, a little town on the coast called Calleblanque. The photos online were beautiful, by the sea, just a short taxi ride from the airport. Lisa, the owner of the apartment, seems nice. She says the view from the roof terrace is great and there is a hot tub. I'm just going to spend most of my time in there soaking up the sun, drinking Cava, seizing the day. Swimming in the sea, skinny dipping too, that's what I'll do. I haven't been swimming for years but I'll drag Nell into the sea and we'll both come back bronzed and toned and she won't care about Phil and Nikki any more.

She thought for a moment and then added:

It will be glorious. I can practise speaking Spanish again. And Nell and I can go walking and eat out in the evenings, make new friends, have adventures. If we get bored, we can go to France – it's not far away – or Morocco. We can travel to anywhere we like. She'll be happy again in no time.

Molly closed the notebook and brought it to her lips, thinking for a moment about the activities she and Nell might do, the new places they might visit. Then, the hint of a smile on her face, she slipped the little diary into her handbag. She was ready to go.

There was a rhythmic thudding from the stairs, then Nell appeared, dragging her huge case into the lounge. She met Molly's eyes. 'What?'

'Nothing...' Molly shrugged. 'The case looks a bit... full.'

'I need choices about what to wear.' Nell's gaze was defiant. 'Besides, it has wheels. I won't need to lift it.'

'I expect Vanessa's ready.' Molly checked the clock on the wall. 'It's almost seven o'clock. It was kind of her to offer us a lift this early in the morning.'

Nell agreed, yawning. 'It's too early for me. Most Saturday mornings I'm not even up until almost eleven. Phil brings me up a coffee and...' She sighed. 'Oh, well, that's behind me now. New beginnings, eh, Molly?'

'New beginnings,' Molly grinned, her face shining. She was impatient to go.

Vanessa was waiting just outside the gate, perched in the driver's seat of her Škoda Octavia, waving her hand and grinning. Jack wriggled out of the front seat and took the cases from Molly and Nell, lifting them easily into the boot: he and Mel had insisted on coming with them to carry their luggage into the airport and to keep Vanessa company on the return journey. He then slid in the back, next to Mel, and Molly joined them, allowing Nell the front seat next to Vanessa. Jack was already thanking her again for upgrading the insurance on the Berlingo so that he could drive it and for letting him and Melissa stay in the house.

'We just can't believe our luck,' Jack enthused. 'We have our own place until Christmas. We're so grateful, Molly. You won't recognise the garden when you come back. It'll be the best garden in Somerset.'

'And Crumper will be the happiest cat.' Mel slipped her fingers through Jack's.

'It was kind of you to give us a lift,' Nell offered.

'Oh, not at all. It's the least I can do.' Vanessa pointed at an older man and a younger companion, standing at the front door of a small house. 'Look. It's the colonel. He's come to wave us off.'

'Yoo-hoo.' Molly waved a hand. 'Perhaps he'd like us to bring him some Sangria back?'

'I love Sangria.' Mel turned to Jack. 'Remember the fortnight we spent in the Costa del Sol? The Sangria there was wonderful.'

'You drank quite a lot of it, I remember,' Jack agreed.

Vanessa turned the Škoda onto the main road. 'Mel has found a job.'

'I have.' Mel beamed. 'I'm waiting on tables in the Globe. The manager, Darren, is really nice. He said they are busy at the moment and I'd be able to do shifts at lunchtimes and in the evenings, especially on Sundays, which means Jack and I can save lots of money.'

'We are going to try to save as much as we can for a place of our own,' Jack continued.

'They are sensible kids,' Vanessa said from the front.

Nell suddenly had a thought. 'Oh, I didn't bring a wrap. It might be chilly in the evenings.'

'You never know,' Vanessa suggested. 'There may be a nearby gentleman who will offer to lend you his jacket.'

Nell frowned. 'I hope not. I've no time for men and their rubbishy romantic gestures. It's all just a trick to make you like them and when you do, that's always followed by lies and deceit. I'm off men for good.'

Vanessa sighed. 'But you might change your mind. Spanish

men can be very dashing. And I've heard that they are very courteous and romantic.'

'I doubt it,' Nell grimaced. 'All men are the same. Fine manners at first, just for show, then they let you down.'

'But it might be nice to have a holiday romance...' Vanessa glanced at Nell. 'Do you think I'm too old to find someone now?'

Jack reached for Mel's hand and rolled his eyes: his mother was always asking the same question. Mel nodded in tacit agreement: they both thought the idea of romance involving old people was very disconcerting. The Škoda accelerated onto the motorway. The engine thrummed softly as they reached a steady seventy miles per hour, the wheels vibrating against tarmac, making a low drone.

'I wouldn't give anyone the time of day now, to be honest,' Nell replied. 'I'm done with them all, their lies and their two-timing.'

'But there has to be someone out there for us both,' Vanessa wailed. 'Someone kind and good-natured and perhaps even good looking...'

Jack reached over, placed a kiss on Mel's forehead and winked: older people talking about dating and falling in love was completely ludicrous, especially his mother. Mel caught his pained expression, imagined Jack's mother in a torrid embrace and suppressed the urge to laugh.

'I'm thinking about myself from now on.' Nell folded her arms. 'You wait, when I'm back at Christmas, I'll be a new woman.'

'Well, you have a great time, both of you,' Jack piped up from the back seat. A Transit van overtook them, weaving into the middle lane. The male passenger, sunglasses on his head, caught Vanessa's eye and leaned out of the window, pursing his lips and preening before the van sped away. Vanessa smiled back: he couldn't have been a day over twenty-five. Her fingers strayed to her hair, smoothing it, her cheeks flushing pink.

'Not all men are bad, though, Nell.' She smiled into the driver's mirror. 'Some of them are really quite nice. I certainly haven't given up hope yet. What do you think, Molly?'

Molly didn't answer. Her head was lolling to one side, on Jack's shoulder, her mouth open, and she was making little snuffling noises. She was fast asleep.

9

Saturday 21st August

Spain, here we come. We had a celebratory glass of wine on the plane. I'm buzzing with excitement now – the adventure begins. I can hardly wait to see our new home for the next four months. I'll make sure Nell will enjoy herself and I hope she'll find some peace too...

The nap in the car had done her the world of good. Molly was wide awake throughout the trip, reading the inflight magazine, sipping wine, then sparkling water, staring through the window at the pink-tinged clouds while Nell dozed.

Once they'd cleared passport control in Murcia airport, Nell's case clattering behind her and Molly lugging hers with both hands, they stepped out into the late afternoon sunlight and stopped to catch a breath. Molly looked down at her baggy sweatshirt and leggings, which had been very comfortable to travel in, and gasped. 'I'm too hot.'

'We can change into something cooler when we get to the

apartment.' Nell looked hopefully around, heaving her jacket off and still feeling clammy in the gauzy blouse. Both women gazed up at a cloudless azure sky, feeling the sun's warmth burning the concrete pavements. Molly gathered up her thick slate-grey tresses, winding them into a knot, securing it with a thin band from her wrist. She fanned her warm face with her hand. 'This is bliss.'

Then Nell pointed out a taxi rank. She followed Molly, who surged forward and thrust her head into an open window of a cab, surprising the driver who was smoking a cigarette, his eyes closed behind his sunglasses. Molly thought the man, who had thick dark hair and a bored expression, might have been there for a long time and would be glad to find a customer. '*Hola, Señor,*' she yelled.

The man sat upright in sudden shock, his cigarette almost tumbling onto his T-shirt. He muttered something that sounded like '*ee-oh-de-poot*' and pulled off his sunglasses, wiping his brow and replacing them in one move as he puffed on his cigarette. '*Si?*'

'*Hola. Quiero un taxi a Calleblanque.*' She grinned at him, pleased with herself, then added, '*Por favor.*'

The taxi driver gaped at her for a moment as if she was mad. Nell elbowed her sister gently in the back.

'Are you sure he's a taxi driver? I mean, he's not some random person who's just parked here waiting for his family?'

Molly beamed at the taxi driver hopefully. 'Are you a taxi driver?'

He heaved a heavy sigh. 'English?'

'*Si.*' Molly agreed. 'Both of us. We're both English.'

He nodded. 'I speak English. Okay. You get in the car and I take you to Calleblanque.'

The way he said the name of the place sounded nothing like

how Molly had been pronouncing it. He spoke the word in soft syllables with no 'que' on the end. She nudged herself to the far seat, tugging her case in front of her as Nell followed, heaving her own luggage with a mighty effort. It was a little cramped in the back.

The driver puffed on his cigarette and started the engine. 'Cal-l'blan', by the sea?'

'*Si*,' Molly replied, then for clarity she called out, '*Aparta-mentos Melocotón.*'

'Okay.' The driver steered the car out of his parking space with a jerk of the wheel towards a line of traffic.

'What does that mean, *Melocotón*?' Nell asked. 'It sounds lovely.'

'It's the Spanish word for peach.' Molly hugged her case on her knees. 'We're staying at the Peachy Apartments.'

The taxi lurched around a corner and began to overtake a lorry. Nell flung herself against Molly without intending to. The driver grinned, clearly finding it funny.

Molly gazed out of the window. They were hurtling past traffic on some sort of major road. There were heavy vehicles close by on either side. It was intensely hot inside the cab, the air fogged with cigarette smoke. Molly tried to open the windows but the handle came off in her hand. She decided to make conversation with the driver. 'So – are you local?'

He laughed loudly. 'Local. From Spain.' His voice grew louder. 'Spanish all my life.'

He overtook a long lorry that had the word '*Mercado*' in green on the side. Nell caught Molly's eye and indicated to her that she felt queasy by patting her chest and puffing out her cheeks. Molly reached for her hand and squeezed it. 'We'll be there soon.'

More smoke billowed from the front. The driver shouted

something at a passing lorry, his tone frustrated. Molly raised her voice. 'What time do we arrive in Calleblanque, driver?'

'One hour.'

Nell was horrified. 'One hour?'

The taxi driver accelerated past a small car, too close. 'Maybe forty minutes if I go fast.'

Molly frowned. 'I thought Calleblanque was near the airport.'

'Very near.' The driver grunted. 'One hour is near.'

Nell coughed. 'Could you slow down a little?'

'Slow is longer time, cost more. My wife cooks nice paella for the dinner. I want to be home when it is hot.'

Molly stared out of the widow. They were passing a small town to the left, a group of grey-looking industrial buildings. She called out in her clearest voice. 'Driver, when do we start to see the coast? I mean, when do we see the sea?'

The driver punched the steering wheel one time with his fist. 'We see the sea when we arrive at the coast.'

Molly wriggled against the bulk of her case. She found sunglasses in her handbag and settled back in the lumpy seat, giving Nell a slight nudge and inviting her to do the same. It was going to be a long journey.

Forty minutes later, they pulled up in front of a three-storey concrete complex with a few plants growing outside, behind a low dirty-white brick wall. There were probably eighteen apartments, all uniform peach. The ground floor flats had grubby white doors and the above floors were embellished with equally jaded-looking barred balcony rails. The driver wrenched the handbrake. '*Apartamentos Melocotón*,' he said with a flourish. 'We are here now. There is sea beyond the apartments.'

Nell stared out of her window at the building which had clearly been painted long ago, a dull pinkish hue, with small rectangular windows and a severe staircase at the side. 'Is this it? It looks like a prison, Molly.'

Molly secretly agreed and thought that it looked drab and poky: it had appeared idyllic in the photo Lisa had sent her, but she decided to be as positive as possible. 'It'll be lovely inside, I'm sure.'

The driver grunted impatiently, his crackling voice resounding from the front seat. He stared at Molly. 'Sixty euro.'

Molly was horrified and began to rummage in her handbag for her purse, but Nell was already out of the taxi. She handed the driver three twenty-euro notes. 'Here you are, driver.' She stared at him, offering her best haughty gaze. 'Keep the change.'

He seemed perplexed behind the sunglasses, taking the money without a comment. Nell added dryly, 'Enjoy your paella.'

Molly gave her sister a look of pure admiration: Nell was made of stronger stuff than she'd thought.

Nell and Molly stumbled with their cases towards the apartment block, hearing the taxi roar away behind them. Nell shrugged. 'What poor service. He didn't even help us with our cases and he smoked the entire time. I'll need some sea air as a decongestant.'

'I just picked the wrong driver.' Molly shrugged. 'Spanish people are all incredibly friendly. It'll be wonderful here. Right. We're in flat number fourteen. Top floor with a roof terrace.'

Nell was suddenly anxious. 'Do you have a key?'

'No – I assumed Lisa would meet us here.' Molly frowned. 'Maybe there's a caretaker?'

'A warden, perhaps?' Nell suggested.

They approached the entrance tentatively. An envelope had been secured to the door with sticky tape. The name on the front read, 'FAO Molly Mitchell.'

She took the envelope down and tore it open. Inside were two keys on a small thin metal ring and a little note that read, 'Enjoy your stay. Lisa.' Molly brandished the keys. 'We're in.'

Nell was horrified. 'That's ludicrous. Anyone could have found the keys.'

Molly agreed. 'But there's no harm done. Come on in. Let's get these clothes off and find the hot tub.'

They dragged their cases up a flight of stone stairs flanked by dirty peach-coloured walls and when they arrived at the top, they saw a corridor lined with doors. Molly bounded halfway down, her case thudding on the stone floor, and stopped at a pink door. 'Here we are, Nell. Apartment number fourteen.'

She wriggled one of the keys into the lock and turned. The door sprung ajar. 'We're in. This is it. Home, sweet, home.'

She stepped gingerly into a narrow, open-plan lounge and kitchen. The walls were a dirty apricot colour and there was a red sofa, a glass coffee table and a wooden cupboard that housed a small television and a few pottery ornaments. The floor was a patchwork of matt grey tiles and a print had been hung on the wall depicting a woman with a flower in her dark hair, her face morose. At the end of the living space was a square white table with two seats and, behind it, a hanging bamboo curtain. Molly rushed across, pushing the beads to one side to gaze at a tiny kitchen with three apricot-coloured cabinets, a rusty hob, a tiny fridge, a white worktop and a microwave oven. Nell was behind her, staring over her shoulder.

'It's not too bad,' Molly affirmed, pointing to the bottle of red wine and two glasses on the worktop. 'Look, Lisa's left us some *vino tinto*.'

'Where's the dishwasher?' Nell was distraught.

'We'll eat out.'

Nell had moved away and was investigating the bathroom.

Molly heard her shout 'Ugh! Pokey!' and she'd moved on to the bedrooms. 'Right, I'm having this one.'

Molly followed as Nell heaved her case onto a double bed with a peach-coloured cover, a wicker chair in the corner with a red heart-shaped cushion embroidered with the word *Love*. Nell was staring out of the window and her voice was low and unimpressed. 'Is this the view of the pool?'

'Shared pool,' Molly enthused. 'Get into your shorts, Nell, and we'll go upstairs onto the sun terrace, take the bottle of red with us and investigate the hot tub.' She beamed. 'Then we'll go out for some food.'

Nell was unpacking her clothes, folding them neatly, so Molly lugged her case into the second bedroom, threw it on the bed and blinked as bright light filtered into the room, a thin pale stream against the gloom. There was a single bed, a tiny table with an orange lamp on a wooden base and red curtains, an attempt to complement the pale peach walls. Molly opened the curtains onto a single door leading to a tiny balcony. She pushed it open, breathing in the warm air, and stepped out, immediately leaning on the railings and staring at the road and the small garden below with a few plants. It wasn't too bad.

Molly went back to her case, clicked open the lock and inverted the contents, allowing clothes to tumble onto the bed and the cold tile floor. She found a black swimsuit and a huge silky fringed scarf in a variety of colours. She gazed around the room. There was a tiny built-in wardrobe and no mirror. She grinned, remembering the moment with the cricket bat. She'd tell herself she looked a million dollars every morning and there would be no evidence to the contrary. She was on holiday and the feeling of freedom made her feel light, optimistic, filled with excitement.

She struggled into the swimsuit: she hadn't worn it for

years. It fitted but the Lycra was cracked and stiff, and once she had the suit on, it sagged around the bust. She wrapped the scarf around her as a sarong and unwound her hair, shaking it loose. She was a Hawaiian princess ready to bask in the late afternoon sunshine. Molly smiled at the thought of the day turning into night-time; before long, Spain would be coming to life. The evening would be warm, scented with spicy cooking, and there would be places where they could eat delicious paella and drink wine, perhaps listening to the sound of the Spanish guitar and a soulful female voice or a husky male tenor.

'Are you ready, Nell?'

Nell was in the lounge wearing a white vest and blue denim shorts, her feet encased in pretty strappy sandals. She would have looked the perfect English woman abroad, pale and pretty, apart from the scowl on her face. 'There's no air conditioning.'

'Oh, there must be,' Molly reassured her. 'Come on. Let's go and find the roof terrace and the hot tub.'

Molly uncorked the bottle of red wine and grasped the two opaque glasses from the worktop, then she and Nell made for the door. Molly made sure she had the keys safely in her handbag and pulled the front door shut behind her, checking it was locked. She grinned at Nell. 'There are stairs at the end of this corridor. I bet that's the way to our roof terrace.'

Nell grunted and pulled the sunglasses from her head to cover her eyes. She was trying her best to match Molly's optimism, but she had the distinct feeling that she was about to have the headache to end all headaches. It had been stuffy in the taxi and she'd been feeling nauseous for the whole journey. She followed Molly as she bounded up the stairs, hoping that a glass of red wine and twenty minutes spent dangling her feet in the soothing bubbling water of a hot tub might revive her a little.

The roof terrace was vast, the walls painted terracotta, and Molly whooped. 'This is great, Nell.'

She rushed to the far wall, peering over. 'Look, you can see all the other buildings around here. Roof after roof.' She whirled around. 'And look at our terrace. We've got sun loungers, a sunshade, a patio table...' Nell stood, immobile, as Molly scurried to another tangerine wall. 'The sea. Nell, I can see the sea. It's just like Lisa said, it's a five-minute walk away. You just have to cross the road and go past a few shops and there's the beach. Oh, and look at it. All that sand and glistening waves.'

Nell gave in to her sister's enthusiasm and plodded over to join her. 'That's lovely, Molly. Great location.'

Molly flexed her arms in the swimsuit. 'The girl did well, eh, Nell? Now where's the hot tub? Come on, Nell. It'll be just round this corner.'

She led the way, swaying excitedly as she moved, her arms out holding the glasses and the bottle of red wine. Then she saw it, the hot tub shaped like an old tyre, grey on the outside, and inside the deep blue of an ocean. It wasn't a large tub; in fact, Molly thought it was probably just big enough for two people. And there was one person in it already.

Molly frowned at the white-haired man with the neat beard and intensely blue eyes who was relaxing in the hot tub with his arms stretched out. He was probably in his fifties, and he had an angular build and square shoulders. He was smiling at Molly and Nell, whose feet were glued to the red tiled floor of the roof terrace, gaping back.

Molly broke the silence. 'Hello.'

The man replied, clearly unperturbed. 'Hello.'

There was a long pause, so the man murmured. 'Can I help you?'

'We're staying here, flat fourteen. This is our roof terrace.'

'Oh, yes, you must be in Lisa's apartment. She said she was going away and there would be new people coming to stay.' The man smiled broadly. Molly couldn't discern his accent. Northern European perhaps.

Molly waited and when the white-haired man said nothing, she tried again. 'I think this is our roof terrace.'

'Yes, that is correct,' the man replied, his ice blue gaze quite disconcerting.

Molly added, 'And our hot tub.'

'Yes, correct again,' the man conceded.

Molly heard Nell's intake of breath before her words rushed out impatiently. 'So why are you in it?'

The man turned his eyes to Nell. 'Shared facility,' he explained. 'I live in number twelve. I am your neighbour. I'm Bernt.'

'Burned? Oh, I'm sorry to hear that.' Molly's jaw dropped, unsure whether the hot tub was in fact too hot or whether the man had spent too much time in the sun. Then she realised it was his name and laughed. 'Oh, pleased to meet you, Bernt. I'm Molly and this is Nell. We've just come out to spend some time in the hot tub together.'

'Ah, yes; all the apartments in this block share the roof terrace.' Bernt nodded and waved an arm, indicating the limited space on either side of him. 'Please – be my guests.'

Nell gasped in horror and Molly clutched the wine bottle to her chest. Molly spoke first. 'We – we'd rather hoped you... you'd finished here.'

Bernt's eyes remained focused on them a little longer, his expression unchanged, then he nodded slowly as if he had understood something deep and important. 'I see.' He stood up and Molly could see that he was a tall, sinewy man, his legs lean and muscled. He met her eyes. 'Of course. Please do help yourselves.'

He rose out of the hot tub in one easy step and walked past them without another word, his gait loping and steady. Molly turned and watched him move away, past the sun loungers and the parasol shade. She watched the slow stride of his long legs, stared at the pale orbs of his bottom, then she grasped Nell's arm, caught her breath and covered her face with her hands. Bernt was completely naked.

10

Saturday 21st August

*We're here. The apartment's great, and conveniently close
to the beach. Nell seems happy to be here and our neighbour
is a handsome Swedish man who sits naked in the hot tub on
the roof terrace. What's not to like about Spain?*

Molly and Nell sat at the square table in the apartment, the
opened bottle of wine between them. Nell hadn't touched her
glass. Molly took a gulp. 'I tell you, Nell, he had nothing on.'

Nell put her hands to her head. 'Nonsense, he had a skin-
coloured thong on.'

'I saw his bottom.'

Nell sighed. 'Peach-coloured. Everything here has to be some
shade of peach or another. It's probably the law.'

Molly couldn't help laughing. She was enjoying her holiday
already. '*Apartamentos Melocotón.*' She sipped more wine. 'Can we
go back up to the roof terrace again? We could have another half
an hour in the hot tub and finish the wine before we eat?'

Nell reached over and took her sister's hand. 'Sorry, Moll. I wanted to come back down because I have a headache coming on, a really bad one. I think I'll just take a couple of painkillers and have an early night.'

'But you need to eat...?'

'I'll be better tomorrow, I promise.' Nell forced a smile. 'Then we can start to enjoy Spain.'

Molly chewed her lip. 'Do you mind if I go out and explore a bit then? Get myself a sandwich or something?'

'That's a good idea. Have a look round the area, perhaps, and get some bearings? Then tomorrow we'll both go out.'

'Are you sure you'll be all right by yourself, Nell?'

'I need to rest. Just for tonight.'

Molly leaped up, ready to go, then remembered her wine and finished the remains in the glass. 'I'll put the cork back in the bottle and we'll have the rest tomorrow. Then I'll get my jacket.'

'Molly?' A frown had appeared between Nell's eyes, as if thinking caused her pain. 'Leave the keys, please. I mean, I'd feel happier if you didn't lock me in.'

Molly agreed. 'I'll leave my bag and phone too – I'll just shove a couple of notes in my pocket and be off.' She gazed down at herself. 'Oh, I'd better get changed. I can't go out in a swimsuit and sarong – the T-shirt and jeans combo will be fine, won't it?'

Nell nodded, eased herself to standing position. 'Sorry, Moll. I picked the best bedroom and left you with the single bed. I shouldn't have done that...'

Molly's laughter trilled. 'It's no problem. I'm always saying that the double at home is too big now.' She thought for a moment and then she grinned, throwing her arms round Nell, kissing the side of her hair. 'You rest and get well. I'll tell you all about the town tomorrow.'

Nell slunk into her bedroom, her shoulders hunched like a scolded child. She sat on the edge of her bed on the peach cover and closed her eyes. Her head was pounding. She'd clean her teeth in a moment and then take some painkillers. She turned off the overhead light and lay down on the bed. The room was gloomy, a little light filtering in from under the red curtains. Somewhere in the distance she heard the door click. Molly had gone out. She was alone again. She could hear sounds of music from below through the thin windowpane; there was activity at the poolside, laughter and voices. She hoped she'd be ready for her holiday tomorrow.

But it didn't feel like a holiday. Here she was, lying on a lumpy bed in a horrible cramped apartment in Spain, where there was no air conditioning and the sun terrace wasn't even private. She had been a visitor at Molly's house for over a week; she had no home any more and now she was stuck in a hot hellhole for three months while her zany sister insisted that it was all great fun. Nell exhaled slowly. It wasn't Molly's fault. Molly was wonderful; she took life's knocks, scrambled up and laughed as if she'd just grazed her knee. But Nell thought sadly that she wasn't made of such strong stuff.

Just two weeks ago, her life had been safe and settled, and now it had been changed utterly. Phil had started his life again with Nikki and Nell was left behind, rootless, with no home.

The pillow was damp with hot tears and Nell realised she was sobbing. She felt lonely, broken, unwanted, and her sobs became harder. Her voice rose to a wail and she wondered for a second if Bernt, the man they'd seen in the peach-coloured posing pouch in the hot tub, was next door and if he could hear her bawling. The thought made her howl again. She felt sorry for herself, split in two by the unfairness of it all.

Finally, she sniffed twice and stopped crying, opening her eyes. The bedroom was gloomy and stuffy. If only she could be more like Molly. Molly who, if she'd been abandoned inside the

Black Hole of Calcutta, would be marvelling at how wonderfully dark and deep it was. Nell forced a harsh laugh. Molly had said that she should see the break with Phil as an opportunity and she wondered for a moment what shape it might take. At the same time a thought was seeping into her mind: what if she didn't really love Phil any more anyway? She liked him, she was used to him, she enjoyed the presence of another person in the house – it was a buffer against the loneliness – but she didn't honestly, truly need him, did she? She had lost herself in their marriage and now perhaps that was the loss she was mourning, the loss of her old life, not of Phil.

The thought came, sharp as a lightning flash, that she needed to find herself, to rediscover who she really was. She rolled over, her eyes closed, concentrating. It was a terrifying thought but it was also exhilarating. She was in Spain, she could do whatever she wished, and she was free to rediscover herself.

Nell rubbed her temples and tried to imagine who she wanted to be. Someone new: glamorous, intriguing, witty, independent. She wouldn't be penniless; Phil had promised her money from the house and she had some investments that had been shared between her and Molly after her mum had died five years ago. Nell thought of her mother and wondered what she would say to her now, if she knew that Phil had abandoned her. She'd be kind, sweet, supportive; she'd stroke Nell's hair with a soft hand and tell her she'd be fine. And she would be right.

Nell rolled over again, now determined that Spain would be the making of her. She was far away from Yeovil, away from Phil, and she'd rediscover herself, and then, by Christmas, she could return to the UK with her head held high, a survivor – better than that: a strong, new, happy person.

Nell decided it didn't matter if no one else loved her ever again. The golden, glistening, glorious Nell who'd return home from Spain would surprise everyone. Then she'd find her own place to live, build her own life. The idea fluttered into her head that she might even have enough funds to buy somewhere small in Spain, if she wanted to stay. She had the world at her feet. She could do whatever she liked. And that was what mattered. She was immediately filled with a sense of purpose and belief; she could do it, she was determined that she would.

Nell closed her eyes and breathed deeply. The headache had shrunk to a small twinge behind her eyes. She sensed that her body was relaxing, and she tugged the thin peach cover around her. As she felt her body sinking into the lumpiness of the mattress, a smile twitched across her lips and she exhaled softly, then she was asleep.

* * *

It was dark now, past nine; the street was lit by soft yellow lights, and the town was beginning to stir with a bustle of shoppers and diners excited by the prospect of a Saturday night out. Molly sauntered down the little boulevard, parallel with the sea, gazing into all the shop windows, stopping at every café in the parade, trying to memorise each place. She had noticed a little bar that sold *tapas* and *raciones*, where she and Nell might eat lunch. There was a cheap souvenir shop with a window full of scarves, jewellery and long skirts, the sort of things they might buy to wear on holiday. There was an open-fronted café with an incredible sweet smell seeping into the night air. Molly followed her nose, wandered inside and bought a portion of *churros* wrapped in a cone of paper. Out in the warm air again, she held a finger of hot fried dough between her fingers and nibbled, feeling the sensation of cinnamon and hot sugar against her lips.

Her mind was filled with the buzz of the little town and she

wondered what aspects of it Nell might enjoy. Molly texted
Vanessa that Spain was wonderful and their new neighbour was
even better. She wondered, after she'd pressed send, if Vanessa
wouldn't interpret it the wrong way, as a criticism of herself, and
she hoped not. She'd take a few photos tomorrow and send them
to Vanessa and to Samantha with a chirpy message. Molly walked
on, determined to bring Nell back tomorrow and start their
holiday properly. There was so much more they'd discover
together in the bright sunshine of the following day but, for now,
she was soaking up the nightlife. She passed a bar where couples
and families sat at tables outside. Lively music filled her ears and
she inhaled the savoury smells of something cooking. A blonde
woman and her shiny-domed husband, their skin scorched red
against white strips where straps had been, were tucking into
steak and chips. A lively family were laughing and chattering
nearby, and Molly watched as a waiter brought a huge tray of
burgers in bread rolls. Molly recognised their English voices, a
man asking for more beer, the children begging for ice cream.
She smiled and walked further along the parade.

The shops had become less frequent now. A young couple
were sitting on a bench, their heads down, talking quietly. Molly
passed them and muttered, '*Buenos noches*,' but there was no
reply. She glanced at a hoarding to her left, smiling faces advertising fishing and boat trips around the coast in English and
Spanish; another offering snorkelling and diving. Molly hoped
they could try them all: she intended to be fitter when she
returned to England. She threw the *churros* wrapper into a metal
bin marked *basura*: a discarded piece of cloth had been left on the
ground next to it, a dishevelled blaze of red and yellow. She
noticed the beginning of a path flanked by wooden posts: Molly
paused to listen. She could hear the sound of waves murmuring.
She was almost on the beach. She straddled a wall and rushed

down the path towards the ocean. Her feet were already sinking into sand.

The moon was huge overhead, shimmering amongst coils of clouds in a black sky, and she felt tugged towards the sea. The crinkled shifting surface of the waves was illuminated by a strip of silver light from the moon. It was dark and chilly on the beach and Molly pulled her jacket around her. She felt her feet sinking into the softness of the sand as she stared around, trying to discern shapes. The beach was deserted. There were mountainous shadows of rocks to the left and, to the right, the twinkling lights of Calleblanque. In front of her, Molly gazed at the shadowy beach blending into the ocean. An idea struck her. She would go for a swim.

She stood in one place for a moment, kicking off her shoes. She listened hard and stared around; there was definitely no one else on the beach. Suddenly, an image came to her, a moment on the roof terrace this afternoon: she recalled her neighbour, the casual way he had strolled out of the tub, seemingly naked, as if it was the most natural thing in the world. The sense of freedom, the idea of water against her skin was thrilling and, in two quick movements, she tugged off her T-shirt, jeans and underwear, hurled them on the sand, wrapped her arms around her chest and set off at a running pace towards the whispering waves.

Her feet felt it first, the water's icy coldness, and she shouted out loud with shock and joy. She rushed in until the freezing water lapped around her knees, then her thighs, horrified by the immediate numbing cold and then, before she knew it, she was swimming in the ocean. The water licked her flesh and made it suddenly tingle. Of course, cold water bathing was so good for circulation. She threshed her arms and legs furiously as a wave buffeted her in the face and salty water spluttered into her mouth and up her nose. She hadn't been swimming in an ocean for years and she'd forgotten what hard work it was.

Molly rolled onto her back, gaping up at the disc of the moon and noticing that it really did have indentations, just like cheese. The night sky was completely black, apart from a snaggle of clouds that grazed the darkness. She allowed the water to hold her, letting it lap over her face, as she bellowed her favourite U2 song from the top of her lungs – 'I Still Haven't Found What I'm Looking For'. She felt happy, lifted by the water, wrapped by the velvet sky overhead, exhilarated by the sheer joy of being in Spain. It made her skin fizz with excitement and she closed her eyes and floated for a while, humming the tune. Time drifted as she allowed the water to cradle her, then she became aware that she could hardly feel her feet and her fingers, so she reluctantly pushed hard against the strong lift of the waves back towards the shore.

Moments later, she was standing upright, cold air against her skin, water around her ankles, then she was running back towards the beach at full pelt. The moon slipped behind a cloud and everywhere was suddenly dark. Molly blinked, stopped, looked around and began to stagger forward, her hands out in front of her, trying to recognise the bundle of her clothes in the shadows. She approached what she thought were her jeans and jacket, but it was a dark pile of pebbles.

Molly stood still, nonplussed. Her clothes had disappeared – she certainly couldn't find them. She wandered around, searching, her skin prickling with cold. She wondered what to do next – she was alone, on the edge of a dark beach, close to the road and completely naked. She stopped for a moment and considered her options.

Molly crouched behind the wall like a stalker and peered into the street, illuminated by soft lighting. Then she saw a couple approaching, an older man and woman, talking quietly in Spanish. As they drew level, she called from behind the wall, her tone desperate. '*Disculpe* – er – excuse me...'

The couple stopped, confused by a strange voice that seemed to come from nowhere. They glanced around, clinging to each other nervously. Then Molly popped her head over the wall, an apologetic grin on her face and muttered, 'Ah, can you help? I lost my clothes on the beach – *la ropa*...'

The man stared at Molly, her wet hair, the maniacal smile, and grasped his wife's arm. Molly heard the woman catch her breath – her fingers moved to her throat and she whispered, '*Madre de dios*.' She looked away quickly, then they both scuttled forwards at a fast pace, clinging to each other, heads down, muttering anxiously.

Molly watched them go. A cyclist whizzed by: he shouted something in her direction, his words taken by the wind. Molly skulked back further behind the wall and shivered, her thoughts racing: she'd try one more time to find her clothes.

She slunk back to the beach and rummaged around on all fours in the dark. Her clothes had to be somewhere. But after ten minutes of fumbling around, sand sticking to her palms and shins, she gave up and staggered back to the wall, defeated. Like a furtive animal, her damp hair around her shoulders, she hid in the shadows, her teeth chattering. Then she remembered throwing away the *churros* paper. It came to her: it was a crazy idea, but she was desperate enough to try anything. When there was no one around, during a gap in the traffic, Molly straddled the wall, crept towards the metal bin, and seized the discarded cloth that had been left on the ground. She shook out an old beach towel in the design of the Spanish flag and held it up; it was red and yellow, emblazoned with a crown, still slightly damp. Beneath it was one abandoned flip-flop, large, bright blue and well-worn. Molly rushed back to her safe place behind the wall and wrapped the towel tightly around herself, securing it in a small knot at the front, like a sarong. Despite the flag being damp, she felt instantly warmer. Then she wriggled her foot into the single flip-flop. At least one of her feet would be safely shod. Molly gritted her teeth: beggars couldn't be choosers.

She glanced around: the coast was fairly clear, so she climbed out onto the pavement and strode briskly towards the parade of shops and cafés. Molly set off at a fast pace dressed in the dirty towel, wet hair dripping over her face and shoulders, hoping that she'd appear almost normal, that she might even blend in.

A car honked a horn. Molly waved back graciously, her strut becoming a swagger, then a flounce: she was a catwalk model flaunting the latest fashion. She was on a roll. Molly sashayed past shoppers, diners, families and tourists, offering everyone her most engaging smile. Someone made a comment in Spanish and Molly merely waved her hand and replied, '*Viva España*,' as if it was the most normal thing in the world to be out for a night on the town wearing the national flag.

She limped across the road that led to *Apartamentos Melocotón*; one heel was embedded with shards of gravel, but the single flip-flop had protected the other sole well. Then she made a run for it, leaping high across the small lawn of plants, tramping through a flower bed, belting full-pelt towards the entrance. She rushed up three flights of steps and banged her fists on the door of number fourteen, hoping that Nell would be awake and would let her in before Bernt peered through the window to see what the noise was. She was freezing, her skin prickling goose flesh, but she was safe now. Molly sighed, so relieved to be back at the apartment.

Nell opened the door in pyjamas, her eyes wide, and gasped. 'What the hell, Molly...?'

'Hi, Nell – sorry to wake you.'

Molly rushed past, her laughter tinkling, full of triumph – she had just made it through Calleblanque in front of hundreds of people, dressed only in an old damp towel, and now she was heading for the shower. She dived under scalding hot water, gasping with delight as she rubbed her tingling body with Nell's scented soap. Molly began to sing '*Y Viva España*', enjoying the intensity of heat and steam. She was pleased with herself, then a sudden thought occurred to her: she wondered if anyone had managed to take a sneaky photo, if she would see herself in all her glory splashed all over the front page of the local newspaper tomorrow morning. She hoped not.

Molly smeared shampoo over her hair and rubbed her scalp with strong fingers. She was happy: she was here in Spain and she was already having adventures. In truth, it was exactly what she needed.

11

Sunday 22nd August

The swim last night was truly beautiful – I so enjoyed the sense of freedom, the tingling water on my skin, the moon overhead. Never mind about what happened next – I gave a few of the locals a good laugh. I'll pop back today and see if I can find my clothes...

The morning light was intensely bright in the apartment. Nell wrapped her dressing gown around her and stumbled, blinking, into the kitchen. It was gone eight o'clock: she had slept for nine hours straight. The dirty apricot-coloured walls glowed peachy pink in the sunlight and she smiled: this was the first day of her brand-new self and the apartment seemed warm and bright. She heard the sound of running water – slopping water – from the kitchen and she pushed open the bamboo curtains to reveal Molly, wearing shorts and a T-shirt, bending over the sink washing a pair of jeans. Nell folded her arms good-humouredly.

'So, are you going to tell me what happened last night? When

I let you in, you were soaking wet and dressed in the Spanish flag.'

'It's a long story, best forgotten.' Molly gave a rueful smile. She decided to change the subject. 'By the way, I just phoned Samantha. I'd forgotten to tell her we were in Spain. She didn't seem to mind. They are busy on the farm right now. Then I texted Lisa about the air conditioning and she said the switch is in the lounge behind the wooden bookcase. It's hidden behind the jewelled green flamenco ornament – I checked, and it really is there.'

She was rinsing out underwear, jeans, a T-shirt. 'The jacket's a mess – I can't get all the sand out... it's in the pockets and the seams.'

Nell frowned: she knew Molly too well to ask her the finer details of how she'd ruined her clothes. 'Let's take the lot up to the roof terrace and hang them out up there. I remember seeing a line and pegs. It'll be the best place for it to dry.'

'Great idea.' Molly dumped the heavy washing into a plastic bowl. 'Then we'll go out for breakfast. I've seen a great little place called *Ajo Rojo*, where they do a fry-up.'

Nell agreed. 'Anything will do for me – an espresso would be good.'

The sisters were striding up the stairs two at a time. The sun was blindingly bright and it warmed their skin. When they reached the top, they saw two people sitting at the patio table, sipping coffee. Molly recognised one of them, despite the fact that he was wearing clothes: a light blue T-shirt and shorts.

'Hello, Bernt.'

He waved a hand. 'Good to see you again. Most of the residents don't seem to use the sunroof. It's always a pleasure to have company.'

Molly wondered if he was being sarcastic after the hot tub

incident yesterday or if he was genuinely being kind. She met the eyes of the woman next to him, a slim, elegant woman probably in her fifties, with white hair, cut in a short angular style with a thick fringe. She waved an arm. 'Hello. I'm Ulla. Won't you join us for breakfast?'

Molly was hanging her washing. Nell looked at the friendly couple, at their coffee pot and the bowl of plump fresh fruit, and smiled enthusiastically. 'That would be lovely. Thank you.'

Ulla glanced at Bernt. 'Darling, would you mind going down-stairs and bringing up more plates and cups? I want to stay here and get to know our new neighbours.'

Bernt stood up, taller and more muscular than Nell had remembered him, and gave a little smile, strolling towards the stairway. Ulla indicated that Nell should sit. Molly had finished pegging up her twisted wet clothes and she joined them. Ulla leaned forward and held out her hand.

'Ulla Nilsson. Bernt and I own the apartment next to yours, number twelve. We're based in Stockholm, but we come out here as much as we can.' She nodded knowingly. 'The weather is very beneficial. And this is a lovely area, very friendly, and the beaches are nice.'

'We're off to the beach this morning,' Molly interjected.

Nell took Ulla's hand. 'Nell...' She was about to say 'Nell Spencer' but she paused, thinking. Today was the first day of the new Nell. She'd use her own name, her maiden name. Phil was in the past now, along with his name and his mistress. Her voice came out strongly, assured. 'Nell Mitchell, and this is my sister Molly.' She was pleased with herself. 'We're here for a few months, for the same reason really.'

'We've booked the apartment from Lisa, probably until Christmas,' Molly added, noting her sister's use of her maiden name with a tinge of admiration. It gave her a warm feeling, that somehow their shared name brought her and Nell even closer. Molly was sure this was going to be a special holiday for them both.

'Oh, that's wonderful.' Ulla flicked long fingers through the white hair, touching the sunglasses perched on top of her head. 'There is so much to do here, places to visit, and my favourite activity, shopping.'

Nell gave a light laugh and Molly thought about the little souvenir shop she'd passed last night on the parade with its jewellery and long skirts and scarves. She didn't shop for herself much, but she might pop in there later. Ulla was still discussing their surroundings. 'There are great water sports locally. Bernt likes the sense of freedom, being on the water, but I'm happier on the beach or in a spa or a shopping mall.'

'I couldn't agree more,' Nell enthused.

Bernt arrived back, his stride leisurely and relaxed, carrying a tray with cups and plates, another coffee pot, fruit, bread rolls, some sort of jam and a plate of *churros*. He placed the tray on the table and sat down.

'It is nice to share breakfast with our new neighbours.' He raised an eyebrow. '*Que aproveche*, as they say here. Enjoy.' He began to pour coffee into cups and, as Ulla reached for a grape, Nell did the same. Molly nodded enthusiastically and extended a hand towards the plate, picking up two warm, cinnamon-sugared churros.

* * *

For the next two weeks, Molly and Nell fell into a routine that pleased them both. They'd have breakfast on the roof terrace each morning, frequently meeting up with Ulla and Bernt for a conversation and coffee; they'd spend mornings by the pool at

Apartamentos Melocotón, afternoons down at the beach, and evenings eating either in the apartment or at various restaurants. Molly was becoming fond of *Ajo Rojo*, a café run by a friendly Spanish family, which served tortillas, patatas bravas and salads, whereas Nell was keen to try out different places, her palate requiring new tastes to tempt her to eat. They dined occasionally with Ulla and Bernt, who served up mashed potatoes or pasta with fish or chicken. Molly wasn't accustomed to Swedish food but Nell appeared to enjoy it and complimented Ulla and Bernt effusively on their cooking.

Within two weeks, both women had started to look and feel healthier. The sun had bronzed their skin, Molly's deep tan making her appear Spanish, which caused countless problems in bars and shops as the locals expected her to respond fluently to their conversation. Her thick, dark grey hair had been bleached by the strong sun, streaking it white, tingeing the darker bits indigo: it shone in the sunlight, a pretty colour that suited her skin tone. Nell marvelled at it, repeatedly telling her sister that she should take every step possible to keep it that way.

Nell's fair skin had turned pink, then salmon, then a pretty golden brown, making her eyes bright and her hair glow, and she had developed a spring to her step, a confidence in her poise and a new cheerfulness in her demeanour. Spain was suiting them both.

Ulla had invited them on several occasions to go with her to a spa session and shopping trip. Initially they had declined, feeling the need simply to do nothing, to rest by the pool or sprawl on the beach. But yesterday Nell had accepted, accompanying Ulla to a spa for a facial. She had returned full of enthusiasm, her sun-kissed skin radiant, protesting to Molly that she should have gone with them, but Molly had spent the afternoon asleep on the beach, a book open across her stomach, and arrived back long after the women had prepared a healthy salad in number four-teen, complete with white wine.

It was therefore no great surprise that, when Ulla called round the following morning and suggested that Nell and Molly accompany her to a nearby town for a shopping trip, Nell was very keen to go. They stood in the lounge of their apartment while Nell reached for her handbag.

'Come on, Molly – it'll be great.'

Molly wrinkled her nose. 'To be honest, Nell, I'd rather just go to the beach.'

Ulla took Molly's hand. 'Oh, no – come along. It will be fun. There are some lovely things in the shops. You could replace that old jacket you ruined on the beach.'

Molly shrugged. 'I've had to throw it away.' She thought for a moment. 'I don't need a jacket. No, seriously – you three go.'

'Three?' Ulla burst into laughter. 'Bernt won't come. He's off to hire a boat for the day. This is strictly a girls' outing.'

Molly wondered if she wouldn't prefer to take the boat trip. She forced a smile. 'I tell you what – I'll come next time. You two go and have fun.'

Nell hugged her. 'Right. Thanks, Molly. We'll check out the shops for you.' She swung her handbag over her shoulder. 'Let's get going then, Ulla. I'm very keen to get myself some classy new beachwear.'

'Wonderful.' Ulla was full of enthusiasm. 'There's a great shop – *Vela Nueva* – that sells really good things. Bernt buys his swimming trunks there.'

Molly remembered the peach pouch he'd worn in the hot tub, virtually invisible against his skin, and stifled a smile. Nell and Ulla were on their way towards the staircase, chattering excitedly. Molly listened to their footsteps on the stairs and then closed the door. She was glad Nell had a new friend and was enjoying herself. She sank into a chair and wondered whether to make a cup of tea or to go down to the pool and buy a cocktail. She was already feeling restless, unsure what she wanted to do next.

Her feet took her to the beach instead. She'd wandered aimlessly past the swimming pool, where she had heard the joyful sounds of children squealing with delight as they hurled themselves like little clenched fists into the water. Molly had decided to keep walking. She passed through the front gardens with the patches of greenery, through the narrow path between buildings that led to the parade of shops and then across the road, over the familiar wall and onto the beach.

Molly laid out her towel and stretched full length, enjoying the feeling of heat on her skin. She closed her eyes and removed her sunglasses, pushing back her thick hair. The sound of the sea soothed her and she began to relax.

Then her thoughts came rapidly; she couldn't hold one idea still for long before another took its place. She thought of Samantha, her daughter, working on the farm with her husband, and her two grown sons who lived in the adjoining cottages. Samantha's life was rigorous, repetitive, routine, a long way from the relaxing sunshine of Calleblanque. Molly wondered if her daughter ever craved a holiday. She imagined Nell and Ulla, enjoying shopping, buying swimwear, stopping somewhere for a coffee and chattering. Bernt would have hired a boat. He'd be standing on the deck, the wind in his face, his skin leathery against the buffeting salt water spray. Molly wondered if she should have joined the women, tried harder to be part of a group that held up dresses and enthused about how gorgeous they would look. But she was happy where she was, dozing, allowing sunshine to soak into her skin like liquid honey.

Molly's thoughts drifted to her mother, Kezia Lovell, and how her father had once said Molly was exactly like her. Molly had always taken his words as criticism. She recalled an incident when she was a child: her father had been sitting in his chair, arms folded, his pipe a bowl in his hand, watching her dance to music on the radio. He had muttered, 'Molly's just like her mother.' She had been seven years old, but she'd never forgotten the incident or the strange feeling, pride mixed with a sense of guilt and inadequacy. Molly had assumed that he was commenting on her wildness, her unpredictability, her impulsiveness. After all, Kezia Lovell had abandoned both him and her baby. But a thought fidgeted in her mind now; what if his words conveyed admiration, love, even?

Molly recalled the woman she had called 'Mum' as far back as she could remember, but who was really Nell's mother, Jean. She was small and fair, like Nell, but by the time the girls were teenagers she was greying and had started to look tired. Molly had loved her: Jean had always been kind; she had treated both girls equally, her hands soft as she cupped a chin and muttered encouragement or endearments. She'd helped them with homework, hugged them when they had grazed knees; her eyes had glowed with something like longing as the girls played records by the Beatles and the Rolling Stones on the stereogram their father had bought, as they danced around the living room, Nell twisting her hips expertly, Molly thrashing her arms in the air and laughing. Jean had been a good mum, and she'd never allowed Molly to feel that both girls weren't equally her own. But Molly always knew; like a thorn stuck in her shoe, the thought was always there: it always pricked her into remembering.

Molly's father, Thomas, had died in his fifties. Molly had been frantically busy with Samantha then, doing her blind best to be a good mother. It was before she was living with Dave and she'd found those times by herself hard, trying to hold down a job and foster a close relationship with an aloof and uninterested daughter. Those days passed so quickly, like a cine-film on fast play, and her strongest memory was of trying too hard to supply the laughter in a quiet house.

Jean had helped Molly with childcare and had been a source of constant support, but later she grew frail, continuing to live alone after Thomas died. Molly and Nell, both separately and together, had made sure they'd visited their mother regularly as she became more and more fragile. Five years ago, Jean had taken to her bed feeling unwell and had never got up: two weeks later, she'd died of pneumonia. It was in the same month that Richie had passed away and Molly had been too distraught to organise her mother's affairs; she had allowed Nell to do the necessary jobs of arranging the funeral and clearing and selling the house. Nell missed her mother badly, but Phil had been supportive and she'd concentrated all her efforts on being busy. Molly had found it difficult to think straight: when faced with tasks of organisation, she had left things out, made mistakes or just forgot.

Molly sighed. She hadn't been the best of parents or the best of children. Perhaps she could be the best of sisters. The thought made her happy.

Sunlight filtered through her lashes and her lids became heavy. She thought she heard herself snore, a soft sound in her nose. She was here in Spain, sleepy, contented, relaxed. The sea breathed in and out, a chorus of whispers, and the sand held her still as she dozed, bathed in warm light.

12

Tuesday 7th September

Today was much more interesting than I could ever have planned. I was feeling restless, that old sensation of itchy feet, needing something new to interest me, and I thought it was just going to be another ordinary sunny day on the beach. But it's funny what can happen when you talk to strangers, especially attractive ones on a boat...

Molly woke suddenly. She'd rolled over from her beach towel and her hair was full of sand. Her mouth was dry. She sat up and shook her hair. She peered down at the old red swimsuit, baggy at the bust, and the bright floral sarong that had twisted and tied itself in a knot around her thighs. She stood up slowly and brushed herself clean. She'd take a walk around the parade of shops and buy an ice cream.

Molly wandered past the shop that sold *churros*, the strong, sweet smell filling her nostrils. She was hungry but she'd had enough of fried food. She'd have a cool ice lolly now, and then share a meal with Nell later that evening. She passed a bustling café where people were eating at metal tables outside, and she realised it was lunchtime. Gazing at the menu in the café window, Molly imagined herself eating at one of the shiny silver tables, sampling *calamari, gazpacho, paella, chorizo*. She and Nell would be dressed in colourful dresses, a bottle of Cava between them, their heads close together, talking. In her imagination, Bernt and Ulla arrived to join them, everyone laughing and hugging each other, and the Nilssons ordered *pulpo a la Gallega*, sitting upright to eat their octopus, poised and sophisticated, commenting on how well it was cooked.

Molly thought instantly of Richie. He'd have grabbed her hand at lunchtime in a gesture of romantic impetuosity and dragged her, laughing, to an isolated table in the corner, calling for wine immediately, '*Vino tinto, Señor*,' grinning at her as red wine splashed into two glasses. Then he'd have ordered *berenjenas fritas* and *espinacas con garbanzos* with the lazy confidence of a man who spoke perfect Spanish. He'd have pushed a hand through his dark, curly hair, then stretched it out to circle Molly's wrist across the table. As the waiter brought the fried aubergines and spinach with chickpeas, he'd have winked at her, thanked the waiter politely, sipped his wine and then started to eat with gusto, proclaiming that vegetarian food was both delicious and best for health.

Molly had stopped being a strict vegetarian when Richie died. It hadn't kept him alive, although she suspected that the heart attack he'd suffered in his seventies had been a similar family ailment to the one that killed his father at fifty and his grandfather at forty-five. After Richie was gone, Molly had lapsed into accepting whatever was put in front of her – although when she cooked vegetarian food at home, it often brought back a bittersweet memory of Richie and his *joie de vivre*. She thought about him and missed him every day.

Molly paused at the souvenir shop that sold silver jewellery and bright clothes, hesitating at a rail of colourful skirts outside and examining several wrap-around styles. For a moment, she imagined herself in a flowing skirt on the beach, in the apartment and by the swimming pool, then she went inside the shop to browse.

The shop was long and narrow; she passed a counter where a woman wearing a bright headscarf and huge earrings greeted her with a smile. '*Buenos días, Señora.*' Molly lifted a hand in greeting and drifted towards the back of the shop. She searched through a rack of colourful long dresses, skirts and loose trousers and then turned to face a rail of hats in various styles. Suddenly she burst out laughing. The final rail in the shop was labelled *Disfraces* and it appeared to be an array of wild fancy dress costumes. There was a Superman suit, a witch's get-up, a fairy tutu comprising pink net and tinsel, and even a crocodile outfit. Molly turned back to the rail of dresses and frowned, selecting something she could take home to prove to Nell that she'd had a productive day. She had money in her purse and the clothes were relatively cheap; she would spoil herself.

Half an hour later, she stepped into the bright sunlight carrying a shopping bag containing two long skirts, a loose top and a denim jacket. A black, wide-brimmed hat was perched on her head; huge round sunglasses shielded her eyes and she sauntered forward with a smile on her face. She glimpsed herself in a shop window and thought she looked like Yoko Ono in the 1970s. She decided it wasn't a bad look at all: it suited her and brought a swing to her hips that made her feel as if she was a modern woman at leisure.

She strolled past the parade of shops towards the sign advertising boats for hire. It occurred to her that it might be very pleasant to watch distant boats gliding along, dotted against the line of the ocean. She wondered if she might see Bernt there. She'd forgotten to buy herself an ice lolly, but she imagined inviting him for coffee and sitting at a pleasant rickety beach bar, drinking lattes and laughing about how much nicer it was to be on the beach than bustling in the town centre trying on swimwear.

Molly turned down the narrow, sandy path with the wooden posts where she'd been skinny dipping and lost her clothes. It led to an open expanse of beach. She wandered along the sand until she came to a rocky cove where various boats were lined up in a little harbour. Molly strolled along a wooden walkway, past several moored boats. She paused next to a blue sailing boat to listen to the rippling sound of the waves lapping against it. A man in a cap was half-sitting, half-sprawled on the deck, his legs crossed, propped up against a toolbox, munching on a sandwich. Molly examined his boat, the scrubbed white deck, the blue paint, the name of the vessel painted on the side in huge black capitals: *Carpe Diem*. The name made Molly exclaim with delight. The man turned to stare at her, then a smile broke across his craggy face and he addressed her in a gravelly voice.

'*¿Quieres un paseo, Señora?*'

Molly frowned behind the sunglasses and thought for a moment, translating his words steadily. As far as she could make out through the dark lenses, she thought the man was about her age; he had dark grey curls beneath the peaked cap, a broad weather-beaten face, a muscular body beneath a grey T-shirt and cut-off jeans.

'No, no, I don't want a boat ride, thanks. I was just admiring the name of your boat.'

'You're English,' the man replied in perfect English. He stood up and moved to the edge of the boat, leaning forwards and holding out his hand. 'Thank goodness. My Spanish isn't great. And it's always good to meet another Brit…'

Molly took his hand. It was dry and hard-skinned, and easily covered her own. The sunglasses slipped down her nose and she pushed them back up. 'I'm Molly.'

'Ronnie Barnes.' His voice reminded her of cinder toffee somehow, burned, crackly and smooth all at the same time. She recognised the burr in his voice.

'Are you from Bristol?'

He smiled. 'Devon, Molly. Lived there all of my life until I came here. I have to be close to the sea – I lived in Teignmouth.'

'I know it well.' Molly beamed. She recalled walking on the beach at Teignmouth some ten years ago, holding Richie's hand, eating an ice cream. He had just sold a painting to a professor of sociology in Starcross. She met Ronnie's eyes. 'I live in Yeovil.'

'A Somerset maid?' Ronnie's eyebrows disappeared beneath his cap. 'Are you on holiday here?'

'Yes.' Molly waved her hands to show that she was staying for an indefinite period.

'By yourself or with your husband?'

'With my sister.' Molly waved her hands again, indicating her sister wasn't with her at the moment. 'She's gone shopping.'

'Would you like to come aboard? I'll show you around this beast of a boat, shall I?'

He stretched out a tanned arm, grasped her wrist in a clasp of his fist and tugged her towards the boat. Molly heaved herself forwards and stepped onto the deck. She caught her breath as she felt the lilt of the waves. The movement beneath her feet was exciting, the swaying surge suggesting that she was about to travel to new lands.

'This is lovely.'

'Welcome to the *Carpe Diem*.'

'Oh, it's such a great name – seize the day,' Molly gasped.

'My motto in life,' Ronnie explained. 'Have you had lunch?'

'No, not yet.' Molly studied the sandwich box he thrust under her nose.

'Crab on rye?' he offered. 'Glass of white?'

Molly perched herself on a wooden seat carved into the side of the boat. 'Don't mind if I do.' She took a sandwich and bit into the crusty bread, reaching her hand out for a glass of *vino blanco*. 'Lovely.'

She looked around at the neat deck, the coils of rope, past the crisp white sails and out into the vast expanse of sea beyond, chewing thoughtfully. 'Shouldn't you be out there on the ocean blue, Ronnie? I mean, if you do boat tours then why aren't you touring the boat?'

'Business is a bit slack at the moment.' He wiped his mouth with the back of his hand. 'It doesn't bother me. I have my house and cars and a nice life here in Spain. The boat touring business is a hobby, really – something to do during the day, where I get to be out on my boat.'

'Do you have family here?' Molly asked without thinking, sipping her wine.

'My daughters are in the UK. Verity has just finished university in Leeds and Storm is doing Drama at LIPA. She's very like me, Storm – a bit of a show-off. Verity's like her mother, a bit more sophisticated.'

Molly frowned. 'You have young daughters.'

'I was an older dad, second marriage,' Ronnie admitted.

Molly thought of Nell's husband Phil in his late sixties, and of Nikki's expanding waistline, the prospect of dirty nappies and sleepless nights. The next question popped out of her mouth. 'So it's just you and your wife here in Spain then?'

Ronnie shook his head. 'No, Tracy didn't like it here. She

stayed here for a bit but she didn't really settle to Spanish life. She left me and took the girls back to England. She's back in Torquay now, living with a plasterer called John.' Molly noticed the deep laughter creases around his eyes. 'Life was too laid-back for Tracy here. It suits me fine, though.'

Molly had almost finished her wine. 'So, you live by yourself, Ronnie?'

'I do, just me rattling around in a big old *finca* with too many bedrooms and a pool. My cleaner, Pilar, comes in three times a week to keep me on my toes.' His eyes met Molly's. 'And you? Do you live with your sister?'

'I do now.' A slow smile spread across her face. 'She's split up from her husband. I was by myself before that.'

'Single?'

'Widowed,' Molly explained.

Ronnie's face became serious. 'I'm sorry about that.' Then his expression brightened. 'Look, Molly, we've had a spot of lunch. How about we have a mini cruise in the old boat? I'll take you out for a quick tour of the coastline.'

'How much will it cost?' Molly thought about her empty purse. She had almost spent every euro in her purse in the clothes shop on the parade.

'Oh, no, I don't want paying – it's on the house,' Ronnie grinned. 'I'm not doing anything else and it's nice to have another Brit for company. I can take us out to some pretty coves and there's a lovely sandy beach where hardly any tourists go. It's very peaceful there. Half an hour's run, and we can finish off that bottle of wine. How about it?'

Molly drained the wine in her glass and nodded. 'Thank you, Ronnie. I'd be delighted.'

Ten minutes later, Ronnie was at the wheel, steering the boat out to sea. The sails flapped overhead and Molly watched his broad back, the cap firmly on his head, dark grey curls beneath, above square shoulders. The ocean was intensely blue, indigo against the turquoise of the sky. The sun was at its height, the white deck of the boat reflecting searing hot rays. Molly took a few photos to send to Vanessa and Samantha, then she stretched out, smoothing her sarong over her thighs, and pushed the black, wide-brimmed hat firmly on her head against the breeze, adjusting the sunglasses. She felt like a film star or a Bond girl. Molly gazed out to sea, towards the deep blue line of the horizon. The sensation of the waves below the decks stirred something deep in her, lifting, dipping, pushing the boat onwards, the curve of the coast on the horizon, the promise of a land beyond. She yearned for new places, new experiences. The sunshine glinted on the waves and kissed the surface of her skin and she sighed. This was the life.

13

─────────

Wednesday 8th September

He reminds me of R, just a little. The creases around his eyes when he smiles. His friendly grin, the way he is so laid-back about life. He's quite nice... and the boat trip was lovely, just drifting, afloat on the waves, new horizons, the open sea.

Molly scuttled past the parade of shops towards *Apartamentos Melocotón*, talking breathlessly into her phone. 'I didn't realise the time, Nell. How long have you been back at the apartment? Oh, that long? Sorry...'

She listened while Nell babbled excitedly about her shopping trip and the seafood lunch in town and how she and Ulla had returned to the apartment at four o'clock and spent the last two hours with Bernt basking on the roof terrace in their new bikinis, wondering where Molly was. It was past six and Nell had begun to feel anxious, which was why she was phoning her now.

'So, where are you, Molly?'

'I – ah – I fell asleep on the beach. I'm on my way back now. I'll only be ten minutes.' Molly didn't know why she'd just lied to her sister about how she'd spent the afternoon. She hadn't meant to lie but, for some reason, she wasn't ready to tell Nell about Ronnie Barnes, his craggy face, his crab sandwiches, his cinder toffee voice and the bottle of wine they'd consumed during the tour around golden coves. She recalled the breath-taking excitement of being far out at sea, surrounded by miles of water, a solitary boat bobbing on the vast ocean, and Ronnie making her laugh about his escapades in Spain over the past few years. They'd been on the boat for several hours.

Molly wasn't sure at all why she wanted to keep Ronnie a secret. It was foolish: she wasn't magnetically attracted to him but he was nice and, somehow, telling Nell she'd been in the company of a new man would feel awkward. So she breathed her excuses into the phone as she hurtled down the road that led to the apartments. 'I'm only a few minutes away. Sorry I'm late.'

'We're making paella. It's almost ready.' Nell's voice was loud in her ear. 'I'll see you in a minute or two then?'

Molly swung her bag of clothes and increased her pace. 'Yes, yes – thanks, Nell, and sorry I didn't pick up your texts.'

She heard Nell laugh good-naturedly and say something about plating up and eating their meal on the roof terrace with a bottle of white wine. Molly wasn't sure she wanted any more wine after the lunch she'd shared with Ronnie.

But she had to admit, Ronnie had been good fun. The thought of their final conversation as he helped her from the boat bubbled in her mind again and she smiled. It had been a dare, a flirtation. She'd asked Ronnie what he was going to do to drum up more business and Ronnie had said that he didn't care: he was quite well-off as he was and he was happy to take attractive women on boat tours without payment. Molly had retorted that it would be incredibly easy to persuade punters – she'd actually used that word – to take a boat trip and he'd replied that she was very welcome to try if she knew a way to bring him more business. She had whipped off her sunglasses and met his gaze, then she'd said, 'If I bring the hordes in to ride on your boat tomorrow, you owe me dinner.'

His eyes had twinkled. 'It's a deal, Molly Mitchell,' he had said in a mischievous way that had made her skin prickle.

She'd flashed a sassy look and said, 'Be careful what you wish for, Ronnie. You'll have customers galore tomorrow afternoon.'

He'd nodded incredulously and asked for her number. 'Just so that I can call you tomorrow and tell you where I've booked for dinner... for two.'

She had given him her mobile number and whirled away, vivacious and playful, feeling his eyes on her as she swung her hips. Then she had realised it was six o'clock and had increased her speed. At that point, her phone had buzzed and she'd picked it up to hear Nell's anxious voice in her ear.

Molly rushed past the plants in the front garden of the apartments – but her mind wasn't on the roof terrace supper Nell had prepared. No, she was cooking up a plan. She'd be up bright and early tomorrow morning and she knew what to do: she'd be busy drumming up so many customers that Ronnie Barnes would be amazed and dazzled by her brilliant business acumen. She chortled softly as she bounded up the stairs towards number fourteen. She had a mission now, and it made her steps light: she was really beginning to enjoy this holiday.

Nell stretched her arms and legs, warm inside the double bed. The morning sun streamed a dust-speckled, creamy yellow beam through the windows and onto the peach cover. Nell glanced at the clock. It was past eight. She smiled and a small sigh built in her chest and filtered through her lips. She was enjoying Spain.

Her mind flitted back to the delicious supper they'd eaten last night. She'd worn the dress she'd bought yesterday while shopping with Ulla; it was a short, navy linen sleeveless dress with cream piping. She'd never have worn anything like that six months ago but then she'd been in England, she'd been Mrs Phil Spencer and she'd been sensible and boring and stuck in a routine. Now she was a scintillating, bronze-skinned woman on holiday who would wear exactly what she pleased. And when Ulla and Bernt had offered her an open invitation to visit them in Sweden, she had said, 'Why not?'

It occurred to Nell that she had no idea what Sweden was like but Bernt and Ulla were warm, adventurous, progressive and fun, so she imagined Sweden would be just the same. She rolled over onto her elbows. Molly had been in a trance-like state throughout the meal. Nell had touched her arm gently and Molly had bubbled to life, joining in the conversation for a little while. Then she'd lifted a fork of paella and returned to her dreamy state. The fork had remained in position for a full five minutes before Molly had brought it down to her plate again without eating it. Nell was intrigued: that was exactly how Molly behaved when she was restless or when she was plotting a new venture.

Nell knew Molly of old; she'd arrived home late with an expression of studied nonchalance; she was certainly hiding something. Nell was determined to get to the bottom of Molly's little secret. An idea came to her. She'd wake Molly and take her out to breakfast; they'd share quality time together and she'd ask what she was up to. Left to her own devices, Molly was capable of being zany and impulsive and Nell was always fascinated by what her capricious sister did. The self-painting was a perfect example, typical of Molly, whimsical and unpredictable as ever, covering herself in cling film and rolling on the canvas. And Nell knew she'd ruined her clothes on the beach, although she shuddered to think how that might have happened. Nell smiled, a mixture of affection and admiration. Then a sense of guilt filled her mind – she had been neglecting Molly. Nell thought that perhaps she'd felt left out yesterday, spending the whole day by herself. She didn't want her sister to feel unimportant: she'd been so sweet, especially since the Phil episode, and her idea of coming to Spain had been perfect. Breakfast together might be the ideal treat.

Nell heard the apartment door click. She frowned, then she swung her legs out of bed and reached for her dressing gown. She padded past Molly's little room. The bed was unmade and empty. She trotted into the lounge area. Molly wasn't there, but there was an almost-empty glass of orange juice on the table, next to the silk-covered book she used as a diary, and a ballpoint pen. The book was placed face-down, open.

Nell picked up the diary and turned it over in her hands. She glanced at the open page and her eyes read a few words.

Wednesday 8th September

Things are starting to heat up! I may have something really interesting to write about later. Meanwhile, to put my plan into action…

Nell closed the diary firmly. Molly had written the entry this morning, probably just minutes ago. She touched the turquoise silk cover with her fingertips and was thoughtful for a moment. It was tempting to delve into the diary, into Molly's unfathomable mind, but no, Nell wouldn't do that. She flicked open the back of the diary and noticed that several pages had been torn out. It seemed such a shame to spoil a beautiful book. Nell ran her fingers over the smooth page and felt indentations: something had been heavily written on the torn page and had scored itself onto the blank page below. She held the book close to her narrowed eyes and read the words '*Carpe Diem*'. She shook her head, replacing the diary where she'd found it, pages open, its cover spread like the wings of a bright blue bird.

Nell toyed with the idea of having a quick shower and then setting off down to the beach to find her sister. She would persuade Molly to go to a café and they'd chat together over coffee and toast. Molly was definitely up to something and the best way to find out would be to ask her over a meal. There was certainly no need to snoop in her diary, even if Molly had left it open for anyone to read. She had clearly been in a rush to go somewhere.

Nell mused for a moment about the meaning of Molly's words: *Things are starting to heat up!* Nell doubted that she meant the weather. As she threw her dressing gown on the floor and rushed into the little bathroom, squeezing into the shower cubicle and turning on the scalding water, Nell began to hum a little tune.

* * *

Molly was waiting outside the jewellery and clothes shop when it opened. The woman with the colourful headscarf and huge earrings waved her inside with a cheerful, '*Buenos días, Señora.*'

She rushed to the back of the shop, stopping at the clothes rail marked '*Disfraces*', and began to sort through the various costumes. Some of them were tiny; the fairy costume was clearly for a child and besides, she didn't want a fairy outfit. Nor did she want to be Superman, Batman, a witch or a naughty nurse with a short skirt and stockings. They wouldn't be appropriate. There was a latex face mask of Donald Trump, and another of a skeleton head with a stitched mouth, and a third of a smiling red-lipped blonde woman, possibly Madonna. Molly shook her head: these were not what she was looking for.

She pushed more costumes along the rail and then she saw it, right near the end. It felt rubbery and the colour glowed, turquoise and silver sheen. She pulled the whole costume out. The body suit was pliable and soft, probably latex. There were two holes for arms and two more for feet at the bottom. The rest was a long tube of silver and blue shining scales and a thin flapping fin. Molly lifted out the mask that fitted over the entire head. There were two staring oversized eyes and the oval gaping mouth. It was unmistakably a fish: a cod or a guppy, she thought.

The woman with the colourful headscarf was standing behind her, hands on hips. Molly turned round and beamed. She had her Spanish phrase ready. '*Quiero alquilar este... pescado.*' The shop owner frowned so Molly translated. 'I'd like to hire this fish.'

The woman shook her head. 'It will not fit you, *Señora*. It is for a youth.'

Molly smiled, all breath and positivity. 'I need to hire it. It's very stretchy. I think I can squeeze into it. How much for the day?'

The woman fingered one earring. 'Twenty euros. Also, twenty euros deposit in case you don't return. Forty euros.'

Molly's hand was already in her purse, pulling out notes. 'Here.'

The woman was unsure. 'It will be tight fit.'

Molly nodded enthusiastically and pointed to a green velvet curtain with the wooden sign overhead, '*Probadores*'. She waved the hand clutching the cod suit. 'Can I try?'

The woman nodded and Molly pushed the curtain aside. The changing room was very small, just large enough for one person to turn around. There was an upright clothes stand and a huge ornate mirror. Molly beamed optimistically at her own reflection and began to tug off her T-shirt and jeans.

It took a full fifteen minutes to squeeze into the cod. It was a case of holding her breath, rolling down the latex and inching it over her flesh slowly, tucking herself in as she went.

Finally, she gazed in the mirror and smiled. She could hardly breathe, but the suit was on. It would probably never come off again, but Molly decided she'd worry about that later. The latex was tight around her torso and bending would be difficult. Her hands and her arms protruded through the small holes and her ankles and feet in sandals poked out at the bottom. Molly knew she looked ridiculous but she felt the thrill of an escapade: it made her eager to put her plan into action right away. She moved tentatively, twisting at the waist, the rubbery material constricting her stomach, and pulled the fish head on, wriggling it down over her face and neck. She could barely see through the pinprick eye holes but the mouth was a longish spout with a hole at the end so at least she could breathe. Inside the fish, there was a strange heavy smell of plastic and chemicals. Molly peered at her reflection: she certainly looked like a prize carp.

She wriggled down to bend forward and managed to open her huge denim bag then delved into the bottom for a handful of the thirty leaflets she'd made earlier. She squinted at them through the tiny eye holes, pleased with her thick scrawl.

SET SAIL ON THE CARPE DIEM.
BEST BOAT TOUR IN SPAIN.
SKIPPER – RONNIE BARNES.
CRUISE AROUND THE BAY. TRY IT. YOU'LL LOVE IT.

She pushed her jeans and T-shirt into the bag and she was ready. She used her shoulder to open the curtain and began waddling past the owner towards the open door. Molly was grinning with optimism. She was sure her plan would work.

As she left the shop, a young female customer paused and watched her shuffling towards the road. She caught the eye of the shop owner and they shook their heads. By way of explanation, the woman with the bright headscarf and earrings shrugged and muttered, '*Inglesa.*'

14

Wednesday 8th September

I've never worried about love. When I was young, relationships came so easily and I'd jump in and grab at happiness with both hands. I'd put my whole self in. Then, if things didn't work out, I'd see myself from the outside, stuck somewhere I had leaped into without thinking, so, as quick as lightning, I'd pull my whole self out again. It's the same with life – I just seem to put my feet down in one place then I yearn for a change, for something new…

Molly was standing on the beach in the cod suit. She had taken her life in her hands to get there, launching herself across the road amid hooting cars and then jumping in little hops down the gritty path with humps of grass on either side to reach an expanse of sand. She found a place, not far from the rolling waves, held out the hand containing the leaflets and began to bob about in an imitation of a fish on the end of a hook.

At first, people passed her with trepidation, turning around to look at a bloated cod precariously leaping on the spot, shouting,

'Get your boat trip. The best boat in town.' Children snickered and pointed, and an older couple gazed at each other anxiously and huddled close before moving away. Inside the suit, Molly felt the salt of the sea breeze but her cheeks were intensely sweaty inside the mask. She waved her arms like a flipping fish as a family passed. 'Boat trip?'

A man stopped, his hand holding the clenched fist of a little boy, and chuckled. 'What are you supposed to be? A gutted grouper?'

Molly gave him her best smile from inside the mask. 'Oh, you're English – that's great,' she enthused. 'I'm advertising the *Carpe Diem*, the best boat in Spain. It does wonderful trips around the coast, really good value. And your kids can snorkel.'

One of the children, a little girl with red hair, piped up, 'I want to snorkel, Dad.'

The mother, who Molly thought might also be a redhead from what she could see from inside the mask, raised her voice. 'I'll have a leaflet. We could go on a boat trip this afternoon, Andy. It might keep the kids quiet.'

Molly was jubilant. 'The *Carpe Diem*. Skippered by Ronnie Barnes. He's English, from Devon. An experienced sailor.'

The couple took a leaflet and moved on. Molly felt someone pat her shoulder. 'What's all this then, love? Why are you dressed as a kipper?'

Molly shrugged: of course, she had expected fish jokes. Clearly a woman in a cod suit was going to provoke some humour from people. Molly turned to see a man, probably in his sixties, in a light jacket. She gave him her best cod smile. 'I'm advertising boat trips.'

'Booze cruise?' The man asked, suddenly keen.

'Go and ask Ronnie, the skipper. I bet he'd take you and a few mates out in his boat. There's no reason why you shouldn't have a beer or two.'

'Don't mind if I do.' The man tugged a leaflet from her hand. '*Crappy dame*? That's a funny name for a boat.'

He was off on his way, chuckling to himself. Molly moved the fish head from side to side, seeking new customers. She spotted a young couple holding hands, walking towards her. She wobbled over, doing her little skip and jump, and greeted them breathlessly. 'Hello. Are you English?'

'We're from Finland.' The man's English was perfect.

'What are you selling?' The woman spoke equally perfectly.

'I'm advertising cruises on the *Carpe Diem*. The skipper is great. I went on a trip yesterday and it was lovely. We discovered little coves and a sandy beach where no one else goes.'

'It sounds glorious,' the woman murmured.

'Would you like to go on a boat trip, honey?' The man looked tenderly at the woman.

'Yes. It would be very romantic.' She turned to Molly. 'Thank you. We will take one of your leaflets.'

Molly wanted to leap for joy but the fish suit made it difficult to bend her knees. From the corner of her eye, she spotted a family of four building sandcastles a few feet away and heard the friendly twang of a London accent. She waddled towards them.

'Hello. Can I interest you in a lovely family cruise? A sandy beach all to yourselves. Ronnie Barnes, the skipper, knows all about this area and you can swim in the sea and snorkel...' The children sat up to greet her and the woman held out her hand for a leaflet.

Molly was on a roll. She spoke to a charming young man, a middle-aged couple and two family groups, all Spanish, all delightful, all speaking better English than she could speak Spanish, all very keen to try a cruise on the *Carpe Diem*. Her hand-scrawled leaflets had almost all gone. She was so pleased with herself that she leaped up and down again, wriggling inside her fish suit, waving her arms frantically and yelling, 'Get yourself the best cruise in Spain.'

A few yards away, Nell folded her arms and squinted. She was sure it was her. Certainly, there was a familiarity about the way the fish moved. There was something about the way the cod inclined its head that Nell had seen many times before and she recognised the denim bag that hung over the fish's shoulder. Then there were the hands clutching the makeshift paper leaflets, the sandaled feet protruding from the tail. Nell knew them almost as well as she knew her own hands and feet.

Nell frowned: there would be no harm in approaching the fish and asking her what she was doing on the beach wearing a very snug scaly costume and shouting. And then she'd invite her to share breakfast. Nell took a step forward.

Then she saw the fish swivel round and stop dead in its tracks. The round eyes met her gaze directly. Nell noticed the body of the fish tense a little; it leaned backwards and twisted around, pulling back as if it was struggling on the end of a hook. Then it started to wriggle away, making small jumps and hops. The cod turned back to look in Nell's direction one time, stumbled, and fell flat on its back, floundering on the sand.

Nell immediately wanted to rush over but two joggers, young women in shorts and vests, had stopped to help the thrashing fish stand up. All three women struggled wildly and then the cod was back on its feet. Nell decided that it might be better to take herself off somewhere and have a coffee alone and discuss the fate of the floundering fish with her sister later. Or perhaps it might be better to say nothing at all for now: discretion was usually a wise move where Molly's antics were concerned.

* * *

Back in the clothes shop several hours later, Molly and the shop owner were in the tiny changing room together, struggling with the fish costume. Molly couldn't get it off. She had managed, with the help of the horrified woman with the colourful headscarf and earrings, to struggle out of the arm holes and the costume was sitting snugly around her waist, glued to her flesh while both women attempted to roll the latex down. The shop owner was heaving the costume over her stomach, stripping back latex firmly in a way that closely resembled a waxing in a beauty parlour. Molly was aware that her skin was sticky and damp and she was covered in indentations that resembled fish scales. The shop owner muttered something in Spanish as both women pushed the suit down over Molly's hips. Molly wriggled for all she was worth, falling back into the curtain and almost into the shop, and the owner met her eyes and spoke worriedly. '*No rompalo.*'

Molly grabbed the curtain for stability, pulling it down from a couple of hooks. 'No, it's fine, I won't tear the fish: I can climb out now.' With a desperate tug, she pulled the costume over her bottom and eased it over her thighs. 'There. It's fine.'

The shop owner nodded, leaving Molly in the changing room without closing the green velvet curtain. Molly dragged it across to protect herself from any customers' stray gazes and squirmed gratefully into her T-shirt and jeans. As she left the changing room, the owner was there, mistrust in her eyes, holding out a twenty euro note. Molly took it, smiling, as the woman grasped the fish costume.

Molly decided that, to placate the woman with the earrings, she'd spend the twenty euros in the shop. Her gaze fell upon a dress in the sale rail and she took it out and held it against herself. It was orange, sleeveless and short, in a fitted, semi-wrap-around style. She imagined wearing it for dinner with Ronnie, looking stunning. She eased her phone from the bottom of her denim bag and checked to see if there were any messages. There were none. Molly assumed that Ronnie was so busy with people booking trips on his boat that he wouldn't have time to text her. She paid for the dress, smiling sweetly at the owner, who had cheered up, and left the shop humming a little tune. Today had been a success.

Molly was still singing half an hour later in the shower, back at the apartment. She felt much better with the scalding water bouncing against her skin, rubbing soap over her stomach to rid herself of the smell of latex. She grinned, recalling painting herself, wrapped in cling film: covering herself with smelly plastic was becoming a habit. She assumed that Nell was down at the pool or with Ulla and Bernt at the beach: she'd be relaxing, oblivious of Molly's adventures. Molly wrapped herself in two towels, one round her body and the other almost containing her dripping hair and padded through the lounge and into the kitchen. She opened the fridge and found a yogurt and a small dish of left-over paella. She took both, plus a fork and spoon to the table and started to eat. She was starving. She checked her phone to see if there were any messages as she chewed. Nothing from Ronnie.

The door clicked and Nell breezed into the room, her skin glowing from the sunshine. She sat at the table and watched Molly shovel cold paella into her mouth, her phone in her other hand.

'You're hungry,' she observed.

'Starving.'

Nell almost blurted that she didn't know that fish liked paella, but she stopped herself: sarcasm wasn't the way forward. She was waiting for Molly to tell her where she'd been. But Molly was clearly holding back. She forked the last of the food into her mouth and opened the yogurt, tucking into it with relish. When she'd finished, her eyes met Nell's and she said, 'Have you had lunch yet?' Then, without waiting for Nell's reply, 'I'm still hungry. I think I'll make some toast – do you want some?'

Nell watched Molly wrap the towel around her body again, pushing in the end under her arm, dabbing at her hair with the other towel which she dropped onto the floor as she fled into the kitchen. Nell listened to her sister clattering around, filling a kettle and bustling with cups. Molly emerged seconds later, her hair dishevelled around her shoulders.

'Toast is on. Coffee made. I'll just get my dressing gown.'

Molly stepped over the damp towel on her way to her bedroom, then turned around, picked it up and skipped away, humming a tune.

Nell pressed her lips together. The denim bag was on the table, next to another plastic bag marked '*Rosamira Ropa*'. Nell peeked inside, then pushed a hand in and pulled out the orange dress. She held it up against her, marvelling at the bright colour and the short style. The price tag read twenty euros.

Molly rushed into the room, wrapped in a grey dressing gown covered in pink hearts, and beamed at Nell. 'Try it on if you like. I bought it in the sale.'

'It's very cheerful, Molly. Have you bought it for a special occasion?'

Molly was already in the kitchen; Nell heard her banging the fridge door. She returned seconds later with two steaming mugs of coffee, a pile of toast and a jar of peanut butter. Her eyes met Nell's, a quizzical glance. 'Pardon? Sorry. I just have to eat some-thing else. I forgot about breakfast, and lunch too. Have you eaten?'

Nell brought her lips together in a straight line. 'I had breakfast down by the beach.' Her eyes met Molly's who was looking deliberately at a piece of charred toast as she smeared peanut butter thickly across the surface. Nell took a deep breath. 'Do you know, I saw something really strange on the beach this morning? Quite surreal. It was a fish...'

'A fish?' Molly gave a high peal of laughter and looked away. 'What sort of fish?'

Nell folded her arms. 'A human-sized one, on the beach, shouting and handing out leaflets.' She paused, trying to read Molly's reaction, then she added, 'Carrying a denim bag, just like yours.'

'Oh?' Molly let out a little squeal: the coincidence was amazing. She slapped a hand against her thigh as if it was the funniest thing she had heard in a long time. Then suddenly a tune rang out from the mobile on the table: it was a jangly version of 'YMCA' by the Village People. Molly snatched at her phone and spoke quickly. 'Hello?'

Nell could hear a lively male voice rattling at the other end. She watched Molly carefully: her eyes shone, her cheeks were glowing as she nodded eagerly and listened. Then she laughed, a throaty sound, and said, 'That's great news. I'm so glad it worked.'

The man spoke some more, his voice crackling, then Molly flashed a wide smile. 'I'll be there. I'm definitely looking forward to it. Yes. Yes, me too.'

Molly put the phone down and turned to Nell, whose eyes were intently examining her face, trying to work out what was going on. Molly picked up her toast, munching contentedly, her face a picture of innocence.

'Who was that?' Nell asked, leaning forward eagerly.

'Oh, nobody.'

'Molly!' Nell shook her head and grabbed her sister's hand. 'Don't keep me in suspense. I need to know what's going on. Why the new dress? Why the fish costume? And who's calling you on the phone with a deep sexy voice? Now you're grinning all over your face and saying you're looking forward to something. What's happening?'

Molly picked up her mug and sighed exaggeratedly, then she turned to Nell, and pushed back her damp wild hair. She looked pleased with herself. 'I have a hot date, Nell.' She watched her sister's expression change from puzzled to amazed and she smiled. 'I'm going out to the best restaurant in town with a handsome sailor tonight. He's picking me up outside at eight. So there you have it all, from the horse's mouth.' She pulled an impish expression. 'Or, if you prefer, the fish's mouth...' Then she began to laugh and thrash her arms around in an exaggerated impression of a cod.

15

Thursday 9th September

Ronnie's a nice man, really nice. Warm, generous, good company. And he's fun to spend time with, easy-going. But as for a second date… I've no idea what to do.

Molly rushed out of the apartment block, the cool evening air tingling against her skin, heels clacking, wearing the orange dress and a black wrap. Nell's voice was still ringing in her ears, telling her she looked fabulous but who was the mystery man and she'd wait up to hear all about it when she returned. Molly was still smiling as she reached the kerbside; an open-top car glided to a stop and a gravelly voice called out, 'Hello, there – your taxi awaits.'

She slid onto the soft leather seat of the silver convertible and glanced at Ronnie, who was smiling from the driver's side. He was wearing wrap-around sunglasses and an expensive-looking leather jacket, with a black cap covering his head, and he smelled of something very pungent that reminded Molly of the insecticide the farmers put on their fields in Somerset. She grinned at him. 'Hello, Ronnie. Where are we going?'

'*Pulpo Azul*,' he grinned. 'The Blue Octopus. I reserved a table. They do the best seafood you can get.'

Molly snuggled down into the softness of the seat. She recalled nervously that she hadn't been on a date since Richie had died. She gave Ronnie a sideways glance, observing his profile, the rugged face, the confident way his hands slid over the steering wheel and reached for the gearstick, the car growling and purring in response to his smooth movements. The wind blew her hair and tousled it across her face. She gazed at the parade of shops, the orange lights of restaurants as Ronnie accelerated out of town towards the distant sparkling line of the horizon.

They were shown to a table overlooking the ocean and Ronnie greeted the waiter. 'A bottle of Rioja, Miguel.' He smiled at Molly. 'I'm driving so it's just one small glass for me – you can drink as much as you like.'

Molly sat down, watching as Ronnie removed his jacket and cap. His hair was sparse at the front; his black jacket and tie impeccable with skinny jeans. She wondered how old he was: his face was tanned and rugged, but he was clearly fit and powerfully built. He gave Miguel a familiar smile. 'Right. We'll start with the lobster bisque.' He raised an eyebrow and glanced at Molly. 'If that's okay with you, Molly.'

'Fine by me.' She met the waiter's eyes. '*Si, Caldereta de langosta, por favor.*'

Ronnie was impressed. 'You speak Spanish?'

'*Un poco*,' Molly winked, then wondered if she was flirting; that wasn't her style. She composed her face and picked up the menu, determined to order her own food from now on, and spoke directly to Miguel who was pouring wine into crystal glasses. '*Prefiero un pescado blanco con arroz.*'

Miguel nodded. '*Claro, Señora.*'

Ronnie frowned. 'Was that the white fish with rice? I've picked up a bit of Spanish but it's only really food and drink. I'll have the oysters, please.' He watched the waiter walk away and then gave Molly his full attention. 'Well, what do you think?'

She wrinkled her noise. 'Think?'

'Of the restaurant, the *Pulpo Azul*?' He raised his brows and Molly noticed his eyes were the colour of rainwater.

Molly looked around, considering the décor. The walls were roughly plastered white and there was a huge design of a blue octopus with a smiling face by the bar. The restaurant was already busy; people sat at white tables, chattering and drinking. Music played loudly through tall speakers, a mariachi band, trumpets and a man singing a cheerful song. Molly gazed through the window beyond the sea wall at the azure depths of the ocean. The sun was dipping low, a melting orange sphere: the sunset would be spectacular. Ronnie read her thoughts.

'When the sun goes down, it's really quite something,' he breathed.

Molly sipped from the wine glass. 'It's a busy place. Very popular.' Her thoughts moved to Nell, who'd be cooking something simple for herself in the little kitchen. 'My sister would like it here.'

Ronnie leaned forward, his brows raised. 'Tell me about your sister. And yourself, of course. Tell me all about Molly.'

She waved a hand in front of her face. 'Oh, there's not much to tell.'

He grinned encouragingly, waiting, and Molly launched in. 'Well, I live in Somerset – that is, I used to live there, I'm letting my house to the neighbour's son. I've done all sorts of jobs from

office work to waiting on tables, to being an artist's model.' She
paused a moment. She had been more than Richie's model. She'd
been his muse. She caught Ronnie's expression: he was
impressed, so she carried on.

'I'm in my... sixties and I live by myself. I have a daughter,
Samantha, and she married a farmer she met at a Young Farmers'
dance in Somerset and moved to Cumbria. Samantha has two
sons and she's fifty-something...' She stopped. Ronnie was laughing. 'What?'

'Were you ten years old when you had Sammy?'

'No, not at all.' Molly wasn't thinking about arithmetic or the
fact that she'd adjusted her age; she was imagining how indignant her daughter would be if she heard her name being abbrevi-
ated. Samantha was Samantha, no fuss, no frills. Molly decided to
change the subject.

'My sister Ellen, Nell, she's my half-sister, came to stay with
me because her marriage is over.' Molly paused. It wasn't her
place to tell Nell's story. 'You'd like Nell. She's really sweet.' She
noticed the waiter arriving with two bowls of lobster bisque and
suddenly felt hungry. 'So – tell me all about yourself, Ronnie.'

'Not much to tell.' Ronnie's eyes were focused on hers as the
waiter put the bowls on the table. 'I love the sea, the ocean. I
came here years ago with my wife and two daughters to start a
new life. Tracy didn't like it and went back to the UK after a while
and took the girls with her. I loved it here and stayed. It's a fine
life here. I live well. I have a five-bedroomed *finca* out in the hills
with a pool, two cars, a boat.' He raised his eyebrows. 'A good
prospect for any woman, I'd say.'

Molly spoke without thinking. 'But not Tracy.'

They both began to eat. Molly watched how Ronnie lifted the
spoon, the way the orange liquid trickled back into the plate, the
soft slurping sound he made, the twist of his mouth as he ate. She

couldn't stop the comparison that tipped like a set of scales in her head: Molly remembered Richie, the curve of his lips, the cute thumbprint dent in his chin, the little pale scar over his brow he'd had since he was a child. Molly sighed and thought the same thought she always had about champagne and lemonade.

Later, they watched the sea soak up the orange glow of the sky, Molly huddled in the passenger seat of the convertible, listening to Ronnie's crackling voice telling her stories about some of the boat trips he'd taken. Molly decided he was good company. The blood-red sun dipped behind the horizon, dissolving into the inky sea and was gone in a moment. Ronnie was explaining how he once took a honeymoon couple on a cruise in his boat and the young man had split his speedos while diving, and had to make the rest of the journey back to Calle-blanque wearing his wife's bikini bottoms. Molly was about to ask what the wife had worn instead when she realised she was cold.

Ronnie noticed that she was shivering and wrapped an arm around her. 'Is that better, Molly?'

Molly wasn't sure she wanted him to hug her. She offered a breezy smile. 'Oh, I'm fine, thanks.' He was staring at her, his expression serious. She opted for a change of subject. 'So, the boat trips were a success then?'

'Thanks to you.' Ronnie's eyes were on her face. He moved closer.

'You should have seen me in the fish costume on the beach,' she spluttered, playing for time.

'I bet you were beautiful...' Ronnie murmured. He reached out a hand. 'All that lovely hair...'

'I was wearing a fish head.' Molly blurted. She was desperate to keep the conversation going and Ronnie at a distance: he was pawing her hair with his huge hand.

'I think you're lovely, Molly.'

His lips approached her face, two suction pads. Molly pulled away. 'Did I ever tell you about the time I lost all my clothes on the beach?' She saw his face brighten at the thought, so she added, 'I had to sprint home wearing the Spanish flag.'

'Ah,' Ronnie frowned, his expression disappointed. 'Are you having a nice time tonight?'

'To tell you the truth, I'm a bit tired now.' She offered him a wide smile. 'Impersonating a fish really took it out of me today.'

'Okay. We can always have dinner again, another time, maybe?' Ronnie was optimistic as he started the engine. 'Shall I take you home?'

They pulled up outside the apartments and Molly leaned over and pecked his cheek. 'Thanks for a lovely evening, Ronnie.'

He patted her knee, a friendly gesture. 'We must definitely have dinner again, Molly.' He raised his eyebrows hopefully. 'And maybe you can do some more work for me? I could get you another costume and an advertising board and we can do the publicity thing properly.'

Molly shrugged and wriggled out of the car. 'Maybe.'

Ronnie met her eyes. 'And I can take you out on another boat trip, a longer one, a whole-day cruise sometime.'

Molly nodded. 'Yes, that would be nice.'

'I'll text you,' Ronnie called out as the engine rumbled and the car pulled away. Molly watched him drive into the distance and let out a slow sigh. It had been a pleasant enough evening. The food had been lovely and the company had been fun. She wondered if Ronnie could become a friend. She was certain he would never be anything more.

Molly stayed where she was for a while, staring across the road at the twinkling lights and the sea in the distance, thinking about Richie. She imagined him eating with her at the *Pulpo Azul*, in Ronnie's place, sharing a simple meal. He'd have loved being with her this evening, sitting quietly, simply watching the sun slip into the sea.

He'd have entwined his fingers in hers across the table and they'd have shared a bottle of wine together. After the meal, they'd have walked along the beach hand in hand until the darkness had swallowed the light. They would have stretched out on their backs on the sand and stared at the canopy of stars, trying to work out which was the Plough and Orion and Cassiopeia. She'd have snuggled under his arm, warmed by the touch of his flesh, as they strolled back to the apartment, the shushing of the sea in their ears. The only sound on the beach would have been Molly's tinkling laughter and the low sound of Richie's voice.

Richie had been special. He'd never have spoken in English to the waiter. He'd never have driven an ostentatious car or owned a flash boat. He was simply happy spending days by himself, painting, cooking, reading, listening to music. He loved Stravinsky and Tchaikovsky, U2 and the Rolling Stones; he loved to travel and he loved Molly. Molly wondered what music Ronnie liked. She hugged the shawl around her and wandered back to the apartment, running up the steps to number fourteen.

Nell was sitting at the table, her hands around a cup of hot chocolate, wearing her dressing gown. As Molly rushed into the apartment, she called out softly.

'I'll make you a hot drink. Then you can tell me all about the date.'

'There's not much to tell.' Molly plonked herself at the table.

'Not true love, then?' Nell was next to her, pushing a cup of hot chocolate in her direction. She seemed disappointed.

'No, I don't think so.' Molly shook her head. 'He's a nice bloke. He's a local; he owns a boat. We ate seafood in a restaurant a little further up the coast. It was pleasant.'

'Just pleasant? What a shame.' Nell made a face. 'I was hoping you'd cheer me up, Molly. I wanted to hear about how this man had whisked you off your feet, how dashing and handsome he was.'

'He's called Ronnie. I ate lobster and white fish with rice and watched the sun set. You'd have loved it.' Molly studied Nell's face. Her brow was knitted in a determined frown. 'All right – what's worrying you, Nell? Tell me all about it.'

'I've had a few messages from Phil, just routine stuff about the divorce and about money. Apparently, he wants to do everything quickly so that he can marry Nikki. I've no idea why there's such a rush. He's offered me her house: it's a small terraced cottage in the centre of town. She doesn't need it now. I told him no: I'm not living there – I don't want to start single life in her cast-off house. I told Phil I want a fresh start, a clean break. So, they are selling her place and using the money to buy me out.'

She put a hand over Molly's. 'I'm so glad you dragged me out to Spain, Moll – even if the apartment is a bit small. I'm having a great time here, and I've come to terms with Phil, and the split. Ulla and Bernt are lovely and now you've met a man with a boat. So maybe there's hope for me, too.' She squeezed Molly's hand excitedly. 'I'm sure we're going to have a great time. Come Christmas, when we go home, I'll be fit and tanned and I'll have my share of the money, my ticket to independence; I'll buy myself a little place in Yeovil. Or maybe I could even buy somewhere here in Spain, in the sunshine, and start a new life?'

Molly hugged her sister, enjoying the softness of Nell's hair against her face, pleased that she was coping so well. But Nell's mention of Christmas, the future and returning to Yeovil had stirred an old feeling: she didn't want to go back to her solitary home yet. She was ready to explore new pastures.

Nell was thoughtful: she stretched her arms above her head in a languid expression of freedom that Molly hadn't noticed before.

'Well, if you're dating the locals, why shouldn't I have some fun too? We're still young, comparatively...' Her expression was determined. 'We're free and single. The world is our oyster.'

Molly thought of the oysters she'd seen on Ronnie's plate, empty shells shucked and discarded: there were so many men who wouldn't be her type now. Nell might be ready to date, to meet someone, to fall in love again, but she certainly wasn't: she wasn't sure she would ever be. And, more than ever, Molly felt that something else, something different, was out there for her, another place, another future, another home. She just had no idea what it was.

16

Friday 17th September

We go to the beach most days. Or the pool. Then it's a meal and something to drink. I fall asleep before midnight and wake early with the sun streaming in through the window. It's so much nicer than being in the UK with the cold weather and the rain. Nell is happy, settled, blossoming – Spain really suits her and I'm so delighted we came here. Three months ago, I'd have thought this life was idyllic. It is. So what's wrong with me? What more do I want? I suddenly feel ready to move on again. Perhaps I'm just like my mother, like Kezia – fickle and easily bored.

I'm not sure what I'm looking for. It's just that Spain doesn't feel like home...

Nell emerged from the sea in her white tankini and pushed wet hair back from her face. As she strolled towards the beach, the foam swirling around her ankles, she wondered if this was how it felt to be a film star. It was certainly liberating, wearing something she might have worn thirty years ago, feeling confident.

She strode across the sand, the sun warming the droplets on her golden skin. Out of the corner of her eye, she saw a large man in colourful shorts sprawling in a deckchair sit up and turn to study her, giving her an appreciative gaze. Nell noticed the woman next to him elbow the man angrily and he flopped back, deflated. Nell smiled, a spring in her step. She might be in her sixties but – what was the phrase buzzing in her mind? She still had it, whatever *it* was. It had been a long time since she'd even thought about wearing skimpy clothes and being attractive.

Weeks ago, at the beginning of August, when she was still living with Phil, every day had been the same, a steady routine, and she had been horrified when her comfortable version of normality had suddenly slipped from her grasp. But now here she was in Spain, feeling really good about herself and receiving admiring glances from men she didn't know. Suddenly, like the hug of the sun's heat on her back, she felt alive and glowing. She strode smiling across the beach and it occurred to her that Phil, unintentionally, had given her the gift of a second chance; he had taken her old life and held it up, revealing its shortcomings, and now she had the opportunity to find something better.

She flopped onto the spare beach mat next to the others and grinned. Molly was lying on her front in vest and shorts reading a book with a bright cover. Bernt was asleep with his sunglasses on, a white trilby hat on his head. Ulla was smearing suntan oil on her arms, stretching out her legs below a crisp yellow swimsuit. She smiled at Nell. 'Did you enjoy the swim?'

Nell nodded. 'I'm not a very good swimmer but it's great exercise. I'm sure my arms and legs are more toned than they were when I arrived.'

Molly grunted something about the water being very cold the last time she'd gone in and Nell patted her shoulder. 'The water is lovely today. I'll have another dip again later this afternoon. You should come with me.'

Molly glanced up. 'I'm reading this book about Van Gogh and his time painting and living in Arles. He had such an interesting life; so sad, though. Arles is somewhere I'd love to visit. Apparently, the light is incredible.'

'You should go to the Van Gogh museum in Amsterdam.' Bernt wasn't asleep after all. He spoke from behind the sunglasses without moving his position. 'There are many of his paintings there. It is fascinating.'

'Yes, I've been, but I'd love to go there again,' Molly murmured thoughtfully. 'I went seven years ago. I cried when I saw the sunflowers and his self-portrait, the one with him in the straw hat. His paintings are so vibrant and moving.'

Ulla sat upright. 'You paint a bit yourself, don't you, Molly? You should bring a canvas down to the beach and paint the sunrise.'

'I might just do that,' Molly agreed. 'Although maybe I could do the sunset instead – then I wouldn't have to get up so early.'

'Talking of getting up early...' Bernt reached out and took Ulla's hand. 'We should be going, darling. Our massage is booked for half two. We don't want to be late.'

Ulla brushed sand from her ankles and pushed her feet into yellow espadrilles. 'Are you sure you won't come with us, Molly? Nell? I'm sure the team could squeeze you in for aromatherapy?'

'Next time,' Nell promised, and Molly muttered that it sounded like a plan as she turned over the page of her book.

Bernt was standing at his full height, blocking the sun's glare, gazing down. 'We'll see you later, maybe. Come for a drink this evening if you're around.'

'That'd be nice,' Molly mumbled, still without looking up. She was wondering if there was a train that went to Arles, perhaps via Valencia and Barcelona. She could stay for a few days and explore.

Nell called after them as they walked away, 'Enjoy the massage.' Nell watched her sister, her hair piled on her head and her sunglasses perched on top, as she read avidly. Nell poked her with a finger. 'Have you got enough sunscreen on?'

'Yep.'

'I mean, you don't want to burn your shoulders.'

'I'm okay.'

'But are you, Molly? Are you sure?'

Molly glanced up from the book. 'Huh? Sorry – I'm a bit engrossed in Van Gogh...'

Nell met her eyes. 'Are you really okay?'

Molly beamed at her to show she was perfectly fine then returned her eyes to the page and continued reading.

Nell sighed. 'You aren't missing Ronnie the sailor?'

Molly squinted up towards the sunlight and wrinkled her nose. 'Nope.'

'I mean, it's over a week since you had dinner with him. Ten days, in fact.'

Molly didn't look up. 'And?'

'And you haven't heard from him...'

Molly turned another page. 'He texted me.'

'What?'

'He texted me.'

'When?'

'Three days ago, four, maybe five. A week?' She breathed out slowly. 'Twice, I think, maybe three times.'

Nell gasped. 'And?'

Molly pushed herself up on to her elbows. 'And nothing. I just haven't replied yet.'

'Why not?'

'I don't know. I haven't got round to it, I suppose.' Molly shrugged. 'He invited us to go out on his boat with him sometime.'

Nell sat upright. 'And you didn't reply?'

'I will, at some point.' Molly brushed sand from the page with her palm. 'Maybe when I find out what happens to poor Vincent. At the moment he's in Arles and madly in love with a prostitute called Gabrielle...' She exhaled. 'I wonder what it's like in Arles now?'

'Right.' Nell took a breath. When Molly didn't respond, she began to unpack a thin top and a pair of shorts from her beach bag and pulled them on over the white tankini. She reached for her sandals. 'Come on, Molly.'

Molly still had the book open. 'What? Where are we going?'

Nell took her sister's book and gently placed it in the beach bag, then pressed her arm in a gesture of impatience. 'The boat place isn't far from here, is it? What did you say Ronnie's boat was called?'

'*Carpe Diem.*'

'Then that's what we're going to do,' Nell said emphatically. 'We're going to seize the day. I fancy a boat ride.'

Nell bustled along the sand, her beach bag swinging on her shoulder. Molly scuttled behind, trying to keep up: she had to admit, a boat ride would be quite pleasant; she thought of the calm blue of the sea and the cloud-mottled skies, but she was asking herself why she wasn't excited about seeing Ronnie again. She thought about it for a while. She liked him well enough and he had been interested in her. So she wasn't sure why she hadn't been keen to go on a second date.

Molly thought it might be a good idea to write down her thoughts in her diary soon. Perhaps that would be a way of making sense of her feelings, and of understanding what was behind her current listlessness. Certainly, she'd neglected writing for a few days and she needed to collect her thoughts. Something was bothering her, something she needed to resolve. She wondered if it might help to talk to Vanessa or even Samantha, who would at least give her a down-to-earth opinion.

Molly trailed behind Nell, marvelling at her energy and enthusiasm, while in her mind, Molly was writing an entry in her diary. Several weeks ago, she'd been restless, dissatisfied with her life at home, back in Somerset; she'd been looking for a new hobby or a project to interest her. She'd thrown herself into supporting her sister in her hour of marital rejection and the idea of coming to Spain for several months had seemed a perfect solution to her edginess and dissatisfaction. In its own way, their holiday to Spain was a great success. They were having fun, relaxing, and feeling very healthy, so why was she restless again?

Molly wondered, as she saw Nell rush on ahead towards the little harbour where the sailing boats were moored, whether her sister's new independence had left her feeling a little redundant, without something to focus her attention on. She knew it was good that Nell was finding a new lease of life, that she'd got her mojo back and didn't need Molly's shoulder to cry on. Nell was having fun; she was making friends; she spent a lot of time with Ulla and Bernt now and, while Molly didn't feel left out and wasn't at all keen to join in with the shopping trips or visits to the spa, she had the distinct feeling that she'd need to do something different before very long. Her wanderlust was returning. As her feet pattered on the wooden boards leading to the boats, Molly made her mind up that a boat trip might be the perfect solution for today: the sea air would blow her thoughts around and help her to clear her mind.

Nell turned to her sister and linked an arm through hers. She put her mouth close to Molly's ear and whispered, 'Which one is the *Carpe Diem*? Where's Ronnie?' She was gazing at each boat, her face flushed with enthusiasm.

Molly pointed to a boat with blue and white paint where a man in a navy cap was standing on board winding a length of rope around a tanned arm. 'Over there. Hi, Ronnie.' He glanced up and a smile creased his face. In three bounds, he had crossed the deck to meet them and held out a rough hand.

'Molly. How nice to see you again. Come on board for a moment.' He tugged her onto the boat and aimed a grin in Nell's direction. 'You must be Nell. Welcome aboard.'

Nell tripped lightly onto the deck. Ronnie pushed his hands into the pockets of his denim shorts and shrugged. 'I wasn't expecting you. You should have texted me to say you were coming. How about a beer?'

'Don't mind if I do,' Nell trilled and watched as Ronnie bent down to pull a can of lager from a small fridge, rip open the ring and pass her the fizzing drink. He repeated the action for Molly as she said, 'We wondered if there was any chance of a boat trip.'

Nell gazed out to sea, and then turned her eyes on Ronnie hopefully as he shook his head. 'Not today, I'm afraid. I've got a family coming to meet me in twenty minutes and I'll be out with them for the rest of the afternoon.'

'Oh.' Nell sounded disappointed.

Molly shrugged. 'Another time might be nice, next week, perhaps? We could book in advance?' She turned, intending to step back onto the wooden harbour.

Ronnie gave a sharp cough. 'Why don't you both come up to my place tonight for dinner instead?' He met Molly's eyes with a meaningful gaze and she was reminded again of the colour of rainwater in puddles. He grinned in Nell's direction. 'I can put some steaks on the barbie if you like.'

Nell pushed a hand through her hair as the sea breeze lifted it and replaced it over her eyes. 'That might be nice. What do you think, Molly?'

Molly was about to say she'd be happy with anything when Ronnie chimed, 'I'll pick you up outside the apartment at seven, shall I? Then I can drive you to the *finca*. It's about twenty minutes outside town. And bring your swimmers. We can have a dip in the pool before dinner.' He rolled his eyes mischievously. 'Or the hot tub. And if you like, I'll make up two beds in the *casita* and you can stay over – then we can all enjoy a drink or two.'

'Sounds fab,' Nell said.

Molly wrinkled her nose. She had never heard Nell use the word *fab* before. She hadn't a clue why Nell was behaving so spontaneously but, she told herself as she drained the last of the lager from the can, it was a good sign that her sister was flourishing and developing a new sophistication. In fact, Nell was positively glowing nowadays. She was clearly in holiday mood and determined to revel in every moment. Molly was pleased that Nell was so keen. Perhaps an evening at Ronnie's *finca*, chatting and sipping Cava amid the spluttering bubbles of the hot tub, might be just what she needed too. With Nell in tow to make sure Ronnie didn't see the evening as an opportunity for romance, it might be really good fun.

'Thanks, Ronnie,' she grinned. 'Nell and I will look forward to it.'

He gave her his most charming smile and pressed her hand. 'But not half as much as I will, Molly.'

17

Saturday 18th September
  Dinner at Ronnie's finca. Nell and I are dressed up, ready to
  go. I wonder what tonight will bring...

Molly had to admit, she was really enjoying herself. She and Nell
and Ronnie were wallowing in the turquoise swimming pool, the
water sparkling in the sunshine, and the fun had developed into a
game that Ronnie called water polo, although it was just an
excuse to leap up and down, hurl the ball across the water and
splash your opponent's face. Ronnie had thrown himself into the
game, his toned torso rising from the water with a glimpse of red
swim shorts, his hair thinly plastered to his head, long wet curls
at the back, his eyes shaded by expensive sunglasses. Nell
mischievously suggested that she and Molly take on Ronnie as an
opponent, and she had deliberately aimed the ball at her adver-
sary in an attempt to knock off the Ray-Bans; Molly discovered
that, although her aim was poor, her punch packed some power
behind the ball's strong trajectory.

Ronnie's voice was throaty with delight. 'I'm not taking on you two any more; you're both far too dangerous. I think it's time for a drink.'

Nell swam stylishly to the edge of the pool and hoisted herself up onto the white patio tiles. Little droplets fell from the black swimsuit and ran in rivulets down her legs. She moved easily towards a covered area under a wide white arch. She called over her shoulder. 'Shall I make us a cocktail, Ronnie?'

Ronnie rolled on his back and floated, his eyes closed. 'I'll have a Bloody Mary please, Nell. You'll find it's all there, behind the bar in the *naya* – that's the glazed terrace. There's a fridge below the counter.' He winked in Molly's direction. 'What will you have, Moll?'

Molly was delighted to see Nell making herself at home at the *finca*. 'Anything – the same as you're having, Nell.' She swam towards the shallow end and clambered out of the pool, water streaming from the back of her orange swimsuit, wondering how Nell had managed to look so elegant.

She pulled a towel round her body and shook the droplets from her hair. From the poolside, she gazed at the *finca*, a long farmhouse with arched entrances, orange roof tiles, and a second storey reached by white steps, and then at the view across the pool towards the orchard, the vineyards, the almond groves and the vast looming hills beyond. To one side of the *finca* there were geraniums and bougainvillea in bloom. Molly plonked herself down at a little table with a parasol and sighed.

'This is a lovely place, Ronnie. Idyllic.'

He was out of the pool and sitting beside her in an instant, his shoulders broad and covered with glistening droplets. 'I like it here. It's a great place to relax.'

Nell walked over carrying a tray with three glasses, which she placed on the table. 'Aren't you lonely here all by yourself, Ronnie?'

'I have Pilar to keep me company.' He grinned. 'She was here earlier. I asked her to make the two bedrooms in the *casita* up for you both tonight.'

'Who's Pilar?' Nell reached for her Bloody Mary.

'She's my cleaner. She comes here three times a week on her little scooter.' He offered a broad smile. 'I love her to bits. Especially the way she nags me and pretends she really hates me.'

Nell licked her lips. 'Why does she hate you? That's ridiculous.'

Ronnie shook his head. 'It's just her sense of humour. She often tells me how wicked I am. And she swears like a trooper. She learned it all from my youngest daughter, Storm. Pilar's English is really good, much better than my Spanish. She does a great job on the house though. She's been working at the *finca* since Tracy and the girls were here so, I guess, she disapproves of my being single now.' He swigged from his glass. 'I pay her well and she has four children and a husband to look after, so she keeps coming back, despite giving me a hard time.' He made a low sound of contentment. 'This Bloody Mary is perfect, Nell.'

Molly reached for her cocktail. 'I love the way the mountains rise up behind the *finca* here. It's beautiful. It's like being snuggled in the arms of the countryside with something really exciting just beyond the horizon.'

'You're a romantic, Molly.' Ronnie lifted his glass. 'I agree with you, though. I enjoy the best life can offer out here and I'm on the sea all day in my boat. It's perfect. I'm very glad I came to Spain.'

'You're right, it's perfect,' Nell repeated, sipping her Bloody Mary.

Molly sat upright. 'So, Nell and I are staying in the *casita* tonight?'

'Yes, it's a little two-bedroom self-contained apartment. I'll be

in the main part of the *finca*. My bedroom is on the second floor.'
He gave a rasping laugh. 'So you won't be able to hear me snore.'

'Do you snore, Ronnie?' Nell raised an eyebrow.

'I've no one to tell me if I do or don't.' He replied. 'My ex used
to complain all the time, though.'

'Phil used to snore dreadfully.' Nell frowned. 'That's why he
moved into the spare room.'

Molly said nothing. She remembered snuggling up with
Richie, their legs entwined, listening to his steady breathing, and
feeling warm and safe and blessed. Then one day the breathing
stopped, just like that. She wondered briefly what it would be like
to share a bed with someone now. It would certainly keep her feet
warm; her toes were often like ice at night. The memory of a
having a human hot water bottle made her smile as she swallowed a mouthful of the cocktail. The tomato juice was bitter and
tangy on her tongue.

Ronnie finished the contents of his glass and grinned. 'How
about we go up to the sunroof and cook some steaks? We could
take more cocktails up there. I have the table set for dinner and
the barbecue fired up; we can watch the sun setting over the hills.
It's very dramatic.'

'It sounds lovely,' Nell purred.

'And we'll take a towel each. The hot tub is up there. We can
relax after we've eaten and leap into the tub and drink some
Cava.'

Nell stood up. 'Great. I'm up for all of that. And I'm starving.'

Molly pushed her glass away. 'I'll follow you up in a few
minutes, Ronnie, if that's okay. I just want to have a wander
through the gardens and down towards the orchards. It's so beautiful.' She met his eyes. 'Would that be okay?'

'Be my guest.' Ronnie waved his hand. 'I'll be up on the sun
terrace – just go up the white stairs to the left of the house. I'll

start on the steaks. There's some other food in the kitchen, some bread and salad and beans. Do you mind fetching it, Nell, and meeting me up on the terrace? You can help me cook.'

Nell trilled. 'I'd love to.' She smiled in Molly's direction. 'We can have a walk around the orchard tomorrow morning, if you like – before breakfast.'

Ronnie winked at Molly. 'Your sister is getting the hang of *finca* life, Molly.' He stood up and stretched. 'Right. I'm hungry. Let's get this party started.'

Molly pulled on a long skirt over her swimsuit and pushed her feet into sandals, then wandered away from the *finca* and the pool, turning left before the wrought iron gates and strolling through the gardens. In the distance, the hills loomed high, covered with scrubby green trees, the summits cutting through sparse clouds. Molly wondered what lay beyond. The air was still warm, although it was gone eight o'clock, and there was the heavy scent of flowers. There were almond trees standing in a row, straight as sentries.

She walked into the orchard, breathing in the sweet succulent smell of ripening fruit, gazing at the rows of orange trees. She wandered further; there were clusters of lemons hanging down and another fruit that she thought might be quince. She took one and held it in her hand. It was soft, bright yellow and wrinkled at one end, but not unappetising. Molly took a bite and pulled a face. The juice exploded on her tongue, too tart, and she lifted her arm behind her head and hurled the fruit into the distance.

She turned back and retraced her steps softly, blinking at the *finca*, blindingly white in the sunlight with its terracotta tiled roof. The aroma of barbecue cooking hung on the air, drifting towards her. All of a sudden, Molly felt her appetite return. She was hungry.

* * *

The view from the rooftop was spectacular; the sun held its position, a soft red glow above black hills, before dipping between two peaks and leaving a trail of mottled golden clouds in its wake. Nell pushed her empty plate away and sighed. 'I've never eaten so much in my life, Ronnie. That was gorgeous.'

Molly licked her lips, still tasting olive oil and balsamic vinegar. 'That was lovely.'

'Are you both warm enough?' Ronnie looked anxiously at the two women who had wrapped towels around their bare shoulders. 'I could go and fetch you a jumper each.'

'I'm okay for now, thanks,' Nell smiled and Molly nodded in agreement.

Ronnie was already pouring Cava into glasses and tugging off his top. 'Perhaps it's a good time to move to the hot tub then?'

Nell took a glass of sparkling wine, her face grateful. 'What a great idea.'

Molly followed them both to the square hot tub, a glass in her hand, and positioned herself in a corner, leaning back to look up at the sky. It was dappled blue with blotchy blood-red clouds, the horizon streaked with leaking orange as if someone had spilled paint and divided the canvas with a careless brush stroke. She closed her eyes.

Nell and Ronnie were chattering, and Molly could hear her sister asking excited questions about the boat, whether Ronnie took it out each day, demanding to know about the best places to visit.

'There's a cove not far from Palomar, where Molly and I went for the fish supper at the *Pulpo Azul*. It's quite a private place. I often take honeymoon couples there; the beach is totally deserted and the snorkelling is good. There's a wonderful view of the blue rocks and I've seen whales and dolphins from time to time.'

'Oh, Ronnie – I'd love to go.'

Molly heard Ronnie's soft voice. 'I'll take you both next week, if you like.'

Molly opened her eyes. 'How's business now, Ronnie?'

'Improved, thanks to your advertising stunt, Molly.' He met her gaze and lifted his glass with a little laugh. 'I was wondering whether to take you on full-time.'

Molly winked at Nell. 'I'd need a better fish suit.'

Ronnie reached for the bottle of Cava. 'I thought you'd be great in a mermaid costume, Molly. I could get one for you. You know, just a tail and you'd wear your swimsuit. You could sit on the sand and I'd get you a proper board advertising the boat. With all that long hair, I think you'd look authentic. What do you think?'

'She'd be a lovely mermaid.' Nell took a breath. 'I was just thinking, Ronnie – you could really step up the business with honeymoon couples and families, or whale-spotting trips. And what about an evening trip with cocktails and music? Imagine welcoming them on board with a drink and nibbles, maybe in evening dress, doing the hospitality. It could be really good.'

Ronnie turned his attention fully to Nell. 'That's a great idea, Nell. I can imagine you all dressed up, serving cocktails, cheese and pineapple on a stick.'

'Fab.' Nell had said it again, her eyes shining. 'Shall we try it, Ronnie? Oh, I'd love to give it a whirl.'

Molly considered Nell's words and was thoughtful for a moment then she turned to Ronnie. 'Your offer to borrow a warm sweater – is it still on? It's a bit chilly now.'

Ronnie leapt over the side of the hot tub. 'Right away. You too, Nell? Shall I get you both one?'

'Oh, yes please, Ronnie. That'd be great,' Nell enthused.

As Ronnie disappeared towards the white steps leading down from the sun terrace, Molly leaned over towards her sister, her voice a low whisper.

'Nell, are you feeling all right?'

Nell grabbed Molly's wrist and leaned over, her breath smelling of sweet wine. 'Oh, I'm having such a lovely time.' She was suddenly anxious. 'Am I being a bit over the top? You don't think I'm trying too hard, Moll?'

Molly was suddenly concerned. 'What do you mean, trying too hard? Aren't you enjoying yourself?'

The grip on Molly's wrist tightened as Nell brought her mouth closer to her sister's ear. 'Molly, do you like Ronnie?'

'Yes, he's good fun...'

'I mean, do you fancy him?'

'Not really... no.' Molly stared at her sister. 'He's a nice man and we're all having fun together...'

'So, you wouldn't mind if I...?' Nell's voice trailed into silence.

'If you what?'

Nell's grip on Molly's wrist was a vice. 'I really like him. I mean *really*. I'm not sure if he likes me but... you wouldn't mind if I...?'

The Cava had dulled Molly's thoughts. 'If you what?'

'Oh, Molly.' Nell met her sister's eyes. 'I think Ronnie's lovely. I mean, I really like him. It's been a long time since I... you know... Phil was my first boyfriend really and so... I thought I might even... well, I was thinking about Ronnie, you know, I was thinking about... about trying to seduce him...'

Ronnie appeared at the top of the steps, two chunky sweatshirts across his arm. He deposited them neatly in a pile on a chair and stepped briskly back into the hot tub between Nell and Molly. He eased himself beneath the foaming surface and groaned softly. 'Ah, this is the life. It was getting quite nippy out there.'

The bubbles rippled and Molly stared up at the darkening sky. Then she turned to Ronnie. 'Do you know, I might just have an early night? Thanks for everything, Ronnie. Great food, great company.' She gave Nell a conspiratorial hug, her eyes gleaming with mischief. 'Good night, Nell. I think I'll head off to bed now if you don't mind. Don't worry about me, though. I can find my own way to the *casita*. You two stay up here under the stars and enjoy the evening.'

She stood up, feeling the water trickle from her swimsuit, and stepped onto the sun terrace. The tiles were cold beneath her feet. She picked up a towel and one of Ronnie's sweatshirts, which she swung around her shoulders.

'Well,' she thought with a smile as she began to stroll away. 'Nell and Ronnie, together? I certainly didn't see that coming.'

18

Sunday 19th September

I wasn't expecting things to turn out as they did at Ronnie's. I'm thrilled for Nell, of course. She seems so happy and that's what I want for her. She loves Spain: she fits in here. But I still feel unsettled. I don't want the same things as Nell. Perhaps that's the problem. Perhaps I need a change of direction.

Molly opened her eyes and smiled. Sunlight streamed like honey through the huge window of the *casita* directly onto the white duvet. She gazed around at the cream stone walls, the mahogany door, and a huge dark wooden wardrobe. She stretched her arms and legs and swung herself out of the bed, her feet cold on the flagstones, reaching for her clothes. Her swimsuit was on the floor, still damp, and Ronnie's sweatshirt had been discarded at the foot of the bed, but she had left her long skirt, a T-shirt and sandals on a wicker chair in the corner along with her underwear and an overnight bag. She struggled into her clothes, hopping from one foot to the other as she pushed her toes into sandals.

She dragged her fingers through her hair and shuffled over to the wardrobe mirror.

Molly saw herself in the glass, remembering the time when she'd thought about smashing the wardrobe mirror at home. She smiled at her reflection, and a woman with tanned skin and sparkling eyes grinned back. Molly gave a little shimmy, allowing the long skirt to swirl around her ankles, and she put her hands on her hips. The woman in the mirror had plenty of sass, her hair was thick and glossy around her shoulders; her teeth were good, and her face was confident and happy. She looked again – she wasn't perfect, but she would do. Molly wondered briefly if Ronnie was in the *finca* kitchen making breakfast. She was hungry. She delved into the overnight bag, found her toothbrush and a comb and went off in search of a bathroom.

She passed the second bedroom, the door slightly ajar. It was dark inside, the heavy curtains drawn, but Molly could make out the shape of a bed. She pushed the door gently and gazed into a pretty room, not dissimilar to her own. The bed was smooth, empty and unslept in: Nell had not returned to the *casita*. Molly gave a little laugh; she assumed Nell had seduced Ronnie or perhaps it had been the other way around, but either way it could probably be counted as a satisfactory outcome.

A small frown puckered her brow: perhaps Nell's fascination with Ronnie was a good thing, although it was possibly a little soon after the breakup with Phil, but Molly assumed there was a strong mutual attraction: she had certainly sensed a spark between them last night. She pulled the bedroom door closed with a crisp clunk, putting an end to any further thoughts about the compatibility of her sister and the sailor. It would be what it would be and she wished them every happiness. She turned the corner in her search for a bathroom and saw a dark-haired woman bending over the sink, a cloth in her hand, polishing. Molly smiled at her and said, 'Hello.'

The woman looked up, her face intrigued. Molly noticed a firmness about her mouth, a muscular tension held tight in a permanent refusal to smile. The woman had short hair, cut in a neat, unfussy style, and dark eyes. She was probably in her late thirties and wore an apron around her waist over blue jeans, a green shirt and thick training shoes. She met Molly's eyes. 'Who bloody hell are you?'

Molly paused, thinking. The woman's accent was clearly Spanish, her mouth moving disdainfully with each syllable. Molly decided on simplicity. 'I'm Molly.'

The woman turned her back to the sink and held up the damp cloth. 'You are Ronnie's new woman?'

Molly laughed, indicating that the idea was ridiculous. 'No.'

The woman put her hands on her hips. 'He had a party here last night, Ronnie. He leaves the sun terrace like a house for pigs. It is filthy. I was cleaning it since early this morning.'

Molly moved her mouth thinking of an answer. All she could say was, 'Oh.'

The woman snorted. 'Ronnie...' She rolled her Rs as if there were four of them in his name and wrinkled her nose as if any mention of him smelled bad. 'Ronnie, he is no good. Don't go fall in love with him. He is a big cheat.'

'Cheat?' Molly shrugged and then a smile broke out on her face. 'Oh, I remember – I think he mentioned you. You must be Pilar.'

The woman squeezed the cloth tight in her palms as if she were throttling Ronnie's neck. Her face clouded. 'I clean his house but he is a dirty cheat. All men are the same. Big dirty cheats. They leave their things everywhere. Then I come here and clean it all up.'

Molly folded her arms. 'Why is he a cheat?'

Pilar snorted, a low growl in her nose and throat. 'He is a man. They do nothing but make bloody cheat. They leave the place untidy; they leave their cheat all over the place.'

Molly frowned. 'How...?'

'He treat me like cheat. He treat his wife like bloody cheat. Ronnie will never change. He leaves all his cheat here and I come and clean it all up.'

Molly nodded, understanding. 'Ah, cheat... ha, ha, I see...'

'Bloody cheat. Bloody man.' Pilar spat her words and turned back to the sink to polish the taps.

'It was nice to meet you, Pilar,' Molly smiled.

Pilar whirled round, her eyes suddenly kind. 'I tell you, don't stay with that man. Don't sleep with him. He will treat you like bloody cheat too.'

'Thanks for the advice.' Molly gave Pilar her most friendly smile. 'I won't pick any men who are big cheats. I'm too long in the tooth for that.'

Pilar shrugged, muttering something that sounded like 'What is wrong with the bloody tooth?' and went back to polishing the taps. Molly saw the front door to the *casita* had been left gaping open; the sunlight outside was blinding white and she stepped into the heat. She thought she might wander into the orchard or perhaps go up onto the sunroof and sit for a while gazing at the mauve hills. Then she'd go back to the *finca* and try to rouse Nell.

* * *

Nell was lying on her front in the king-sized bed, thinking. Ronnie was asleep, his back turned towards her, snoring softly, purring like a satisfied cat. Nell smiled. It wasn't a bad sound and here she was, warm, her flesh resting against the flesh of another human being. She felt safe, connected. She rolled over and gazed at the clock. It was after nine. She and Ronnie had stayed on the terrace last night until the sun had set and the sky was crammed with little stars. They had talked and talked until the early hours, Ronnie telling her about his life in Spain shortly after he had arrived with his family and how Tracy had changed, how she'd become more remote, how her decision to leave him had been a slow, gradual turning away from the *finca*, the business, everything he'd wanted to bring to their marriage. Nell had said that her experience had been just the opposite: she had thought everything had been fine, routine, but Phil had been hiding his secret, his infatuation with his new love Nikki, and he had sprung the news on her in an instant.

Ronnie had been sitting next to her at the table, a beer bottle in his hand. She had been wearing his sweatshirt over her swimsuit and he'd leaned towards her, his arm almost against hers, and he had told her that Phil must be crazy to leave her for someone else. Nell had met his eyes and muttered that Nikki was much younger than she was: she'd forced a dry laugh and said that Phil had chosen a newer model. Ronnie's gaze had fixed on her, his eyes shining, and he had murmured that Nell was beautiful, that if he had such a woman in his life, he would never have let her go: he'd treat her just as she deserved, like a queen, and Nell had caught her breath as he had leaned forward, put his lips against hers and wrapped his arms around her shoulders. She recalled the warmth of their embrace, their hands cold in the night air as they reached for each other.

Nell sighed softly. It had been predictable, even clichéd, their first kiss, but it had very quickly become frantic passion. Ronnie had whispered tender endearments; he had led her to his room and there had been desperation in their undressing and their clumsy caresses in the dark. But Nell had felt needed and loved.

Ronnie was a good man. She closed her eyes for a moment and imagined living with him in the *finca*. Every day would be just like a holiday. She'd have breakfast on the sun terrace then swim in the pool. They'd drive into Calleblanque and take the boat out, exploring crystal seas and white sandy coves. It would be idyllic, snorkelling and then sharing a picnic lunch and kisses. She would help him build his boat trip business into the best in the area. They could be a partnership. The thought came to her that Phil was at home in Somerset in his square box house with his homely young lover, the rain hammering against the double-glazed bedroom window, and she was free to enjoy the high life in Spain with rugged sailor Ronnie. Perhaps something good had come from being dumped. Perhaps she would be all right now.

Nell put out a hand and touched the warm flesh of Ronnie's forearm, the broad expanse of his back, a dolphin tattoo on his shoulder, and she heard him murmur with contentment. She pressed her lips against the skin. Last night after their lovemaking he had whispered that it would be very easy to fall in love with her. Nell sighed. That was what she wanted, to be loved, to be cared for. It wasn't too much to hope for, not now.

It occurred to her that she needed to get to know her way around the *finca*, particularly if she was going to spend a lot of time there. She had briefly seen a huge kitchen, beyond the living room, and she decided that she'd go there now, find a tray and load it with coffee and orange juice and something to eat. She could cook eggs and toast and bring them back to the bedroom. Ronnie would be delighted and they'd share the domestic bliss other couples took for granted.

She slid out of bed and found a dressing gown of Ronnie's hanging on the door; it was a black kimono design that tied around her waist and ended below her knees. She grinned at his choice, but the cool touch of silk against her skin felt pleasant.

Her feet cold on the tiled floor, she padded softly to the door. It creaked as she opened it; she sidled through and moved softly across the landing and towards the stone staircase.

Nell shuffled through the open-plan living room where the walls and the sofa and even the rugs were white, into the dining room. She paused at the long wooden dining table, gazing at a low chandelier hanging from rustic beams on a white plaster ceiling. She touched the table with her fingertips and imagined hosting dinner parties. Ulla and Bernt could come over; there would be new people she would meet in the future, sophisticated, fun-loving couples who would soon become close friends.

The kitchen was spacious, with white walls, oak cabinets and warm brown mosaic floor tiles. The quartz work surfaces were spotless, and Nell wondered how Ronnie managed to keep the *finca* so clean. She assumed it was because he lived by himself and then she remembered he had a cleaner, Pilar, who Ronnie had said was an angel in disguise. He paid her well: she had several children and a lazy husband so, Ronnie had joked, she was often vocal in her hatred of men but, he assured her, she had a heart of gold.

Nell opened cupboards and found a frying pan, eggs, bread. The toaster and kettle were side by side, the stainless-steel spotless. She found a coffee grinder and beans, quickly setting about making a pot of Colombian roast and popping sliced bread into the toaster. As she bustled about, she hummed softly. She felt at home in the *finca*; the space seemed to hug her like Ronnie's arms; it was safe, homely, comfortable.

She heard a step behind her and swirled round, a grin already on her face and her arms open. She was not expecting Molly to rush over to her, chuckling. Molly hugged her tight. 'So, it worked then – the seduction plan?'

Nell pulled back, her cheeks pink and tingling, and tugged at the black kimono, adjusting the belt to tie it tightly. 'Molly. I was just making breakfast – to have in bed...'

'You're an item then, you and Ronnie?' Molly cackled, her eyes watering.

Nell's cheeks flushed pink. 'Would that be all right? I mean, you don't mind, do you?'

'Not at all.' Molly was clearly delighted. 'I think you make a lovely couple. But there is one thing, Nell...'

'What's that?' Nell's forehead puckered with anxiety.

Molly hugged her again, squeezing tightly. 'Put some extra toast on for me, will you? And a couple of eggs and some coffee. I'm starving.'

19

Thursday 7th October

I've finished another book today and sunbathed and I swam in the sea. I've texted Samantha three times, sent her lots of photos and she sent me a picture of the farm. I texted Vanessa and she messaged back that she's dying to tell me all the local gossip. I promised to ring her for a proper chat soon. It seems strange, though, thinking of my old home – it all feels so distant, so long ago, so unimportant. I miss Crumper but, honestly, that's about all I miss.

Raul, the waiter at the café I visit for breakfast most mornings brings me my coffee, eggs and toast each morning before I've even asked him for it. He knows my name now and even gives me a newspaper to read each day. My Spanish is improving. I read an entire copy of the Correo from front to back yesterday, even the sports pages, before I started my second slice of toast. I'm off for a brisk walk now and I'm meeting Nell for lunch tomorrow.

Molly had only occasionally seen Nell over the last two weeks. Her sister stayed at Ronnie's *finca* most nights and, apparently, they were making new plans to develop the boat trip business for couples and honeymooners. Nell had said it was her idea and it would be very lucrative. It involved her playing a hostess role. She had added that she and Ronnie were becoming close very quickly: Molly had met her sister for lunch two days ago, and Nell had talked non-stop about life in the *finca* and how attentive Ronnie was and how Pilar had become her new best friend. Nell had become used to her saying 'bloody' and 'shit' and blaming men all the time and now, she said, they were thick as thieves. Molly had hardly time to talk about what she had been doing, although she was delighted to hear that Nell's life had settled into a routine of domestic bliss.

In fact, she had been very busy with a new self-care programme, based on a magazine article Ulla had shown her. It explained how she should put herself first and that each day she should lavish the same love upon herself that she might lavish on a child. Molly thought about Samantha and the phone call they'd just had. It was cold in Cumbria now and Samantha was telling her all about the progress of the flock of pregnant sheep. As the monologue had continued, Molly had thought how nice it would be to hug her daughter and share lunch and a long chat, but Samantha always said she had no time in her busy life for such luxuries.

Molly had just eaten some fresh fruit for breakfast, and she was sitting in the apartment in her swimsuit and a long skirt, the turquoise silk diary open. She stared at the date she had just written.

Friday 8th October

She chewed the end of the pen and thought for a moment. Then she wrote a few words.

The new healthy regime is going well. I swam in the sea twice yesterday and once in the pool. I ate vegetables, fruit and rice all day and I only drank water.

She considered what she'd written for a moment and pulled a face, unimpressed, then she continued.

I'm having a late lunch with Nell and Ronnie on his boat this afternoon. I'm looking forward to spending time with them. I'll take another book in case I have nothing to do!

She smiled, reading her words again.

I'm so pleased for them both. Being by myself is fine. At least Nell is happy and she isn't thinking about Phil all the time and she doesn't know about pregnant Nikki. Best way, I think. I'm trying to adopt the self-care programme Ulla told me about in her magazine. I'm feeling full of energy so far. Off to the pool now to lounge about and maybe have a swim and then a cocktail – non-alcoholic, of course!

Molly put the pen down and glanced at the wall clock. It was almost ten. She would relax for a few hours on a sun lounger by the pool. Ulla and Bernt would be there. She might have a chat with Ulla about her own regime. She and Bernt both seemed so healthy. They were going back to Stockholm in two weeks: Molly thought sadly that there would be no one next door to talk to; when she climbed to the roof terrace in the late afternoon, Bernt was always lounging in the hot tub in his thong and often they'd chat about politics, art or novels. Bernt made life in Sweden sound very cool.

Molly wondered about her ginger cat, Crumper, if he was missing her and, on impulse, she picked up the phone and dialled Vanessa's number. The answer came at once. 'Hello?'

'It's Molly. I promised I'd ring. How are you getting on? How are Jack and Melissa? How's my Crumper?'

'Molly!' Vanessa sounded delighted. 'How lovely to hear from you. Yes, everything is fine. Jack and Mel say Crumper sleeps on their bed every night – your bed. Oh, but the weather is getting so chilly here. Spain must be gorgeous. How are you? How's Nell?'

Molly hesitated. Her life in Somerset seemed so far away. 'All's fine here, Vanessa. We're having a lovely time.' Her mind searched for some news that didn't involve Nell and Ronnie, or Molly being alone. 'Nell and I are having a boat trip this afternoon. It's glorious being here.'

'Oh, I'd love a holiday.' Vanessa enthused. 'I'm saving up though. We were thinking we might go somewhere nice after Easter.'

'You and Jack and Melissa?'

'Oh, no.' Vanessa's voice pealed with laughter, as loud as if she was in the same room. 'Of course, you don't know, do you? I've found myself a – well, a man-friend. I've been seeing Darren. He manages the Globe where Mel works. She introduced us and...' Vanessa sounded excited. 'We've been a couple for over a month now.'

Molly sighed. 'It's all happening in the Yeovil area, then?'

'Oh, yes.' Vanessa's words came quickly. 'And Colonel Brimble-Dicks has gone away on holiday too. Joe has taken him to Brighton for a week for the sea air. And your garden is perfect. Jack has made it so tidy.' She took a breath. 'I can't say how grateful I am for all you've done, letting them stay in the house.

Jack loves his job, Mel too – they are planning Christmas already and of course I get to see them most days...'

'That's great.' Molly was aware that she was smiling, although there was no one in the room to see her grinning face.

'I must go.' Vanessa sounded in a rush. 'I'm meeting Darren. He and I have got things to do, plans to make...'

Molly could hear her smiling on the other end of the phone. 'Bye then, Vanessa. We'll talk soon...'

She heard a click and there was sudden silence. Molly gazed around the little apartment and felt a long way from home. She wasn't sure any more where home was. It wasn't in Spain and it wasn't in Somerset, not really. Molly thought sadly that her house hadn't really felt like home since Richie died. Now it was just a house that she'd failed to clean and love, a house she existed in from one day to the next. It had been easy to give it up. She shrugged, picked up her keys, sunscreen, sunglasses and made her way towards the door.

There was a lot of activity in the swimming pool. Molly picked her way towards an empty sunbed and plonked herself down, sunglasses in place. She heard a shout and saw Bernt in the deep end, waving in her direction. Ulla was swimming furiously, her legs like a fin weaving below the water's surface; Molly gestured back and began applying sun cream to her legs.

A husky voice next to her said something in Spanish. Molly heard the words '*no quiere quemaduras*' and glanced up to see a tall, elegant woman in a navy swimsuit, who had lean legs like a model's. Molly grinned at the woman, whose head was covered by a huge hat and her face shaded by enormous sunglasses. The woman gave her a wide smile back.

Molly understood that the woman was saying something about sunburn. She glanced at the woman's deep tan and assumed she wasn't speaking about herself. She nodded. 'No, I don't want to burn. Er – *no quiero quemaduras de sol* – er, *soy inglesa*, I'm English.'

'Oh,' the woman cooed. 'You look so Spanish. I beg your pardon. I thought I had found a fellow countrywoman.'

Molly stared at the woman. Her accent was certainly Spanish. She was poised and confident, waiting for Molly to reply. Molly thrust out a hand.

'I'm Molly. Pleased to meet you.'

'Lourdes,' the woman purred. 'I own one of the apartments on the ground floor. I don't get to use it very often.' She gave an apologetic smile. 'I live in Barcelona. I'm a translator – part-time. I should have retired years ago, but I like to keep busy.'

Molly studied the woman. Behind the glasses she had the shining tightened face of a woman who had treated herself to Botox many times. Her damson-red lips were plump, a sultry pout. Her raven hair was swept up under her hat. Lourdes put out a hand, square shaped with manicured crimson nails, and said, 'How old do you think I am?'

Molly shook her head. 'I don't know. It seems rude to guess someone's age.'

Lourdes made a rich throaty sound. 'You English are too hesitant when it comes to matters of honesty. Go on, guess – I won't be offended.'

'Fifty?'

Molly's words made Lourdes laugh. She removed her glasses and wiped the corner of her eyes, which Molly could see were a chocolate colour.

'I am seventy-five years old.'

'Really?' Molly was genuinely shocked.

'You are much younger than I am,' Lourdes told her. 'I think you are in your mid-sixties.'

'Seventy,' Molly replied, realising that she was telling the truth about her age for the first time in years.

'You look good,' Lourdes told her with another tap of her fingers. 'It is important for a woman to look good.'

'Is it?' Molly had no idea why she'd asked the question.

'Of course,' Lourdes said, her voice serious. 'For ourselves. We women need to be confident. We don't look good so that we are just a portrait gallery for a man to look at.'

Molly thought about Lourdes' words for a moment and then asked. 'Are you married?'

Lourdes found the question even funnier than Molly's guess about her age. 'Of course not,' she said defiantly. 'I don't want anyone to cramp my style.' She surveyed Molly, the mane of silver hair beneath her hat, the swimsuit, the long skirt. 'You are not married.'

Molly shrugged. 'I was once. He died.' She sat upright, surprised that she was revealing so much about herself to a complete stranger.

Lourdes gave a loud sigh. 'You have an air of independence. You make your own choices in life. You are a woman who does what she wants on a whim. That is good.'

'How do you know all this?' Molly was amazed.

'Your aura, your bearing. You are a strong woman, wilful.' Lourdes gripped her arm. 'I like you. You are on holiday here alone?'

'With my sister.'

Lourdes nodded slowly. 'And where is she, the sister?'

Molly beamed. 'She's found a new man. She stays at his *finca* a lot.'

'And you? What are you doing while your sister is with this man?'

'I'm practising self-care,' Molly explained. 'I'm looking after myself.'

'What does that mean?'

Molly shrugged. 'I eat vegetables and fruit and swim a lot.'

Lourdes' laughter rang out. 'Is that self-care, to eat vegetables?'

Molly shook her head. 'That's what it said to do in the article I read.'

Lourdes reached into her handbag and took out a lipstick and a mirror. She gazed at her mouth as she applied a deep plum colour to her pout. 'It is so important to put ourselves first. So many women believe it is their job to prop up a man, to cook for him, to organise his life.'

'Have you never been married?' Molly was genuinely interested.

Again, Lourdes seemed to find Molly's comment ridiculous. 'No, never. I have my own life. What is the English expression? I plough my own furrow.' Lourdes put her lipstick away and took a breath. 'I do what I please, when I please. No one is there to tell me I should do things differently. I am my own person. If you like, I am in love with myself. I don't need anyone else to tell me I'm beautiful.'

Molly scrutinised Lourdes. She was beautiful: there was something in her confidence that exuded loveliness. Molly thought about herself for a moment, her ill-fitting swimsuit, the long skirt covering a multitude of imperfections. A question popped into Molly's mind and she blurted it out. 'Don't you ever feel lonely?'

'No.' Lourdes' face was serious. 'Because in life, we should always have a project.'

'Do you have a project?'

'I have my work, my apartment in Barcelona,' Lourdes

explained. 'I have my place here to relax from time to time. But also, I have other projects that absorb me. I write for a magazine. I look after myself and I pay a doctor to make me look this good. It takes time and money and it keeps me busy. I go to a club where I meet many friends. I ski a little still and I certainly enjoy the après-ski; I also like to spend time alone, to read, to dine out, to drink good wine.'

'It sounds like you're very busy,' Molly agreed.

'I am.'

'You have no children? Grandchildren?'

'None.' Lourdes seemed to think this was the most ludicrous idea. Then suddenly her face became serious. 'You have told me your sister is here with you on holiday and now she has found romance. Does that leave you feeling alone?'

Molly shrugged. 'A little, I suppose – not all the time...'

'Use the time you have well.' Lourdes' vice grip was on her wrist again. 'Why not travel? Why not see the world?' She smiled at a sudden memory. 'Iceland is particularly beautiful this time of year. If I were you, I'd fly to Reykjavik. Treat myself to a long soak in the Blue Lagoon. Then I'd go on a cruise, perhaps. Or I'd go to Canada. Canada is the most beautiful country. The people are so welcoming. Or Australia. It is the only place to go for a beach party. Oh, I've had so much fun in Australia. I've been half a dozen times.'

Molly was impressed. 'My goodness me.'

Lourdes was pleased with herself. 'I take good care of myself. Self-care is more than just eating vegetables.' She eased herself from the lounger and stood tall, her eyes on a distant place.

'You're right.' Molly noticed Bernt and Ulla clambering from the pool. 'It was so nice to meet you, Lourdes.'

Lourdes reached for her bag. 'Now I am going to care for myself some more. I will buy myself a cocktail – with gin – and then I will visit Manu, my hairdresser here, who always makes me look a million dollars.' She extended her hand. 'By the way, I have to say, your hair looks wonderful. Blonde with those dark blue strands. Adorable. Well, it was nice to meet you. I hope we shall meet again, Molly. And then again...' She gave a deep throaty laugh. 'And then maybe I hope we don't meet again. Maybe instead you will be having new adventures, travelling to Venezuela or treating yourself to a month on the beach in Bali. I wish you the best in your travels. *Adios, amiga.*'

Molly watched Lourdes walk away, tall on heels, elegant, and she was thoughtful for a moment. Lourdes' life was completely different from her own but her words made perfect sense. She had spoken about thinking only of herself, following her own heart, travelling to different places: Canada, Australia, Iceland. Molly closed her eyes, dreaming...

Ulla plonked herself next to Molly in the lounger Lourdes had vacated and shook the droplets of water from her glowing skin. She grinned. 'Who were you talking to?'

Molly's face was serious. 'A most inspirational Spanish lady.'

Ulla met her gaze. 'Bernt has gone to get us all a drink. I thought we could do with a freshly squeezed orange juice. What do you say, Molly?'

'Great idea,' Molly beamed. 'But ask him to put a big glug of gin in mine, please. I'm practising self-care.'

20

Friday 8th October

*What to do, what to do, what to do? Today I feel far out to
sea, just like Ronnie's boat. I need to swim to a different shore
to see new places. I'd love to go somewhere exciting. Perhaps
Spain belongs just to Nell now…*

The *Carpe Diem* was drifting towards a secluded sandy cove
surrounded by jagged rocks. The sea was an endless stretch of
sparkling sapphire against a cloudless sky. Molly lay on her
stomach on a rug she'd placed on the wooden boards of the deck;
she stretched out languidly, feeling the sun's heat on the back of
her thighs, listening to waves slapping against the side of the
boat. She was dozing, almost asleep, but in the hazy background
she could hear Ronnie and Nell moving about. She knew from
the excited chatter that Ronnie was steering the boat into the cove
where they would stop. Nell was fussing with food, arranging
bite-sized nibbles on plates, playing hostess and enjoying herself.
Once there was a sudden silence after whispered voices and
Molly assumed the lovers were kissing. She wondered if she

should go home, to give Nell some space. But Molly wasn't sure where home was any more. It certainly wasn't in her old house, in Somerset. That would be simply going back to where she'd come from, a backwards step. She breathed in the fresh salty sea air and felt her eyelids become heavy.

There was a gentle hand on her arm and she pulled herself from sleep. She lifted her head, her cheek flattened by the coarse fibres of the rug, and peered through one eye at Nell, who was squatting down holding out a tall glass full of pale liquid and a sprig of mint. Molly lifted herself slowly like a cat roused from a comfortable spot and wriggled to sit up. She took the glass in her fingers and sipped the liquid. It was tangy and pleasant at the same time.

'Thanks, Nell.'

Nell lay down beside her and raised a glass to her lips. Molly twisted her neck to look over her shoulder: Ronnie had his back to them. He was wearing a cap, shorts and striped shirt, the picture of an accomplished sailor. Nell snuggled next to Molly, wriggling onto the rug to keep her pristine white shorts clean. She pressed her shoulder against her sister's arm and smiled. 'Is the homemade lemonade okay?'

'Mmmm.' Molly was drinking.

'It's shaken but not stirred,' Nell joked.

'Delicious,' Molly chirped. There was a silence and Molly wondered if Nell felt awkward; for a moment her demeanour suggested she was holding something back or was about to share a secret. Molly broke the silence. 'I don't usually like lemonade but this is nice. It's not too sweet.'

'We'll be mooring in ten minutes and we can have lunch,' Nell explained. Molly thought that her sister had taken on the role of hostess perfectly. Her skin glowed gold, her hair pushed back by sunglasses and she seemed reassured and happy. Molly put her lips against the glass.

Nell took a breath. 'Molly, can I ask you something?'

Molly smiled: she had been right. Nell had something on her mind.

'Anything.'

'It's about Ronnie and me...'

Molly rolled her eyes mischievously. 'You're getting married?'

Nell burst into peals of laughter. 'How can I? I'm still married to Phil.' She leaned even closer to Molly, pushing her slightly sideways. 'Mind you, I've sent photos of myself at the *finca* and on the boat to my friend Liz from the tennis club. I know she'll show the others and it will get back to Phil.' She gave a defiant sniff, like a naughty schoolgirl. 'I want him to know what a great time I'm having. After all, he ended our marriage and so it's only right that he knows I'm better off now and that I don't care that he's out of my life.'

'Does Phil really matter any more?' Molly was hoping Nell wouldn't investigate Phil's situation too much; Nikki would be noticeably pregnant now and it would surely be the talk of all Nell's friends back in Yeovil.

'I guess not.'

'What's on your mind?'

'I just wanted to check... you don't mind about Ronnie and me being together? I mean – I really feel a bit awful, to be honest. You and I came on holiday and I've deserted you. I'm virtually living with Ronnie at the *finca* and you're left at the apartment all by yourself most of the time. It doesn't seem fair and I do feel terrible.'

Molly beamed to show that she was perfectly happy. 'You know me, Nell. I'm used to my own company.' She gave a little chortle, a sound of resignation. 'I've been virtually by myself for most of my life. Richie's gone now, and he was the only person I stayed with. Samantha was with me as a child and a teenager. She's much happier leading her own life on the farm. Even my real mother abandoned me. So, as they say, it's the story of my life, being alone. I'm used to it.' Molly finished her drink with a flourish to show that she didn't care; she was independent and accustomed to being self-sufficient.

Nell pouted. 'I feel so bad.'

'Don't.' Molly stretched out an arm holding the glass, to ask for more lemonade. The hazy sunlight and her earlier doze had left her lethargic. 'I'm fine.'

Nell leaped up, slinked away in her perfect white vest and shorts, and returned with two full glasses. She handed one to Molly. 'Besides, it's not completely true. Your mother didn't leave you.'

'She did.' Molly sighed loudly. 'You weren't born then so you don't know what happened.'

'Mum told me. I promise you. She didn't abandon you. Not like you think she did.'

'Mum told you that, Nell? When? What did she say?' Suddenly, Molly felt sharply awake.

Nell took a breath. 'When Mum was very ill, and you were... well, you know, Richie had just passed, I spent the last days with her at the bungalow and Mum said lots of things to me about her and Dad and about their relationship. It was like she wanted to confide in me before she died. You know she always felt second best, that Dad loved your mother the most, that he adored her and after she'd gone, Mum was a second choice?'

'No, I didn't know that. She didn't tell me anything.' Molly frowned. 'Why did she feel second best? Dad was always lovely to her; he was good to all of us. He was considerate and sweet... they both were, the best parents we could have had.'

'But your mother, Kezia Lovell, was his first love. They had you as a result of their passion.'

'Then she left him. And me. Then Dad married Mum and they had you...'

'That's not quite how it happened, Moll. Mum gave me a photo of you and Kezia Lovell – you were in her arms...'

'You have a photo? I knew Dad had one – I saw it once. I assumed it was lost. Nell, how come you have it?'

Nell chewed her bottom lip. 'Mum gave it to me before she died. It was at the house, mine and Phil's, with lots of other photos and I'd always meant to give it to you but – Richie had just passed – I didn't think it was the right time to bother you with it. I filed it away and forgot. Then when I left Phil, it was in a folder in one of the suitcases you brought. It's in my handbag now.'

'I'd really like to see it, Nell...' Molly put a hand to her head. The thought of seeing the photograph again had hit her like a sharp blast of wind.

Nell scuttled over in Ronnie's direction and bent over, searching in her bag. Molly swallowed lemonade, her mind desperate for answers. She had always thought her mother had left her because she didn't want to look after a baby and she had tired of her father. Whenever she'd asked questions about her mother, as any normal inquisitive child would, he had always smiled, his eyes filled with sadness, and said, 'Your mother was a free spirit. She stayed for a while but then I couldn't keep her.' Then he'd slipped into silent thought and Molly had been acutely aware of his loss. She had thought it better to ask no more about a woman she couldn't remember and whom she would never see again.

Nell was beside her. She slipped a black and white photo into Molly's hand and suddenly there she was, a tiny puckered face rolled in a shawl, clasped in the arms of a woman with defiant eyes, a mane of loose dark hair around her shoulders just like Molly's used to be, and the ghost of a smile on her lips, as if she wanted to smile for all she was worth, as if she was so proud of her baby, but for some reason she wasn't allowed to show her feelings. Molly gaped at the young woman in the photo. This was Kezia Lovell. This woman was her mother and now, over seventy years later, she was looking at a stranger in a photograph whom she'd never seen properly before. Molly wondered if she was still alive. Probably not – the young woman would be in her nineties now. Yet... it wasn't completely impossible.

Molly asked herself how she felt, and she wasn't sure. She didn't feel angry, she wasn't sad; she certainly didn't blame anyone. She just felt a little numb, as if the two people in the photograph and the life she'd once had, the mother she had once known, were strangers who had never existed. She gazed up at Nell and frowned.

'I wish Mum had spoken to me about her.'

'It was difficult for her, Moll. Doubly so after Richie had passed away. And Mum was so weak by that time; I suppose she wanted to finally lay the past to rest...'

'I have so many questions, though...' Molly's eyes were drawn back to the photo, to the small child swaddled in a lace shawl, to the woman with the serious eyes who was her mother, holding the child close to her body; this was the mother she'd always believed had abandoned her.

Ronnie's voice called over cheerily. 'Lunchtime, ladies. Shall we have a bite to eat, Nell? The sea air always gives me an appetite.' He was beside them, crouching behind Nell, kissing the top of her head. Molly heard him murmur, 'I'm hungry, and not just for food...'

Molly held the photo against her heart. There were so many

questions. So many things she needed to know, but it would have to wait.

* * *

Nell and Ronnie had decided to go for a swim in the sea after lunch. They stripped off their outer clothes and suddenly Ronnie was wearing rainbow swim shorts and Nell a new yellow bikini. They had dived in, yelping, the cold water against their skin, thrashing about, laughing and shouting. Both of them repeatedly called to Molly to come and join them. Ronnie had shouted that it was 'glorious' although Nell's screams every time he splashed her and tugged her playfully beneath the waves implied that, despite the sunshine, it was cold.

Molly had returned to the rug on the deck and was sprawled on her stomach with a cup of coffee and a newspaper. It was a local weekly called *Calle Correo* and it was printed in Spanish. Molly had asked Ronnie if she could borrow it and he'd immediately replied that it didn't belong to him – his Spanish wasn't good enough to justify him buying a newspaper: a client had left it on board after a cruise yesterday afternoon. Molly was intrigued to test her ability to translate Spanish and, so far, she understood about half of what she was reading.

She had perused a front-page article about an English child who had been lost and found on the beach. Molly had worked out that he was a six-year-old boy and his mother had brought him on holiday for two weeks at Palomar, just up the coast. She read the *Deportivo* pages, reviewing a local football match and a game called *baloncesto,* which Molly decided was probably basketball. Then her eyes fell on a page with a column marked *Casas para alquilar.* There were photos of houses to let, *fincas* like Ronnie's and apartments like the one she was renting from Lisa.

It was easy to translate most of the words, the number of *habitaciones,* the *baños,* the *jardín.* She was enjoying scrutinising the pictures of rooms, bathrooms and gardens and working out how much it might cost in pounds to rent a different house. Some houses were local, others in the north of Spain, one in Majorca, two in Portugal and several in the Canary Islands.

Then her eyes fell on a striking picture of a modern kitchen with rustic tiles in a mosaic style. She translated eagerly and realised she was looking at an apartment not far from a beach, with two bedrooms, but this one was a very long way from Calleblanque. Molly's pulse raced with the idea of a new journey, a different place completely. The apartment was modestly priced because the owner would be away on business until Christmas and wanted someone to live in the house in his or her absence. The owner was called G. Lòpez and there was an email address. Molly pored over the information, making sure she had translated each word properly. The apartment seemed to be a lovely place, close to all the local amenities.

In an instant, Molly rolled onto her back and squeezed her eyes shut. She could feel the blood pumping harder, coursing around her body. For a moment she thought of her mother, Kezia Lovell. They shared the same wild heart, the same untamed spirit, the same desire to seek out new adventures, new pastures. Her mind was filling with thoughts, scrambling and bumping against each other. Nell would not miss her if she moved somewhere far away from Calleblanque. In fact, it would be ideal for her and Ronnie to have time together alone, to develop their relationship without worrying about Molly the gooseberry. Ulla and Bernt were going back to Sweden soon and the *Melocotón* apartment was paid for until Christmas, so Nell would have a base for herself if she needed it: she wasn't in a position where she had to live at the *finca* with Ronnie. She had a choice: she was independent.

Molly sat upright. She had enough money to cover all the expenses, she was sure. Richie had left her financially comfortable. A plan had formed already. She would email G. Lòpez tonight in her best Spanish and enquire about renting the apartment. Her thoughts raced. Today was the eighth of October. The apartment was to be let from the sixteenth, next Saturday. She would have plenty of time to organise everything.

An image flashed into her mind: she pictured the elegant Spanish woman, Lourdes, whom she had met by the pool that morning. She recalled her long legs and wide-brimmed hat, the enormous sunglasses and raven hair. Molly could almost hear her husky voice, her contagious enthusiasm as she gripped her arm and insisted that she should follow her dreams. What had she said? *I am my own project*, that was it. Molly picked up the newspaper and, without thinking, tore out the page with the advert for the beautiful apartment and stuffed the paper in her shorts pocket, breathing deeply. She'd only tell Nell once it was all sorted out. She didn't want anyone to try to change her mind. It was what she wanted to do desperately: all of a sudden, she was sure.

Molly stretched out on the rug and listened to Nell and Ronnie splashing and laughing in the sea beyond the boat. *Carpe Diem* – seize the day. It was a wise motto, she decided, and one which would spur her forwards. Richie would have approved of her plan, and it was the perfect solution to her itchy feet. Yes, she was off to spend two and a half months in an apartment by the beach, a long way from Spain, thirty minutes from Cancún, in Mexico.

Thursday 14th October

The flight's booked: it's going to be a long haul, and two days of travelling. I'm really excited. Nell and Ronnie have wished me luck, although Nell was a bit tearful this morning. But it's an ideal opportunity for us both – she'll be able to concentrate on her new relationship (which seems to be going really well!) and I will be off to sample the delights of Cancún. Guadalupe Lòpez, the owner of the apartment, seems really nice. She knows Spain well – she has a friend in Calleblanque and often visits. I spoke to her on the phone – she's offered to meet me at the airport and give me a lift to Puerto Palacio. I am so excited about Mexico – it'll be a chance to go somewhere I've never been and to have new adventures. R would have really loved it… I'll enjoy it for us both.

Ronnie had driven them all to the station and Nell had sobbed into her hanky for the entire journey. She had protested that she didn't want to stay in Spain without Molly and Ronnie had been bewildered the whole time, not knowing how to comfort her. Molly had been taken by surprise too, reassuring her sister that she'd be fine. Nell's face, streaked with tears, and the desperate way she had hugged her as they left each other at the station made Molly unsure that she was doing the right thing by leaving. She'd assumed Nell would be fine: she had her new relationship with Ronnie; they were an item, completely loved-up; they needed to spend time by themselves.

But Nell had howled and sniffed, repeating that she wished that Molly had confided in her earlier so that she could have persuaded her to stay. Nell then became even more upset, asking Molly when she would stop changing her mind; when would she finally settle down. Then, worst of all, Nell began to blame herself for Molly's sudden departure: she had neglected her, she had been selfish, making Molly feel like a gooseberry. Molly had denied it desperately, glancing at Ronnie's face in the mirror from the back seat of his car; he had looked hurt and completely confused.

During the train ride from Calleblanque to Madrid, Molly had wondered if she was going to regret leaving Spain, given Nell's tearfulness. And the overnight stay in a cheap hotel with faulty air conditioning had been stuffy; the long flight from Madrid to Dallas, with the blood flow to her ankles constricted by tight flight socks, had seemed like an eternity. The final journey from Dallas to Cancún had been dull: she'd eventually fallen asleep with her head on the shoulder of a portly gentleman who had spoken continuously about what a great holiday he'd had last time he'd visited Mexico. But despite the tedious long journey, the blood thrumming in her veins told Molly that she had made the right decision. She couldn't wait for a new adventure...

And now, at half past eight on Saturday evening, she was

happily dragging her luggage through Cancún airport, her legs stiff and aching and her heart soaring with new expectation. She'd pulled off the tight travel socks in a cubicle in the ladies' toilet, shoving them into her jacket pocket, and was marching briskly out beyond the passport control when she saw a woman in the waiting crowd holding a piece of paper with the name 'Milly Mitchell' in thick felt pen. Molly paused and glanced at the woman. She was probably in her late forties or early fifties, her chestnut hair wound in a coil. She wore a long expensive-looking camel-coloured coat; her face was serious and her lips were vermillion. Molly grinned and walked over to her. 'Guadalupe Lòpez? I'm Molly.'

The woman folded her paper carefully, then held out a hand. 'Pleased to meet you. I hope you've had a good flight?'

Molly took in her perfect English, her American accent, and decided that she would not spoil their early relationship by regaling the poor woman with how awful the journey had been. She was here now, so she breathed out gratefully and said, 'Yes, wonderful, thanks.'

Guadalupe Lòpez turned quickly and began to walk at a fast pace, her voice drifting back to Molly. 'I'll take you back to the apartment in my car and then I need to go to bed early. My own flight leaves first thing tomorrow morning and I have to be in New York for an important meeting.'

'No, I mean, yes, it's very kind of you to meet me and give me a lift...' Molly was trotting to keep up.

Guadalupe was still talking. 'I need someone to live in the apartment while I'm away. It's good that you'll be there and I can forget about the place and concentrate on my work.'

'What is it you do, Guadalupe?' Guadalupe's pace had quickened even more. They had reached a car park and she was forging ahead.

'I work in fashion,' she muttered by way of explanation. She had paused next to a silver car, a Kia Rio. In seconds she was in the driver's seat and Molly had rushed around to the passenger side and was fastening her seat belt, her luggage piled on the rear seats. Guadalupe manoeuvred the car out into the road and was negotiating the city traffic as she spoke to Molly. 'I have a place in New York. That's where I work most of the time. The apartment here is where I come to relax. It's a nice place – you'll like it. Puerto Palacio is a great location. It's nowhere near as frantic as Cancún. The apartment's not far from the beach. It's a very friendly community; there's plenty to do.' She paused for a moment, then added, 'I saw the references you attached but you didn't say what you do for a living in your email. Are you retired?'

'Yes, I'm a lady of leisure,' Molly joked but Guadalupe's expression remained the same. Molly pressed her nose against the window to stare out at the twinkling lights of Cancún. The sky was dark now; people were crossing roads and the traffic was busy. She noticed several white buildings, high-rise blocks of apartments, hotels. There were many shops and cafés and palm trees growing at intervals on every street. Her heart suddenly began to beat faster: the sense of adventure was beginning to return. She grinned at Guadalupe. 'I'm sure I'll have plenty to do here until Christmas.'

Guadalupe spoke to the windscreen. 'The last people who stayed were a couple from Barcelona. They stayed for three months, June to August. I always advertise my apartment in Spain. The clients are so keen to come to Mexico. The last people did a lot of snorkelling but, apparently, the thing they enjoyed most was the cooking classes where you get to make authentic Mayan cuisine.'

'Oh.' Molly wasn't sure the cooking class was for her; come to think of it, she didn't snorkel either but, she supposed, there was a first time for everything.

Guadalupe had increased her speed: she was on a main road, passing other cars. 'Are you married?'

'No.' Molly thought that would be the easiest answer. She didn't want to explain about Richie, how much she wished he was with her at the moment, how much fun it would be to share the adventure with him.

'Nor am I,' Guadalupe's lips came together in a line. 'Husbands are more trouble than they are worth, if you ask me.' She thought about her words for a moment. 'I'm not in a relationship or looking for one.'

Molly agreed, deciding it would be polite to show an interest in Guadalupe. After all, she was renting her apartment. 'So, are you an American living in Mexico or a Mexican living in New York?'

Guadalupe raised an eyebrow. 'I'm Mexican. But my work is in New York and I've lived there for many years. Let's say I come to Mexico to chill out. In New York I have to be the professional me.'

Molly watched Guadalupe as she turned the car into another road, her hands gripping the wheel, her nails sparkling pink. She wondered whether the apartment would reflect the owner: matter-of-fact, efficient, glamorous. She recalled the photo in the Spanish newspaper and online, the tiled kitchen and the plastered white walls of a large lounge: she had imagined the owner to be male and practical.

The car came to a halt outside a block of houses, square white buildings, each with a small parking space in front, flanked by green foliage. Molly grabbed her cases and followed Guadalupe inside through a sturdy dark door. They were standing in a huge white room with a flagstone floor; Molly gazed at a minimalist design, a modern dining table with six curved wooden chairs, a huge black leather sofa and a small coffee table. Molly approached a painting on the wall showing a woman wearing an orange scarf, her black hair in braids twisted over her head, entwined with orange flowers. Her face was serious, her eyebrows heavy. Molly breathed out. 'I love Frida Kahlo: well, I love her paintings.'

Guadalupe turned to face her and almost smiled. 'I think she is an inspiration to women.' She gave her single laugh again. 'My ex-husband used to tell me she reminded him of me. He said I had her free spirit.' She waved an arm in Molly's direction. 'Let me give you a quick tour of the apartment. Then, if you don't mind, I'll get an early night.'

Molly followed Guadalupe through the room, past a spacious kitchen with mosaic tiles, a stainless-steel cooker and fridge and white walls, through a hallway and into a vast bedroom. The walls were white and there was a double bed with a slatted wooden headboard and a huge tapestry cover; behind another door, Molly glimpsed another mosaic-tiled room with a shower and a bath.

'This is all yours. You're welcome to use my bedroom of course while I'm away – you're renting the place – but I think you'll be more comfortable here. It is very pleasant, with a new en suite.'

Molly was delighted. 'Thank you. It's beautiful.'

She turned to go. 'Oh, at the back of the apartment you'll find a patio garden. It has a little table for dining and a hammock. It's a real sun trap.' She gave a small snorting laugh. 'We're at the end of the rainy season, almost, and we haven't had a hurricane here for a while, so you'll get plenty of sunshine, hopefully.' She noticed Molly's shocked expression and offered a half-smile. 'It's a pleasant time of year to be here. The rain is less frequent, it's warm, and the place isn't bustling with holidaymakers. You have

a great stay, now.' She placed a key ring in Molly's palm. 'If
there's anything you need, do email me. New York's not so far
away.'

Molly glanced round the room. 'Thanks. Yes, I'll have a great
time...'

Guadalupe nodded. 'I guess I'll turn in for the night. Help
yourself to whatever you need. The fridge is stocked. So – it's your
place now. Enjoy.'

And she was gone, whirling through the doorway, leaving
Molly standing in the room with two cases at her feet, wondering
what to do next. She sighed and looked around: here she was,
ready for new adventures in Mexico. She ought to feel
triumphant, excited, delighted, independent, but she didn't. She
felt tired, her head buzzing with too much travel.

Molly wandered into the en suite, noticing the pretty little
tiles, the shower, the white bath and basin with gold taps. She
zipped open one of her suitcases, took out her toothbrush and
her travel cosmetic bag and placed it next to the taps, hoping that
she'd feel more at home. She rooted out a pair of pyjamas, a T-
shirt and shorts set with a print of sheep that reminded her of
Samantha's farm in Cumbria and placed them on the bed. An
exciting thought made her heart beat faster. This was her room
now, until Christmas.

Molly padded to the door, walking through the hallway and
back to the lounge. There was a television she hadn't noticed
before; the curtains were made of heavy white material, like the
sails of a ship. Molly's mind moved to Ronnie, his boat, and then
to Nell. She made a mental note to text Nell, to let her know she'd
arrived safely and to promise to ring soon. She wanted to make
sure that Nell was all right; the image of her tear-streaked face
was still strong in her memory. She reminded herself that Nell
would have an ideal opportunity to cement her relationship with

Ronnie now. She'd be fine once she'd become used to the idea that Molly was in Mexico.

Molly plodded into the kitchen on tired, spongy legs and opened a wooden cupboard, feeling quite at home. She found a glass and was on her way to the sink to fill it when she stopped dead and wondered if the water was suitable to drink. She ambled over to the fridge and opened the door. Guadalupe had been right: it was well stocked, mostly with fresh vegetables and several bottles of beer and water. Molly took out a small bottle of lager and smiled. Despite the fuzziness in her head, she was beginning to feel a surge of excitement. She was here in Mexico and the world was her oyster. She just needed a good night's sleep and then tomorrow her adventure would begin.

She found a bottle opener and flipped off the lid, bringing the lager bottle to her lips. The cool fizz hit the back of her throat: it was instantly refreshing. Molly wandered back to her room, the bottle clutched in her hand. Her legs felt heavy and she was tired but her mind was still buzzing. She sat on the bed and wondered what to do.

It came to her. She'd write an entry in her diary to calm her rushing thoughts before she fell asleep. She'd record the vagaries of her journey and her first impressions of Puerto Palacio or, at least, of the apartment and of Guadalupe Lòpez. She delved into her first case, throwing shorts and shirts around the room, and then sat up straight, chewing her lip in confusion. The blue turquoise diary was not there with the other books she'd brought to read and her drawing pad and the little dog-eared Spanish dictionary.

Molly sat down on the bed and, as she brought the stubby bottle of beer to her lips, she remembered. It was clear in her mind now: she knew exactly where the turquoise silk notebook was. She'd left it in Spain, in the apartment on the little table, along with the pen she always used and her best sunglasses. She put her fingers to her temples, massaging with a firm pressure. She couldn't function without a notebook in which to write her thoughts down. That would be her first mission tomorrow, to go out into Puerto Palacio and to search through the shops. She'd treat herself to a brand-new diary.

22

Sunday 17th October

I've left my diary behind. It's a strange feeling, like missing a friend. I have no way of recording how I feel. I'll stick this scrap of paper into my new diary, the one I'm going to buy today. New diary, new page, new beginnings. New me. Bring it on!

Molly slept deeply until past midday. She woke, stretched her arms and legs and rolled onto her back, a wide smile on her face. She was in Mexico, in a lovely apartment, and the sun was a pale slice of yellow between the window and her tapestry cover. The world was good.

She wriggled out of bed, pulled the pyjama shorts back into place from the uncomfortable position they had twisted into, tugged the top down to cover her midriff and, placing her bare feet on the cool tiles, made her way to the kitchen. The door to Guadalupe's bedroom was open and the space was tidy: she had left already.

Molly set a coffee pot to boil on the stainless-steel stove and found some avocados and tomatoes in the fridge. She cut them up and put some bread in the toaster. It would make a perfect breakfast. Twenty minutes later, she was sitting on the patio at a small table, gazing at sumptuous green foliage and a calico hammock coiled between two trees, sipping steaming coffee. The sun was warm on her skin and she sighed. She'd eat, have a shower and then, leaving everything as it was in her room, her clothes strewn everywhere from wide-open cases, she would head into town, buy a new diary and then set off towards the beach.

She checked her phone: there was a message from Nell on WhatsApp that had come in earlier. Nell was apologising for her tearful goodbye at the station and hoped she'd had a good flight. She said she'd been silly, too emotional: she was fine now. She had sent evidence: there was a photograph attached. Molly gazed at the picture of Nell, Ronnie, Ulla and Bernt smiling, seated on the sun terrace at Ronnie's *finca*, holding up glasses of something that was probably Cava. The caption below read '*Bon voyage* and happy holiday from us all'. Molly nodded: Nell was all right; she was settled. She and Ronnie had invited Ulla and Bernt over for a convivial dinner and Nell was calm again. Molly imagined Ronnie in his shorts barbecuing steaks and Bernt hovering, wearing just the thong, asking if there was any fish for the barbecue as he was practising self-care, while Nell and Ulla sat in the hot tub, topping up their drinks as the crimson sun melted into the hills behind them. Molly replied straight away: the flight had been fine and she was staying in a lovely apartment not far from the beach. She would send a picture of herself on the patio.

It occurred to Molly that a selfie in the hammock holding a bottle of beer would be the perfect way forward. She went back to her bedroom and dressed quickly in a T-shirt and a long swirling skirt. A straw hat on her head, she checked her reflection in the wardrobe mirror: she looked the part, an independent woman ready to explore an exotic new destination. She visited the fridge in the kitchen and took out a beer. It was too early to drink it but she intended to use it to strike a merry pose.

Back on the patio, Molly hoisted up her skirt to her thighs, the phone in one hand and the bottle of beer in the other and straddled the hammock. With care, she lowered herself onto the centre of the material and eased herself in place, sensing herself sagging dangerously close to the ground. She wriggled, feeling fairly secure, and held out the phone to her arm's length and smiled. The image wasn't a good one – Molly's straw hat was askew, her face was in shadow and from the angle she was holding the phone, her chin nestled into her neck and it wasn't a flattering look. Besides, she had wanted to incorporate the long spindly plant with the shining silver foliage behind her into the picture to create the flavour of Mexico.

Molly's fist closed around the beer bottle as she hoisted herself onto her side and stretched out the arm with the phone on the end. She beamed into the lens and noticed that there was just the edge of a single leaf visible in the corner of the picture. She leaned back into the hammock, which had started to sway a little, and extended her arm further, twisting her body round and leaning to one side, incorporating more of the foliage. She pressed the button and the camera sprang to life just as she toppled from the hammock and fell flat onto her side, her knees grazing the ground. Molly breathed out and glanced at the picture. It was an excellent snap of the shrubbery perfectly framed, Molly in mid-air, her hair in a blurred streak. She grinned. She'd take another from the patio table. It would be safer and more dignified.

An hour later, she was strolling through the main street in Puerto Palacio. There were rows of shops on either side, cafés, hotels, the buildings all in lively colours: red, terracotta, white. There were tall trees at regular intervals, their long branches dangling green foliage towards the pavements. Molly was surprised by the amount of activity for a Sunday afternoon in October. Shoppers strolled around the streets; many cafés and restaurants were busy, people sitting outside at tables, families eating and laughing together. She passed a shop selling T-shirts bearing slogans in English and Spanish, a young woman outside calling to her in English to come and find the perfect present.

There was a market selling fruit and vegetables and a parade of open-fronted shops. Molly ambled past a shop on a corner called Sally's Silver Shop and another proclaiming that the well-stocked Tequileria had the greatest variety of booze in the world. On the side of the road was a building with a huge painting of a Mexican man in a sombrero riding a horse, holding up a bottle of Tequila. She could hear music from speakers in shops on every corner: trumpets, strummed guitars, salsa music. Voices came from every doorway: the lilting chatter of Spanish, the more leisurely drawl of Americans on holiday. There were coloured flags and bunting overhead. Molly was surprised by how pulsating and lively the atmosphere was. It was completely different to the more relaxed pace of Calleblanque.

She was standing outside a shop with the words *Cielito Lindo* in blue letters over the doorway. She translated slowly – the pretty little sky. The shop clearly sold T-shirts and knick-knacks. The words *Regalos* and *Bolsas* were scrawled in black capitals on posters in the widows: gifts and bags. Molly frowned. A woman probably in her thirties was standing in the doorway, her hand on her hip, and she called out, 'Can I help you, *Señora*?'

Molly grinned. She wasn't sure what the Spanish word for notebook was – *librito*? Little book? She decided to answer in English.

'Do you sell notebooks?'

'Of course,' the woman retorted, pushing a dark fringe from her eyes. 'We sell everything.'

Molly followed the woman into the shop, passing rows of pretty shells and wind chimes made of wood and ceramics, stopping at a shelf full of exercise books of various sizes. Molly frowned. She wanted something attractive and beautifully bound, something equal to her turquoise silk notepad, but all she could find was a selection of cheap lined jotters and a few hard-backed A4 books. She gazed around. There were diaries, but it was October already so there seemed little point investing in one. In the end, she bought a large A4 pad with a picture of several battling Pokémon on the front. It would have to do. She bought two pairs of sunglasses, three pens, a black silk scarf, an orange beach towel and a beach bag in a canvas material with a red flower design. As she was about to leave the shop, Molly pointed to a life-sized cardboard cut-out shape by the counter. It was a skeleton wearing a smart suit and smoking a cigar, a top hat crowned with orange flowers perched at an angle on his head. Molly was perplexed.

'Is this for sale? It's very scary.'

'No, it is not for sale.' The assistant was very serious as she pushed her hair back. 'Next month we celebrate the Day of the Dead.' She fixed her eyes on Molly's, her voice low. '*El Día de los Muertos.*'

Molly shivered. She glanced at the huge figure of Death in his suit, leering, a cigar clenched between tombstone teeth. She was a foreigner, travelling alone; a single woman abroad. Suddenly, she felt a lot less safe. She decided it was time to take her purchases and go down to the beach where there would be lots of tourists.

A young man offering *helados* from a counter on a small

single-fronted shop sold her a huge cone with chocolate flakes on the top, and Molly seated herself on the orange towel, wearing the sunglasses, licking melting ice cream from her fingers. Behind her were palm trees and a couple of simple shelters on poles that looked as if they were made of coconut matting. Further back was a line of hotels and then the main road. The white sand was so soft it felt like talcum powder. Children were playing, running and yelling, throwing beach balls and rushing into the water. At intervals, people were stretched out on the beach in couples or by themselves, lying on loungers or towels, basking in the sunshine.

Beyond, the ocean was ruffled with rolling waves. The sea was the most incredible turquoise colour, blending into inky indigo as the water became deeper. A few small clouds grazed the sky, little clenched white fists, and the sunlight was so intense that she could feel its heat even behind the shades. She was aware that the heat was baking her skin and immediately she regretted not buying sunscreen. Something to read, an interesting novel or something about local life might have been a good idea too. She would stock up more tomorrow. A slight breeze lifted her hair, rearranged it across her face, cooling her cheeks. She finished the ice cream and lay back on the towel, her eyes closed, listening to the waves rolling and the occasional squeal of children in the background. She felt her body relax.

But her mind was active: several thoughts were jumbled. She was wondering what to do with her time while she was in Mexico. She would be staying in Puerto Palacio for well over two months, so she needed a plan and, at the moment, she didn't have one. It was acceptable today to get up late and have breakfast and stroll around the shopping centre and onto the beach, she thought, but two more days of it and she'd be bored. She'd find out about trips; she'd visit places. There was a rich local culture and history: she could learn about the lives and the art of the Aztecs, the Mayans.

She didn't know much about them at all so she could go on excursions. Perhaps she needed to join a group and meet some people. That made sense. If all else failed she could take a Mayan cooking class, as Guadalupe had suggested. Molly wrinkled her nose as she lay on her back. That wasn't at the top of her priorities list.

Another thought wriggled like a worm at the back of her mind. The photograph of herself and her mother, Kezia Lovell, now carefully placed between two pages of a book for safe-keeping in her suitcase, was worrying her. It was something to do with the expression on her mother's face, the mixture of pride and strength and determination in her eyes and on her brow as she held her child wrapped in a bundle, the little face peering out into the world. It wasn't the expression of a woman who would turn her back on a baby, who would give her up easily. And Nell had said that their mother, the woman Molly had always called Mum and who had treated her in just the same gentle way as she had Nell, had said that Kezia Lovell hadn't walked away. What were Nell's exact words? 'She didn't abandon you. Not like you think she did.' So, what had really happened? Molly frowned, her thoughts jumbling. She should have asked Nell straight away; she should have found out exactly what their mother had told her. But Nell had been so absorbed with Ronnie; Molly had not wanted to butt in, she'd been waiting for the right time when they'd have more time together, and then it had been time to leave. But she needed to know.

Molly felt her stomach rumble: she was hungry and she still felt tired after the long journey. But her mind was fizzing with thoughts. She would ask Nell about her real mother soon, when the time was right. She thought about the huge stainless-steel fridge in Guadalupe's apartment – in *her rented apartment* – full of fresh vegetables and beer. She'd go back and make a salad, have a beer and then she'd go to bed early. Tomorrow would be an important day. There were decisions to make, not least what she was going to do with the time she had left to spend in Mexico. There were plans to make and adventures to organise. But, right now, all she wanted to do was to eat and then fall into bed and sleep.

23

Sunday 17th October

I have a new diary, even if it isn't as beautiful as the old one. It's a clean page. Mexico – my clean page.

I felt tired today and, to be honest, a bit lonely. I sent Samantha some photos of the beach. She hasn't replied yet. I sent Vanessa the same photos of the same beach, Puerto Palacio, and she replied with a smiley face. I expect it's normal to feel a little strange, being alone in a new country. Typical me, I took off on a plane and expected everything to be perfect. I didn't think it through. Off to bed now. Tomorrow will be a lovely day, I'm sure.

Molly opened her eyes and stared into blackness, listening hard. She'd heard a sound coming from somewhere in the apartment. She was snuggled beneath the tapestry cover, wriggling on her side to check the time on the digital alarm. It was 2:43. She had fallen asleep minutes after she'd climbed into bed and slept deeply but now she was wide awake. She blinked, staring hard into the darkness of the room, as if it might improve her hearing.

There it was again: the sharp shuffling sound. It wasn't coming from the hallway; it wasn't outside her room: it was further away, in the kitchen perhaps.

Molly inhaled. Her breathing had become ragged, shallow in her chest. She listened harder, wondering if she'd locked the apartment door properly when she came in. She recalled turning the key and leaving it on the table – at least, she thought she had. The sound came again, a soft bump, the light tread of a foot, a door closing. Molly sat up in bed, her senses keen.

Her first thought was that Guadalupe must have returned, but why should she? She'd be in New York by now. She'd said she was working a busy schedule until Christmas, so there seemed little reason for her to return. Molly wished she had a torch so that she could creep through the darkened hallway or, even better, a poker or a rolling pin to defend herself against the intruder. She could threaten them, at least.

She pictured the scene. There would be a burglar, a man with a crumpled nasty face hunched over an open drawer in the living room, rifling through Guadalupe's possessions, hunting for money or jewellery. Worse still, it might be two men, gaunt faced, armed with pistols, jumpy and fraught, drug addicts desperate for anything that would buy them their next fix. Molly imagined throwing the door wide, facing them and standing there crossly, asking them what they were doing. She wondered if that would be an unwise move. But then, what if a bird had flown in or a small animal was trapped? Molly held her breath, telling herself that all her imagined ideas were ridiculous. It was probably Guadalupe.

Then she heard another noise, a sharp cough. Molly's mind unwittingly offered up the stark image of the cardboard Death she'd seen in the shop yesterday, a top hat on his head, a smart suit over his bones, a fat cigar between his teeth. Molly wondered if the supernatural creature existed and if he was, in fact, in Guadalupe's kitchen right now waiting to greet her.

She threw back the tapestry cover and slid out of bed, her feet connecting with the cold tiles. Whoever it was out there, Molly would confront them. She had no weapon: she would have to use her wits. She pushed the bedroom door open and tiptoed in the darkness down the hall. The kitchen door was ajar; a fluorescent light was on and she peered in. She could see the cooker, the edge of the fridge. Then she heard another sound, a click, and a figure walked straight past, a burly shape in dark clothes. Molly couldn't stop herself. Surprise was the best form of attack. She shoved the door hard so that it banged against the wall and rushed into the kitchen. Her hands on her hips, she faced a man in a black suit holding a bottle of beer in his hand. She frowned at him and in her most indignant voice, she asked, 'Who the hell are you?'

The man stared at her, open-mouthed, and Molly stared back. He was around her age, tall, broad-chested, his once-dark hair flecked with grey, and his beard neatly clipped. He wasn't smiling. He shook his head and pressed his lips together, his face confused.

'I could ask you the same question.'

Molly folded her arms and immediately realised that she was wearing the sheep-print pyjama set, her legs and feet bare. Her hair was dishevelled, strands tumbling over her face. She noticed him staring so she said, 'I live here.'

He brought the beer to his lips. Molly registered his weary expression, his smart clothing; his accent had been American, a slow, pleasant drawl. Suddenly, he gave a single soft laugh, a deep resonant sound coming from his chest, spluttering through his lips.

'I'm sorry. I must have startled you. Are you renting this place? I owe you an apology.'

'Yes, I'm here until Christmas,' Molly said, making her voice assertive. 'So, who are you?'

The man held out a hand. 'Ryan Stone. I'm Guadalupe's ex-husband. I had no idea she'd gotten someone to stay here. I just stepped off the plane...'

Molly moved furtively into the kitchen and took his hand. 'Molly Mitchell.'

'You're English,' he grinned, and Molly rolled her eyes. It was obvious.

He was still smiling so she said, 'And you're American.'

'Native New Yorker,' he replied. 'That's where Lupe and I met all those years ago. Well, Molly, can I get you a beer?'

'I think you'd better.'

The man moved swiftly to the fridge with the assurance of someone in his own home, taking out a small bottle of lager and flipping the lid expertly, handing it to Molly. 'I guess we should sit down and talk this thing through.' He raised concerned eyebrows. 'If that's okay?'

Molly followed him to the living room. He sat on the sofa and patted the space next to him. Molly was conscious of her skimpy pyjamas decorated with grinning sheep. She sat on a rug and sipped her beer. 'So – Mr Stone – I suppose Guadalupe didn't tell you I was here?'

'Ryan, please.' He took a glug from his bottle. 'To tell the truth, I came here on a whim. I'd been working too many hours and I needed a break. I'd no idea she was renting the apartment out. I thought she'd be away and the place would be empty.' He shrugged. 'I didn't tell her I was coming. After all, we both own it jointly: it was our bolt hole in the sun.'

Molly wasn't sure if his tone was sad; his expression certainly was one of regret. She felt sorry for him. He looked tired and unhappy. He dug his hand in his pockets and waved a key. 'See, I still have access to the front door. Molly, I'm so sorry. You must have wondered what was going on, a strange man wandering round the apartment drinking your beer.'

'I had no idea who you were.'

'Hey.' Ryan leaned forwards. 'I'm pretty bushed. My flight just got in. Would you mind if I stayed here tonight, in Lupe's room, my old room? Then tomorrow, I'll find a hotel in Cancún?'

'I suppose that would be okay.' Molly nodded.

Ryan grinned. 'I promise I won't sneak in on you during the night.'

At first, Molly had no idea what he'd meant, then she shook her head. 'The thought hadn't even occurred to me.' She met his eyes. 'Do I need to bolt my door?'

Ryan laughed to show he'd been flippant. Then, his face straight again, he breathed out, a low grateful sound. 'No. Thanks, Molly, for agreeing to let me stay. I'm sorry for cracking a bad joke – I guess I'm just a bit tired. I'll turn in now and then tomorrow I'll be out of your hair.' His eyes sparkled. 'Nice hair, I must say. Nice pyjamas too.'

Molly stood up, too tired to take in his words. 'Goodnight, Ryan. I'm sure we can sort it all out tomorrow.' She finished her beer and took the bottle into the kitchen, calling, 'Sleep well,' over her shoulder.

As she padded through the hallway, she heard him call back, 'I sure will.'

* * *

Molly woke to the smell of cooking coming from the kitchen. The coffee filled her nostrils first, followed by the aroma of something frying in hot oil. She wriggled from her bed, pulled on a top and jeans and followed the scent, which became stronger as she approached the door. She rushed into the kitchen, cannoning into Ryan, who was standing with a spatula in his hand, wearing only Bermuda shorts. He offered her a warm smile.

'Morning, Molly. I was just about to wake you. I guess fried eggs over easy on wholemeal bread is okay for you. I know you Brits are partial to a cooked breakfast.'

'I'm starving.' Molly gazed at the hairy torso for a moment, taking in the deep tan, and helped herself to a mug of coffee from the pot. Ryan was piling food onto plates.

'Sit yourself down and I'll serve up. It's the least I could do for you after you let me stay last night.'

Molly looked at the food he had just placed in front of her: two eggs, perfectly cooked, the toast golden, a pat of butter melting in the centre. 'This is great. Thanks, Ryan.'

They ate in silence for a moment and then Molly said, 'So – where did you fly from yesterday? How come you got in so late?'

'Dubai,' Ryan said between mouthfuls. 'I'm based in New York, but I have business there. I'm in finance.'

'You must work hard. Do you travel a lot?'

'More than is good for my health.' Ryan rapped his bare chest with his fist. 'Of course, I should have retired ten years ago but Lupe is much younger than me and she has her work in fashion, so I kept going. After we split, I just kept working – it's my routine, I guess. I'm seventy-three – would you believe it?'

Molly nodded, then shook her head, thinking it might be more polite.

'I'm guessing you're much younger. Sixty? Late fifties?'

Molly stifled a grin and nodded again. He was clearly flattering her.

'Too much work takes its toll, though – it's about time I quit.'

'You haven't married again? I mean...'

'No, I haven't found the right woman to put up with me yet.

What about you, Molly?' His eyes met hers and Molly noticed they were hazel. 'You seem to be travelling alone…'

'I'm widowed.' Molly resorted to her usual explanation. 'I do things by myself now. After champagne, I'm not about to settle for flat lemonade.'

'Very wise.' Ryan chewed his toast thoughtfully, crumbs tumbling on his chest. 'But, do you know, I believe there's someone out there for us all. It's just about finding the right person. And who knows when they're going to arrive on your doorstep?'

Molly decided Ryan must be an optimist. An optimist who had just cooked great eggs and toast. And who was, in fact, quite good looking. She pushed away her plate and reached for the coffee. 'I wonder if you can help me, Ryan…'

'I'd be glad to…'

'Well, I just arrived here yesterday. I don't know the area at all yet, so… I'm not sure what to do with my spare time. I'm here for a few months. What are the best activities I can sign up for? I need… a project.'

'Do you speak Spanish?'

'*Un poco*,' Molly smiled. 'A bit. I started learning years ago when we first visited Spain. I've forgotten a lot of it – I seem to be out of practice.'

'You could take Spanish classes. There are salsa classes, cooking classes…'

Molly rolled her eyes. 'Mayan cookery?'

'Don't knock it.' Ryan grinned. 'The food round here is wonderful. Have you tried the mole?'

'Mole?'

'As in holy mole – it's a Mexican sauce they have on just about everything around here, and it's to die for.'

Molly shook her head. 'I'll certainly give it a go.' She gazed down at her empty plate, streaked with smears of egg yolk.

'Then there are boat tours around the coastline.'

'Boat tours...' Molly thought of Ronnie and Nell, wondering what they were doing now. She imagined them on the sun terrace, barbecuing steaks and drinking cocktails.

'There's a lot to do – places to eat, places to visit. You could take a speedboat ride, visit Xel Há Park and go snorkelling, visit the Mayan pyramid at Chichén Itzá. There's good horse-riding around here too, Western-style. Plenty to keep you busy.'

Molly's face filled with a broad grin. 'That all sounds wonderful.' She wriggled in her seat. 'I'm going to do all of that – except the horses.'

Ryan was looking at her steadily. 'Hey, I was wondering...' He rubbed his chin thoughtfully. 'I have a video conference with some guy in Dubai later on and I need to find myself a hotel for tonight but...' He scrutinised Molly's face, gauging her reaction. 'We could spend the afternoon together if you like. I could show you the area and we could drive along the coast for an hour or two. How would that be?'

Molly shrugged. 'If you wouldn't mind, it might be nice to get some local knowledge.'

'We have ourselves a date, then.' Ryan sat back in his seat and smiled, looking pleased with himself. He ran a hand through his neat dark hair. 'What do you say, Molly?'

Molly nodded slowly, taking in his neat beard, his broad chest and the twinkling hazel eyes. She hadn't intended to coax him to show her the sights but, now he had offered, she wondered if it had been in the back of her mind all the time.

'Yes, Ryan, I think we do.'

24

Monday 18th October

Well, I didn't expect to have an overnight guest last night. Ryan with the hairy chest, Guadalupe's ex. He seems really nice. He is handsome too, suave, and he has those serious hazel eyes. He has that cute way with him that R had, seemingly self-assured but with a kind of hidden vulnerability. And he is straightforward and direct, like R was. I oughtn't to get carried away, but I'm wondering if Ryan – another R – mightn't be an interesting prospect during my time in Mexico. Careful, Molly. Don't jump in! (Oh, what the hell...maybe I will.)

Molly was ready to go, lying in the hammock on the sun-drenched patio waiting for Ryan, who was still inside the apartment making video calls. She had showered, brushed her hair until it shone, and dressed in a fresh T-shirt and denim shorts. At first, she thought she looked inappropriately casual, but she told herself that she was fine and she should stop thinking about it, so she pushed the sunglasses on her face, a floppy hat on her head, and grinned at her image. She'd do.

The sun warmed her skin; she adjusted her position in the hammock and smiled; she was ready for their date.

She had been scribbling in the new Pokémon exercise book, jotting down her current thoughts. She read back what she had written.

Molly wondered if her diary entry was a little naive, like a silly teenager waiting for her first boyfriend to take her out. She thought about ripping out the first page and starting again, writing something more sensible, but she hesitated. Perhaps it was better to wait and see what the day would bring.

She heard steps behind her. Ryan was humming the tune to the Beach Boys' 'California Girls'. Well, not humming exactly: he was singing the tune in a chirpy 'bom-bom-bom' that showed he was cheerful, eager even. He placed a glass of orange liquid in Molly's hand as she pushed the Pokémon exercise book behind her back in the hammock and wriggled to a seated position, trying not to fall out.

'What's this?'

'Fresh orange juice. I just made it.'

'How?'

He grinned. 'Fresh oranges. Juicer.'

Molly took a sip. It was chilled and sweet. 'Lovely.' She met his eyes, her quizzical expression unreadable behind the sunglasses. 'So, you like the Beach Boys?'

Ryan squatted down next to her, his shorts rising up tanned thighs. 'That's my era, Molly. Flower power, the summer of love. You know, I even went to Monterey.'

'Did you?' Molly assumed he was talking about a pop festival. Somewhere in the back of her mind she remembered there had been one in the late sixties, although she'd either been dating Trevor then or changing Samantha's nappies.

'I saw Hendrix, Janis Joplin, the Who, the Grateful Dead,

Jefferson Airplane. The Beach Boys were going to play but they cancelled. I had a great time though. Living was easy in the sixties. I was a young buck. Girls were everywhere, with their long dresses and short dresses and flowers in their hair...' he grinned. 'Let's just say I had my share of good times in those days.'

'I bet you did. All those poor unsuspecting girls...' Molly's face became serious. 'It was such a long time ago though, Ryan – things are very different now. Are we ready to go?'

'Give me half an hour, will you, Molly? I have just one more call to make. It's a pretty big one, some guy back in Dubai, the guy I was talking to earlier this week. I shan't be too long.'

'What time is it?'

'Midday.' Ryan took the empty glass. 'We'll be on the road by one, I promise you.'

By two o'clock, Ryan was ready. He and Molly were in his white Mercedes motoring down a long road, the sea to their right. Molly was gazing out of the window marvelling at the deep blue stretch of the sea against the white powder sand. To their left were palm trees, and the occasional high-rise block of a hotel. Ryan was explaining about the vast number of activities Molly could do.

'There are jungle treks. You can hike for miles. They have guided tours. There's one hike where you go way deep into the forest. Plenty of wildlife, iguanas. Have you had your mosquito meds?'

'Yes, I'm up to date with everything.' Molly leaned back in her seat, imagining a trek through a sultry forest, brightly coloured parrots flying by.

'This one place, you climb to the top and then come down on a zip wire. Sounds like fun, eh?'

Molly glanced at Ryan and imagined them both in safety gear, thick gloves, heavy helmets, grinning at each other ready to take a zip wire ride down to the ground. She breathed out slowly. 'I'd certainly give that a go. I've never done it before.'

Ryan grunted. 'Rather you than me, Molly.' Behind the metal frames, his eyes were on the road. 'My days of taking my life in my hands are done. I'm not sure it would be good for me, given my stress levels.'

Molly closed her eyes, thinking of the excitement of whizzing down on a zip wire, hurtling towards a rain forest, either side of her a blurred line of passing foliage, the screeches of birds and monkeys in her ears. She nodded slowly. 'I'd definitely give it a try.'

'You seem to me to be that sort of woman, Molly,' Ryan laughed. 'A woman who enjoys a good time. One who takes a risk now and then.'

'Oh, absolutely.' Molly nodded. 'That's me.'

Ryan smiled. 'I'm impressed that you don't let being a bit older slow you down. I used to play a lot of ball games when I was younger; I played ice hockey and baseball at college.' He paused and then turned his handsome face to her. 'So, you like sports?'

'I swim a bit.' She thought for a moment. 'I liked gymnastics at school. I'm still very flexible.'

He accelerated to pass an enormous coach. 'And you've been married, Molly? You're a widow now?'

'That's right.' Molly turned her head to look at a wide curve of coastline, azure water and soft sand, and wondered when they'd stop. She had brought sunscreen and half an hour or so on a beach would have been perfect. Perhaps Ryan had somewhere in mind that he was taking her to.

'I've been married three times myself. My first wife Peggy was fantastic, a great mom to my kids and a great cook. My second wife Shelley was okay but she had a temper. Then I met Lupe and she was gonna be the one for ever.' He sighed. 'Or so I thought. Sadly, it didn't turn out that way.'

Molly raised her eyebrows. 'You've had a lot of wives.'

'I'm sure we've both had plenty of lovers in our time.' He turned his head to smile. 'You're a stunning woman. You remind me of Frida Kahlo.'

Molly wrinkled her nose. Hadn't Guadalupe said something about her ex saying she reminded him of Frida Kahlo? She decided to ask. 'So, what do you like about Frida?'

'She was a free spirit,' Ryan observed, overtaking a truck. 'Like you.'

'Where are we going?' Molly asked. She'd noticed they'd been driving for a long time and it was time to find out.

'I thought we'd have a tour round the coastline, a nice drive. We'll stop for a coffee in a little place in the next town then I thought we'd head back.'

Molly raised her eyebrows. 'Oh.' She gazed at the beach and imagined walking, swimming or sunbathing, basking in a cooling breeze.

'Then I thought we'd go to a hotel in Cancún, the one I'll book into for the rest of my stay. I thought we could have dinner there.' He shrugged. 'If you'd let me buy you dinner – as a way of saying thanks for letting me stay over last night.'

Molly was bored with sitting in a car: she didn't need to think twice about her answer. 'Yes, please, Ryan. Dinner would be lovely.'

'Swell,' he replied and swung the car into a side road towards a little town where, he said, they served some of the best coffee in Mexico.

* * *

They were sitting at a solitary table in the gardens of a huge white hotel in Cancún, watching a waiter in a dinner jacket pour wine into their glasses. The heavy scent of blooms filled the air. Not far away, beyond the swimming pool and the beach, the last rays of the sun were dipping into the sea, spattering turquoise with drizzles of pink and orange. Ryan pushed his sunglasses back onto his head and smiled, lifting his glass. 'To you, Molly, and to your wonderful company.'

Molly raised her glass and chinked it against his. She wasn't sure how she had been such good company. She had been sitting quietly in the car for most of the afternoon apart from the stop they'd made at a brightly painted café, where Ryan had spoken perfect Spanish and they'd made small talk and drunk from little silver cups. It had been a spectacular drive back; the scenery had been stunning but she'd hoped for a place to stop where she might stretch her legs and walk on the beach.

Ryan was pleasant company and it would have been nice to talk to him, but he drove quite quickly so Molly hadn't initiated conversation too often. She had wanted to find out about him, about his work in New York, about his hobbies, his views on politics and culture, travel and music. She knew he liked the Beach Boys and women but very little else about his life.

Ryan exhaled, indicating the sunset with his wine glass. 'Look over at the ocean. That's spectacular, isn't it?'

'It's magnificent.'

He grinned. 'I bet it's a while since you had dinner with a guy while watching the sun set.'

'Last month, actually.' Molly recalled Ronnie and the *Pulpo Azul*. Ryan looked disappointed so she added, 'This is nicer though. I was in a fish restaurant in Spain with a friend.'

'You are quite a woman,' Ryan observed, raising his eyebrows.

The food arrived, a dish of enchiladas with mole sauce, and

Molly's eyes grew wide with the first mouthful. 'This is incredible, Ryan: it's so delicious – spicy – that will be the chillies, velvety... what else can I taste?'

'Mole for Molly.' Ryan was delighted. 'Chocolate. That's the special ingredient here. I'm a huge fan of mole – you can get all different sorts, black, green, *almendrado, de olla, huaxmole*. I love the stuff. And of course, the best mole is in Mexico. That's one of the reasons I keep coming back. And this restaurant does great mole.'

Molly licked her lips. 'I love it.'

Ryan was watching her, his fork poised in the air. 'You have such *joie de vivre*. It's very contagious.' His eyes shone. 'And very attractive.'

Molly met his eyes and then went back to eating her food. She chewed thoughtfully for a moment and then pushed her plate away, glancing over her shoulder and towards the ocean. Beyond the dark leaves of the palm trees the sun was a pin prick of yellow, the sky above blasted with orange and blue; the sea was smooth and shimmering with gold.

'I need to ask you something, Molly.'

Her thoughts drifted back to reality and she turned her gaze on Ryan, who was watching her thoughtfully. 'Anything.'

'I can't work you out. You're an enigma.'

'Am I?' Molly raised an eyebrow.

'Yeah – you're very confident and happy. I like that a lot. It's very sexy but...'

'But?'

'You can be a little aloof, lost in your own thoughts.'

'Oh, sorry, Ryan. No. I'm fine, really.'

'I was thinking, Molly, I mean – you and I get on and we're single and we like each other...'

'And...?' Molly frowned.

'I wondered if you'd sleep with me tonight.'

Molly stared at him. 'The thought hadn't entered my head, to be honest.'

Ryan leaned across the table and took her hand. 'We've had a great evening. It would be the perfect way to end it.'

'No, Ryan, I won't sleep with you.' Molly pulled her hand away, somewhat taken aback. 'I don't know whether to be offended or to be impressed by your honesty.'

'I just thought I'd ask.' Ryan shrugged. 'Nothing ventured, nothing gained. I really didn't mean to offend.'

'As long as we understand each other.' Molly met his eyes. She wondered at Ryan's past: he clearly hadn't encountered much resistance from women. She thought it was about time he did. She took a breath. 'I agreed to have dinner with you, but sex is clearly not on the table.' She put a hand over her mouth to stop the splutter of laughter as she saw his shocked expression.

'Right,' Ryan exhaled slowly. 'I think I've been told where I stand. Thank you, Molly.'

Molly nodded. 'Okay. Well, I'm glad we've cleared that up.'

'I hope we're still friends.' Ryan raised an eyebrow. 'I hope we can still take a drive sometimes, hang out, meet up for dinner...'

'Of course.' Molly's eyes twinkled. 'You're good company when you don't try to be Casanova all the time. You need to remember that we're not living in the sixties now, Ryan. It's not very flattering to be asked for sex like that – I felt like an after-dinner mint.'

'I'm so sorry if I got things wrong.' Ryan couldn't help grinning. 'You say things so directly. I think you're quite a lady, though.'

Inside the hotel a band had started to play: trumpets rang out, guitars jangled, drums thrummed: it was a lively salsa tune. A smooth male voice was singing in Spanish. Molly moved her shoulders in time with the beat. Ryan reached out and rested his hand on top of her arm.

'Would you like to dance?'

Molly shook her head. 'Oh, I'm not much of a dancer.'

'Just as friends? To show me you're not offended by my crazy and inappropriate suggestion.' His face was optimistic. He tugged at her hand. 'Come on, Molly. We have the moonlight, the sea breeze, the music. What more do we need?'

'All right – as long as you know the rules.'

'I sure do – I promise.'

He took her hand and manoeuvred her away from the table, then put an arm around her waist and linked the fingers of his other hand through hers. They swayed slowly to the rhythm. Then Ryan increased his pressure on Molly's waist, pulling her in towards his body and they moved as one. Molly breathed in the smell of him, the warm scent of nutmeg, and realised how pleasant it was to be held firmly, to be dancing close to a man, her hand on his shoulder while he guided her with skilful steps to the music. She knew he would never become a lover, but as a friend and certainly as a dance partner he was useful to have around. Ryan spoke Spanish well, he knew the local area, and she felt safer out in the evening with someone else. She had made the terms of their friendship clear and he was now being polite and respectful.

Bright lights shone from the hotel and soft coloured beams had been switched on around the pool. Molly and Ryan danced alone, their pace much slower than the fast beat of salsa, and Molly wished for a moment that she could dance well. She imagined herself whirling under his raised arm, twirling and bending, her skirt flaring out as she swivelled.

The tune came to an end and they stood still, his arms holding her in a dance position. He murmured into her ear. 'Shall I take you back to Lupe's apartment?'

'That would be nice, Ryan.'

'There's a vacant room for me here...' In the darkness his eyes glimmered. 'That is, unless...'

She met his gaze directly, her mouth firm. 'Unless?'

Ryan took a breath. 'We get on well, Molly. How about I just stay in Lupe's room? I promise I won't come on to you again. We could share food bills. I could give you half your rent back. And I have my car. We could go out for odd days when I'm not working, like we did today. We could have dinner, hang out together.' He looked hopeful. 'What do you think?'

'I think it's a great idea, Ryan.' The words were out of her mouth before she'd had time to consider them. The extra money from the reimbursed rent would be handy. He was pleasant company. It was nice having someone around in the flat and she'd certainly feel more secure at night-time. They seemed to get on well enough and it could be useful having an expert at hand who knew the area. Besides, he knew the rules now: there would be no chance of any dalliance between them. She nodded. 'Yes, I think we could make that work.'

'Swell.' Ryan wrapped a protective arm around her. 'It's getting chilly now. Shall we head back home?'

'Great,' Molly breathed. 'And now I'm so tired I could sleep and sleep.'

Molly let him lead her towards the car park around the front of the hotel. She could still hear the waves behind them, whispering as they rolled onto the beach and then away again. The sky was indigo now and the moon was low, a flat copper disc. She gazed up at Ryan and grinned: she had a flatmate, transport and more money to spend. Now she could start to enjoy Mexico. And a plan had crept into her head. She knew exactly what she was going to do first thing tomorrow.

25

———

Tuesday 19th October

I have a new flatmate – the lovely Ryan. I think we get on well as friends, but that's all. Now I'll have more money to spend and someone bustling around the place so that I don't feel lonely, and he knows the best places to go in the area. Perfect. I'm settling into Mexico. And today I'm going to start a brand-new project.

Molly had gone straight to bed and slept soundly. In the morning, she had showered, dressed in a flowing skirt and a colourful top and sauntered into the kitchen where Ryan was sitting looking at his computer and drinking orange juice, wearing only purple boxer shorts. He'd wished her a cheery good morning, his face innocent and relaxed as if he hadn't propositioned her the night before, and she'd poured herself a glass, gazed once at the tangle of hair on his torso, refused the cooked breakfast he said he was about to make for them both and cheerily told him she'd see him later. She stepped out into sunlight that was so bright it made her blink. She pulled on sunglasses, a wide-brimmed hat and headed for the shops.

She vaguely remembered seeing the sign somewhere near Sally's Silver Shop on the corner. She'd remembered the name of the place because it had seemed so incongruous next to an English-sounding trinket shop. She paused to look in the window at the jewellery and wondered whether to treat herself. There were beautiful dangling silver earrings, many shaped like shells and stars. Molly gazed at charm bracelets, necklaces with crucifixes, filigree hearts, and ornate silver rings with huge gemstones. She looked at the prices and translated pesos into pounds. The jewellery wasn't cheap, but it was well-made. She noticed a woman inside, her face smartly made-up, auburn hair piled high. She might be the shop owner, Sally, but she was almost certainly Mexican.

She turned the corner into another street and there it was, beyond several shops, up a small flight of stone steps. The white building had a blue door and the sign '*Ritmo*' above in black italic lettering, with a design showing a man and woman together connected at the hands, their feet flailing. She took a breath, climbed the steps and rang the bell. She was about to ring again when a woman answered. She was tall, slim, probably in her thirties, her jet-black hair twisted in a long ponytail. She wore black leggings and a black vest and looked very professional. Molly had prepared what she was going to say, so she launched in optimistically.

'*Quisiero aprender bailar.*'

The woman frowned. 'American?'

Molly offered her warmest smile. '*Inglesa*. English.'

'You want to learn to dance, yes?'

'Yes... please.'

The woman looked at her face, at her clothes, her sandals and then back to her face. 'What dance do you want to learn?'

Molly hadn't been prepared for the question, so she simply replied, 'Salsa.'

'I'm not sure if my father has spaces left for one-to-one tuition.'

'Oh.'

'There might be some space in a group.' The woman turned over her shoulder and shouted something in Spanish. There was a pause, then a brief reply from a male voice somewhere up high in the building. The woman indicated with her head. 'You can come up.'

Molly followed the woman up another flight of stairs, noticing her easy, lithe movements and the way her glossy pony-tail swung behind her. As Molly held up the hemline of her long skirt and struggled to keep up, she was wondering if the dance idea had been such a good one after all.

She followed the woman into a huge, brightly lit hall lined with mirrors. She was conscious of her reflection as she shuffled behind the woman in leggings who had a spring in her step. A slim man was seated on the floor in the corner looking at a book, his legs stretched in front of him. Molly thought he must be a little younger than her, possibly in his sixties. He leaped to his feet and smiled a greeting, holding out a hand.

'*Buenos dias, Señora*. I am Alejandro Estaban. You have met my daughter, Rosa Maria. Welcome to our little school, *Ritmo*. It means rhythm. You want to learn to dance? We do many dances here: salsa, mambo, merengue, rumba, bachata, bomba and plena.'

Molly met his eyes and smiled. He was tall and very hand-some. His hair, which must once have been as black as his daugh-ter's, was now greying, straight and glossy in a fringe and over his ears. He had deep-set sparkling eyes. His smile was warm and sincere.

'Salsa, I think...' she stammered.

'I do one-to-one lessons but there are no spaces left, I am afraid. But there is a group of seven beginners who meet on Wednesday afternoons and I can take one more student to make the number even. It is not salsa, though. It is bachata.'

Molly nodded as if she understood, but she had no idea. 'What is bachata?'

Alejandro smiled again. 'Bachata is a little slower than salsa. It is a three-step with a Cuban hip motion, followed by a tap on the fourth beat. Bachata is a very sensual dance.'

Molly held her breath for a moment. 'Will I be able to do it? I mean, I'm not particularly good at dancing. I might hold everyone back.'

Rosa Maria gave a little snort behind her father's shoulder. Alejandro's smile broadened. 'No, I don't think so. Most people in the class are new to the dance. We try to go at each person's pace so you will be fine, I think. The class costs four hundred and fifty pesos for an hour and a half.'

Molly nodded. 'That sounds good.' She counted on her fingers. That was about eighteen pounds, maybe less. She could afford that easily, certainly now that Ryan was going to reimburse half of her rent. She imagined having dinner in the hotel garden in Cancún with Ryan, music bubbling from inside the building; she'd whisk him to his feet and surprise him with the sensual steps of the bachata. She'd be able to dance with other partners and meet new people. She glanced again at Alejandro's face, at the shining dark eyes that promised mystery, and thought it might be quite pleasant to dance with him too. She hoped he hadn't read her mind.

'So, two o'clock tomorrow afternoon, *Señora*. For the first session, I only charge half price. Two twenty-five pesos. In case you don't like it enough to want to come back.' His grin was mischievous.

'Oh, I'm sure I will,' Molly replied, her face enthusiastic. 'I'm looking forward to learning.'

'Wear comfortable clothing, please. If you can, leggings and a T-shirt are best. We will work quite hard but you can rest when you need to.'

Molly glanced at Alejandro, lightly built, his slender frame in dark top and leggings. He looked very professional and incredibly fit. 'I'll see you tomorrow, *Señor...*'

'Alejandro,' he prompted. 'And your name, *Señora?*'

'Molly Mitchell. Just Molly is fine. Molly.' Molly could hear herself gabbling.

Alejandro took her hand in his nimble fingers, squeezing it briefly. 'That is good. *Hasta mañana* then, Molly. We begin at two o'clock.'

'Great. That's great. I'll see you then, Alejandro. Thank you. *Hasta mañana.*'

Molly scurried away, down the stairs and into the sunshine and breathed out a huge puff of air. She had done it – she had booked herself some dance lessons and with a very interesting teacher. She hoped that tomorrow was going to be a good day, and that she wouldn't make a fool of herself in the dance class. All she needed to do now was to find a clothing shop and buy herself some suitable leggings to dance in.

When she arrived back at the apartment carrying a bag stuffed with three pairs of leggings and some colourful T-shirts, Ryan was waiting for her, his brow furrowed.

'Hi. I was worried you'd moved out.'

'No, I – I've been shopping.'

'It's past two,' Ryan told her. 'I was hoping you'd be back soon.

I have a little something for you here.' He handed her a brown envelope. 'It's all in pesos. I figured you'd spend it while you were here, but I can always change it back...' Seeing her puzzled expression, he added. 'My contribution to your rent. You've been kind enough to let me stay. I mean, it's not your fault my ex-wife rented our home out to you without consulting me, so it's only fair I show my appreciation.'

Molly beamed at him. 'Thanks, Ryan.'

'And I wondered if you'd eaten since breakfast – you only had a glass of juice.'

Molly hadn't eaten: her stomach had been growling all the way back to the apartment. She shook her head.

'Then I have a treat for you,' Ryan raised his eyebrows. 'We'll walk down to a great little place in town. It's a tapas bar. I know you said you're into your healthy foods. Well, it does really cool tapas. It's called *Sabores*. It's only been open a couple months.'

Molly rushed into her bedroom, threw her bags of shopping on her unmade bed and reappeared in seconds. 'Tapas and healthy eating?' She laughed. 'Then I'm ready to go. Lead on, Ryan.'

26

Tuesday 19th October

Rang Vanessa and told her all about dancing the bachata. She was so thrilled to hear about the teacher Alejandro. Of course, I let her know how talented and sexy he is. I rang Samantha, who listened to me chattering and said she'd love to learn to dance, which quite surprised me. Then I rang Nell and told her the same thing. She was a bit quiet. Hope she's not overdoing things.

Molly was nibbling a little savoury biscuit topped with cream cheese and salmon, watching Ryan who was watching the owner of the tapas bar. A slim Mexican woman in her late thirties or early forties was busily rushing around serving drinks to customers and fetching plates of food, bending over in tight jeans. Every time she turned her back or leaned over the bar, Ryan tipped himself forward on his bar stool and raised his eyebrows. Molly gave him a gentle nudge with her elbow. He glanced at her apologetically, as if he'd forgotten she was there. 'Molly?'

'She seems like a nice woman.' Molly met his eyes.

Ryan scratched his beard. 'Can I help it if I admire pretty women?' He shrugged. 'I like women, Molly. I always have. It's been my downfall.'

Molly munched her biscuit. 'I like men but I don't ogle them.' She thought for a moment about Alejandro Estaban, how handsome he had looked, and she hoped she hadn't flirted with him in the dance studio. 'It can be quite unpleasant, being stared at, you know – intimidating.'

'Oh, I do hope I'm not intimidating.' Ryan's eyes were wide with apology. 'Women used to find my attentions flattering. Do you think that's different now I'm older?'

'I think maybe it's because times have changed, Ryan. You need to change with them. This isn't the swinging sixties. You can't really expect women to fall at your feet just because you want them to.' She thought for a moment. 'It was a tough time for women then.'

'What, all that free love and flower power? Women didn't like that? You're kidding me.'

Ryan seemed horrified, so Molly reached for her beer and explained. 'Women like to be admired for the person they are, not just for how well their jeans fit.'

Ryan nodded slowly, as if it was a difficult maths problem he was attempting to solve.

The woman approached Molly with a plate of different tapas and smiled. 'Would you like to try?'

'What do we have here?' Molly glanced at the plate. The tapas were certainly unusual for Mexican fare and she'd never seen anything quite like them in Spain: there was a Scotch egg, divided in half, slices of salami, beetroot-coloured chorizo.

The woman placed the plate down. 'Try. Tell me what you think. These are really popular.'

Molly nibbled the Scotch egg tentatively. The crunchy coating and savoury filling were delicious. Ryan had eaten the chorizo and had started on the salami. He leaned forward and offered the woman a suave smile. 'These are the most delicious tapas I've ever had. Did you make them? This is the best place in town.'

The woman's face shone with delight. She had soft chocolate-coloured eyes under a thick golden-brown fringe, her long hair tied back. 'And the egg?'

'Incredible.' Molly wiped her mouth with a paper napkin. 'Really tasty.'

'And no meat or eggs.' The woman seemed pleased with herself.

'I don't believe it.' Ryan was interested. 'I just had the best chorizo ever.'

The woman's dark eyes glowed with happiness. 'All the tapas here are plant-based.'

'How come?' Molly immediately thought of Richie, how he'd have loved this tapas bar; how he'd have wanted to eat there every day. But he'd have spoken to the woman in Spanish: the owner was chatting easily in perfect English. She smiled at Molly.

'I'm so glad you like it. The egg is tofu – the yellow yolk part is coloured with turmeric. The chorizo and salami are made from wheat gluten.'

'And the salmon and cheese?' Molly asked.

'Salmon is ribbons of carrot marinated for days in seaweed liquid. The cream cheese is from cashew nuts.'

'I don't believe it,' Ryan enthused. 'I honestly couldn't tell the difference.'

'Much healthier for you,' Molly advised him and then she turned to the woman. 'What else do you have?'

'My chef and I are constantly working on new things. He comes up with new ideas – he is a genius. He is training a new chef too so we can have more dishes. Our next dish will be mini tacos filled with shredded jackfruit and a mole sauce.'

'I love mole.' Ryan's interest was increasing by the second.

'I'll definitely come back for some of that,' Molly promised. 'This is a great place you have here.' She looked around at the bar; several people were seated at wooden tables; there were bright red curtains at the windows, brown wooden floorboards. It was a humble place lit by storm lamps in alcoves in the wall. Jazz music bubbled in the background. Molly thought briefly that the place didn't seem Mexican at all.

'I want this place to work.' The woman leaned on the bar. 'I've been back in Puerto Palacio for eight months. My chef has been here for three months and we've been open here for two – we work together on new dishes each week with Javi, our trainee. I'm hoping to incorporate some sweet things into the menu too – some chocolate mousse made with aquafaba, some tiramisu and French-style pastries filled with cashew cream.'

Molly licked her lips. 'It sounds like my kind of place.'

The woman thrust out her hand. 'I'm Liliana. Pleased to meet you. I'm so glad you like my little café.'

Molly shook her hand. 'I'm Molly.'

'Ryan Stone.' Ryan leaned over the bar. 'From New York.'

'Pleased to meet you,' Liliana said before turning her gaze back to Molly. 'You are English?'

'Yes.'

'Where are you from?'

Molly realised she hadn't thought about home in a long time. 'Somerset. In the south-west.' She frowned, surprised at how she felt no feelings of homesickness. She knew she'd go back there sometime but, other than hugs with Crumper, she missed very little about it.

'I worked in London for a long time.' Liliana smiled. 'I trained in a big hotel there – that's where I met my chef, Kristof. He taught me everything I know.'

'You'd like New York,' Ryan insisted. 'We have some great hotels there.'

'Oh, yes,' Liliana agreed. 'I have worked there. Kristof too. I took over this place from my mother – she isn't able to work now. It used to be a little café with drinks and now I have made it into a tapas bar. I wanted to try something new. Healthy eating is something I am interested in, and it's becoming more popular all the time. Everything we make here is just the same as the dishes you'd find all over the world but – no dairy, meat or fish.'

Molly was impressed. 'You are doing brilliantly.'

Liliana had an idea. 'Would you like to try a fennel breadstick with chilli dip? Or how about a canapé filled with walnut pâté? We perfected the recipe just last week.'

'I'll try everything you've got to offer,' Ryan suggested with a wink, and Molly frowned at him. His intentions were becoming far too obvious. As Liliana walked across the bar, she could see Ryan noting every movement of her jeans. She returned, placing a plate of small nibbles between them. 'Enjoy.'

She was about to walk away when Ryan called out, 'I'd enjoy it so much more if you'd have dinner with me.'

Liliana glanced over her shoulder. 'I am already in a relationship. The chef and I are an item.' Her face was fierce. 'Stay there with your wife. She is too good for you.'

Ryan grinned and indicated Molly. 'Oh, she's not my wife. She's just the woman I live with.'

Molly glanced at Ryan. His dismissive words had struck a sharp note. He was right – she was a guest staying in the spare room in his apartment, just as Nell had come to stay in her home months ago. The thought left her feeling suddenly spare, unwanted. Although she had desperately needed to travel and she was enjoying being in Mexico, she felt isolated – a visitor in her own life, looking in from the outside at a woman making the best effort to enjoy herself. Molly forced a smile and reached for a canapé.

Molly was lying on her bed, an orange juice and a sandwich on the bedside table. Ryan had taken himself out for dinner. Molly hadn't wanted to go with him – she'd eaten her fill of tapas several hours ago and, since she'd returned, a strange feeling of solitude was settling on her, making her feel distinctly uncomfortable. She had her diary open and was attempting to compose her thoughts. Now she felt anxious, a strange fear squeezing the breath from her lungs. She wasn't sure what was making her feel apprehensive. She wrote slowly, examining every sentence.

Tuesday 19th October

Tomorrow is the first dance class. I should be looking forward to it. I thought I'd just be able to pick up a difficult new dance. Now I'm really not sure it's for me at all.

She paused and felt a sadness squat on her shoulders, pressing her down. She tried again.

I'm worried about going to the class. I usually like meeting new people but now I feel strangely nervous.

Ryan's constant flirting in the tapas bar has left me feeling past my sell-by date, I suppose. I hadn't really stopped to think about that until now. He was only interested in me because he's single and a bit desperate. Ronnie was the same. Ryan and Ronnie are nice men but they're not relationship material

*for me. That's my problem – no one can ever be. So, I'm alone
and I've constantly told myself that I'm happy alone because I
know I'll always be alone now. And yet the honest truth is – I'm
starting to feel that something is missing.*

Molly reread her words. She'd hadn't written so much in a
long time: she was airing her feelings on the page. She put a hand
to her face and discovered, to her surprise, that there were tears
on her cheeks.

Here she was in Mexico, rootless, adrift, by herself. It would
be nice to have someone special to spend time with, to laugh
with, to share things with.

It came to her in a lightning bolt of loss and bitterness and
suddenly she was sobbing. She needed another Richie but, of
course, she'd never find anyone like him again. She'd dated
Ronnie for the company. That was why she'd readily agreed to
have dinner with Ryan too, why she was so glad to invite him to
stay at Guadalupe's apartment. Now she felt awkward about
dancing in front of others in the bachata class with Alejandro
Estaban, whom she had only met once: he was unfamiliar, a
stranger, and she knew he was bound to be unimpressed by her
efforts and she'd feel humiliated.

She told herself she was being silly. She was alone, feeling
raw, exposed, that was the truth of it and the sudden knowledge
hurt. Molly sobbed into the pillow, realising that she hadn't cried
since Richie had died and now she wasn't just crying because she
missed him, she was crying because she missed the warmth of
another human being, someone who would love her. She was
crying for herself.

Nell had found it easy to find love again. Phil had been
quickly replaced by Ronnie, who was kind and good-natured. But
Ronnie didn't have what Molly needed. She asked herself what it

was, the elusive thing her soul yearned for in another human being, something that wasn't there in all the Ronnies and the Ryans. Would she recognise it if she found it? Would she ever find it? She was seventy years old, and women of her age didn't usually find a soulmate, did they?

It was unfair that older men weren't the same as older women – they were still allowed to be attractive, to seek a younger woman who would value their age, their experience, their silver fox looks. Guadalupe was much younger than Ryan; the evidence was obvious: she had been his third wife. Phil had been the same: he had Nikki and a baby on the way. But Molly would be alone for ever. It would have been better if she hadn't realised it but, by coming away on holiday by herself, by writing her thoughts and feelings in a diary, it had hit her in the face like a splash of cold water: she was truly lonely.

Molly left the sandwich and orange juice on the bedside cabinet, wriggled out of her clothes and slid between the covers, shivering. She hadn't cleaned her teeth, washed her face or brushed her hair. It didn't matter.

She hugged the pillow and sobbed again. Tomorrow, she decided, it would be better not to go to the dance class. Alejandro Estaban and the others would probably laugh at her clumsiness as she tried to dance the bachata. She'd never dance with anyone again, so what was the point? The best times of her life were in the past now. At least this way she wouldn't be a failure.

The pillow was damp and still Molly wept, feeling wretched. Darkness slinked into every corner, filling the room with ice cold air. She let herself cry for another twenty minutes and then, wrapping her arms around herself, she fell into a deep sleep.

27

Wednesday 20th October

The dance class has been booked for today. To go or not to go, that is the question. I'm not really feeling my usual enthusiasm. But I'm here in Mexico, and it would be a shame to miss out. Come on, Molly – you can do this. Pull yourself together and put your best left foot forward.

Molly sat on the edge of the bed staring at her phone. It was past midday. She had been thinking about how she felt for the last hour. She didn't want to go back to England. The cottage didn't feel like home. It was just the house she lived in by herself, after Richie. But she missed something about the familiarity of the people, something reassuringly solid and safe.

She thought about Spain. She missed Nell and thought about ringing her for a chat. She knew everyone in Spain and in England would still be asleep; the time difference put them several hours ahead of her in Mexico. She pictured Nell and Ronnie, slumbering together in each other's arms in the *finca*;

Jack and Mel would be tucked up in her bed with Crumper purring by their feet; Samantha would be in the farm with her husband, the wind rattling the thin window panes. Molly felt a sudden need to connect with the people who knew her. She texted a short message to Nell, hoping she was well, explaining how much fun it was to be in Mexico and that she hoped they could catch up soon. She copied it, then sent exactly the same message to Samantha and to Vanessa. She sniffed and practised deep breathing for a moment: she felt a little better than she had last night, a bit more like her old self again.

She could smell coffee brewing. Ryan was bumping around in the kitchen, making lunch. She hoped he'd go out soon. She wasn't sure why she wanted to be by herself this morning; it seemed at odds with her feelings of loneliness. But she guessed that he'd be excessively cheerful; he might invite her to spend time with him and she didn't feel particularly sociable. She glanced down at her legs in the gold and black leggings, at the T-shirt that swamped her. She'd go to the dance class, just once; Alejandro Estaban had said the first session was half price, so she'd force herself to turn up and try it, so that she could at least say that she hadn't backed out. But she wouldn't go a second time.

Half an hour later, there was no sound in the apartment and Molly assumed that the coast was clear. She grabbed her handbag and tiptoed through the kitchen into the lounge. Ryan was reclining on the leather sofa, all tanned hairy chest and black boxers, legs sprawled in front of him, his phone in his hand. He met her eyes cheerily, covering the mouthpiece with his palm and whispered. 'Hey, Molly – I wasn't sure what you were up to. I'd have made you some lunch.'

'Oh, thanks – no – I'm going out – I'll get something later.'

Ryan rolled his eyes and began to speak into his phone with

hurried enthusiasm. 'Oh no, not at all. Yeah, honey, sure I'm still out in the Middle East. Yeah, of course I'll let you know... Christmas? No plans at all, not yet...'

Molly raised her hand in goodbye. He gestured to her to wait, breathing quickly. 'Yeah, honey, sure I will, yeah. Yeah, I'll phone you when I know when I'm finished. Yeah, so long.' He hung up and turned desperate eyes towards Molly. 'That was Lupe.'

'From New York? Is she all right?' Molly asked breezily.

'Yeah, she was asking me about something to do with her solicitor and the divorce – it's not final yet – but I didn't tell her I was here, staying in the apartment, with you.'

'Why not?'

Ryan's face was troubled. 'She'd go crazy. She thinks I'm still in Dubai. She was asking me what I'm doing for Christmas, I guess because she wants to come here and she's checking out that I don't intend to be here at the same time.' He shrugged sadly. 'I annoy her.'

Molly was sympathetic. 'How come you two aren't divorced yet?'

He sighed. 'Well, I guess we're too busy arguing – we haven't gotten round to it. We've been apart for almost a year now. She threw me out after a New Year party went a little awry last year. She said I was flirting and she was furious and I guess I'd just pushed her too far once too often.'

'What did you do?' Molly put her hands on her hips.

'I just – well, we were at a big party and there was drink and mistletoe and dancing and this young woman put her arms around me so, I guess I just reciprocated. I'm a fool.'

Molly rolled her eyes. 'Big mistake.'

Ryan nodded. 'I tried everything – apologies, flowers, jewellery, but Lupe wasn't having any of it.'

'What would she say if she knew you were here?'

Ryan sighed. 'Well, it's technically our apartment but... Lupe has a low opinion of me now – she thinks I'm a louse, she even called me that, and she won't meet me face to face to talk, even though I've tried. She said she doesn't want our paths to cross ever again. I have to talk to her on the phone.' He grimaced. 'But I need a break from working and I've always been able to relax here. Besides...' He grinned at Molly. 'You're good fun to hang out with.'

Molly didn't feel as if she was good fun, but she forced a cheery grin. 'Well, I'm going out now. Maybe we can have a beer later and share some supper.'

He nodded. 'Great. I have a few calls to make this afternoon then I'm done. I'll make us something to eat in, around six.'

'I'll see you later, then.'

Molly shrugged her bag on her shoulder. Outside, it was quite cool and she wished she'd brought a jacket but the dancing would be energetic and she'd soon warm up. She asked herself how she felt, if she was looking forward to learning the bachata. She realised sadly that she felt nothing at all; she was just a little numb and with no expectations. She told herself that was no bad thing – at least she wouldn't be disappointed. Molly wrinkled her nose and hoped the sunny weather would return soon and with it her almost unfaltering optimism.

She walked quickly through the centre of town, turning into the narrow street at the corner of Sally's Silver Shop, stopping at the stairs to look up at the dance studio, *Ritmo*. A window was open on the first floor where she assumed the dancing would take place, and lively guitar music floated onto the street. Molly frowned – it wasn't quite two o'clock, but the class had started. She rushed up the stairs and into the studio.

Five people were standing in a half circle on the hard floor watching two couples dancing in the centre. Molly recognised Alejandro Estaban, slim and tall in tight-fitting dark clothes, swaying with a young woman who was probably in her twenties. She was slender, wearing a crop top and red leggings, a sweatshirt tied around her waist, her hair in a ponytail. His daughter Rosa Maria was wearing a short skirt and a dark top, dancing with a young man in a yellow T-shirt and black jogging bottoms who wiggled his shoulders excessively, his feet clumsy and heavy on the floorboards. The other three dancers moved their bodies easily towards each other and away, sinewy snake-like movements, provocatively linking hands, moving their bodies forward and back with a flick of a hip.

Molly watched, magnetised; through the speakers, voices sang a chorus over the strumming guitars. She heard the words *amor* and *besito a besito* repeatedly. Love, kisses: it was clearly a flirtatious song, a dance intended to seduce and attract, peacocking dancers with their arms in the air, their eyes locked and their shoulders and hips making their intentions clear. Molly's eyes were fastened on Alejandro as he cavorted and swayed. His attitude was one of a man completely confident in his wooing of the young woman; he could lure her and seduce her and she, quite clearly, was able to flirt and tantalise him. Molly knew it was just a dance, but Alejandro was hypnotic, twirling the young woman beneath his arm and staring at her in an alluring manner.

Suddenly, the music ended: the dancers stopped, their expressions neutral again; they held hands briefly and gave a respectful little bow to their partners. The audience applauded with appreciation and Alejandro said something in Spanish that was so fast Molly didn't understand a word of it. He turned to her as she stood in the doorway clutching her handbag.

'Molly, hello. Welcome. *Benvenido.* Come and join the group. Everyone, this is Molly.' He translated into Spanish easily and the other group members nodded in her direction, smiling. A woman ran towards her and grasped her hand, yelling with enthusiasm.

'Oh, thank God – another woman and someone who speaks English. You can dance with me.'

Molly looked at the woman who, by her accent, was American. She was about Molly's age, petite in navy leggings and a pretty pink top, with honey-coloured hair in a sleek bob and perfect make-up. Her voice resonated with confidence and enthusiasm. 'I'm Betty Henderson. I'm so pleased to meet you.'

'Molly Mitchell.'

Her hand was in Molly's, cool and dry. She smiled warmly. 'Can you dance? I'm still trying to get the hang of the bachata. I have two left feet. No one really wants to dance with me – I trip over everyone. Of course, Alejandro's a wonderful teacher. You'll have to be the man – you're taller than I am.'

Molly glanced over her shoulder. The other dancers were forming pairs. Betty followed her gaze, still chattering. 'Oh, you'll like the gang here. Most of them don't speak a lot of English but Alejandro always translates everything just for me. Do you see the couple over there? They've been married for centuries. They never dance with anyone else, only each other.'

She pointed out a couple at least in their eighties, who were facing each other and holding hands, practising the movements slowly. Betty indicated two middle-aged women in the corner who were taking off their sweatshirts and swinging their arms to loosen up. 'Those two are Carmen and Ana. They are making good progress – they were so hesitant when they first arrived; and the couple you saw partnering Alejandro and Rosa Maria when you came in...' Betty waved her hand towards the young man and woman Molly had seen dancing. 'They are José and Valeria. They are getting married in a couple of weeks and they'll be dancing together at their reception. They need the practice – that's why Alejandro and Rosa Maria were helping them before the lesson started. Valeria's really quite good but poor José isn't naturally gifted with his feet, shall we say? I'm sure he has other qualities, though.'

Molly glanced at the other dancers to see if anyone had heard Betty's remarks, if anyone was staring in their direction or seemed offended, but there was the light buzz of chatter in Spanish, the couples engrossed in each other's practise of basic steps. Betty squeezed her hand again.

'Are you here on holiday from England? Are you here all by yourself?'

'Yes – to both,' Molly murmured, her eyes searching for Alejandro, who appeared to be calling the class together to begin the session.

'Lovely. I come to Mexico whenever I can. I'm from Austin, Texas. I'm a widow, have been for two years. I have a condo at the edge of town – my husband bought it years ago and we always came here. I adore Mexico. What do you think of it here, Molly? How are you enjoying Puerto Palacio?'

'It's great,' Molly began but Alejandro had started to speak in his hurried Spanish. Then he smiled in her direction and waved an arm.

'Molly, Betty. We begin now. Please join us.'

The session began and Molly and Betty took up a position opposite each other. At first, Molly stared at Betty, her face straight, her shoulders back and stomach tucked in as Alejandro advised, and she copied his every move as he took them through the shoulder movements, the hip flick and the rhythm of the steps. Then Molly and Betty were instructed, with the rest of the group, to begin the dance and the music started loudly. Betty focused her gaze on Molly, her eyes glaring wildly, apparently determined to appear sensual. Molly stifled a laugh and tried the same expression: it was an integral part of the performance.

Betty, her small face set in a provocative grin, was desperate to master the bachata, but the hip movement on the fourth beat appeared to trouble her. The third time of trying to wiggle seductively in Molly's direction, Betty fell over her feet and cannoned headlong into Molly's arms, almost head-butting her in the stomach. Both women started to laugh and then Betty's eyes filled with tears and she snorted loudly. They fell against each other, sniggering like schoolgirls. Alejandro grinned in their direction.

'Take five please, ladies, and return when you're ready to concentrate. This is normal, of course, the first time, Molly. Betty, you should know better by now.'

Molly and Betty dragged each other to the corner of the dance hall, trying not to laugh while watching the other dancers sidle seductively around each other. Soon, they were snorting, in hysterics. Molly would stop and hold her breath then Betty would start to hoot every few seconds, clasping Molly's hand, repeating, 'I never had so much fun in this class. I can't dance but I'm sure enjoying trying.'

A few minutes later, Molly hauled Betty back onto the wooden floor. She had been watching Alejandro and Rosa Maria dancing together in perfect rhythm and she thought she'd got the hang of their steps. She gripped Betty by her shoulders and took her methodically through the movements, drilling her on each pace, each position. Soon, they were both writhing around each other, arms in the air, their steps synchronised and their hips swaying smoothly. Betty met Molly's eyes, her own wide with surprise at her newly acquired skills, her cheeks flushed with pleasure and pride, muttering, 'Well, will you look at me go?'

Molly's smile filled her face as her feet seemed to move by

themselves: she was dancing the bachata and, she had to admit to herself, she was really quite good at it.

28

Wednesday 20th October

I love the bachata. It seems I have rhythm after all and now I've started dancing, I don't want to stop. I felt like Cinderella at the ball today. I'm so glad I went!

'I couldn't believe it, Molly. He kept us back at the end to tell us how pleased he was with our dancing. Then when he took your hand and spun you round and showed you how to perfect that move, I almost fell over with jealousy.' Betty smiled as Molly led her through the door of *Sabores*. 'Well, will you look at this place? It's so lovely. And I'm so starved I could eat a whole steer.'

Molly caught Liliana's eye and smiled as she manoeuvred Betty towards the bar. 'I doubt you'll get one in here, Betty.'

'Oh, I'm so glad you brought me though. *Sabores*, what a lovely sounding word. Do you think that means tapas bar?'

'It means flavours.'

'I'd no idea this place even existed. I love tapas. Oh Molly, it's so cute here.' Betty clapped her hands together, gazing at the small tables and chairs, the glowing storm lamps placed in alcoves. 'You know, you're my new best friend.'

Molly scrambled up on a stool at the bar and waited for Liliana to finish serving a customer. She was thrilled to have met Betty, who was so positive and full of fun. She smiled at the shorter woman's enthusiasm. 'No, seriously, Betty, I had a great time today and it's all thanks to you, cheering me up. It's a pleasure to buy you some tapas.'

'I enjoyed myself,' Betty murmured. 'And do you know, I think Alejandro has taken quite a shine to you. He never ever asks students to stay back and I've never heard of him giving extra tuition after the lesson has finished.'

Molly closed her eyes, recalling Alejandro's light touch on her waist as he showed her how to spin and flick her hips. He was, certainly, very easy to dance with. Betty had held her small fists to her face, watching every move, her feet tapping to the music.

Liliana leaned against the bar, offering her most welcoming smile. 'Hello, again. What can I get you?'

'Can we have a selection of tapas?' Molly asked. 'Especially the salmon that's not salmon and the egg that's not egg.'

Betty was watching Molly, her mouth open; she turned to Liliana. 'Do you do steaks that aren't steaks? I'm from Texas.'

'Kristof does a mean ranch steak made from cauliflower but it's not on the menu at the moment.' Liliana pursed her lips. 'We're doing a baked camembert dip with herbs today, made from cashews– would you like to try that?'

'I would.' Betty grasped Molly's arm. 'What a great place you've brought me to.' She moved her head to stare around the café, gazing at the white walls, the red curtains and the clusters of people sitting around tables, chatting and eating. Jazz music was blustering through speakers, a saxophone bubbling and a woman crooning about an old devil called love. Suddenly, Betty squealed and waved an arm. 'Molly, look – over there at that table in the corner. It's Valeria and José, isn't it?'

Molly followed Betty's pointing finger and noticed the young couple from the dance group talking earnestly to a grey-haired man in white clothes, his back turned. José was waving his hands and chattering excitedly while Valeria leaned forward, her face serious and composed. Liliana placed two plates of nibbles in front of them.

'The couple over there? They are organising a wedding feast on the beach. Kristof is planning the menu with them.' She indicated the food. 'Enjoy your tapas.'

Molly picked up the little biscuit with mock-salmon and cream cheese while Betty pushed a piece of celery into a small baked camembert and devoured it, licking her lips. 'This is such a great place, Molly. I want to eat here every day.'

Liliana heard the comment and smiled. 'You're very welcome. I'll introduce you to Kristof when he's finished. He'll be so pleased you like the food.' Her face was serious. 'To be honest, when I took over here, I wasn't sure whether people would be happy with meatless tapas. My friends said I was crazy but...' She beamed, indicating the café and the tables crammed with customers. 'It seems to be working.'

'You serve delicious food, that's why.' Molly dabbed her mouth as Betty reached over and stole half a Scotch 'egg' from her plate. Her own dish was empty.

Betty's eyes closed in ecstasy. 'This is so gorgeous.'

Molly ordered two beers and Liliana returned with glasses full of foaming liquid the colour of sunshine, and a small plate. 'Maybe you'd like to try these new tapas? It's our version of battered squid, but here we have artichoke tempura in a beer batter. Let me know what you think.'

Both women stretched out eager fingers and picked up piping

hot tempura, dipping it in chilli sauce and biting into the crunchy coating. They closed their eyes at the same time and murmured, 'Mmmm.'

'I'd marry someone who can cook like this,' Betty hooted.

Molly reached for her beer. 'I'm glad we've been dancing. We've burned the calories first, so we can have treats and tapas afterwards.'

Betty leaned towards Molly, resting her head against her new friend's arm. 'I'm so glad you came to the bachata class, Molly. I used to feel a little left out. Everyone there is Mexican and I can only speak a few words of Spanish. I was determined to stick it out but I did feel the odd one out. Do you know, I'm seventy-six years old next birthday, two days after Thanksgiving? I'm going back to Texas for that. I may come across as brimming with self-confidence but really, I'm just a shy girl from Austin with two left feet.' She licked oil from her fingers. 'And now I'm dancing like an expert and sharing tapas with my new friend from England.'

Molly was delighted. 'Maybe we can make it a weekly event – bachata and tapas on a Wednesday afternoon?'

'Oh, that would be so fabulous.' Betty clapped her hands together.

Liliana was standing behind the counter talking in Spanish to a tall, good-looking man, probably in his late sixties, with crinkly grey hair. She heard the word *azúcar*, which she knew meant sugar. By the man's expression, he seemed to be making a joke. Liliana turned to Molly. 'This is my chef, Kristof van den Broeck.'

He met Molly's gaze, his own eyes chocolate brown, shining with mischief. 'Hello. I'm glad you enjoy the tapas.'

'Oh, we do!' Betty enthused.

The chef turned the same dancing eyes on her. 'Thank you.'

Molly decided to ask the question. 'So, where are you from, Kristof?'

'Bruges originally, but I have lived in other places for many years.'

'Bruges? Is that in France?' Betty asked.

Kristof's eyes twinkled and he gave an easy smile. 'Belgium. At least it was last time I was there.'

Betty clapped her hands together. 'I love your humour.' She wriggled on her seat. 'And your tapas. Is this how you eat all the time?'

'It is, nowadays.' Kristof's grin broadened. 'I've been a chef for many years and too many *croquembouches* stuffed with cream are not great for the body.'

Molly noticed that, beneath his chef's whites he seemed quite slim, with broad shoulders. She was about to tell him she thought he looked fine, but she decided against it.

Betty spoke aloud what Molly was thinking. 'You look good to me. All this healthy food must be paying off.'

Kristof lifted a hand, waving his fingers. 'I left my trainee chef in the kitchen practising sugar skulls for *La Calavera Catrina*. I ought to check on him. If you'll excuse me...'

Molly nodded, although she had no idea what he was talking about. Betty wasn't ready for him to leave. She called out, 'Have you ever been to Texas, Kristof?'

The chef turned back, his face bright with enthusiasm. 'Yes, I have. Do you know Navasota?'

'I do. It's about two hours away from Austin.' Betty was thrilled. 'What did you do there?'

Kristof's eyes shone with the memory. 'I worked in the States for a while. I went to Navasota to do some horse-riding.'

'Western-style. Did you enjoy it?'

'Very much.' Kristof met Betty's excited gaze. 'Do you ride too?'

'Oh, I used to. I wish I knew somewhere round here I could do some Western-style riding.'

Liliana was back at the bar. 'My brother Samuel owns a little place down the coast a short drive from here. He has several mares and stallions, and people ride them out on the beach. Why don't you check him out?'

'I'd love to.' Betty's face glowed. 'Is there a bus that goes past there? I could get a taxi, maybe.'

Liliana grabbed the chef's arm. 'Kristof goes there on Sundays. He could give you a lift.'

'Oh, would you?'

Kristof shrugged. 'I could, of course.'

Betty patted Molly's hand. 'Do you ride, Molly?'

'A little.' Molly had no idea why she'd said that. The words flew from her mouth. She'd ridden a donkey on the beach as a ten-year-old and been terrified the whole time.

'Then we could both go together.' She gazed entreatingly at Kristof. 'If you'd take us there. Would you mind?'

'Not at all.' Kristof met Betty's eyes, then looked at Molly and back to Betty. 'If you'd like to go, of course you can come with me. I leave at nine-thirty on Sunday morning. If you're outside the café, I'll take you there. I live in the flat upstairs. It would be my pleasure.' He smiled. 'If you'll excuse me, I have to go and check that Javi hasn't set the kitchen on fire.'

Betty watched him go. 'Oh, that's so kind,' she breathed.

Molly folded her arms. She had no idea what she'd just committed to do. She couldn't ride a horse. To her, they were huge, muscly, unpredictable animals and she was far too long in the tooth to start to understand them. But Betty was wriggling on her stool, her hands clasped with joy, already murmuring about how she'd been on horseback since she could stand up and what a great experience it was to be in the saddle.

Molly breathed out. 'I'm not very good at it, Betty – I mean, it's been ages since I've ridden...'

'Have you done Western-style riding before?'

'What's that?' Molly was suddenly terrified.

'Cowgirl style. The saddle's bigger and much heavier – the whole technique is different than the way you ride in England. You Brits have more contact with the horse – Western-style you don't.'

Molly imagined herself on horseback with no way of holding on. She'd fall straight off and probably be trampled by a frenzied wild-eyed stallion who would sense immediately that she was lying about her skills. Horses had an instinct about that sort of thing, didn't they? She wondered how she could back out of Sunday's arrangement.

'Betty, er – I'm not sure I...'

'Oh, don't worry, you'll be fine.' Betty's voice was emotional. 'I haven't been riding for almost a year. It'll be so nice to get back on a horse. Oh, Molly, I'm just so glad we're going together.'

'I've no kit – no jodhpurs... no boots... here with me...' Molly blurted, hoping her excuses would suffice.

'Wear what you have on now. You'll be fine. All stables supply hats...' Betty met Liliana's eyes, hoping for support.

Liliana picked up the empty plates and turned to go. She swivelled back and flashed a smile. 'Don't worry. Kristof will take care of you. He knows his way around horses.'

Molly screwed up her mouth into a small shape and said nothing. She wasn't sure that Liliana's partner, kind and calm as he was, could do anything to prevent her from making the biggest fool of herself. She sighed and finished her beer, wondering if she'd be able to attend a bachata class again after an hour or two straddling a stallion. She rather doubted it.

That evening, after a quiet supper with Ryan, Molly returned to her room to call Nell on WhatsApp. It was lunchtime in Spain and she could see Nell on the screen eating a salad on the sun terrace. Molly was full of her day's exploits, her words spilling from her lips. 'I danced the bachata, Nell. It's such a sultry dance. And the teacher is quite sultry too.'

She could hear Nell laugh. 'What's he called?'

'Alejandro.'

'Alejandro,' Nell repeated in her most husky Spanish accent and rolled her eyes. 'Is he sexy?'

'He's very attractive,' Molly admitted. She heard Ronnie murmur something from a distant place off-screen and Nell muttered something back. Molly frowned. 'Everything okay, Nell?'

Nell made a sound between her lips. 'Mmm. Ronnie's in a bad mood. Nothing new.'

The indentation between Molly's brows deepened further. 'Nell?'

'Maybe my expectations are too high. I don't know...' She heard her sister sigh. 'We just had a bit of a lover's tiff. Nothing to worry about. So, Molly – tell me more about Mexico. Who's this man you're living with, the one you mentioned in your text?'

'We're not living together in that way, just as friends. He's called Ryan. He's from New York. He's into finance – he's in his seventies but he still works abroad, flying all over the world.'

Nell sighed. 'How the other half live. And it's his apartment you're staying in?'

'His ex-wife's, actually.'

'He has an ex-wife? He sounds very interesting.'

Molly heard Ronnie grumble again and Nell moved her head; Molly wasn't sure she hadn't rolled her eyes in the direction of his voice. Then she said, 'You sound as if you're having a great time.'

'Oh, I am. I eat in this great tapas bar. They do the most

amazing food. And I've made a really good friend, a lovely Texan lady called Betty. She's so sweet. And she and I are going horse-riding on the beach on Sunday.'

'I didn't know you could ride, Molly.'

'Ah – yes, there is a bit of a problem...'

'And those horses will probably swim in the sea too,' Nell told her. 'I've heard about it.'

'Swimming on horseback? Surely not.'

'They do,' Nell persisted. 'A friend of Phil's went to Cancún and – well, never mind. I've forgotten about Phil. He's ancient history.'

'The horses swim? With the riders still attached?'

'Just a second, Molly – Ronnie's just saying that – oh, never mind. I'll have to go. He's having one of his teenage tantrums. We'll call each other on Sunday, shall we? About this time?'

'Great,' Molly beamed as Nell's face disappeared from the screen. The confident, reassuring smile slid away as she pictured herself dangling from a horse, losing control as its hooves thundered along the beach. She imagined clinging on as it swam in the sea, suddenly falling beneath its belly, gulping salty water as it filled her lungs. She made a grim face and murmured, 'Yes, we'll definitely catch up on Sunday. That's if I'm still alive.'

29

Saturday 23rd October

I'm going horse-riding tomorrow with Betty Henderson, my new friend, and a man called Kristof van den Broeck, the chef from Sabores tapas bar, who seems nice. I like horses but I can't say I'm looking forward to riding one. Hopefully, it will just be a steady plod. I must remember to ring Nell tomorrow. She didn't seem too happy. Perhaps I can cheer her up when I tell her all about me trying to ride. I just know I'm going to fall off!

Molly and Betty stood outside *Sabores*, the tapas bar, in leggings and sweatshirts. There was a sign on the door: *Cerrado* – closed. After all, it was Sunday morning. Molly's teeth chattered despite the heat.

'They can't be a couple,' Betty moaned, rolling her eyes. 'I was hoping he was single. He's very nice.' She shrugged. 'Not that I'm in the market for a new man – I'm not – but it sure is nice to flirt a little sometimes.'

'I'm sure Liliana said they were together.' Molly scratched her head. She was already feeling nervous about clambering on a horse and sliding off the other side.

'No way. He's older than her. I mean, she can't be more than forty and he's, well, our age.'

Molly shrugged. Wasn't that the way with most of the men she knew at the moment: Phil and Nikki, Ryan and his ex, Guadalupe, and now Kristof and Liliana. Men seemed to be able to pull it off: the other way round, and people might laugh or call the woman a cougar, whatever that meant. It wasn't really fair. Molly reminded herself all that didn't matter. She was wondering if she could just sit on the beach at a safe distance and watch the others riding. Perhaps she could claim she felt stiff after dancing the bachata several days ago. In truth, she felt fine, apart from the fear that had frozen her spine to brittle ice at the very thought of trying to stay upright on a horse.

She stole a quick glance at Betty, who'd said she was seventy-six two days after Thanksgiving, which Molly knew was next month. Beneath the sheen of make-up, Betty's skin was fine, almost papery. Her arms were sinewy and, under the T-shirt and leggings, the smallness of her frame prompted Molly to wonder how well she'd ride a horse, let alone control one if it should surge into the sea. But Betty was confident; she had ridden horses all her life. Right now, she was chattering about how her father first put her on a pony at the tender age of two. Molly had a sinking feeling, her stomach currently plummeting towards her feet, as a white van pulled up, sporting a graphic design of a horse with fire around its head and the words *Caballos Samuel* in black block letters.

Kristof pushed his head through the open window, all iron-grey wavy hair and wide grin. 'Jump in. This is what I drive in Mexico – Liliana's brother's spare van. Inside is very comfortable.'

But, after half an hour of rocketing along a bumpy coastal

road, Molly didn't feel comfortable at all. Betty was in the front seat, chatting to Kristof about places they'd both been to in Texas, her laughter bubbling to the surface at intervals, and Molly was peering from the back seat at the road ahead, holding her body stiff against the jarring and jolting. Occasionally, Kristof's cheery voice would lilt from the driver's seat, 'You okay back there, Molly?' and she'd grunt an affirmation and force a smile.

Then he called out, 'Just ahead is Samuel's place.' Molly peered out of the window. The beach stretched to the left, the sea sparkling in the sunlight. Ahead to the right was a white three-sided building wrapped around a courtyard, its interior dirt-dark. Molly thought it looked like a rotten molar. They came to a stop outside a white board gate, the sign *Caballos Samuel* stripped and bleached by the sun. A man was standing, arms folded, in jeans, a checked shirt and heavy boots. His hair was cropped short, like thick dark fur. Kristof shook his hand eagerly and they chatted in Spanish. As soon as Molly and Betty had reached him, Kristof introduced them. 'This is Samuel, Liliana's brother.'

Both women chorused, '*Hola*, Samuel,' Betty flashing her most enthusiastic grin and Molly smiling through gritted teeth. The wind was warm and arid but she'd started to shake with cold. Kristof noticed her edginess and put a gentle hand on her arm.

'Sam has already saddled up horses for you both. I usually ride Trueno, the black one. Sam has prepared the grey for you, Betty – she's called Nieve – and Molly, you can ride Oro who is like his name, good as gold. Oh, and he has some riding hats for you to try. Pick the one that is the best fit.'

Twenty minutes later, Betty was perched on Nieve, smiling and patting the horse's neck, clucking softly with her tongue. Kristof glanced at Molly, who was frowning suspiciously at a light brown horse with a saddle on its back that looked like a huge bucket seat with an enormous bobble on the front. His voice was hushed in her ear. 'I'll help you up. The stirrups are long so you can stretch your legs straight – that's how it's done but I'll adjust them for you. Take the reins with one hand and hold on to the saddle at the front. Oro is very calm. You'll be fine.'

Molly attempted to put a foot in the stirrup as she'd seen Betty do. It had looked easy as she'd swung her small leg across Nieve's back. But Molly couldn't even reach the stirrup with her foot. She hopped, launched herself desperately at Oro's solid belly and fell onto Kristof, who held a hand against her back. Molly felt ungainly as she heaved herself forward, pulling hard on the saddle, grunting hopelessly, then she felt a light grip on her leg and she was airborne. She threw herself across the saddle and Samuel was on the other side, sliding her foot into the stirrup and adjusting the length. Molly felt herself wobble. She didn't feel at all secure, balanced on a saddle which, in turn, was balanced on a horse's spine. She leaned forward and grabbed the mane, which was a rich chocolate brown, much darker than Oro's body. Molly leaned forward precariously and whispered to the horse. 'I hope we can be friends. *Amigos.*'

Oro twitched his ears and there was a snuffling snort from his mouth. Molly felt her heart beating too fast in her chest. Samuel and Kristof were talking in Spanish, Samuel's expression serious and Kristof laughing as usual, his eyes gleaming. Then he turned to Molly.

'Okay, we'll go onto the beach now. Samuel will take you across the road and we'll be all right from there.'

Molly wasn't sure she'd be all right at all but, with Samuel leading Oro across the road at a steady plod, she gripped the reins in one hand and the humpy handle of the huge saddle in the other and hoped she could hang on. Ahead, Betty was chattering to Kristof, saying what a lovely mare Nieve was and would it be all right for her to go off at a canter on the beach. Molly heard Kristof's confident laugh.

Then they were on a stretch of white sand, the waves rolling to their left. Betty's shrill voice yelled something, and she and her mare took off ahead. Kristof on Trueno, a huge black muscular beast of a horse followed at a pace, the pair of them hurtling forwards while Molly sat squat on Oro's back, wobbling from side to side at each step as they plodded along.

Then Kristof turned his horse around and thundered back to Molly. He tugged the reins and Trueno came to a stop obediently. He grinned. 'Do you want to try a little trot? Are you okay?'

'Yes.' Molly meant that she was okay, not that she wanted to trot, but Kristof murmured something to her horse and it lurched forward. Kristof was next to her on the black stallion, but Molly was concentrating all her efforts on heaving herself upright. She clung to the reins desperately with one hand, hanging on for dear life to the hump on the saddle with the other as she tipped backwards. Everything in her body seemed to bounce, each muscle and sinew was now a separate entity, and the clichéd image of a sack of jiggling potatoes flashed into her mind. Her helmet, strapped below her chin, tilted back, taking her head and neck with it and she flung her weight forward furiously so that she wouldn't topple from Oro's rump.

Her next immediate concern was that she wasn't wearing a sports bra; the flimsy lacy undergarment in a pleasant shade of rose pink which would usually keep her comfortably in place was, as she was hurled up and down on Oro's back, no more use than a thin elastic band. Molly's breasts pitched in every direction as if they had a mind of their own; she clung to the saddle and squeezed her thighs against the horse's sides in a desperate attempt to keep herself upright. Kristof leaned over and touched the reins as Oro slowed down to a trudge.

Molly was aware that her face was damp. Her breath was ragged. 'You go off and ride. I'll be fine here. Oro and I will just...' She glanced down at the horse, who had hung his head down to sniff something. 'We'll just have a chat.'

Kristof nodded. 'Okay. I'll be back soon.'

She watched him gallop into the distance; Betty was ahead, a tiny shape on a slightly bigger horse. Kristof and Trueno were like a centaur, moving as one with perfect rhythm. Molly sighed and thought that she must be a burden to them. She didn't want to spoil their fun simply because she was a useless rider. At least, sitting still astride the horse, she wouldn't be a liability.

'Well, Oro, what do you think? It's very nice here, isn't it?' The horse twitched his ears, his neck still bent. Molly was determined to be positive. 'Do you like it here, Oro? I mean, your life must be pretty good, with a beach to run around on. Not that I'm much of a horsewoman so you won't get a great ride with me today. But look at the sea, how lovely it looks. Do you know, a swim might be nice, cooling down in the ocean? I expect you understand Spanish, not English. *Agua*, that's water, isn't it?'

Oro's ears flicked and he began to traipse forward, turning his nose towards the sea; Molly felt her body roll from one side to the other. Then, without any warning, Oro began to bolt towards the waves, his hooves thundering on the sand below. Molly hung on tight, yelling as the horse hurled himself into the water, foam splashing in her face as they plunged deeper into the sea. Then Oro was swimming, the water lapping over Molly's legs, to the top of her thighs, and to her horror, her legs and body were submerged below the foam. The waves came to Oro's neck and Molly felt herself slipping. The saddle, the horse, everything she'd clung to for safety had now become smooth and slippery. Her feet came out of the stirrups and she felt herself starting to slide away from the horse's back.

She clung to the dark mane with both hands, staring into Oro's wild eye as the horse feverishly surged forwards. The waves splashed in Molly's face, flicking saltwater in her eyes and she blinked hard and looked up towards the sound of a voice. Kristof was next to her on Trueno, only the stallion's black head visible, water up to his waist, on the other side of Oro. He grabbed the reins, turning the horse around. 'Hang on to his neck, Molly. We're heading back now. He'll bring you back to the beach.'

Molly clung on for dear life, clenching her teeth, her muscles, as Oro swam back to shore. Then she slid from the saddle and staggered behind her horse as he trudged steadily across the sand and stopped. Bedraggled and wet, Molly slumped to the ground, Oro standing next to her, his flesh steaming from the heat of the sun. The horse opened his mouth and showed huge teeth: he didn't look at all contrite. Betty was staring at Molly from up high, still astride Nieve, repeatedly asking her if she was all right in the most concerned voice. As Kristof knelt next to her, Molly forced a brave laugh. 'I didn't realise I was giving the horse an instruction – I just said the word for water – I said I fancied a swim.'

Kristof, his jeans soaked, put an arm around her. 'Are you okay?'

Molly spluttered; her nose was still full of seawater. 'It's just my pride that's hurt.' She shrugged. 'And my teeth are still rattling.' She met his eyes, warm with concern, and attempted to make the situation light. 'And my bottom is sore. I don't know how I'm ever going to sit down comfortably again.'

Kristof made a soft sound of sympathy. 'I have an idea.' He glanced up at Betty. 'And I might have a change of clothes in the back of the van. Of course,' he raised his eyebrows, 'they'll be too big for you Molly, but at least you won't be wet to the skin.'

Molly put a hand to her hair; it fell in thick soggy tendrils over her face. Her leggings were encrusted with sand and her T-shirt was dark with water. She knew she looked a mess. She gazed up at Betty, crisp and cool on her mare, and Kristof, who was holding out a hand to help her up, then at Oro, who seemed to be leering triumphantly in her direction, and she offered her most positive smile.

She had expected the worst and it had been even worse than she'd expected.

30

Sunday 24th October

Never again will I sit on a horse! I may possibly never sit down again. Thank goodness for Kristof...

The horses were safely back in the stables and Molly was comfortably dressed in an old set of Kristof's chef's whites, rolled up at the legs and the sleeves. Kristof had found a pair of faded swim shorts to wear instead of his soaked jeans. The three of them set off in the van, driving up the coastal road and Kristof parked on a stretch of beach where several palm trees twisted in the wind and miles of white sand met emerald water. Betty patted his arm. 'Kristof, it's perfect here.'

'I think we deserve lunch.' He glanced over his shoulder and winked at Molly. 'Horse-riding can give you an appetite.'

He tugged a rug from the back of the van and a hamper, and they set up a picnic between swaying palm trees. Molly eased herself into a sitting position with a little groan. Kristof stretched out tanned muscular legs and handed her a glass of pink liquid.

She drank thirstily. It tasted delicious; it was cold and fruity. She poured herself a second glass. 'What's this?'

'Just filtered water that has had pomegranate seeds immersed in it overnight.' Kristof was piling tapas onto plates.

'This is divine,' Betty purred. 'How thoughtful of you, Kristof.'

He gave his easy grin. 'We ride, we eat, we rest.'

Molly took her plate of food and nibbled a little pastry filled with something savoury that might have been mushrooms and cream. She hoped she'd feel better soon. Her limbs ached beneath the chef's white top and trousers but her battered pride hurt her more. She took a breath. 'I hope I haven't ruined your day...'

'Oh, not at all,' Betty chirruped. 'In fact, you made my day great. It was so funny, the way the horse dived into the water with you on its back.' She noticed Molly's pained expression and made her tone as warm and enthusiastic as she could. 'And you were so brave, the way you hung on to his mane. I'm so proud of you.'

Molly wasn't sure but she forced a smile.

'The horses are trained to swim in the water with riders.' Kristof met her eyes. 'I should have known it might happen. Still – no damage done.' He grinned. 'And you look pretty cool in chef's whites.'

Molly was beginning to feel better. The sun was warm on her face. 'Thanks, Kristof.'

'Samuel is a nice man. He looks very much like Liliana.' Betty chewed thoughtfully. 'Does your wife not ride, Kristof? She could've come with us today.'

'Liliana lives with her mother, who isn't well – she has bad arthritis.' He shook his head, a single movement. 'She is not my wife, Betty. She is like a daughter to me. I met her in London years ago, when she was just a kid. I trained her – she's a very talented chef.'

Betty turned to Molly. 'Didn't you tell me these guys were married?'

'Partners – an item, Liliana said – I must have misunderstood,' Molly mumbled.

Kristof's face brightened. 'Was there some guy around, trying to chat Liliana up, when she told you that?'

Molly considered his command of the English vernacular but then, she thought, he had lived in the UK. 'Yes – the man who shares the apartment with me, Ryan.'

'Of course,' Kristof smiled. 'She's used that line a lot. When we worked in London, most of the chefs were male and Liliana used to tell them we were together to keep them at arm's length.' He noticed Betty's interested expression. 'She and I always kept in touch over the years. When she took over her mother's café, I came over for a few months to make new recipes and to train Javi while she manages the tapas bar.'

'How long have you been here in Mexico?' Betty accepted tapas from the plate he was holding out.

'Since August. I'm going back home before the end of the year.' His smile was rueful. 'It's about time I saw my kids.'

'You have kids?' Betty clapped her hands together. 'I have a son, Jason. He's fifty-four years old and he's a lawyer. Tell me about yours, Kristof.'

He exhaled. 'My son Joël is forty-two. He has a little girl, Estella, my granddaughter, who is six. I send her photos from Mexico every day. My daughter Carine is thirty-five. She works for a charity raising awareness of autism. I'm hoping we'll all meet up in Bruges in December.'

'So, are you married?' Betty asked. Molly watched thoughtfully, amazed at Betty's ability to ask brazen questions without feeling awkward. Kristof didn't seem to mind.

'I was. Clémence and I were together for over twenty years.'

'What happened?' Betty leaned forward.

'She married one of my best friends.'

'How awful.'

Kristof shook his head. 'Not at all, Betty. They are very happy together and I am happy for them. We all get on well. She and her husband Gerrit will probably have dinner with me and our kids on Christmas Day. We are all one big family.'

'So, what made you guys split?' Betty's eyes were round with interest.

'My work, mostly.' Kristof put a hand to his forehead. 'I was a good chef, ambitious. I worked lots of hours, I set lots of targets for myself, achieved lots of things, but none of them were to do with my family. I was never at home and my wife fell in love with someone who gave her more time and, I had to agree, they were good together. After Clémence left, I had to change. I was a little bit lost – I was chasing the wrong things. There was too much stress in my life, and I wasn't focusing on what mattered most.'

'And did you manage to change?' Betty asked.

'Yeah, I changed the food I cooked and ate, the places I worked and mostly I changed the attitudes I had to myself and to other people. I had everything wrong in those days.' He thought for a moment. 'Food is not first a business; it is nourishment and health. Life is not a race, it's a celebration. I am not the total of my achievements; I am only the person I am today.'

Molly considered his words carefully, then she spoke for what seemed like the first time in a while. 'But don't you get lonely sometimes, by yourself?'

Kristof met her eyes. 'I suppose everyone is lonely at some point. If I feel too much alone then I seek out new experiences. I travel a lot. I don't work unless I want to and I meet cool people.' He waved his hand towards Betty and Molly to prove his point, a playful grin on his face.

Betty intervened, her face excited. 'And love? Do you have anyone special, Kristof?'

'No, it's not something I set out to look for.' A slight smile moved across his lips. 'First to love someone you have to love yourself. Not in an arrogant way; in an accepting way of yourself. I know if I try to do that and live the best life I can, then I am in a good place maybe to meet someone in the future.'

Molly sipped her water. Betty reached for more tapas and Kristof stared out towards the sea. They were quiet for a moment, then Kristof turned to Molly, his eyes dancing with mischief. 'Molly, I want to show you something – and ask you a big question.' He pulled his mobile phone from his pocket, pressed a button and showed her a photo. She noticed a bracelet made from knotted red cord on his wrist. 'I'd like to send this picture to my granddaughter, Estella. But only if you agree.'

Molly stared at a photo of herself; it was just her head and shoulders above the water, her riding hat pushed back, her hair wet as she hung on to Oro's neck. Her face was serene, calm: she assumed it was the moment the horse turned around to tow her back to shore. She stared at Kristof. 'You want to show your granddaughter a picture of the crazy woman who nearly fell off a horse into the water?'

Kristof closed his eyes for a moment. When he opened them, his voice was soft. 'I will message her I met a beautiful mermaid in the ocean who saved a drowning horse. Every day I send her a photo from Mexico and something about her grandfather's life.' He smiled. 'Of course, it is all stories. But I like to tell her stories. Imagination is a wonderful thing.'

Molly nodded in agreement. 'I think that's lovely.' She reached for the plate of tapas; her appetite was returning. 'I guess that's the last time I go horse-riding.'

'I have so enjoyed today,' Betty enthused.

'So.' Kristof turned from Betty to Molly. 'Next Sunday I am busy preparing for the Day of the Dead. We will serve our version of traditional food for the celebrations so there is much work to do, so I cannot come here. But I'd like to take you somewhere another day – are you free on Thursday morning next week?'

'I certainly am,' Betty gushed.

Kristof turned to Molly and she nodded. 'I think so.'

'Can I pick you up very early – I mean just before four in the morning, if that isn't too early for you? I'll collect you from where you live and we'll go somewhere really special. We'll be back in time for the lunch service around one o'clock; Liliana and Javi will be fine until then.' Kristof reached out and laid a gentle hand on Molly's arm. 'I can apologise, make it up to you for today. There will be no horses. Just incredible history and beautiful views.'

'There's nothing to apologise for...' Molly paused. Another trip out with Kristof and Betty would be lovely, especially if there was no horse-riding and no accidental swimming in the ocean. It would be her chance to put things right too – she would be charming, sophisticated, intriguing and definitely not awkward and foolish, as she had been today. Her mouth was moving already with her answer. 'Kristof, that would be lovely. I'd love to go. I can be up and ready to go by four. Thank you.'

* * *

When she arrived back at the apartment, Ryan was slumped on the sofa, a bottle of beer in his hand. His face held an unhappy expression, a frown between his eyes. Molly breezed into the kitchen and took a beer from the fridge, then returned. Ryan hadn't changed position. She collapsed next to him.

'What's the matter, Ryan?'

He stared at her clothes. 'Have you found yourself a job? Are you working in a kitchen somewhere?'

'My own clothes got wet – I have a history of losing my clothes on the beach.' Molly saw his expression change to one of interest and decided that the less she said the better. 'It's a long story. So – what's the problem?'

'I was going to ask you to have lunch with me but you weren't around. So I went by myself to the hotel in Cancún, you know, the one where we danced together?'

'Lovely place. So – was it closed? You don't look happy.'

'Oh, I ate a great meal. Dessert too. Then I came home and had a beer or three. That was hours ago.'

'And now?'

Ryan pressed a hand to his stomach. 'I have awful indigestion. All around my stomach to my back. I shouldn't have eaten so much.'

'Have you taken anything for it?'

'Yeah, I had some pink antacid stuff in a bottle. My gut still hurts like hell.'

'Perhaps you should go to bed, lie down?'

Ryan looked at her hopefully. 'You could come with me, maybe?'

'You're on your own with that one,' Molly retorted, standing up. She decided to go to her room; she'd promised to ring Nell. She reached the door and turned back, a kindly smile on her face. 'But I could make you a nice cup of tea...'

Ryan guffawed, waved a hand in her direction and lifted the beer bottle to his lips. Molly reached her room and thought what she might say to Nell on the phone. She could mention visiting the stables with her friend Betty and the picnic on the beach, but she'd leave out everything to do with Kristof and the swimming horses. Nell might ask too many questions.

31

Wednesday 27th October

Still stiff after the horse-riding, especially my legs and my poor bottom. I'm trying not to think about the mad dash into the sea – I must have looked really silly. Kristof was very kind. I didn't let the pain bother me too much at the bachata class this afternoon although I was tired out by the end. Alejandro told everyone I was his new star pupil. Betty pretended that she was insanely jealous. I'm still troubled about what Nell said on the phone last Sunday…

Molly wanted to write about her conversation with Nell in her diary. She wasn't sure why there was a nagging worry in her mind and she hoped that writing it down would help her to clarify what bothered her.

Apparently, Lisa's back in the Spanish apartment. Her mother is feeling better and she told Nell the weather in England was too grim to bear. Nell has moved into the finca with Ronnie and Lisa has given her two months' rent back so she seems happy enough. But it was something she said on Sunday. 'Maybe my expectations are too high.' Does she mean life in Spain? Ronnie? Or something else? I hope she's all right

Molly chewed the end of her pen. Suddenly her mind flashed elsewhere.

Ryan is moping around the apartment, usually just wearing his shorts. He has heartburn a lot. I think he's really unhappy. I told him he should take up a hobby, maybe Mayan cookery classes or swimming in the ocean with horses! Betty and I are wondering where Kristof is going to take us tomorrow. She thinks it might be Xel Há, the water park. I told her I was off all things to do with water for a while. Betty's really nice. I think she likes Kristof. She likes Alejandro too.

Molly put her pen down. She was thinking about Kristof, how he'd helped her when she was in the water, how he'd later called her a beautiful mermaid. Being a mermaid made a change from dressing up as a cod, which she'd readily done in Spain to help Ronnie. She smiled, then pushed the thoughts from her mind: she needed an early night. She and Betty were being collected just before four o'clock. Molly's mind was racing in anticipation: she had no idea where they were going, especially at such a ridiculously early hour: it would certainly be an adventure. She changed into her sheep pyjamas and climbed into bed but her mind was a tumbling bumper-car battle of thoughts, and she couldn't sleep.

* * *

At four in the morning, Molly stepped out into darkness and Kristof was waiting in the white van with the picture of a horse's head surrounded by flames painted on the side. Betty was sitting in the front seat, so Molly clambered into the back. She had considered wearing the orange dress and putting on lipstick, but in a moment of rush and panic she'd opted for jeans and a sweatshirt, remembering at the last minute to pick up the freshly laundered chef's uniform she'd borrowed from Kristof. She glanced at Betty, pristine in a cream trouser suit and careful make-up. Kristof negotiated a twist of side roads before pulling out on the main road. 'It's a two-hour journey.' His voice was soft. 'We don't want to be late.'

Betty touched his shoulder with perfectly manicured fingers. 'Are you going to tell us where we're going, Kristof?'

'It's a surprise.' He called over his shoulder, 'Have you had breakfast, Molly?'

'No...' She'd hardly had time to dress properly or brush the tangles from her hair. She noticed her sweatshirt was on inside out and back to front, the label hanging out below her chin. She was about to tug it over her head when Kristof's voice came from the front.

'There's a bag of pastries on the seat next to you and some fruit, Molly. Help yourself.'

'Thanks.'

Betty twisted round and lunged into the paper bag Molly was holding up. 'Croissants, Kristof? Did you make these?'

He replied with a soft sound of confirmation through his lips as he overtook a truck.

'Aren't they fattening? All that butter?'

'Vegetable-based butter and yes, perhaps a little fattening, but I think you will be all right with just one, Betty.'

'But how did you do it?'

Kristof's voice was soft. 'I am Belgian and a chef.'

Molly smiled and took a croissant. As she bit into it, she found it was flaky and still warm. She wondered what time Kristof must have been up that morning, baking pastries. She gazed out of the window; the traffic was mostly lorries and vans hurtling at pace. High in the sky, the moon was a silver shard. As they drove along the road, the street lights glowed yellow, harsh in the centre, the outside glimmer soft as a sponge. Molly's lids became heavy; she'd slept fitfully last night, and the van was rocking her, a warm cradle filled with Betty's murmuring chatter and the aroma of warm dough. Molly felt herself sinking into sleep.

She was woken by Betty's excited voice yelling, 'We're here, Molly. Wake up!' She shook herself, stumbled out of the van into darkness and stared around. She had no idea where she was.

Kristof put a hand on her shoulder and spoke gently. 'Still asleep? Come on – we don't have much time.'

Molly allowed herself to be shepherded forwards, blinking as she plodded, listening to Betty cooing with delight. Kristof handed tickets to a man in a uniform and said something in Spanish, then they were walking through an *Entrada*. Her legs were stiff, and her face was cold in the chilly air. Betty tucked an arm through Molly's, hugging herself close for warmth.

'But there's hardly anyone here – it's so early. So, where are we going? I don't understand, Kristof.'

'You will.'

The three of them were standing on grass in darkness, Kristof in the middle, gazing at the silhouette of a grey stone tower, a stepped pyramid looming tall against the sky. To the left were more huge, dusky shapes, temples and a sort of rock statue. Molly blinked. She could see very little in the grainy darkness. Several other people had joined them to make a group, standing in silence or whispering in low voices. Kristof put his arms around the two women. 'It's almost six o'clock. And this is why we came so early.'

Tiny golden thread-like skeins surrounded the outline of the pyramid so that it seemed illuminated from behind by a blinding spotlight. Then, at one corner of the silhouette, the pitch-black sky started to split and the sun became visible, a single pure shaft of light. Molly held her breath as streaks of colour spread across the sky, first becoming dappled grey clouds, then merging into mottled orange and red blurring into blue, an artist's brush dripping one colour into another. She felt Kristof's arm around her. She assumed he must be hugging Betty equally enthusiastically as she heard her friend breathe, 'Oh, my goodness. It's so beautiful.'

The sun rose too quickly. Molly would have liked to slow it down and to hold on to each moment; the darkness faded fast, leaving trails of sun-streaked clouds tinged with blotches of fire-red. The pyramid was bathed in a golden light that faded to grey stone as daylight stretched across the sky. She gazed up at Kristof and had a sudden impulse to rest her head against his shoulder. The thought made her pull away from him and she spoke quickly. 'That was worth leaving the house at four o'clock...'

He grinned, his eyes meeting hers. 'Sunrise at Chichén Itzá is special. I thought you had to see it while you were here in Mexico. Besides, there are no horses swimming here.'

Molly returned his smile. 'So, what is this place?'

'It's ancient Mayan ruins, isn't it?' Betty explained.

Kristof nodded. 'We can go and explore now. There's the Temple of Jaguars, the Temple of Warriors, the Thousand Columns, the Wall of Skulls. It's over fifteen hundred years old.'

'I've read about it but it's so nice to be able to visit.' Betty's eyes shone. 'I'll never forget this.'

'It has a powerful atmosphere,' Kristof agreed. 'Itzá means

"water magicians". Shall we go and take a look around? We have five hours. Then I'll get us back in time for you to have lunch at the café and I must help Javi with the preparations for Monday and Tuesday.'

'The Day of the Dead. I'm not sure at all that it's for me.' Betty breathed. 'Isn't it all rather morbid, Kristof?'

'Not at all. It's a special celebration. You must both come to the café – we'll have an altar of sugar skulls and we make special bread. It is a wonderful time, where everyone is reunited with the souls of those gone before us. It is very beautiful.'

Molly wasn't convinced. She thought about Richie. If they were reunited, she'd never want to let him go again. Kristof's words pulled her from her thoughts. 'Molly? Are you all right?'

'Oh, fine, absolutely fine. This place is perfect. Thank you, Kristof.'

'Okay, the fun starts here. We can check out all the ruins, buy a souvenir each and I'll take a photo of us all to send to my granddaughter. I'll tell her three Mayan warriors appeared from the great pyramid to bring her good luck.'

Molly gazed up at the huge stone structure, the stepped terraces, the square castle on the top, and she nodded. She felt like a warrior surrounded by symbolic ancient monuments. Kristof was right –it had a powerful atmosphere, an aura of mysticism. She breathed in and closed her eyes. When she opened them, she met his gaze and he was grinning, the same easy smile he always had. Then she realised her sweatshirt was still inside out.

They chattered all the way back about the ruins and the history of Chichén Itzá, and what a great time they'd had. Kristof had persuaded a tourist to take the perfect photo of the three of them to send to his granddaughter, their arms raised in the air like warriors. Betty had bought a huge wooden Mayan mask that she wanted to give to her son Jason as a present at Thanksgiving when she returned to Texas. She insisted that Kristof should let her pay for the tickets – she was a wealthy widow, after all, but he told them a convoluted tale about being given them by a customer in the café in exchange for a birthday cake he'd made for a child's party.

The two-hour journey back to Puerto Palacio passed quickly, Molly and Betty chattering and laughing, Kristof at the steering wheel listening and adding to the conversation from time to time. As soon as they reached the tapas bar, Kristof grinned a brief farewell and disappeared into the kitchen, leaving Liliana to serve them lunch that he'd insisted was on the house. Molly arrived home after three o'clock. Ryan had gone out so she had a shower, took herself off to bed and fell fast asleep in seconds.

* * *

The following day, Molly found Ryan seated on the sofa wearing only a pair of shorts, hunched over the laptop, a deep frown between his eyes. She was in a surprisingly happy mood, humming a tune as she put her clothes in the washing machine and swept the kitchen. He, however, looked miserable as she placed a cup of coffee in his hand. She laid a friendly hand on his bare shoulder. 'You work too hard.'

Ryan met her eyes. 'You're right. I need to slow down.' He moved his laptop away and gazed at her. 'You're a breath of fresh air, Molly. Always so cheerful. I wish I had some of what you have.'

She sat on the floor opposite him, crossed her legs and leaned forward. 'I went to Chichén Itzá yesterday. It was great.'

He seemed irritated. 'Who did you go with?'

'My friend Betty from dance class.' Molly thought that was

enough information. She was thinking about how much fun
she'd had, how nice Kristof had been. She was remembering how
she'd almost leaned her head against his shoulder as they
watched the first beams of the sun emerge from behind the dark
pyramid, and how her heart had started to bump at that moment.
She pushed the thoughts away and looked at Ryan. Her next
words were a complete lie, intended only to cheer him up. 'I wish
you'd come with us. It would have been nice for you to take a
break.'

He scratched his beard. 'I'm supposed to be here in Mexico to
vacation. Look at me now. It's all work.'

'How's the stomach? The indigestion?' Molly noticed Ryan's
complexion was sallow. He had a light line of perspiration beads
on his brow.

'Better. I'm dosed up to the hilt on that pink liquid.'

Molly had an idea. 'Why don't we go out to the hotel we went
to in Cancún, the one where we ate mole and danced?' His eyes
widened, his expression suddenly surprised, so she explained.
'My treat. I owe you dinner. It might cheer you up.'

'Are you hitting on me, Molly?'

'No. I'm not. But we can have dinner and dance together – as
friends, as flatmates.'

Ryan's expression was one of gratitude. 'I could use a friend,
to be honest with you. I phoned Lupe earlier and asked her if we
could meet, just to talk. I'm still not over her.'

'What did she say?'

'She told me to go to hell. No wonder I have indigestion.'

Molly sighed; she felt sorry for Ryan, bent over, his face
haggard. 'So – can I buy you dinner and we'll dance? Purely as
friends?'

Ryan gazed at her and then a smile broke on his face. 'That's a
swell idea. I'd love dinner.' Suddenly, he was serious again. 'I'm

flying to San Francisco tomorrow for two weeks – I may be away for longer.'

'Business?' Molly asked.

'Kind of – with an old college buddy of mine who's just gotten divorced. We have a deal to make and then we'll concentrate purely on pleasure, catch up, paint the town red for a while.' He thought for a moment. 'So yeah, dinner with you would be great before I go, just as friends. That is, unless you'd like to sleep with me afterwards?'

Molly burst out laughing. 'No, Ryan, I wouldn't. Dinner is dinner and sex is sex. Never the twain shall meet.'

32

Sunday 31st October

I've been very busy lately, what with watching the sunrise with new friends and dancing the bachata and taking Ryan out to dinner. He is clearly in love with his ex and missing her. It will be strange, not bumping into him for the next two weeks, all hairy chest and boxers, but it'll nice to have the place to myself for a short while now he's gone.

Molly was enjoying the temporary independence of living in the apartment by herself. She'd spent most of Saturday reading and texting as the rain fell heavily outside. Samantha had messaged that her eldest son, James, was going to be a father. Molly would be a great-grandmother. She wondered if she'd be like Kristof, sending daily photos and stories to an excited child. It seemed more likely that any grandchild of Samantha's would be more practical and down to earth. Samantha had never been particularly interested in anything to do with creativity and both of her sons had been keener to mend machinery and build Lego. Samantha took after her father, Trevor. Molly wondered where he was now; she knew he kept in touch with his daughter but, she imagined, they simply spoke over the phone about sensible things like what was on the news and how the weather was.

Momentarily, she thought of her younger, sillier, impulsive teenage self and wondered why she had ever considered Trev to be boyfriend material. Of course, she knew why: it had been his huge brown eyes and handsome, serious face. She had thrown herself at him, conceived a child and raised Samantha, all of it based on the vagaries of his physiognomy. Molly laughed out loud at the absurdity of the idea.

On Sunday the sunshine returned in all its glory and she walked into town to buy groceries. There was excitable chatter everywhere; people had decorated shop windows with ornate skulls, golden marigolds, huge photographs of skeletal dancers and thousands of candles; music was playing from speakers in all the shops and bunting had been stretched across the street, flapping flags of vivid colours. She was tempted to pop into *Sabores* for some tapas, but for some reason her feet brought her straight home instead. That evening she cooked paella, wrote in her diary and had an early night.

On Monday, Molly phoned Betty and asked if she'd like to meet her in town the next day and experience the opening of the festivities, but Betty said she was tired and would give it a miss. So Molly spent the morning lazing in the hammock in the sunshine, reading a book about an Irish girl who lost her mind when her sailor lover didn't return from a fishing trip. She padded into the kitchen for a slice of toast and a mug of coffee at two o'clock and went back to the hammock, deciding that a whole day spent reading a good book never hurt anyone.

At five o'clock, she had a shower, wrapped herself in a towel and made herself a mug of coffee. She was sitting at the table when she heard a knock at the door. She gazed down at herself, water from her hair dripping onto the damp towel around her torso and decided that perhaps it was people drumming up a crowd for the Day of the Dead, or children asking for sweets or money for a collection. She rushed to the door, tugged it open, and looked into the smiling eyes of a tall, smartly dressed man who was standing in the darkness. She caught her breath.

'Kristof?'

He glanced at the towel wrapped tightly around her and grinned. 'I remembered this is where you live. I've come to take you to the procession. I don't want you to miss it.' Molly was staring at him. He met her gaze. 'But you can't go dressed like that. It's best clothes tonight; this evening the dead are honoured guests.'

She glanced at his black jacket and trousers, white shirt, and nodded. 'I have an orange dress.'

'The colour of marigolds. Perfect.'

She slammed the door, leaving him smiling on the step and rushed into her bedroom, struggling into the orange wrap-around dress, throwing clothes everywhere as she searched for a suitable wrap for her shoulders and some shoes that would be both comfortable and pretty. She rubbed the towel over her hair and gazed in the mirror. She would have to do. Her heart was beating fast as she opened the door: Kristof hadn't moved; he was still grinning. He held out a vibrant orange flower. 'I brought you this to wear in your hair.'

She noticed he had a similar flower in his buttonhole. She took it in her fingers, wriggling the stem into her thick silver mane, tucking it behind her ear.

'Why marigolds?'

He held out his arm and Molly slipped hers through the crook as they walked along. 'Marigolds represent the fragility of life. Their smell and colour guides spirits to their altars.'

She glanced up at him. 'Betty thought this might be a bit morbid, all this talk of the dead.' She took a breath. 'Have you ever lost anyone you love, Kristof?'

'My father. My mother, last year. An older brother, forty years ago.'

'So...' Her eyes were round with sympathy: in front of them, the procession had started. There was loud music, drums banging, bells rattling, and throngs of people were filling the road. 'Is this ceremony supposed to comfort you?'

'It's a big part of Mexican culture. For me, of course, I miss people I love. It's part of life: we remember them every day. But it's harder for you, Molly. I think you grieve for someone special you loved very much.'

'How do you know that?'

Kristof shrugged. 'Something I heard in the car coming back from the Mayan ruins, when Betty was talking about how she missed her husband. You understood her feelings. I guessed it was the same for you.'

She nodded. 'Richie and I were together for a long time.'

'What was his favourite food?'

Molly thought that was a strange question, but she answered, 'Vegetables.'

'Maybe we leave him a small offering. The *ofrendas* are altars and we leave gifts to those we love. We can say thank you and I love you.'

They had reached crowds of people thronged in the streets, walking steadily forward. The music was loud, jangling. Molly hugged Kristof's arm tighter as she stared into white skull faces with stitched mouths wearing white hats or crowns of flowers on their heads. The candles they carried illuminated grotesque faces, exaggerating their gaping cavernous eyes and leering smiles. The spectres were dressed in white or in vibrant colours, moving menacingly.

Kristof pushed a hand into his pocket and held out a piece of knotted red cord. 'For you, Molly. It is for protection.'

'Protection? Do I need protecting?' She laughed, imagining Ryan's advances.

He smiled. 'The Mexicans believe it will protect us from *mal de ojo*, the evil eye, negative energy. We are in Mexico; it is good to embrace traditions. I think many cultures wear something like it for luck.'

She let him put the bracelet around her left wrist, noticing that he was wearing an identical one. Suddenly, a lean skeleton in a white wide-brimmed hat grasped Molly's shoulder and she gasped. He leaned forward and spoke to her in a Mexican accent, his voice filled with warmth.

'Hello, Molly, it's good to see you.'

'Alejandro?'

Molly recognised her dance teacher's handsome face behind the white make-up. He indicated a slim woman next to him dressed in a flowing pale robe and a black hat with roses around the brim. Her face was cadaverous, a corpse bride. 'This is my wife, Carmen.'

'Pleased to meet you.' Molly held out a hand to the skeletal woman, noticing she too was wearing a red cord around her wrist. She decided it would be polite to speak in Spanish. '*Encantada.*'

'It is good to see you here.' Alejandro held out a hand to Kristof. 'And this is your husband?'

'No, this is Kristof,' Molly spoke quickly. She had no idea how to introduce him so she added, 'He's a chef. From Belgium.'

Kristof shook Alejandro's hand warmly, then Carmen's, and said something in Spanish. Molly recognised a few words – *fiesta* and *una celebración* – before Alejandro and his wife slipped back into the crowd. Molly watched the procession, an explosion of colour and sound crammed with creatures with grotesque faces. Several skeletons staggered on stilts, towering high above the parade. She supposed that everyone was mourning someone; each one knew the pain of loss. Some people were wearing ghastly masks; others' faces had been intricately decorated as beautiful lost souls. In the tightly packed crowd, children accompanied parents, all in costume, ephemeral angelic spirits with tiny skull faces illuminated golden by the light from the candles they were carrying. Molly felt a swelling in her throat: this was a manifestation of so much loss, so much love, but above all, so much invested in the celebration of life and death. She turned to Kristof. He seemed to read her thoughts, his mouth close to her ear.

'The fiesta helps children to understand about life and death. They know the cycle is a part of life.'

Molly threaded her arm through his and moved closer. The clattering music became louder as the parade grew in size. Molly was puzzled, 'Where will they all go now?'

'To the cemetery to decorate tombstones. It will be magical.'

'Are we going there?'

He grinned. 'No, Molly – we are going for tapas.'

They rounded the corner into the side street and arrived at *Sabores*. Candles shone in the windows beneath the most incredible display of piled sugar skulls, little faces with hollowed eyes and tombstone teeth, decorated with flowers in a rainbow of colours. Molly gasped. 'Did you make all these?'

'Team effort – Javi and Liliana too. Wait until you see inside.'

Loud jazz music was fizzing from the speakers. Molly stood in the doorway, gazing around. Plates of food had been set out on the tapas bar, huge mounds of rice, vegetable dishes and oversized loaves of bread. People were seated at tables, laughing and chattering. At the far end of the room was a long white marble bench, the surface glimmering with soft light from many candles. Luminous skulls seemed to hover around the altar on all sides. Kristof took her hand. 'Maybe you'd like something to drink? Some food?'

She turned and Liliana was next to her, hugging her. Her chestnut hair was entwined with marigolds; a white dress hung down to her heels and her face was deathly pale apart from the tiny yellow flowers painted around her darkened eyes.

'Molly – good to see you. I love the marigold orange dress.' She pushed a mug into Molly's hands, a red cord around her wrist. 'Hot chocolate. Enjoy. All the food is free tonight. We have sweet bread, tamales, rice, tacos, enchiladas, cookies, pumpkin candy. Help yourself. And if you fancy something stronger to drink later, just speak to me...' She lowered her voice. 'Behind the bar I have shots of mezcal with chilli salt.'

Molly gazed around. The café was busy, loud chatter mingling with the sultry sound of jazz saxophone. Kristof had been talking to a young dark-haired man in a white suit, a top hat and sharp cheekbones beneath a skull face. He wrapped his arms around the boy in a gesture of affection and then returned to Molly, smiling.

'That was Javi. I wanted to tell him how well he has done with all the food.'

'He made it all?'

Kristof winked at her. 'Not all by himself.' He raised his eyebrows, his face suddenly serious. 'Do you want to visit the *ofrenda*?'

She met his eyes, puzzled, and he pushed something into her cupped hands. She was holding an avocado, a chilli pepper, a potato and a mushroom. Suddenly, a sense of panic made her heart beat faster. Kristof guided her over to the white bench, weaving between chattering diners, and she was standing in front of glossy marble decorated with shimmering candles and skulls. Molly noticed that there were photographs placed on the altar, small plates of food, flowers; glasses of drink had been left in honour of those who had been loved and had died.

'What do I do?' Molly asked but Kristof had gone. She took a deep breath; of course, she had to do this by herself.

She placed the vegetables in a row on the altar, the mushroom first. Richie had loved mushrooms best. Then she picked them up, one at a time and pressed her lips against the cool flesh before putting them back gently. They were a gift for him, from the living to the dead. She gazed into the candles' flickering soft light, staring into the cavernous sockets of the sugar skulls, and her lips moved without sound, the shape of his name in her mouth: Richie.

Molly closed her eyes, but the candlelight was still there, a hypnotic cloud of gleaming gold. She thought of Richie, how much she had loved him and, her mind fully concentrated, she sent him a message. Wherever he was, he would always be in her heart. A single tear trickled down her cheek and she imagined him somewhere a long way away, smiling at her, sending back the same thoughts of love. The remembrance of his voice filled her head, how he'd spoken her name, the sound of his laughter.

And suddenly it was all right. She understood. She had loved him all she could and it had been a privilege and a blessing. Now she could celebrate what they meant to each other, but the suffocating pain restricting her breathing, pressing against her chest had gone. Lightness spread through her body, as if a weight had been lifted from around her heart. She mouthed his name once more and somehow she knew he had answered her. Her breath was calm, her thoughts steady. She opened her eyes and turned around. At the other end of the bar, Kristof was watching her, a smile on his lips, his expression full of kindness.

* * *

Molly had wanted to walk home alone. She had hugged Kristof once, feeling the warmth of his body against her, then she had turned to go. He had grasped her hand, his face close to hers, his eyes shining. 'Come here for tapas next week?' She had nodded, cheered by the thought of seeing him soon. She turned her back on the festivities, images from the evening filling her head, and set off into the cold night air.

The parade was still in full swing, but Molly hardly noticed. The music echoed in her ears but she was cocooned in her own thoughts: the past was in its place, behind her, just like the dead souls' procession. The past was treasured and put away, a keep-sake in a drawer. But what now, what of the present? What of the future? Molly's heart thudded as she considered the options. Something had changed, shifted. She could move forward now.

As she approached the apartment, she stopped, frozen to the spot – a small spectre with golden hair was sitting hunched up on her doorstep. For a moment, Molly wondered if a little spirit child had strayed from the cemetery, a wraith with a message from the dead at her door. Then she noticed the suitcase and was running full-pelt and shouting.

'Nell!'

33

Tuesday 2nd November

The Day of the Dead celebrations are still going on outside. Yesterday was memorable in so many ways. Kristof and I were whisked up into the thrill of Mexican culture and then, out of nowhere, Nell was on my doorstep – all the way from Spain! It's so wonderful to see her again.

They both spoke at once, hugging each other, their eyes wide.

'Where have you been, Molly?'

'Nell, oh, Nell, it's so good to see you – you should have told me you were coming here – I didn't expect you.'

'I'm bloody freezing – and there are people everywhere dressed up as ghosts. I'm so glad you left a forwarding address.'

'Let's get you inside. What's happened? Where's Ronnie?'

'I got a taxi from Cancún. I wanted to surprise you – I thought you'd be in, or at least the American man would be here. It's over between me and Ronnie. Where have you been?'

Molly pushed open the door with one hand, dragging the case with the other.

'Ryan's in San Francisco for a while, and I've been out. It's a big celebration here – that's what the ghost costumes are all about. Come in, Nell – you're cold – let me get you a hot drink. We have lots to talk about.'

'You are so right about that, Molly.' Nell rolled her eyes in a way that Molly knew meant that she was tired or irritated or both. Nell gazed around the living room and wandered into the kitchen. 'Not bad. It's better than the apricot apartments.'

Molly was still remembering the Day of the Dead procession and how she had thought about Richie at the altar in the tapas bar. She tugged her thoughts back to Nell. 'Ah, good.'

Nell had found Ryan's room. 'Is this where I'm sleeping?'

'Yes. Luckily, I put on some fresh bedding – will you be all right?'

'Definitely.' Nell watched, dazed, as Molly tugged her case into her room and then put her hands on her sister's shoulders. 'Do you mind if I get an early night? The journey from Spain was... long.'

Molly nodded. She remembered her own journey: she had been beyond tired. 'Great idea, Nell. We'll have breakfast tomorrow on the patio. We'll catch up then.'

'We certainly will.' Nell noticed her sister's sparkling gaze. She thought how well Molly looked, bright eyed and tanned. She smiled briefly and closed the bedroom door.

Nell cleaned her teeth, stripped off her clothes and slid between the sheets in her underwear. She was too tired to unpack properly: she just wanted to sleep. The bed was comfortable, spacious, smelling faintly of nutmeg. It was good to rest at last. She closed her eyes.

Ronnie's face popped into the space of her imagination, his sad expression at the station in Calleblanque as he begged her to stay. She recalled her voice, miserably telling him it wouldn't work, how sorry she was, how she wasn't ready for a relationship yet, wasn't ready for commitment. She squeezed her lids tightly. She had been a fool; she had invested in the idea of a lifestyle, blindly hoping for love at the first opportunity, and she had hurt Ronnie. Even Pilar had told her that she was a 'bad woman to leave poor Ronnie feeling like cheat'. Kind, loyal Pilar. Nell had felt even worse; she had fled to Molly for help.

She couldn't go back to Yeovil now. She knew too much. She recalled the moment she'd reached into her handbag on the plane and pulled out Molly's diary. Normally, she wouldn't have read her sister's private thoughts, but she was bored, the journey was long and she'd just opened the little book at one page and read one line: *At least Nell is happy and she isn't thinking about Phil all the time and she doesn't know about pregnant Nikki.* Her eyes had blurred; she'd read it again and, even supported by the seat in the plane, she had felt her legs give way and the space around her spin. She'd endured five miscarriages! She'd called the cabin crew immediately and asked for a brandy. Then she had read the whole diary.

Nell didn't blame Molly for keeping it from her. Molly was the kindest person; she was trying to support her. Nell understood exactly why she had dragged her to Spain. Now Nell didn't think she could ever go home again. All she wanted to do now was to have a proper holiday, have fun with her big sister, pay her back with some quality time. She wanted to laugh, to enjoy herself and to forget about Phil and Nikki and their baby. The situation had been made worse by emails from her solicitor in Taunton, unravelling the stark details of the divorce.

Nell was desperate to be single again and, behind the anonymous formality of the solicitor, it was clear that Phil was in a hurry to move on too. The fact that Nell now knew why her husband was so keen to marry his young girlfriend had made her cry. But Molly would take care of her; she'd understand, although Nell wasn't sure she was ready to let her sister know that she'd read the diary, not yet. It would hurt too much to speak about it. First, she was going to bury her misery and embrace Mexico as she should have embraced Spain – by throwing herself into daily bouts of fun with her zany sister. She'd go on every trip she could and have a wonderful time. Molly and she would bond together even more – they were both alone and they only truly had each other.

Nell wiped a tear from her face – it had trickled into the crease of her neck. She swiped at it angrily with her palm. She wasn't going to be upset. She was on holiday and she was determined to have a fabulous time. She breathed out angrily and rolled over. Her body was hot, bones aching with tiredness, but her mind was alive with rushing thoughts. She turned over again and gritted her teeth. Tomorrow, she'd start her holiday again, properly.

* * *

Molly felt the warm sunshine on her skin as she placed a jug of orange juice and a pot of coffee on the patio table. She'd wake Nell; it was past ten: her sister had slept for twelve hours. As Molly arranged toast and marmalade, she wished she had some of Kristof's pastries, and her thoughts drifted back to the Day of the Dead and the time she had spent with him. It was his expression that was uppermost in her mind, the moment she'd turned from the altar; his smiling eyes had met hers and she'd felt safe and something else that made her skin tingle.

Her mobile buzzed in her shorts pocket and she pulled it out. Betty's voice trilled in her ear. Molly was delighted. 'How are you?

Do you feel all right now? Betty, I've some good news for you – my...'

'Me first, please.' Betty sounded much better. 'I wanted to say I'm so sorry about yesterday, missing the procession in town, leaving you in the lurch like that...'

Molly thought of Kristof, the red cord bracelet he'd given her, the way she'd hung on to his arm in the crowds. 'Oh, you didn't, not at all.'

'Molly, it was fifty years since Cliff and I married...'

Molly took a deep breath: no wonder Betty hadn't wanted to celebrate the Day of the Dead. 'Oh, Betty – I'm so sorry...'

'My brother-in-law, Teddy, he'd always said I should call him if I needed anything and of course I never did. I'm used to managing by myself. Then, last night, I was so down, I picked up the phone.'

'Does he live in Texas?'

'Yes, and Molly, he is so sweet. I said I'd take a plane back to Texas early but he had this wonderful idea. He's flying to Cancún, then we're hiring a car and taking a couple of days to drive down to Mexico City; we'll stay for a few days. It will be just the tonic I need to banish the blues but—'

'That's great, Betty.'

'But I'll miss you at bachata this week. We'll catch up soon as I'm back, I promise. I'll introduce you to Teddy. He's really so kind.'

Molly was all enthusiasm, her words spilling. 'And I'll introduce you to Nell, my sister. She's just arrived. Oh, Betty, I was worried about you yesterday...'

There was a pause on the other end of the phone. 'We both know how it feels to be alone, to miss someone so badly it chokes. But, you know, Molly, I think I'm going to be okay.'

'Me too,' Molly muttered, recalling the altar of sugar skulls and Kristof's warm gaze. She wondered if she and Nell might call in at the tapas bar later; she was surprised at the sudden feeling of her heart bumping in her chest. She took a breath, pulling her thoughts back to Betty. 'Have a great time in Mexico City.'

'I will. And I can't wait for us to catch up.'

Molly put the phone away. Nell was standing behind her, wearing a short pink dress. 'Who was that?'

'My friend Betty. You'll have to meet her, Nell. She's lovely. I've met so many nice people since I've been here.'

Nell was grinning. In a movement, she threw her arms around Molly. 'I missed you. It's so good to see you again.'

Molly squeezed her in a tight hug then they sat down. Nell began munching toast as Molly poured coffee, her face sympathetic. 'I'm sorry it didn't work out for you and Ronnie.'

'I was stupid, Molly. I imagined myself as queen of the *finca*, as first mate of the *Carpe Diem*. I hurt him and I hate myself for doing that.'

'These things happen sometimes.'

'Like Phil?' Nell's expression was bitter.

'Like Phil. But you've proved you can love someone again. It's possible, Nell, to have a life after Phil.'

'And so what about your flatmate, Moll? Is he nice, this Ryan?'

'Handsome, good-natured: he still believes he's living in the nineteen-sixties. He wanders round the place in his boxers all the time, and he's really kind-hearted, but he's not my type.'

Nell folded her arms. 'So, have you worked out what your type is, Molly?'

Molly laughed, a loud peal, too loud. 'I'll let you know when I do.'

'Oh, I bought you a present...' Nell reached into her pocket and handed Molly a piece of soft tissue paper with something wrapped inside. 'From Spain.'

Molly dropped a delicate bracelet onto her palm. It was fashioned with silver heart-shaped links. 'It's lovely, Nell.'

'You're my wonderful sister.' Nell grinned, pointing to the red cord on Molly's wrist. 'You can throw that old thing away now.'

Molly fingered her cord bracelet thoughtfully. 'This one's for protection.'

'So – time to start planning our holiday,' Nell said excitedly.

Molly reached for a slice of toast. She'd completely forgotten about her own breakfast until now. 'Where do you want to go?'

'Where do you recommend?'

'Chichén Itzá,' Molly spluttered without thinking. 'It's a great place – I watched the sun rise – and chilling on the beach with a picnic is perfect...'

'We'll do all that.' Nell clapped her hands. 'And what about hiring a speedboat? I was reading about Mexico and apparently there are loads of sites you can visit; we can trek through forests and visit water parks and go on coach trips, then there's shopping in Cancún – oh, Molly, I'm so glad I'm here with you. I bet you've been lonely...'

'Well, at first...'

'It's fine now. I'm here. We're going to have such a good time. I can't wait to get started.'

Molly put her toast down, a plan forming. 'We can have lunch in the tapas bar...'

'Oh, I've done tapas to death in Spain.' Nell waved imaginary tapas away with a flourish of her hand. 'It's fine dining for us now – I have the two months' rent back from Lisa for the peachy apartment – so money's no object, as long as you're happy with that – you paid for the accommodation, after all. And we can go to a spa hotel in town or even in Cancún – I'll treat us to all the extras. Molly, we'll have such fun.'

'I think that's a great idea. But, oh, you'd have enjoyed the Day of the Dead last night, Nell – it was so incredible...' Molly's voice trailed off.

'I heard it's a big thing in Mexico. Come on, Molly – finish your coffee, then I'm going to write a long list, put the days of the week down for the next few days and we're going to plan out every fun-filled minute. You and I are going to hit Mexico big time and finally have the holiday we both deserve.'

Nell rushed back into the apartment, presumably to get a pen and paper. Molly sipped her coffee. It was tepid. It was good to see Nell so animated and so excited: a proper holiday together, just the two of them, would be good. So why wasn't she feeling more enthusiastic? She took a deep breath: she had missed Nell and this was the perfect opportunity to make up for lost time. She grinned broadly just as Nell reappeared, paper and pen in one hand and her turquoise silk diary in the other. 'I forgot to give you this, Molly – you left it behind.'

Molly held Nell's gaze a second too long, wondering if she had read it, then she said, 'Oh, I've missed this. I can stop using the Pokémon pad now. Thanks so much.'

Nell brandished her writing implements. 'Right. I'm going to put each day down starting today for the next ten days and we're going to decide what we'll do. I thought today and every other day might be lazy days, beach or spa or something gentle. Then on the alternate days we'd do something strenuous – the water park or a hike in the forest or a coach trip to some ancient ruins. When we've got a plan, we'll go into town and book everything. We'll take everything Mexico's got to give and more. What do you say?'

Nell's enthusiasm was infectious. Molly leaned across the table. 'I totally agree.'

'I've one condition,' Nell suggested.

'Me too,' replied Molly. 'I'm not going swimming with those poor dolphins they keep in enclosures – or with horses.'

'Right. Agreed.'

'And what's yours, Nell – your one condition?'

Nell folded her arms and pressed her lips together. 'It's just me and you this time, Molly. I've learned my lesson. I'm independent, free and single. There will be no bloody men from now on.' Nell raised her coffee cup in a mock toast.

Molly held up her own cup, now empty, and repeated the pledge. 'No bloody men.'

34

Friday 19th November

    Nell and I are having such fun. She's ready to have the time of her life here in Mexico and I'm determined that she will. She deserves it. Life is a rollercoaster of visits at the moment, going somewhere exciting every day. No time to stop, not even to call in for tapas...

Nell was in the shower, washing off the excesses of Xel Há. They'd arrived home late, well after nine o'clock, tired and happy. They had swum in underground rivers, smoothed the feathers of brightly coloured parrots and even braved the zip line, screaming all the way along. The coach had dropped them in the centre of Puerto Palacio and they had strolled home, their arms around each other, laughing.

Molly lay on her bed and touched the turquoise silk cover of her diary, then gazed through her diary entries, written hurriedly over the last ten days. They had certainly enjoyed the best Mexico could offer: they had hired a speedboat, been far out at sea on a catamaran and seen the best and worst of Mexico's November weather, snorkelled for the first time, sunbathed, been to a spa three times and shopping twice. Nell had been amazed by the ancient ruins of Chichén Itzá, although Molly had secretly preferred the sunrise experience and was pleased that Kristof had managed to acquire the rare early-access tickets. But the best thing was that she and Nell were happy. Nell was looking refreshed and relaxed and they were truly closer than they'd ever been.

Molly reread some of her diary entries. On Sunday 7th they had been on a yacht cruise around the *Isla Mujeres*, the crystal water taking their breath away. On Tuesday 9th Nell had booked them in for a beauty day. Molly had laughed as the young hairdresser who had trimmed her hair complimented her on the stunning colour, completely silver now with indigo streaks, refusing to believe that it had been bleached by natural sunlight. Nell had what she called 'getting the whole works done' while Molly had revelled in a hot stones massage. On Monday 15th, they had drunk too many cocktails and danced to seventies music in the Bemba-Bemba nightclub in Cancún: she and Nell had laughed together all evening. Molly gazed at yesterday's entry:

Thursday 18th November

Great to meet up with Betty at the dance class and lovely to see the others again. José and Valeria are very excited about their wedding – the after-party is on the beach on Saturday. We're all invited and Alejandro says we must join in and dance the bachata with them. Betty and I are catching up for breakfast at Sabores on Saturday morning – I'm delighted that Nell can finally meet her. And it will be good to go to the tapas bar again…

Molly lifted her pen and began to write more about her day:

Friday 19th November

*Wonderful day at Xel Há. On the coach coming home Nell
opened up about what went wrong with her and Ronnie. I think
she still feels guilty and a little angry with herself so I told her a
little about Chichén Itzá and the Day of the Dead procession
with Kristof – it seemed strange to mention him to Nell.*

Suddenly a loud scream filled the air. Molly dropped her pen
and rushed into the hallway. The yell had definitely been Nell's
voice and it had come from the vicinity of her bedroom. Molly
reached the lounge to see Ryan, his case in his hand, looking
confused.

'Hi, Molly – there's a naked blonde in my room.' He
composed himself and offered a grin. 'Not that I'm complaining
but she seems a little upset about it all...'

Nell appeared suddenly, wrapped in a short dressing gown,
her face flushed. 'Who the hell is this?'

'Ah...' Molly offered a placatory smile. 'Ryan, this is my sister,
Nell.'

Ryan took in the sparse covering around Nell's torso and said,
'Pleased to meet you.'

Nell was immediately horrified. 'Oh, no – I've stolen your
room. I'm so sorry. Molly...?' She gaped at her sister, begging for
help.

'You and I can share,' Molly offered calmly. 'How are you,
Ryan? How was San Francisco?'

'Great,' he breathed. 'I feel a lot better now.' His eyes fell on
Nell. 'And I'm glad to be back. But please don't worry.' He noticed
Molly's glare and offered Nell his best smile. 'I'll sleep on the
couch. It isn't a problem.'

Molly expected him to have suggested that he and Nell share
the room; but there was something different about the way he

was watching her sister. He was suddenly polite, respectful, his eyes shining with a new interest. 'It's so good to meet you, Nell. You and Molly aren't alike at all. It's incredible that you're sisters...'

'Half-sisters,' Molly interjected between clenched teeth. Nell was holding out a hand to Ryan and smiling warmly.

Ryan cranked his suave attentions to the next level. 'Maybe we could all have dinner together tomorrow night? I know this great little hotel in Cancún...'

'Nell and I are going to a beach party. It's a wedding...' Molly interrupted.

Nell was still allowing Ryan to hold her hand. 'Maybe Ryan could come along too?' she suggested. 'After all, it's on a beach. No one would mind.'

Ryan's eyes were stuck to Nell's face. 'You remind me so much of Frida Kahlo,' he murmured. 'You have her wild spirit.'

Molly groaned and went back to her room. It was definitely time for bed.

* * *

When Molly and Nell arrived at the tapas bar the following morning, Betty was waiting outside, looking refreshed and happy, wearing a neat peach trouser suit. She indicated the door and frowned. 'I guess there are no tapas for us today. The place is closed.'

Molly stared at the sign in the door. *Cerrado.* She peered through the glass. There was no one inside the café; no lights were on. She rapped hard with her knuckles and shouted, 'Anyone there?'

Nell shrugged. 'We can go somewhere else.'

Betty grasped Nell's hand. 'It's so good to meet you at last. I heard so much about you from Molly. Are you having a wonderful time here?'

Molly tapped again and pressed her nose to the glass. Inside, chairs were inverted on tables; the café was in shadow and there was no sound.

'I'm loving being in Mexico,' Nell cooed. 'Molly said you were bringing a guest to breakfast – your brother-in-law?'

'Teddy's resting at the condo this morning. But we had an incredible time in Mexico City. He'll be at the wedding party tonight – you'll meet him there.'

Molly banged her fist harder against the glass. 'The place can't be closed – it's a Saturday.'

Then the door rattled open and Kristof stood in the frame, tall and smiling, wearing his chef's whites. 'Good morning. It's great to see you. Did you want breakfast? Come in.'

Molly, Nell and Betty trooped after Kristof through the bar and into the kitchen, where cookers, fridges and worktops gleamed in impeccable stainless steel. Molly couldn't help smiling as she watched Kristof place a pot of coffee on a hotplate and slide a tray of croissants into an oven. He held his hand out towards Nell.

'You must be Molly's sister. Good to meet you.' He hugged Betty and then Molly. 'Coffee and pastries okay? I'm a bit busy at the moment. I have some mini quiches just ready though if you'd like to try.'

He turned back to the worktop where he was piping green mousse for macarons onto a tray. Molly's eyes shone as she watched him work. His hands were large, but his movements were fluid, efficient. He placed the tray in an eye-level oven, taking out a batch of savoury tarts. He placed a few on a plate and handed it to Betty, whose eyes were wide with anticipation.

'Aperitif,' he grinned. 'Breakfast will follow soon.'

Betty was astonished to see him working alone. 'So where are Liliana and your young trainee chef?'

'Both sick.' Kristof smoothed something that looked like sponge mixture onto a tray with a palette knife. 'The same bug, I think. So, of course, they can't come here. This is why I closed the café. I have a wedding buffet to make by six o'clock this evening.'

'That must be impossible,' Molly couldn't help blurting. 'By yourself...'

'I'll be fine. I'm ahead of schedule.' He moved to the coffee pot, placing it onto a tray with three cups and a pile of croissants he'd taken from the oven. 'Would you like breakfast in the bar?'

'I'd rather eat here and watch you work.' Betty was nibbling a mini quiche. 'What is this?'

'Tofu, onion, broccoli and cashew cheese.'

Molly immediately reached for a tart and bit into crumbly pastry. 'Mmmm.'

'I have to make fifty of those, some opera petit fours, some jackfruit tacos, a few salads and roasted potatoes.' Kristof glanced at a list on the end of his workstation. 'Stuffed pittas, bread rolls, dips, a batch of frittata, sweet pastries, extra vegetables in case we have extra people.'

Molly was pouring coffee. 'Can we help?'

Kristof began to dice vegetables expertly with a hatchet. 'I think I can get it done.'

'I mean it – would you like some help? We wouldn't mind giving you a hand.'

'Thanks, Molly...'

Betty put her hands on her hips. 'We can do the easy things – make salads, slice vegetables... wash up.'

'We could make the extra roasted vegetables,' Molly suggested. 'They are easy to cook and a tray of those with a bit of dressing would feed lots of people.'

'I can butter bread...' Betty offered.

'Okay.' Kristof put down his knife and smiled. 'I have clean uniforms. If you don't mind...' He waved an arm towards the food. 'But first, enjoy your breakfast.'

Half an hour later, Betty was holding up Liliana's spare chef whites against herself. 'What do you think? Is it me?'

Nell was struggling into Javi's trousers, buttoning the top over her dress. 'I've always wanted to be a sous chef.' She grabbed Molly's arm. 'You could pop down to the market and buy those extra vegetables for roasting – you know, courgettes, peppers, that sort of thing.'

'That would be cool.' Kristof pointed towards the door. 'My wallet is in the jacket pocket, Molly, on the peg by the door.'

Nell shook her head at Molly who was staring at her, one leg poised above a spare set of Kristof's chef's trousers. 'Well, I can't go. My Spanish is non-existent.'

'I'll come with you,' Betty offered.

Kristof shrugged. 'There are potatoes to peel, Nell, if you don't mind.' He grinned encouragingly. 'Molly, when you're back, you can help me prepare the chocolate for the opera petit fours.'

Molly returned his smile. She tugged the wallet from Kristof's jacket pocket and Betty took her arm. 'While we're gone, I can tell you all about Mexico City and the great places we stayed on the way. And I can tell you all about Teddy, and how he's been a dear. He's a little older than Cliff, of course. He's been a widower for six years. He's a very considerate man.'

Molly leaned an attentive ear towards Betty as they walked into the café. As soon as she was out of earshot, Nell turned her attention to Kristof, who was dicing vegetables; then she picked up a potato and began hacking the skin from it, exhaling steadily. 'So – how do you know Molly?'

Kristof smiled. He replied without raising his eyes from his work. 'She and Betty come here sometimes to eat. We have been out together, horse-riding, one time to see the Mayan ruins.'

'Molly said you spent the evening with her during the Day of the Dead procession.'

'That's right.' Kristof dropped the vegetables into a sizzling pan and tipped some cashew nuts into a blender.

'So... are you and she...?' Nell was searching for the right words. 'I mean, do you like her?'

Kristof put the jar of cashews quietly onto the counter. 'Molly is great. Yes, I like her.'

Nell chopped a potato in half, making the knife clunk on stainless steel. 'You're not married, are you?'

'No.' Kristof pushed his hands into his pockets and leaned back on the worktop, watching Nell's straight back and her angry movements. Nell decapitated another potato and the one next to it with malice.

'What is worrying you, Nell?' Kristof asked softly.

Nell banged her blade against another potato. 'I don't want you to hurt her.'

He sighed. 'I won't do that.'

'The thing is...' Nell rubbed potato skin from her hands, her back still turned away. 'I'm not sure what your relationship is with my sister, but I've heard her mention you and this place several times over the last two weeks. I think she's developing a soft spot for you. Molly hasn't had a – a man-friend – in a long while. She's a widow and she's strong and independent and doing fine by herself. I don't want you messing with her feelings by offering her all this kindness and attention, promising her something she can't have. She's on holiday. We're going back to England at Christmas. I know what these holiday flings are like, I've just had one myself and it ended badly, and I don't want you to take advantage of her good nature...'

Kristof was staring at her, his gaze level. 'Thank you for telling me this. I am fond of Molly, but I won't hurt her. She is very special. And yes, she's strong and independent. I respect that. And I respect how loyal you are. But don't worry, Nell. I promise, Molly is fine with me – she is safe.'

'As long as we're clear about it,' Nell grunted and chopped another potato in half.

They worked in silence for half an hour, apart from Kristof's soft tuneful humming to the jazz music sifting through speakers, then Molly and Betty bustled through the bar, carrying a bag of vegetables each. Betty had just been telling her about visiting Frida Kahlo's house in Mexico City and that she'd had no idea that Trotsky was murdered in her home.

Molly's eyes widened. 'Oh yes, it was Leon in the study, with the ice pick.' She made a sad face. 'It was horrible, though. Poor Frida had an affair with him. She must have been devastated.' They burst into the kitchen, Molly holding out Kristof's wallet. 'That didn't take too long. I got lots of roast-able veggies. If Betty slices them up and puts them in a tray, I can help you with the chocolate. How would that be?'

'Great. Thanks, Molly.' Kristof took the wallet she was holding out and shoved it in the chef's trouser pocket.

Molly met his gaze and gave him a spontaneous hug; she was beaming with delight. 'I'm so going to enjoy helping you to make a wedding banquet.'

Nell watched her sister through narrowed eyes. Kristof's arms were round Molly, her head on his chest. She frowned. She was worried Molly was becoming keener on the chef than was good for her. She'd learned valuable lessons recently: Phil, Ronnie. It would inevitably end in tears. It always did. She couldn't let this happen to Molly, who had taken so long to recover from losing Richie. It would break her heart.

35

Saturday 20th November

A Mexican wedding feast on the beach is so exciting. I'm going to dance the bachata with Betty. Nell is coming with me, Ryan too. They seem to be getting on very well but Nell assures me they are just friends. And Kristof will be there. I wonder if he dances...

As they reached the beach, Nell was considering the words and phrases she'd choose to speak her mind to Molly: it was the right thing, the sisterly thing, to warn her. Nell gazed at Molly in the new dress she'd bought in Cancún, a grey shift that set off her thick silver mane beautifully. Nell waved a hand through her own sleek blonde bob, a look she'd spent an hour and several products attempting to achieve: Molly was striding forward, having stepped out of a shower and into her dress without a care, confident and happy. Nell didn't want to spoil her good mood, but it was only fair to say something. Molly had been very good to her over Phil and Ronnie; Nell didn't want her sister to make the same mistake.

The bride and groom were already in each other's arms, dancing together on the sand. Valeria was wearing a white silk dress, the material shimmering in the heat of the late afternoon sun. She and José, smart in his suit, were in the centre of a circle of admirers. Molly grinned happily.

'Kristof has set up the food under a palm tree. Everyone will love all those dishes we made. He's a brilliant chef, isn't he? He was so calm the whole time we were cooking, Nell. And when you cut your finger – he's so professional.'

Nell held up her index finger with the blue plaster, her nail varnished pearly pink. She decided to approach the subject of Kristof from another angle. 'Ryan should be coming down soon. He said he had some phone calls to make first.'

'He always makes a lot of business calls.' Molly recognised Alejandro and his wife Carmen. 'I'm so looking forward to this evening.'

'Ryan's very handsome.'

'Mmm.' Molly waved towards Rosa Maria, Alejandro's daughter, who was standing with a group of smartly dressed young women clutching handbags and glasses of champagne. She realised what Nell had said. 'Do you like him, Nell? He's a bit of a ladies' man.'

Nell shook her head. 'I'm off men for good. I don't think I'll have a relationship ever again. After all, you and I are the same, Molly – a man doesn't define us. We're fine by ourselves, aren't we?'

A waiter passed by with a tray of champagne; Molly took one and handed another to Nell. She clearly wasn't listening. Nell inhaled and tried again.

'Are you looking forward to being back in the UK?'

Molly shrugged. 'To be honest, I haven't given it a thought.'

Molly knew that wasn't strictly true; she had thought about it recently and decided she wasn't in a rush to go home. She glanced over towards a cluster of palm trees at the edge of the beach, where the sand ended and the road began. Trestle tables had been set up for the buffet and people were thronging around. She couldn't see Kristof, but his van, the one advertising *Caballos Samuel* on the side, was parked at the edge of the beach, so she assumed he was there. She craned her neck.

'You like him, don't you, Molly?'

'Yes.' Molly realised she'd answered too quickly, her guard lowered, and added, 'Everyone likes Kristof. He's really nice.' She pulled her gaze away from Nell's accusing stare. 'There's Betty, with her brother-in-law, Teddy. Let's go and say hello.'

Nell laid a firm hand on her sister's arm. 'Molly, we're only here for another month. I learned the hard way with Ronnie. A holiday romance might seem like a wonderful thing, but I don't want to see you get hurt.'

Molly returned her sister's gaze, all innocence. 'I've no idea what you mean. Come on – let's say hi to Betty. Then I'm going to dance the bachata.'

Betty and Teddy were eating small cakes from paper plates. She winked in Molly's direction. 'This opera cake is divine. I told Teddy you'd made the chocolate topping.'

Teddy was smiling, a dapper man in a white suit and panama hat. He grinned. 'I hear you girls have been doing all the catering. I'll have to get you all to come up to my next bash in Texas. This food is really something else.'

Betty licked her lips. 'We've sampled all the savouries. Teddy couldn't believe it was all plant-based. He's always been a steak and fries man. Everyone is talking about Kristof's food. You should go get some before it's all gone.'

The sound of lively trumpet playing replaced the smooth smoochy music coming from speakers and Alejandro and Rosa Maria were at Molly's shoulder. She was suddenly excited. 'It's bachata time first. Come on, Betty – we're partners.'

'Oh, but I've eaten too much...'

'Too bad. It's our turn to show the world how to bachata.'

Alejandro led his daughter to the space allocated for dancing. José and Valeria were already shaking and twirling. Molly noticed other dancers: the older couple from the dance class who always partnered each other and the two younger women who were experts by now. She tugged Betty's sleeve. 'Let's show them how it's done.'

The sun had dissolved behind the sea, the golden reflection rippling towards the beach. The darkening sky leaked the last rays of sunlight between pink and dark purple edged clouds; the music had become softer, mellower. Couples were swaying, their bodies close, and Molly watched as Teddy led Betty in a sedate waltz. Ryan had arrived, smart in an expensive suit, and whirled Nell in his arms. Molly gazed over towards the palm trees. Kristof was there, wearing an apron over jeans and a T-shirt. He'd finished serving food; he was talking to a young man wearing a leather jacket and the most ludicrous crash helmet Molly had ever seen. She knew the leering full-face helmet depicted one of the teenage mutant ninja turtles. The green-faced Michelangelo, with an orange eye mask and a grotesque grinning smile, seemed tiny in his motorcycle leathers standing next to Kristof. Molly made her way towards the food tables as the young man removed his helmet. She recognised the sharp cheekbones and dark hair:

it was Javi, Kristof's trainee chef. As she arrived, they were chatting in fast Spanish.

Kristof turned his welcoming smile towards her. 'Javi is feeling a little better. He's come to help me pack the empty dishes into the van.' Molly glanced at the trestle tables. There was one plate of food remaining. 'I saved this for you. I thought you might want to sample the things we made.'

Molly picked up a savoury quiche and took a bite. 'We make a good team, Kristof.'

His eyes gleamed. 'We do.'

Javi spoke quietly, his hands floating from his stomach to his throat. Kristof explained. 'He says he has been unwell all day. His mother has made him some soup so he's off home soon to eat it and go to bed. Tomorrow is Sunday so he will rest and be well again for Monday.'

Molly helped Kristof and Javi pack the empty plates and bowls into boxes in the back of the van. Javi said something to Molly in Spanish which was too quick for her to understand, then he held out his hand to shake hers, pulled the ninja turtle helmet on his head, zipped up his leather jacket and moved towards a small moped that was parked next to the van.

They listened to the spluttering sound of the moped engine and the fading roar as the ninja turtle rode away. They both turned back towards the beach. The sun had disappeared into the ocean and little candles illuminated the dancers, whose silhouettes merged as they swayed. Santana's 'Samba Pa Ti' slipped like syrup from the speakers, the guitar both sad and sultry. Molly was aware that Kristof was staring at her, his eyes shining. She opted for small talk.

'I think we did well. The food was a hit.'

'Yes.'

They gazed at each other. The music lifted and with it, Molly's breathing, which had suddenly become shallow. The sea shifted softly beyond the dancers, dark foam frothing on waves. She wondered if Kristof wanted to dance, if she could invite him to put his arms around her, if they could sway together beneath the palm trees. She imagined leaning her head against his chest as he smoothed her hair with his hand. But his eyes were on her face and he hadn't moved.

Santana's melancholy strains filled her ears, moody and melodic. Above them, a splinter moon slipped behind a cloud, trailing smudges of light in a sky dark and dense as liquorice. Then everything faded, all sounds, all movements; it was as if an invisible silk cord had been wound around them both and was pulling them closer together, as if there was no world remaining beyond the two of them, eyes fastened, standing on sand.

Kristof's voice was a whisper. 'We could go back to my place...'

His words hung on the air; Molly's mind was suddenly at full-pelt, kick-started into rushing thoughts. Yes: she would say yes. She wasn't ready to leave him, to go back to the apartment. He stretched out a hand and she placed her smaller one inside his grasp as they walked towards the van.

* * *

They were sitting on cushions in Kristof's flat above the tapas bar. Molly glanced around, surprised by the simplicity of the large living room: one small table, rugs and squashy cushions on wooden floors, a CD player with huge speakers, a saxophone on a stand against the wall. In the adjoining room, a single lamp outlined the shadows of a wardrobe and a double bed, a door leading to an en suite bathroom. Kristof poured red wine into two glasses; bowls on a small table contained dips and bread sticks. He sat beside her.

'Please help yourself. You didn't eat much at the party. I think I didn't eat properly today. It happens sometimes when I'm so busy.'

Molly reached for her wine glass. It occurred to her that she'd hardly eaten either, but for some reason she didn't feel hungry. Jazz music was seeping softly from the speakers, a woman's husky voice. She sipped the wine and wondered what to say.

'So, Kristof, you make all this great food, but you don't have time to eat much of it?' Molly was annoyed with herself: she was interrogating him, filling silence with pointless chatter.

He gave his usual grin. 'We have to taste our food all the time as chefs. Often, it is easy to taste it too much. I have learned to eat more wisely.'

'Was it a difficult lifestyle, being a professional chef?'

'For me, yes – I was too ambitious, always seeking the next challenge. It wasn't enough to be head chef, teaching others, making pastries for the Queen's garden party, to find my face in a magazine.'

'You did all that?'

'And missed my kids growing up and ignored Clémence. Crazy, really. Then I made some changes. I moved to New York and started again, then I worked in France for a while, then Spain. I wanted to make different food, to be able to combine a good taste with healthy ingredients. It was a good journey for me – I became thinner and wiser and it brought important things into focus.'

Molly watched his mouth form every word. 'What important things?'

He shrugged. 'Making a life I can be happy with.' He smiled softly. 'I am still learning.'

She noticed a half-moon slice beneath his eye, a wrinkle or a scar. Without thinking, she reached out to touch his face, her fingers feeling the indentation. 'What's this?'

'A cut from a bottle.' His eyes shone. 'My brother was in a fight – several people were beating him. It was in the town where we lived – I was about eighteen.'

'And you joined in?'

'He was my brother. I looked out for him. It happened a lot, guys waiting for him to come out of a club or a café at night.'

'Is this your brother who died?'

'Yes, he was sick. Forty years ago. Remi is buried in Bruges. I think about him every day, and I visit his grave when I am back there.'

Molly was quiet for a moment, listening to the sultry voice of the singer and the blustering notes of the saxophone. She looked across the room at the alto sax in its stand and back at Kristof. 'Is that yours? Do you play it?'

'The sax? A little.'

She sighed. 'I wish I could play or sing. I wish I had a talent.'

'I'm sure you have talent, Molly.' He held the glass, not drinking, his eyes still on her.

'I can paint a bit.' She was suddenly shy.

'Tell me about it.'

Molly took a breath. 'I painted a picture of myself once. I rolled in paint and then I lay on the canvas. It was green. So was I.' She was talking too fast. 'I do really mad things sometimes. I lost my clothes when I was skinny dipping, then I dressed up as a fish to advertise a boat trip.'

He grinned. 'I love that about you. So spontaneous. Always happy.'

'Oh, I'm not always happy.' Molly put a hand across her mouth, laughing again. 'Do you know I nearly smashed up the wardrobe at home on my birthday because I saw myself in the mirror?'

A frown appeared between his eyes. 'I don't understand.'

She offered him a shrug as an excuse. 'I just thought I'd become old. So I decided it would be better not to look at myself any more.' She brushed the thought away, a wave of her fingers. 'I was being silly really.'

Kristof stood up slowly and held out a hand. 'Come.'

Molly let him pull her to her feet. He led her into the bedroom, where the tiny lamp glimmered orange, and they stopped in front of the wardrobe, a heavy oak antique.

She gazed in the mirror at a woman in a grey silk shift dress, her feet bare, glossy silver hair around her shoulders, her eyes shining. She was lovely, serene, happy to be who she was and where she was. Behind her stood a tall handsome man smiling, his hand on her shoulder. They both stared at the image.

'Beautiful.' He spoke the word into her hair.

He wrapped both arms around her and her skin prickled. 'You called me a beautiful mermaid once...'

A sigh lifted in her chest. She turned to face him and lifted an arm around his neck. Their eyes connected: she couldn't pull her gaze away. He was so close she felt the warmth of his body, inhaled the musky scent of his skin.

The singer's scratchy voice began to murmur through the speakers in the living room, an achingly sad song about being misunderstood. For some reason, the gravelly tone and the melancholy song stirred something primal in Molly's soul. She knew at once that she wanted to be loved, to love back, to belong. Her fingers threaded through Kristof's hair and she leaned against him, finding his mouth with parted lips. The kiss became stronger; Molly pulled him closer, feeling passion take over and she let go of control. The moment was all that mattered, the thing that was happening now.

The invisible silk skein that had tugged them together on the beach was now a thick band binding them tight, restricting Molly's breathing as she clung to him; she couldn't break free and she didn't want to. She held on with all the strength in her arms as they tumbled back onto the bed and she kissed his mouth again as if it was her last breath.

36

Saturday 20th November

I'm thinking about Kristof. All the time. There seems to be nothing else in my mind.

Nell and Ryan were walking home, his arm around her shoulder against the cold wind that was drifting in from the ocean and buffeting their faces. The only sound was the soft slap of their feet against the pavement, then Ryan sniffed loudly.

'Weddings make me a little miserable. I always think of mine.'

Nell made a face. 'I've forgotten everything about my wedding to Phil. It was so long ago. It's best forgotten, too.' She gazed up at him. 'Was it an extravagant affair, your wedding?'

'Big hotel in New York; three hundred guests. I wanted the best for Lupe. It was to be my last wedding. It was going to be my best.'

Nell breathed out, listening to their feet tapping against concrete.

Ryan's voice took on a plaintive tone. 'Are you sure you won't stay with me tonight, Nell?'

'Absolutely.' She offered him a smile instead. 'You're still in love with your wife anyway.'

'My ex,' Ryan muttered sadly. 'And you're the iron lady nowadays, it seems.'

Nell nodded. 'I won't be hurt again,' she said flatly. 'I had too many years with one man and it didn't amount to much more than a habit. Since we split up, I've rediscovered myself. I don't need anyone now. I know that's right for me. I want to find out who I am and follow my own heart. I'm happier that way.'

'But you're great to dance with – and very attractive.' He reached in his pocket for the key. They stood at the front door of the apartment. Ryan pushed it ajar and stood back to let Nell in.

She wandered into the warmth and glanced at the wall clock. 'It's midnight already. I wonder if Molly's asleep.'

'I'll make us a coffee.' Ryan put a hand to his stomach. 'I think I ate too much, drank too much. I have heartburn coming on again.'

Nell called to him from Molly's room, her voice suddenly anxious. 'She's not here, Ryan. I thought she'd be back by now.' She rushed back into the kitchen where Ryan was clanking cups. 'Molly's not here. Should I ring her?'

Ryan's eyes twinkled. 'I'm guessing she won't be home tonight. Didn't you see her on the beach with the chef?' Nell's face was aghast. Ryan laughed, a satisfied guffaw. 'I bet the two of them are making out right now beneath a palm tree.' He thought for a moment. 'At least someone is getting some action tonight.'

Nell put her hands on her hips and sighed. She hoped Molly would be all right and, most of all, she hoped she and Kristof were only sharing coffee.

* * *

Molly stretched her arms over her head, a luxurious moment of pure happiness. On one side, Kristof was asleep, an arm flung out, the knotted red cord bracelet on his wrist. On the other side, the tiny alarm clock showed it was almost six o'clock. Sunrise. The Spanish word suddenly came to her: *la madrugada*, daybreak, dawn. She formed it with her lips: it was a beautiful word, sensual. She rolled over to gaze at Kristof, his eyes closed, breathing gently, and she realised she was smiling. She hadn't known him long but she was sure about her feelings. She knew it was right: Kristof was champagne, he was pure gold. He made her happy. She reached out a finger touching his lips, his hair. This morning, she felt younger, strong, beautiful: she could do anything she wanted.

As if thunderbolts had smashed through the window, several thoughts came at once. The image of Richie five years ago: they had made love, just as she and Kristof had done last night, and when she'd woken, he had not. Molly had stayed with him for hours in silence, a silence that screamed in her ears as loud as the sobs that followed. One moment, she had been his and he hers and then, in an instant, half of her was missing. She couldn't go through that again.

Nell's words came to her, the disdain on her face as she remembered her fling with Ronnie, her foolish holiday romance; it had been meant as a kindly warning to Molly. And Nell had been right. As she gazed at Kristof, Molly knew in an instant that she had fallen in love with him. And it would end. He would go back to Bruges; she'd return to Somerset; it would be over soon. She couldn't face the idea. Her body had gone cold, frozen by the fear of loss and separation.

She slid from the bed and pulled on her clothes quickly, picking them up from where they had been flung on the floor in hurried passion. At least she'd had that, Molly thought sadly. But once would have to be enough.

She tiptoed into the living room, gazing sadly at the saxophone by the wall, lifting up her handbag, inspecting the empty Nina Simone CD on top of the speaker. Last night, she had been affected by the mood of the music. No, Molly corrected herself: it had not been the tender passion of a song that had made her throw herself at Kristof. It had been the beginning of love, the beginning and the end, both in one night. It hurt to leave him but, if there was a next time, it would certainly hurt more.

Molly paused by the wine glasses, half full, the uneaten food on the table. She wished she could leave him a note. She could write *love you* or *sorry* or just the simple scrawled *x* of a kiss. It was better just to go, to say nothing, to walk and not turn back.

She stepped out of the back door to the café where Kristof had parked the van and walked briskly through a side street and through the town. It was early, Sunday morning and sepulchre-quiet. The sunshine was lighting the pavements, reflecting a glare on window panes; it would be a warm day, but her skin still felt cold. She increased her pace; she would soon be back at the apartment.

* * *

She wasn't hungry at lunchtime, although Nell had made omelettes for everyone and Ryan was pouring freshly squeezed fruit juice into glasses, wearing only a pair of turquoise shorts. Nell was droning on as if Molly was a teenager and she was a disappointed parent. 'I can't believe you slept with him, Molly.'

Molly wanted to sulk, to react with the sullen words, 'I love him,' but Nell leaned forward, putting her lips close to Molly's ear. 'Whatever were you thinking of?'

Molly flashed her sister a wild look of exasperation. Nell felt her cheeks tingle; she had been fourteen when Molly became a pregnant teenager. Six months ago, she was sleeping alone, her husband banished to the spare room. Recently, she had broken Ronnie's heart. She was in no position to lecture Molly.

Ryan laughed, a barking guffaw of admiration. 'Fair play to you, Molly. You have a one-night stand with this guy and then you walk away like a real player. It takes me back to the sixties, to the summer of love. The number of chicks I've...' He caught Molly's flashing eyes and poured juice, his mouth closed and contrite.

'I'm no better than that, am I?' Molly wiped the tears that sprang to her eyes, swallowing hard. 'Love them and leave them? Is that the sort of person I've become – selfish and heartless?'

Nell's face softened. She wrapped her arms around Molly. 'You've done the right thing. I mean, we'll all be on our way soon. It's just a few weeks until Christmas.'

Molly was thinking that a few weeks with Kristof would have been better than nothing. She could have made them last a lifetime. But she kept her thoughts to herself. Nell was probably right. She had to be sensible to protect her feelings and Kristof's by walking away sooner rather than later.

'Eat your omelette, Moll,' Nell coaxed, still in parent-mode.

'She's probably all plant-based now,' Ryan teased. If Nell was a chiding mother, Ryan was an annoying brother. Molly pushed the plate away and glanced at the clock on the wall. It was almost two.

Nell's face brightened. 'How about we all go out this afternoon? Ryan, you're a local. Where do you suggest?'

'We could go to the hotel in Cancún and I could dance with both of you.' He saw Molly's sneer. 'Or we could go for a drive and a coffee? Maybe we could take a speedboat out somewhere?'

Molly couldn't hear him. She was thinking about her horse Oro swimming in the sea and Kristof being there, reaching out. She was remembering the sunrise over Chichén Itzá and his arm around her, and the moment she had caught his gaze at the altar after the procession. She was holding tight to the memory of them together, the warmth in his voice as he'd whispered her name, the way he'd held her like he'd never let go.

Nell was saying something. 'Was that someone knocking? Shall I go and see?'

Ryan made to move from his chair, but Molly was ahead of him, bounding towards the front door, just in case it was Kristof. She had no idea what she'd say, but she tugged the door wide and held her breath. Betty was smiling at her from the step, neat and smart in a pale blue suit.

'Betty.' Molly's mouth was moving faster than her brain; her heart had already started to thud in her ears at the thought of who might be behind the door. 'Come in. I'll make coffee.'

'I can't...' Betty smiled and waved a hand towards a grey BMW parked at the kerb. Teddy was sitting in the driver's seat, wiggling his fingers and smiling. 'We're going back to Texas a little early. We want to plan a big Thanksgiving party for the whole family.'

Molly flung her arms open. 'I'll miss you, Betty.'

'Oh, honey, we'll stay in touch. And you and Kristof must come to Texas. It would be great. I can teach you to ride...' She stopped as Molly had thrust herself back, straight-armed, and was shaking her head. 'What is it? You've got together, you and Kristof, surely?'

Molly nodded her head then shook it again. A frown line deepened between Betty's neat eyebrows. 'I don't understand. You are dating him now, aren't you? I saw you together at the wedding party...'

Molly sniffed, shrugging her shoulders. 'Holiday romance. Brief one. Over.'

Betty's small hands flew to her mouth. 'No, Molly. That can't be right. You and Kristof are perfect together.'

Molly turned away, gazing up the road into the distance. Betty grabbed her wrists with surprising force. 'Now, you listen to me. That guy cares for you, really cares, and unless I'm completely crazy, you're in love with him too. So, do yourself a favour and get right on over there and tell him how you feel. Do you hear me, Molly?'

Molly nodded, although her arms and legs had become numb and her mouth wouldn't move. Betty planted a kiss on her cheek. 'I have to go. Teddy and I have to drop the hire car off at the airport.' She leaned forward and pressed Molly's hand confidentially. 'We're not lovers. Teddy's a companion, a gentleman. We're the best of friends. But you're different – you're ready for something else; you and Kristof are so well suited. I've seen you together, the way you look at each other. You know I'm right, Molly.'

Molly nodded, sniffed in agreement and then flung her arms round her friend. She watched as Betty moved elegantly back to the BMW, offered her a conspiratorial wink, slid into the passenger seat and drove away, leaving one large hoot floating on the air as a final goodbye. Molly waved until the car disappeared around the corner, then she felt her heart sink.

* * *

Later that afternoon, Ryan drove his white Mercedes into Cancún, Nell smiling from the front in designer sunglasses and Molly scowling from the back seat, wearing budget imitations. He treated them to cocktails in a hotel, trying to lighten Molly's mood by offering her sex on the beach. Nell explained in her tinkling laugh that it was a cocktail made from vodka, peach schnapps, orange juice and cranberry juice, and that she'd happily have one. Molly was trying hard not to allow her bad mood to spoil the fun, so she threw herself into the party spirit and drank two large cocktails in quick succession on an empty stomach, which had the immediate effect of making her raucously loud, finding the most ridiculous things funny. She was entertaining Nell and Ryan and everyone else in the bar with her stand-up comedy routine, leaning against her stool and waving her arms frantically.

'Why can't you hear a pterodactyl go to the toilet? Because the pee is silent.'

Ryan coughed. 'I don't think I've heard that one...'

'So, okay, what about this one...? What happens when a frog's car breaks down? It gets toad.'

Nell laughed reluctantly. 'Molly...'

'Here's one for Pilar. You remember Pilar, Nell, Ronnie's lovely cleaner? Okay, so – What did the blanket say as it fell off the bed? "Oh, *sheet!*"'

Nell rolled her eyes: she didn't want to be reminded.

'And here's one for my Texan friend, Betty. What did the buffalo say when his son left? Bi-son! There are buffalos in Texas, aren't there?'

'Yeah, okay, Molly. Do you want another cocktail or shall we get going?'

'I think we should go, Ryan,' Nell muttered, her voice low.

'I met this great woman by the pool in Spain. She was called Lourdes. I bet she'd love this joke.' Molly took a breath. 'Cosmetic surgery used to be such a taboo subject. Now you can talk about Botox and nobody raises an eyebrow.'

Ryan rubbed the top of his stomach. 'I have a bit of heartburn coming on – my gut feels like it's radioactive.'

'What's the most terrifying word in nuclear physics? Oops!' Molly cackled. 'I want another cocktail.'

'We should be going, Moll,' Nell whispered soothingly. 'You can have a coffee back at the apartment.'

'How do you feel when there's no coffee? Depresso.'

Nell sighed. 'I might message Ulla and Bernt tonight; I promised I would.'

'What do you call someone who emigrated to Sweden? Artificial Swedener.'

Ryan wrapped his arms around Nell and Molly. 'Let's go home and grab a movie, shall we?'

'What is Forrest Gump's computer password?' Molly bent forwards, laughing. '1-Forrest-1.'

Ryan thought about it for a moment, then smiled. He shepherded her to the hotel exit, then towards the Mercedes, helping her into the back seat. Nell climbed into the front and shut the door crisply.

Molly snuggled down in her seat and closed her eyes. 'I'm tired. What time is it, Nell? Oh, the sun is going down. Must be around six, then? I'm hungry too.' The thought of food made her remember the last meal she shared with Kristof, staring into his eyes. She felt suddenly sad. 'The problem with love... is that it's just like a barometer...' she began, and she felt instinctively that both Ryan and Nell were sitting upright, listening. 'The barometer goes up and you're warm, happy, on cloud nine, but when it plummets down again, you're left out in the cold, and that's when you know you'll never be happy again.'

She saw Nell and Ryan exchange glances, so she raised her voice a little louder. 'But we three are okay. We're fine. We don't care a hoot for love, do we, guys? We're over it, aren't we? Let's go home and watch a movie and order in pizza and drink beer. That would be great: what do you say?'

'A film's good.' Nell's voice came from the front seat.

'I might pass on the pizza, what with my heartburn,' Ryan suggested.

Molly guffawed. 'Where's the fun in you all? This is our holiday.'

Everyone was suddenly quiet, Ryan and Nell lost in their own thoughts and Molly staring through the window at the traffic and the shops. The car turned around the corner and came to a stop outside the apartment. It was almost dark now, but Molly recognised the figure sitting on the front step, waiting. She stumbled out of the car, gazing at the easy smile, into soft eyes. The temperature dropped, her skin tingled with cold, and she was suddenly shivering, immediately clear-headed. 'Kristof.'

Sunday 21st November

I can't see him any more. I've leaped in again, haven't I? I'm so stupid, I put my best foot in without thinking of the consequences and I have to pull it out again. Nell is right. It has to end – I'm leaving next month and it hurts already. What was I thinking?

I think about Kristof all the time, though, his smile, his dancing eyes, the scent, the warmth of him. I don't want to replace someone I loved in the past – I want someone I can love for the future. But I can't think about him again. Not ever.

They were walking through the town. It was dark now, neon lights glimmering from the shops where doors had been flung open for the last-minute shoppers. Kristof was holding her hand and she was trying to explain, but the words wouldn't form in her mouth. She'd told him she didn't want to go to the beach: they'd been there last night and she was sure it would leave her feeling vulnerable and romantic. She'd shuddered at his offer to go back to his flat and talk; she knew she couldn't trust herself not to throw herself into his arms and into his bed. So they wandered through the empty desolate backstreets; Molly felt empty and desolate.

'It wouldn't work, Kristof.' He didn't answer, so Molly tried again. 'We live in different countries. I don't want a holiday romance.'

He shrugged. 'We can make anything work. The world is small. There are planes, trains, boats.'

Molly wanted to cry. She took a deep breath and said nothing. She felt Kristof's touch as he linked his fingers through hers.

'Molly, last night was special for me.'

'It was just sex.' Molly stopped speaking. If she'd continued, she would have added other words like love and forever and how she didn't want to let him go.

'No, I think we have something special. I think that you and I are special together.'

'I don't feel special. I feel sad.'

They had arrived at a church, a beautiful ornate building with a sweeping flight of steps at the bottom. Tiny lights twinkled from the tower and the cross at the top was illuminated, a golden yellow. Molly pulled her hand from Kristof's grasp and flopped down onto cold stone; he sat beside her. She met his gaze for the first time since he'd been outside the apartment, waiting for her, and the tenderness in his eyes made her heart ache. She exhaled and tried hard to explain, lurching at any words that filled her mouth.

'I just – don't need anyone in my life. I've been alone for five years. I'm fine.'

Kristof closed his eyes for a moment. 'The same is true for me: I have been alone for many years.'

'So, I'm used to being by myself.'

'Perhaps we are both fine alone but better together? Twice as good?' He smiled. 'The day we went to Chichén Itzá to watch the sunrise, it was my seventieth birthday.'

'You didn't say anything...'

'It was a good birthday, just being with you. Even then, Molly, I knew I had feelings for you—'

'Why me?'

He smiled. 'You had your sweatshirt on inside out that day. I wanted to hold you in my arms.'

Molly sighed. 'You should have seen me dressed as a carp in Spain.' She saw his puzzled face: humour wasn't the way forward. She tried honesty. 'It's not that I don't care...'

'Tell me how you feel now.'

'Sad.' Molly answered without thinking. 'Yes, I have feelings for you, Kristof. But what if we stay together? What happens if I come back to your flat now and we fall completely in love?'

A smile flickered across his face. 'That's what I want.'

'And at Christmas time? Tell me, Kristof, what had you planned to do at Christmas? And in January and February? Where will you be?'

He frowned. 'My son Joël is a sports teacher but he wants to buy a little café and turn it into a tapas bar, like we did here. He has some money left by my mother. I might help him.'

'In Bruges?'

Kristof nodded. 'I don't understand.'

'I'll be in England.' Her expression was one of exasperation.

'I want to be with you.'

Molly put her hands to her head, rubbing her temples. 'It can't work.' She took a breath. 'Just let me go, please. It's better this way.'

He held her gaze for what seemed a long time. 'Tell me how I can change your mind. What do you want? I can send flowers to your house. I can sit on your doorstep all night. If you like, I'll fight every day to make you stay.'

'Please don't.' Molly shook her head and stared at her knees. Tears had started to stream down her face.

'I want us to be together.' He wrapped an arm around her, kissing her forehead. 'I know we can make it work, you and me.'

Molly felt herself weakening. Struggling from his embrace, she sighed. 'Please – just go.'

Kristof put a hand on her shoulder, lifted her chin to meet his eyes. 'Is this what you want, Molly? For me to walk away? Really? Tell me the truth.'

She nodded, her cheeks wet.

'Are you sure? Completely sure?'

Molly bit her lip and nodded again, this time more frantically.

'Then I wish you happiness, the best things in life, always.'

Her face was in his hands. He pressed his lips against hers gently and when he pulled away, his eyes were sad with regret. Molly felt more tears brim over and stream down her cheeks. Kristof didn't speak. He stood up quietly, touching his lips against the top of her head and then he moved away. She watched him as he crossed the square and disappeared around a corner. Molly stared up at the vast dark sky, a howl choking in her throat, her face wet with weeping.

* * *

It rained heavily on Monday and Tuesday. Molly spent most of the time in her room reading. When she emerged for meals, she plastered a fake smile on her face and made her voice cheerful. She wasn't sure whether she was trying to fool herself or everyone else. Ryan appeared to be on his mobile talking business most of the time, a mug of coffee in his hand; Nell was painting her toenails or thumbing through messages on her phone. Molly returned to her book, although her mind wasn't on the story.

Wednesday was the day before Thanksgiving, so she messaged Betty, who was back in Texas and excited about being reunited with her son Jason. Teddy was organising a huge celebratory dinner for the extended family, children, grandchildren, cousins, siblings to sit together around the table. Betty said she had so much to be thankful for. Molly agreed with her, but her heart wasn't in it.

She thought about home and felt adrift. Home wasn't the apartment in Mexico; her own house in Somerset was occupied by someone else – even her cat Crumper had adapted well to his new owner. She didn't know where home was any more, so, desperate to talk to her own kin, she rang Samantha, who was unusually delighted to chat and eagerly invited her to come and stay in Cumbria in the New Year. Molly, flushed with success, messaged Vanessa who was equally enthusiastic to share her news. She replied straight away that she was going to move in with Darren, the manager from the Globe, in the New Year and Jack and Mel could have her house, so Molly would have her home back after Christmas.

Molly imagined her little cottage, the paintings on the wall, the garden (now tidy), the wardrobe she'd never chopped up. It seemed so far away. Vanessa's next message interrupted her thoughts; Colonel Brimble-Dicks was in hospital. Joe had been incredible: he had saved him, recognising the symptoms of a stroke, slurred speech and his mouth turned down on one side. Vanessa added that Jack and Mel and Crumper were all doing well, one little happy family. Molly replied that she was pleased, but once she'd finished the conversation she felt a chill settle on her skin: their lives and the area and the house that had once been her home felt so distant, so disconnected to who she was now. Everyone back in Somerset had moved on and Molly wasn't sure where she fitted in any more. She had changed too much now to go back to the routine of her old life.

Molly opened the turquoise diary – it was all she had to share her feelings with – and tried to write down her thoughts. She managed to scrawl *Wednesday 24th November*, then she wrote *I feel*, crossed it out, wrote *Kristof*, was tempted to draw a heart and colour it in, so she threw the diary on the bedside table and had a shower instead, then went to bed. But she could not sleep: her mind was crammed with thoughts of Kristof, imagining him working in the kitchen; she recalled the moment on the beach when their eyes had locked. His expression when he'd left her on the steps of the church troubled her: she had hurt him. Spectres of memories would not leave her alone; they froze her to the bone with sadness and made her want to sob.

On Thursday, Ryan took Molly and Nell out for a drive and dinner. He ate far too much steak and spent the evening eyeing the waitress, while Nell complained about how expensive the food was, given the quality. Molly suggested she'd happily have settled for some plant-based tapas, which turned out to be a conversation killer.

On Friday evening Nell, desperate to cheer everyone up, dragged Molly and Ryan to a hotel with a huge swimming pool in Cancún. There was a barbecue and dancing to a samba band. Ryan took it in turns to dance with Nell and Molly. When they came home, Ryan opened a small bottle of bourbon and filled three glasses. Nell was regaling everyone with details of the Sámi bracelet Bernt had bought Ulla; they had been chatting on WhatsApp and Ulla had mentioned how it was intricately fashioned from reindeer leather and metallic braid. She had sent a photo and Nell thought it was lovely. Molly glanced at the red cord bracelet on her own wrist and wondered where the protection was that Kristof had promised. She didn't feel safe or positive: behind her cheery grin, she felt raw and exposed.

Nell had interrupted her thoughts and asked if she was all right. Molly had offered a breezy smile and said she wanted to buy everyone breakfast in town first thing tomorrow. She saw Nell's expression freeze, a waxwork moment of alarm, and Molly calmed her by assuring her they'd go to a ranch-style place that served pancakes and tortillas, not the tapas bar.

* * *

So, on Saturday morning, Molly put on the orange dress and a black silk wrap and brushed her hair until it shone. Nell wore a smart black dress and Ryan appeared in a jacket, jeans and an open-necked shirt.

'My treat,' Molly announced, explaining that the café was in the centre of town and it was renowned for its pancakes. The truth was, she'd passed it last Sunday night after Kristof had left her, and she'd stared into the window, the incongruous garish lighting and cheerful customers inside making her feel all the more lonely. But, somehow, she had to put her bravest foot forward.

As soon as they'd stepped out into the road, Ryan placed a hand to his stomach. 'I might just have coffee. My indigestion is playing up again.'

'Too much bourbon last night,' Nell scolded playfully.

Molly agreed, grinning. 'A breakfast tortilla will settle you down.'

As the three of them walked side by side, Nell suggested a shopping trip to Cancún might be a good idea later. Molly didn't reply; she was examining every street corner, every passer-by in case she saw Kristof, but she knew he'd be at work in the tapas bar. She told herself she was being stupid; he was the last person she wanted to see. She was trying to heal herself, not open the wound again.

Ryan asked if they could stop by a pharmacist on the way for some Pepto-Bismol. Nell said it was a good idea – she needed more tablets for her headache: the bright sun often made it worse. Ryan said his head was hurting too. Molly offered to buy them each a sun hat and stopped in a shop doorway, trying on a variety of headgear and striking silly poses, making them smile.

Then Ryan put a hand to his face. 'I have to say, I'm not feeling too great.'

Nell grinned. 'You just need breakfast.' She glanced at him and her expression changed. His face was an unhealthy colour, pale beneath his tan. He was sweating heavily.

Molly reached out to touch his brow. 'You're clammy. I don't think you're too well. Do you want to go back?'

Ryan leaned back against the window of the shop, slumping hard against the glass. 'I feel dizzy.'

Molly saw Nell's worried expression and grasped Ryan's arm. 'I think I've seen a doctor's surgery near here. Shall we take you there, Ryan? I'm sure it's only a street away... it's best we get you checked out.'

'No, I...' He lurched forward and both Molly and Nell had to struggle to hold him upright.

Nell flashed Molly an anxious look. 'Where is it, the surgery?'

'Not far.'

Molly and Nell hauled Ryan to an upright position and set off as fast as they could, dragging him between them. He had become heavier, his legs not moving in time with theirs. Molly manoeuvred him into a side street and they stopped in front of a bronze sign: *Francisco Álvarez: Médico.*

Molly heaved the door ajar with her shoulder and she and Nell helped Ryan to stumble up the steps and into a waiting room. Several people were seated in a row on chairs: a woman in dark clothes with a little boy on her knee, her face pinched and anxious; an old man wearing a heavy coat, a young couple holding hands. Molly looked around for a receptionist, a professional, anyone who could help her. Nell, grasping Ryan's arm, heaved him upright against her body. Then his legs gave way and he flopped to the floor. A little scream escaped from Nell's mouth. Molly's head buzzed, searching for the right words, then she yelled, '*Ayúdame por favor, este hombre está enfermo.* Sick – he's sick.'

The doors opened and people were moving quickly. A man in a white coat was kneeling next to Ryan, his fingers feeling for a pulse. A woman had joined him and they were talking in rapid Spanish, too fast for Molly to understand. Then Ryan was on his feet, helped through a door and gone. Molly and Nell sat down together, their faces reflecting each other's concern. A clock ticked on the wall, the second-hand twitching: it wasn't yet ten o'clock.

38

Saturday 27th November

For the last week, I've missed Kristof more than I can say. Life has a way of giving you too much time to think about things that hurt and my head has been achingly full, changing my mind one way and then the other. It's been torture for days, sometimes deciding to go and see him, sometimes trying to forget him forever. Then something happens that you don't expect and everything is suddenly, blindingly, flashlight-in-your-face clear.

'It's been half an hour.' Molly checked the clock again. 'More.'

'I hope he's all right.' Nell pressed her lips together.

Molly thought for a moment. 'He looked awful. His face was a terrible colour.'

Nell agreed. 'Health is everything, Moll. We have to make the most of our time – fill our life with positive things.' She sighed. 'I've got something to tell you.'

Molly met her eyes, waiting.

'I'm going to Sweden. To stay with Bernt and Ulla.'

'When?'

'Next week. They've invited me to be their guest for all of December, over Christmas. I want to go.'

'Oh.'

Nell wrapped an arm around Molly's shoulders. 'You can come with me if you want. It would be lovely...'

'Sweden?' Molly shook her head. She was thinking about how far away Sweden was from Mexico, from where she wanted to be. Her mind moved to Ryan. He was unwell: he was still with the doctor. What if he died? There were important things he should have done with his life. If he were asked right now what he'd miss most, he would say he regretted breaking up with Guadalupe. He'd regret the time he'd wasted not being with her, Molly was sure of it. And, Molly asked herself, what would she regret most?

Nell interrupted her thoughts. 'I have to tell you something else, Molly... I know...'

Molly assumed somehow Nell had just read her thoughts; that she knew she was thinking about Kristof; that she was wondering why she had let him walk away. It had seemed sensible not to embark on a transient holiday romance. It had been the wise thing to do at the time. But Molly didn't want to be wise now. Ryan's health scare had prompted a change of heart: she wanted to do the things she'd miss most if her life ended today. And she knew who she'd miss more than anything.

Nell took her hand. 'About the baby. Phil's baby. Phil and Nikki's.'

'Oh. You know about that?' Molly sighed.

'I don't care about it now. I wish Phil all the best. There's nothing I can do to change it and I don't want to. I'm going to concentrate on my own life. But I won't go back to Yeovil, certainly not yet. I want to wait until after his baby's born and the divorce is settled, then I can buy a place of my own and hold my head high, show I'm independent. I don't need Phil now. I don't think I ever did, really.'

'How did you find out about Nikki being pregnant?'

'I needed something sensational to read on the plane,' Nell blurted, then gazed at her knees and exhaled sharply. 'I read your diary. Sorry, Molly.'

'It's all right.' Molly pressed her lips together. 'I have something to tell you, too.'

'What?'

'I shouldn't have let Kristof go. I want to go and see him. I've decided – I want him back.'

Nell nodded. 'I think you're right. I'm sorry I was so cynical and sour and tried to put you off. You and he aren't like me and Phil or me and Ronnie. I've been stupid...'

Molly shook her head. 'I'm just like Kezia Lovell. I walk out on people I love.'

'You don't walk out on people – look how brilliantly you've supported me. You are a great mum to Samantha, even though you were just a kid yourself when you were pregnant. And Richie adored you...'

'My own mother left me, though...'

Nell moved her head to stare at Molly. 'She didn't leave you, Molly. I thought I told you what Mum said...'

'You never said exactly what happened.'

'Dad told Mum. Mum told me. She was from a Travelling community, Kezia Lovell, and she went to live with Dad, and they had you. But she was already married. She knew what would happen eventually, but she adored Dad – and you. You were sleeping in a cot upstairs. Her brothers caught up with her and they took her back to her husband, prised her away...'

'So, she never left me behind deliberately?'

'She loved you, Molly. She wasn't someone who'd simply move on and leave her family behind. She wanted to stay with Dad and you. She was where she wanted to be. She'd just broken some rules and, in those days, she had no choice – she had to go back.'

'I'm not a drifter, either.' Molly closed her eyes and squeezed Nell's hand hard. 'I'm like my mother – I'm loyal and I take care of those people I love. And I love you, Nell – you're the best of sisters.'

'I've made some mistakes. I shouldn't have hurt Ronnie. Phil was probably a mistake too. I'm still finding out who I am.'

'It's like Kristof said – we're all still learning, all the time.'

'I don't need a man in my life.' Nell's voice was firm. 'I know that now. Being single isn't the opposite of being happy. Being single isn't a temporary state until I find a partner. I am learning to love myself more than that.'

'I thought I didn't need anyone. But Kristof's not just any man – I don't need just anyone. But I do want to be with him.'

'You love him don't you, Moll?'

Molly nodded.

'Then go and see him – tell him how you feel. He's right for you – he's generous, good looking, kind, he cares – what do you have to lose?'

A door opened and a woman came through, pushing a wheel-chair: Ryan was hunched over in the seat, pale, his eyes ringed with dark circles, but he smiled up at Molly. She was by his side. 'How are you?'

He offered a weak smile. 'My heart isn't great. High blood pressure. They are giving me medication.'

Nell exhaled. 'Thank goodness we got you here.'

Ryan held his mobile out towards Molly, his arm weak. 'Do me a favour? Ring Lupe. Tell her about me, that I'm here...'

'Of course.' Molly took the phone. 'But why don't you call her?'

'She's always angry with me.' Ryan sighed. 'She'll listen to you.'

Molly held the phone to her ear, waiting for the repeating burr. Then a sharp voice answered. 'Ryan? Why are you ringing me at work?'

'It's not Ryan, it's me, Molly.'

'Who?'

'Molly Mitchell. I rent your apartment in Puerto Palacio. Ryan's here with me.'

'What?'

Molly took a breath. 'He's staying at the apartment. He's at the doctor's now. He's not well. He collapsed.'

'Collapsed?' Guadalupe's voice was shrill. 'Is he all right? What's happened?'

'Yes, I think he'll be all right. They are giving him medication for his heart—'

'His heart? Tell him to stay where he is, not to move until I get there. I'll be on the next plane to Cancún.'

There was a click. She had gone. Ryan's face was anxious. 'What did Lupe say?'

Molly handed his phone back to him. 'She's on her way here.'

Ryan closed his eyes and smiled. 'She's coming back to me.' He breathed out slowly. 'I'll be fine now. My Lupe's coming home.'

* * *

Molly left Nell with Ryan and hurried across the road towards the tapas bar. She had no idea what she'd say when she arrived, but she knew she'd blurt something out and Kristof's eyes would twinkle and he'd hug her. She was walking as fast as she could; the moment couldn't come quickly enough.

She turned the corner and rushed into *Sabores*. There were a few people at tables, eating and drinking. There was no jazz music; a dreary ballad groaned through speakers. Molly didn't recognise the short-haired young woman at the bar. She leaned forward and tried her best Spanish. '*Dónde está* Liliana?'

'*Está en la cocina.*' The woman pointed towards the kitchen. Molly rushed behind the bar and into the stainless steel kitchen where Liliana and Javi were working, chopping vegetables, pristine in their chef's whites. Liliana's mouth opened in surprise. 'Molly? I didn't expect to see you...'

'Where's Kristof?' Molly grasped Liliana's arm. 'I need to talk to him.'

'He's not here.'

Molly nodded; he'd be upstairs in the flat. She hurried out of the kitchen and over to the door at the back of the café that led upstairs. Her feet hammering on the floorboards, she pelted into the flat and stopped. The living room was different, bare. His saxophone, the CD player and speakers, everything was gone. The cushions were tidied into one corner and the table was empty. Liliana and Javi were behind her; Molly spun round, shocked. 'Where is he?'

'He left, Molly.'

'When?' Molly squeezed her eyes shut. The world had started to spin.

'This morning he tells me he wants to move on. I have to ask my friend Alma to take over at the counter while I help Javi to cook.' Liliana put her hands on her hips. 'I never see Kristof without his smile. What happened?'

Molly blinked hard, her chest heaving. 'Where is he? Can you ring him? Can you tell him to come back?'

Liliana produced her phone and put it against her ear. Molly held her breath. Liliana listened for a moment then waved the phone. 'Still no reply. Three times I call him now.'

'Do you know where he has gone?'

Liliana nodded briefly. 'I think he has gone to see my brother. He will ask to borrow his van and then drive north, I think.'

'He's at the stables?' Molly gripped Liliana's arm. 'At Samuel's stables?'

Liliana nodded 'He may still be there...'

'How can I get to him? I need to see him... I need to tell him to come back.'

Javi was frowning; he muttered something in Spanish to Liliana who rolled her eyes and replied rapidly. Javi thundered down the stairs and returned moments later, holding out his leather jacket and his full-face ninja turtle crash helmet. Molly stared at him. He pushed the helmet and jacket into her arms, his eyes wide with excitement. '*Es importante, no?*'

Molly seized the helmet, the jacket and the keys he was pressing into her hand. 'Thank you. Yes, yes, it's important,' she breathed.

* * *

Cars on the coast road honked their horns as they whizzed past the chugging moped, Molly astride, leaning forwards, her green face leering. She was squinting through the visor of the helmet, straining her eyes to check how far it was to the turn-off for Samuel's stables. Liliana had said the area was called Playa Redonda. She recalled the ranch had looked like a hollowed-out tooth from a distance. She was searching for a sign, anything that would take her there. How she appeared to other motorists was the last thing on her mind.

But the drivers of cars and lorries hooted blaring horns in rapid succession. It wasn't every day they saw a teenage mutant ninja turtle crawling along the highway on a moped. And this turtle, Michelangelo with the green face, the orange mask and the wide grimacing tombstone teeth was wearing a tight leather jacket, an orange dress and a long black scarf that ballooned behind, resembling a cape. The determined ninja turtle leaned forward over the handlebars of the moped, urging it to go faster as it spluttered along at a slow plod. People pointed, their faces incredulous, and a young man hung out of a window, taking a photo and screaming something excitedly in Spanish. A lorry driver waved and shouted something that was probably rude. Several other drivers couldn't resist yelling, 'Cowabunga!'

Molly didn't notice. She was thinking about her mother, about Kezia. She had been wrong – she'd misunderstood her all her life. Kezia hadn't been a wanderer who simply decided to leave, to discard her child and move on. She had loved her family; she had found her true home and she had wanted to stay. Molly had been wrong about herself too: she shared her mother's free spirit, her looks, her passionate ways, but she also shared her capacity to love. Molly knew that now, after all these years, she understood the woman in the photograph clutching the tiny baby, her eyes defiant: they were both the same flesh. She smiled and glanced across the road, continuing to search for the sign for Playa Redonda. She needed to be there soon.

She was passed by a woman driving a large silver car who took her eyes off the road for a moment to stare at the green-faced ninja turtle biker and almost knocked her off the moped. An American man wound down his window and shouted that she had made his day: the ninja turtles he'd seen on TV when he was a kid had never been cross-dressers. Another man yelled that she must be the most mutant ninja turtle he'd ever seen. Molly wasn't listening; she'd seen the sign ahead and a smudge on the road near the beach that could be the ranch.

She swung the little moped onto the narrow road leading towards the beach and through open gates, past a sign, stripped and bleached by the sun, with a picture of a horse, leaping flames and the words *Caballos Samuel*. She drove around a corner and saw a white van with the same logo on it parked up. She stopped the moped and let it fall to the ground, running full-pelt towards the two men who were standing next to a stable with a black horse. Molly called as loudly as she could through the helmet, 'Kristof!'

He turned, his face registering surprise, but she was in his arms, ninja turtle helmet and leather jacket, flying scarf and orange dress, and he was laughing, lifting her up in the air and twirling her round. Then her feet were on the ground and she was smiling up at him. Her fingers found the strap of the helmet and she dragged it from her head, her face warm, her hair damp with perspiration. Kristof took her hand, said something quietly to Samuel, then they walked away towards the beach.

Molly was still breathless. 'I don't want you to leave.'

She realised how much she'd missed his smile, the way his eyes gleamed, the way he always looked so calm and contented. His voice was soft. 'You came to find me.'

'I borrowed Javi's moped.'

'Yes, I saw it.' Kristof wrapped his arms around her and laughed. 'You really are the most amazing woman.'

She took both his hands in hers. 'Don't go away.'

'I won't. Not if you want me to stay.'

'I do want you to stay, Kristof.'

'That's not what you said to me last Sunday.' He exhaled. 'You told me you think this is a holiday romance. That it is just for a few weeks.'

Molly's expression was determined. 'I don't care if it is. I don't care if we only have a short time together and then you have to go back to Belgium. I want to be with you now. I'm happy being with you and that's all I care about.'

His face was suddenly serious. 'You want to go back to Puerto Palacio and be with me there? We can stay together until Christmas?'

'Yes.'

'And after that?'

Molly shrugged. 'I don't care.'

He smoothed her hair, a gentle touch of his palm. 'I care, Molly. There has to be more for us. You and me, we deserve more.'

'We can stay in Mexico, then...'

Kristof smiled. 'There are visas, work permits. We can't be here forever.'

'What then?'

They were standing on warm sand, listening to the waves crashing, watching foam roll across the sand and sweep back into the ocean. Kristof gazed into the distance.

'We could go to Belgium, to Bruges. You could have Christmas dinner with me and my family.' His eyes shone. 'We could help Joël with his café, make food together.'

'Then you could come to Somerset and meet Crumper, my cat, for New Year. You could live with me in my cottage.'

Kristof grinned. 'I have always wanted to write down the tapas recipes for a cookery book. I can do that while you paint yourself green and roll on a canvas. I'm sure the art will sell well.'

'We'll be millionaires, then.' Molly's words were full of enthusiasm. 'We can go to Sweden and see Nell and Ulla and Bernt or fly to Texas and see Betty. You could even meet Ronnie in Spain and we could have a trip on his boat.'

'We could travel to India. The food is incredible.' Kristof pulled her close, lifting a tendril of hair. 'I always wanted to go back to Goa, to set up a beach shack there. We could do that.'

'The important thing is that we do it together.' She kissed his lips. 'We can do anything, go anywhere. It's me and you now.'

He closed his eyes, a contented smile, the cat with the cream. 'That's what I want, Molly.'

'That's what I want too: me, you – and a project.'

'We will do all of it.' He took her hand and they began to walk back towards the van. 'We can put Javi's moped in the back with my stuff.'

'It was kind of him to lend it to me.' Molly glanced up at him. 'Liliana will be glad to see you, too.' She squeezed his hand. 'I'm so glad you're coming back, Kristof.'

He brought her fingers to his lips. 'I didn't want to be there without you.'

'Where would you have gone?'

'I'd have travelled round, discovered new places. But I wouldn't be happy as I am now.'

They wrapped arms around each other and leaned against the van, Kristof grinning as he glanced from the moped to Molly in the leather jacket and orange dress. He kissed her again. 'Shall we go home?'

Molly nodded, her head against his chest, her eyes closed. Home, she thought, was not a fixed point. It wasn't a country, a location on a map. It was not even a house. It was here, now, or anywhere in the world, wherever she and Kristof were together. They were in the middle of Mexico, on the edge of a beach, standing at the entrance to the stables, and she was where she had always wanted to be. She had been searching for so long: from Somerset to Spain to Mexico, she'd been seeking something she couldn't identify, trying to find a reason to stay, to settle. Molly knew in a flash why she had always been so erratic, leaping without thinking, one foot in then out again, changing her mind, unable to decide. Home wasn't a place, it was a person, and finally she'd understood. She was here, now, and it felt absolutely right. She had come home.

ACKNOWLEDGMENTS

Thanks to my agent, Kiran Kataria, for her kindness, wisdom, professionalism and integrity.

Thanks to the brilliant Boldwood team: Amanda Ridout, Nia Beynon, Ellie Foot and Megan Townsend for everything they do.

Special huge thanks to Sarah Ritherdon, editor extraordinaire.

Huge appreciation to everyone who has worked hard to make this book happen. I'm so grateful to designers, editors, technicians, magicians, voice actors, bloggers – thanks to you all.

Thanks to so many lovely friends: Erika, Rich, Kay, Rog, Jan, Jan M, Bill, Ken, Trish, Lexy, Helen, Frank, Shaz, Ian, Susie, Chrissie, Kathy N, Julie and Martin, Rach, Nik R, Pete O', Sarah and Jim, Sarah E, Mart, Cath, Slawka, Beau, Zach, Matt B, Casey B, Ruchi, Stephanie, Ingrid, Katie H, Steve F, Jonno, Edward and Robin.

To everyone in the NAC community; you are always in my thoughts.

Thanks to Ivor at Deep Studios for the Tech and Planet Rock for the music, especially Wyatt and Darren.

Massive thanks to Peter and all the wonderful Solitary Writers, Avril and the Tuesday writing group, the talented community of Boldwood writers and to writer friends of the RNA.

Thanks to my wonderful neighbours, Martin, Lindsay, Kitty, Ian, Nina, James and Jackie, and to Jenny, Sophie, Claire, Paul, Gary and Herman the chef.

Special thanks to our Tony for years of love, banter and bikes; to family, Kim, Ellen, Angela, Norman, Bridget and Debbie.

Love to my mum, who showed me books, and to my dad, who proudly never read one.

Best love to my four: to Liam, Maddie, Cait and Big G.

Huge thanks and special love to anyone who has read and enjoyed any of my books. You have helped to make this journey incredible.

SABORES TAPAS RECIPES

Scotch 'eggs'

Sausage-coating:
A can of chickpeas and one of black beans
Fried onion and celery stick
¼ cup water
Thyme, sage, fennel seeds, paprika, salt, black pepper
1 tbsp liquid smoke
1 cup vital wheat gluten
A packet of Panko or some whole-wheat breadcrumbs
Combine all ingredients except for the breadcrumbs and the vital
wheat gluten in a processor. Mix in the gluten and a few of the
breadcrumbs then knead for two minutes. Chill in refrigerator.

Method:
To create the 'white' of the egg, take a block of drained and
dried firm tofu, slice into six ¾ inch horizontal slices. Marinate in
half a cup of water, a pinch of Himalayan salt, and 2 tbsp nutri-

tional yeast for an hour. Pat dry and leave – if they crack a bit, that's fine.

For the 'yolk', take some boiled potatoes (about two cups) and mash them with 2 tbsp nutritional yeast, half a tsp turmeric, a tbsp plant-based cream cheese. Add a tbsp olive oil and mash together.

Now, to make the 'egg', spoon the yolk on top of the slice of tofu and roll it using plastic wrap to help to form a tube.

To make the Scotch egg, take a handful of the sausage mix and flatten it. Encase a chunk of vegan egg, pressing the mix tightly around it. Roll the whole egg in Panko breadcrumbs and deep fry until golden brown.

Vegan 'chorizo'

Dry ingredients:
1 cup vital wheat gluten
¼ cup gram or chickpea flour
2 tbsp nutritional yeast
2 tsp ground cumin
1 tsp ground coriander
1 tsp paprika
1 tsp chilli powder
½ tsp turmeric
½ tsp black pepper
1 tbsp chilli flakes
2 pounded garlic cloves

Wet ingredients:
2 tbsp apple cider vinegar

2 tbsp soy sauce
½ tsp liquid smoke
1 tbsp tomato paste
A cup of favourite veg stock (keep this on hand – you may not need it all)

Method:
Mix all the dry ingredients in a bowl.
Add vinegar, soy sauce, liquid smoke, tomato paste, a little of the stock and mix well adding a bit of stock until the mix comes together. It should be moist but knead-able.
Knead for 8-12 minutes. Add a bit more wheat gluten if you need to.
Divide into equal portions and roll into chorizo-shaped sausages.
Wrap each chorizo well in tinfoil and squeeze or twist the edges to seal.
Steam for 45 minutes in a pan of water. Turn during this process so that all the chorizo is well cooked.
Cool. Remove from foil.
Shallow fry in chilli oil until brown and perfect.
The chorizo will keep in the fridge or you can freeze them. Use on pizza, in sandwiches, or as you wish.

Vegan 'smoked salmon'

Ingredients:
3 large carrots
2 nori sheets
1 cup hot water
2 tbsp soy sauce
1 tbsp maple syrup

1 tbsp apple cider vinegar
1 tsp smoked paprika
1 tsp garlic powder
⅛ tsp ground black pepper
Sprinkle of sea salt (Himalayan works well)

Method:
Wash the carrots, add some salt to taste, place them onto a lined baking tray and bake for 45 minutes in a pre-heated oven on 180°.
Make the marinade: put the nori, water, tamari, syrup, vinegar, paprika, garlic powder and pepper into a blender and blend until smooth.
Remove the baked carrots from the oven and let them cool. Then use a mandolin or a sharp knife and slice them into thin ribbons or strips.
Put the carrot strips into a bowl and add the marinade. Cover.
Leave in the fridge for 1-4 days.
Serve: roll up the strips of carrot on crackers with a dollop of vegan cream cheese, some fresh dill, chopped red onion and a sprinkle of black pepper.

MORE FROM JUDY LEIGH

We hope you enjoyed reading *Chasing the Sun*. If you did, please leave a review.

If you'd like to gift a copy, this book is also available as an ebook, digital audio download and audiobook CD.

Sign up to Judy Leigh's mailing list for news, competitions and updates on future books:

http://bit.ly/JudyLeighNewsletter

Explore more fun, uplifting reads from Judy Leigh:

ABOUT THE AUTHOR

Judy Leigh is the bestselling author of *A Grand Old Time* and *Five French Hens* and the doyenne of the 'it's never too late' genre of women's fiction. She has lived all over the UK from Liverpool to Cornwall, but currently resides in Somerset.

Visit Judy's website: https://judyleigh.com

Follow Judy on social media:

facebook.com/judyleighuk
twitter.com/judyleighwriter
instagram.com/judyrleigh
bookbub.com/authors/judy-leigh

ABOUT BOLDWOOD BOOKS

Boldwood Books is a fiction publishing company seeking out the best stories from around the world.

Find out more at www.boldwoodbooks.com

Sign up to the Book and Tonic newsletter for news, offers and competitions from Boldwood Books!

http://www.bit.ly/bookandtonic

We'd love to hear from you, follow us on social media:

 facebook.com/BookandTonic
 twitter.com/BoldwoodBooks
 instagram.com/BookandTonic

Printed in Great Britain
by Amazon